CHERIE PRIEST

This special signed edition
is limited to 1000 numbered copies.

This is copy 705 .

HOLY TERROR

HOLY TERROR

Stories by

CHERIE PRIEST

Subterranean Press 2022

First Edition

ISBN
978-1-64524-055-6

Subterranean Press
PO Box 190106
Burton, MI 48519

subterraneanpress.com

Manufactured in the United States of America

Table of Contents

A COME-HITHER TO FEAR

by Kevin Hearne

NO ONE scares me as much as Cherie Priest.

To be clear, she is also a completely delightful person who will happily walk her dogs through a graveyard with you, deliver a brief dissertation on Victorian death symbolism, and then smirk as she points out the tombstone of someone named "Harry Beaver."

But mostly she scares me. With her stories, I mean.

And she does it in the way I like to be scared. A nice creeping dread that builds and builds until you're shouting at the character on the page to *run*. (I have done this before, yelling "Get out of there, dude!" at a protagonist in peril and causing my wife to inquire who I'm talking to.) And unlike some other tales I've read, I cheer pretty hard for Cherie's heroes and heroines to survive.

They're working folks who are struggling to pay bills, aware that the system isn't designed for their ease or comfort, but doing their best to get by. And then some bonus horror comes along, threatening to crush them. Maybe it's a metaphor for the implacable bootheel of capitalism, or maybe we don't need to assign meanings and can just enjoy a cool monster or the soulless evil of some Elder Gods. Regardless, Cherie's hero(in)es gamely try to handle situations that should be overwhelming, but because they have struggled so long, they know that they are on their own. No one else is going to save them, so they might as well be about the business of saving themselves.

Which is entirely relatable; few, if any of us, can truly rely on someone else to save our lives. We all have to make choices in the contexts we live in, and Cherie invites us to ponder some valid questions: What choices would you make if your context suddenly included zombies? Or nameless horrors in the woods? What if you were surrounded by cultists impervious to facts? What if you found a dragon? (It could happen. And if it does, after this you'll be prepared.)

What terrifies us, very often, is that our lives are just a short step away from these fictions. In an age of widespread disinformation, people who are impervious to facts could be next door, or in our own families. And in some of these tales, the idea of an inimical plague infecting everyone around us…? Yeah. That's pretty close to a bullseye.

One of my favorite series by Cherie is her *Maplecroft* books, a reimagining of the true-life ax murders of Lizzie Borden combined with the Elder Gods mythos. They're so well-done that I used passages from them to teach writing students how syntax can develop voice. "The October Devotion" is an early story in that vein and reading it was like coming home but finding it rearranged in a delightfully spooky manner. Similarly, "Bad Sushi" has that Lovecraftian vibe but without his numerous hang-ups or horrendous prose—Lovecraft, in other words, as it should have been done from the beginning.

Two stories from Cherie's popular Clockwork Century universe— "Clementine" and "Reluctance"—give me airships and steampunk fashion, and one offers a massive dose of zombie horror.

A COME-HITHER TO FEAR

"The Immigrant" is one of those stories where you realize a small decision here or there, a single bad choice, could have wrenched the world onto a different timeline. And though the subject is fantastical, I found it incredibly poignant considering what the world has gone through recently (and continues to wrestle with) regarding immigrants. How should we care for them, and what blessings will they bring to us if we welcome them? But what I loved most was that someone found humanity amongst a background of inhumanity.

Apart from some more recognizable genres (like steampunk or zombie fic), Cherie is also incredibly good at what, for lack of a better term, gets called Weird (or sometimes New Weird). "The Catastrophe Box" is an excellent example, serving up apocalyptic themes, Poe-like dread and alienation, and a peek through a doorway into madness. "Wishbones" is another—definitely one of those where I shouted at the protagonist to run—but it also contains a brief observation that sang of truth to me: "Sometimes when you own jackets, you just want to wear them." This is the sort of simple truth that makes me smile in recognition. I grew up in Arizona where there was not much call for jackets, but we wore them anyway when we could. Cherie excels at marinating her characters in such keen reality that when it's time to add some heat, the fantastic becomes plausible.

And sometimes Cherie conducts experiments in narrative structure that I really enjoy. "The Wreck of the Mary Byrd" is one of these, and "Heavy Metal" is another. As a reader I appreciate the different approach to telling a story; as a writer I appreciate the skill it takes to make it work.

I also appreciate it when a writer can move me to catharsis, and "Mother Jones and the Nasty Eclipse" did just that. It's odd to feel a story catch you up and then there's a release, but it's not the story releasing you, it's something inside you being released that you caught long ago and didn't know how to let go of, not until a particular string of words turned the key of a lock in your heart.

All that—and more—lies ahead of you in this marvelous collection. And there are many novels to explore, too, apart from those already mentioned—*The Family Plot* and *The Toll* have recently delighted me, and my collection of Priest books grows by the year. If you like to be scared the way I do, your collection will doubtless grow as well.

Settle in with something snuggly now, and maybe a cup of tea with honey—just in case your throat needs soothing after you've shouted at the characters in these stories to *run*.

—Kevin Hearne

THE OCTOBER DEVOTION

"The October Devotion" was one of the first short stories I ever wrote or sold. (I'd say it's the very first, but I sold two tales quite close together— and I'm not sure, after all this time, which one was actually released first.) In retrospect, I can see all the things I'd do differently now; but honestly, that's true of almost everything I've ever had published. I wanted to include this one in this collection if for no other reason than to show how much my style and instincts have changed through the years.

It was inspired in an oblique way by my upbringing. I was raised in the Seventh Day Adventist church, and although I still have family and friends who worship that way, I've put my experiences with that institution (and its educational system) as far behind me as possible. For reasons.

I have a complex relationship with organized religion. Let's leave it at that.

At any rate, one of the foundational events of that church came courtesy of William Miller, and his Apocalypse That Never Happened on October 22, 1844. Better known as "The Great Disappointment."

CHERIE PRIEST

In the wake of this non-event, the "Millerites" faced considerable persecution and mockery. A number of these people had allegedly given away all their possessions, and there are long rumors of folks climbing mountains or standing on the tallest hills they could find while wearing "ascension robes"—but this may have been anecdotal. Non-believers teased them about it. Mercilessly. They also burned down a few churches (which is bad form, I don't care who you are). But what can you do.

At any rate, the beleaguered Millerites mostly either disbanded, or rallied around a teenage girl who was hit on the head with a rock and began hearing God talking to her.

The girl's name was Ellen G. White. She wrote many books with varying levels of usefulness, helped kickstart sanitariums like the J. H. Kellogg one in Battle Creek, Michigan, about which *The Road to Wellville* was written...and she more or less founded the SDA church—an institution which somewhat ironically still declines to ordain women. Apart from that, the less said about her, the better.

If you really want to learn about this evangelical Victorian lady with a traumatic brain injury, Google is your friend. It's honestly a hell of a story.

But that's not what "The October Devotion" is about. This tale is about another version of the mid-19th century apocalypse. I just imagined all those devout, faithful people, staring up at the sky, waiting for God to return. They got so much wrong! What else did they miss? Maybe instead of looking up for salvation, they should've been looking *down*.

This was my first foray into fiction with a Lovecraftian edge. I'm torn as to how successful I think it is, as a whole, but it is at least a weirdly personal story for me—and I hope you enjoy it.

THE OCTOBER DEVOTION

IT BEGAN in church, as great fears do.

The song they sang was a dirge of Revelation. "Sing to us," they cried, "of the Spirit of Prophecy. Sing of how it comes to us, sent from God, and how it calls us home." And the severe old man with the white face and the black suit beat his great Bible to the thunderous rhythm of Armageddon. But they should not fear. But they should not quake. Does not the Good Book say that the righteous will be caught up? That He goes to prepare a place for them, and He will receive them unto Himself?

That where I am, there ye may be also.

Such a blessing. Such a gift.

Such a horror to the young ones, especially. Short years had not yet gained them the gradual knowledge and sorrow of adulthood, or the idea that a cosmic reward must one day come. Surely it was reward enough for the sermon to end, and a hearty Sunday lunch to follow. Surely the world must not pass away with a preacher's promise.

Yes, yes it must. It must for Mr. Miller.

He brandished his calendar like a weapon. Upon it a date was circled with brilliant red ink: October 22, 1844. A matter of weeks, marked out in red. Red like the savior's blood. Red like the blood of the martyrs.

Red skies at morning, sailors take warning, Prudence thought. She would have rather been a sailor, with concerns no deeper than the weather and waves, or the starfish on the beach. Only fourteen years behind her and eternity stretching before her. How unfair.

Also unfair was the interminable trip to Florida, farther south and twice as hot as hell. But if her grandmother refused to be caught up with the saints to meet the Lord, it was not going to be on the conscience of Prudence's mother. Not on *her* watch would any family members be left behind, whether they liked it or not. Job made sacrifices for his children, and so Frances Harding would petition God on her reluctant loved ones' behalf.

But Grandmother laughed, as clear and sincere as Abraham's wife when she heard that she'd yet be a mother. She laughed, and her age-yellowed teeth reared out of her mouth with mirth.

Then how Frances wailed—and how she had beaten the door frame and begged to come inside, to no effect. In the end she pitched a leather-bound bible clean through the kitchen window. It landed on a counter in a triumphant spray of glass and fluttering, gold-brushed pages. Grandmother left it where it fell and turned aside to take a broom. She answered the assault softly, her words accented by her slow, apathetic sweeping. "Let your Lord come," she said. "If He's half the brute you say He is, I want no part of it. Go with Him and be happy if you must. But as for me and my house, we rest here with the toasty sinners and we will be content."

Amidst the vandalism and rebuke, when her mother's shaking back was turned, Prudence permitted a tiny smile. Her older brother saw this small act of rebellion, but said nothing. It would do no good to antagonize their mother any further, and since their father was dead Elijah was the only man present to console her. There was no reason to make his duty more difficult.

Prudence wondered if he believed.

She stared at him all the time, both when he was looking and when he was not. Every day he resembled their father more, and every day Prudence stared a bit longer. It unnerved her to see a man in the house, where one had almost never been before. The change had come so slowly, then abruptly. Boy to man. Skinny and hairless to bulky with a half-beard of pale brown wires stabbing forth from his square chin.

He rarely spoke and even more rarely did he smile. So perhaps he *did* believe it was true, and that was why he remained so somber, this flesh-and-blood ghost of her father.

THE OCTOBER DEVOTION

In time the prophesied day came.

It dawned splendid and somewhat cool for the gulf coast. Prudence searched the sky for some apocryphal warning, but the morning was disappointingly gold and blue. A lovely day for the world to end. "You'll put these on," Frances announced, holding out two white linen sheathes that matched her own and hung like choir robes. "We'll return to the Lord as pure as our sinful sense of human decency will allow."

Elijah nodded and took the robe and pulled it over his clothes. Prudence did likewise, the bow of her dress making an obscene bunch at her lower back. The robe did not fit well. It clenched too snug at the underarms and hung an inch too long. Her shoes snagged the hem when she stepped, but her mother would hear no complaints.

"We won't be walking much longer anyway. Soon we'll have our wings, and we'll be with the Lord. We'll fly through heaven like fish through the sea." She took her childrens' hands in each of hers and the three of them walked together to the beach. The powder-soft strand was deserted and bright, and the ocean water glistened more clear and fresh than anything that came out of a pump. In great, wide circles above the seagulls soared and called, singing tales of light and new beginnings.

Prudence didn't believe a word of it, at least that's what she told herself. She told it to one of the gulls, too—one that wandered too close. It hopped boldly toward her, cocking its ringed head and parting its pointed beak to swear or bless.

"I don't believe you," the girl whispered. She gripped the sleeves of her robe and pulled them taut, releasing the crease that formed in her armpits.

The bird shrugged and flew away, unimpressed by her skepticism.

The small family settled down to wait and stare at the eastern sky. The sun crept along its course uninterrupted by saints or trumpets for many hours.

"I'm thirsty." Prudence tugged her sleeves again. Although the day grew later, her mother refused to budge from her spot, seated with folded legs in the sand. "I'm real thirsty," Prudence said again, "and my face is hot. I'm getting burned."

"Better you burn here than down with the devil. Stop your fussing. This is too important for you to be fussing. He'll be here any minute to take us home."

"But my face is hot. And I need to *go*." It was hard to hide from the sun when the sand and water both reflected it so readily. Prudence would have sold her soul for a hat, but her mother had given away everything they owned in anticipation of this day—including most of their clothes. Even the horses had been cheerfully signed to new owners, as well as the house and everything it contained.

Elijah avoided his mother's always-suspicious eyes. "She could run back to Grandmother's for some water," he said.

Frances's jaw dropped and her voice rose. "But Jesus is coming!"

"And Jesus can find her at Grandmother's as well as on the beach, don't you think?" He said it with humility and a touch of accusation. Prudence thought that he must be as thirsty and tired and bored as she was. The sky was turning a deeper gold and the sun crouched lower over the water, hovering above the horizon line as if it too were waiting for something grand—holding out as long as possible to signal that the whole thing had been called off.

"The three of us are going to rise up to meet him as a family," she insisted. "You do want to come and meet your father again, don't you Prudence? I know you hardly remember him. It's so important to—it's just important. I want to show you to him. I want him to see that I raised you right and well." She fidgeted with her robe and rubbed her heels into the sand. "I think you should stay here with *us*."

But the more Elijah grew into the mold of her late husband, the less she could refuse him. After a hesitant moment she frowned and half-relented. "Prudence, if you really must go, the trees are right there. But be quick about it. I just know that the moment you leave He's going to appear, and we need to meet Him as a family. Don't you want to see your father again?"

Prudence bobbed her head in the affirmative, but she was already running for the trees. Grandmother's house was only a few hundred yards beyond them, and it wasn't Prudence who had thrown the Bible through the window. With a touch of sacrilegious sweet-talk, Grandmother might give her a glass of water and even let her use the outhouse too.

That very thought propelled her slender legs onward, dodging along the narrow path that wound its way between the trees and deeper inland. Couldn't be far. But it was getting hard to see, harder to navigate between the great old trees with their fluffy tops or dangling branches. She noted with no small measure of satisfaction that the day would soon come to a close. No more than an hour, certainly. Less than that, maybe. Less than that before everything was over—either the whole world, or just her mother's.

If she played her cards right, she might be able to stay at Grandmother's until after sundown. That way if Jesus didn't come she would be free of her mother's grief or rage. And it was true, what she'd told the bird. She didn't really believe. How horrible it was that her mother did, and more horrible yet if she was right.

The way through the woods was darker than she thought it should be and her soft church shoes were not intended to climb across roots, or navigate the big palmetto bushes that bit her heels. The way through the woods was narrow, and the path was worn clear only in occasional places where the white sand showed through the dirt in pale parallel lines.

A great, knobby tree root higher than her knees reared across the trail but Prudence had worked up too much steam to stop and go around. Instead she leaped, and the toe of her shoe tangled in the awful white robe. She cleared the root with one leg and caught it with her other shin.

Down she fell, and farther than she should have.

On the other side of the root the ground dropped away quite steep, into a great bowl-shaped depression that had not been there in the morning.

Down into this hole she fell, and into the center of the earthen bowl. And where she landed a thin, star-shaped crack opened beneath her, spreading to match her sprawling shape of wayward arms and crooked legs. Down in this hole—which really was not so deep—the girl heard a snap, or a crunch; and there she slept through the second coming that never came.

Prudence awoke to screaming, and the noise was not her own.

Upon that awakening she found herself upright, standing on the edge of the white sand pit. Her mother was there, and her brother too—both in night dress and holding lanterns. The frightened yelling came from her mother, which was not surprising under the best of circumstances.

Her brother shuttered the lantern and leaped down into the hole, then scrambled up the other side to meet her. "What are you doing?" he asked, patting at the gauzy white bandage that circled her head like a bonnet. "Why are you out here like this again?"

She had no choice but to stare at him blankly. "Again?"

"Again," he nodded.

Prudence stared past him at their mother, who was growing calmer, or at least more quiet if those two can be the same. Frances stumbled down into the hole and caught her foot in the crack at the bottom. She jerked it free and staggered onward, climbing up the other side with Elijah's assistance.

"Why do you do this?" she panted, setting the light to rest on a fallen tree and dusting her night dress with her hands. "Why did you come here again? And why won't you wake up proper?"

"I *am* awake, Mother." Prudence shook off the searching hands that poked and grasped, and swung her head back and forth to clear it with the motion. "I *am* awake now. But if you say I've done this again, then I wasn't awake the time before." She pressed her palms to the enormous sore spot above her right ear. It throbbed at her touch and her vision wavered like water flowed before it. "I can smell the beach," she said.

Elijah put one long arm around her shoulders and drew her close. His scritchy chin scraped the top of her head in an oddly comforting fashion. "You've been out for a long time. We need to get you back to bed."

"After a fall like that, you need your rest," Frances agreed. Her eyes were losing their buggy fear as she retrieved the lantern. "We need to get you back to Grandmother's."

"Grandmother's."

Yes, she'd been going there when…when there was falling. Great, interminable falling down through a massive fissure. And at the bottom she'd seen sand, and more water. Down at the bottom there were stars and light. There were places for her head to swim—places deep enough and old enough that even the stars could rest. How had they brought her back from such depths, or from such dreams?

"You've been asleep for two days," her brother said. "Ever since you hit your head there. But last night you walked back and we can't imagine what made you do it. I wish you'd tell us why."

She thought about it for a minute, though the effort made her brain ache. "They told me to," she finally replied.

"Who told you to?"

"They did. The starfishes."

Just then their mother caught up with a rustle of fabric tearing through foliage, and she thrust her face forward, afraid that they'd been conspiring without her. "You hit your head hard. You've been delirious for days."

"Yes, that's what Elijah said." Prudence leaned her aching head against her brother's shoulder. He squeezed her arms but added nothing to her response.

"It's true. And at night you wandered out here." Her chin jutted forward and waved like a warning finger. "And you'd better not do it again. Not now that you're awake. I won't have it."

Some small fact jumped about and shouted for Prudence's attention. She chased it around the echoing hurt of her skull until she caught it, and then she dragged it outside—trying not to sound relieved or smug as the words fell into place.

"Jesus didn't come back."

Frances withdrew without a sound, and fell into step behind her children. Her lips pressed close to one another, seeking a comfort that would not come either. The lantern hung by her side and singed her night dress, but she did not seem to care. "We're only human, Prudence, and we make mistakes. We misunderstood, and we were…impatient."

"Impatient," Prudence echoed, understanding there must be irony but uncertain how to address it.

"Stop it," Elijah warned beneath his breath. "Whatever you mean to say, keep it in."

She ignored him and glanced back at her mother. "But what does that mean? What happens now?"

Her mother's jaw was clamped tight enough to cut a lead pipe, and her eyes were bulging again. Prudence had long indulged a notion that her mother's eyes were the only sane part of her body; and when the rage and religion boiled too hot in her brain the poor orbs tried their best to escape. But, unfortunately anchored as they were, they never got farther than a frantic fraction beyond her lids.

"He's still coming, but we know the Bible says it will be like a thief in the night, and that no man knows the day or hour. It was our pride. But he'll come yet—you know he will. We need to be alert for it. At any time—at any moment—he'll be back for us, and we'll see the saints again. I don't wonder but your father must be getting awful impatient."

"Don't push this, Prudence." Elijah murmured another warning for his sister to ignore.

"He left us here, didn't he? And now he's not coming back at all. And that's why we're going back to Grandmother's. You gave away everything we had and Jesus didn't care. He didn't bring back my father, and he didn't come get *you*."

Frances reflexively lifted a fist and might have struck the girl, but Elijah pushed his sister aside and stood between them—raising his own light and holding it out as if it would ward her away. The tropical forest bristled and tensed, and watched for the outcome of the showdown.

"She's hurt, Mother. She doesn't know what she's saying. We'll take her back and put her in bed. We can talk in the morning, if she feels up to it."

"She feels up to blasphemy," Frances growled, but lowered her free fist and clenched her night dress instead. "She feels up to hurting me."

"No," Elijah said. "No one wants to hurt you. It's been a hard time for us all."

It might have been that Frances only missed her husband, or that she was too wounded and drained to pursue the argument. Her son implored her, and for so long she'd been so lonely for the man who had helped her make him. Perhaps it was only that odd trick of heredity that made her relent, but in the end she gave Elijah her hand. He walked them both back to the house, his mother and his sister. And he tried to keep them from touching.

Grandmother was up when they returned, sitting at the table with a pot of steaming tea. She offered it to all or to any, but Frances went to her room without a word. Elijah pulled a chair free for Prudence and bid his Grandmother good night, then left them alone—the oldest and youngest.

"Not too much sugar in it," Grandmother insisted, tossing her head to keep the long white braid from sliding into her cup. "You don't need the sugar. It'll keep you up, and Lord knows you've been up enough these last nights, for a girl who stayed asleep."

"That's what they tell me." She sipped the brew slowly, lest she burn her tongue and earn even more injury.

Grandmother nodded and half-smiled. "Did they tell you it's a sink hole? You need to leave it be. Those things aren't steady, and it might open more. They happen here sometimes, where the water's been running underneath the ground."

"Is that all it is?" she asked.

"Yes, that's all. Just a hole made by water after the water's dried up."

"Oh."

Grandmother took another swig of the murky brown beverage and licked at her bottom lip. "So I guess you've figured now that we're all still earth-bound."

"I figured."

"You don't look any more surprised than I was. But your mother—well."

Prudence accidentally copied her mother's tight-lipped frown and glared at the tea. "Well."

"I could tell you that she's only trying to do right, and I could tell you that she loves you, but it wouldn't matter much, would it?"

The girl could not bring herself to say no, but neither could she muster any argument. "Thank you for the tea," she changed the subject. "I'm going to go back to bed now. Where am I sleeping?"

Grandmother checked the bandage and declared it sound, then led her back to the room her mother occupied, where Prudence had been assigned the bed. Frances rolled over on the creaking cot beneath the window and yanked the covers higher under her face.

Prudence laid her head carefully on the feather pillow and closed her eyes, hoping to dream some more about the stars.

And dream she did.

The stars sang to her while she slept, asking their low, rumbling questions in voices that spoke no human tongue. Or possibly it was the distance—they were so hard to hear from so far away, down below the sandy pit near the shore. In her dreams she would answer them as best she could, straining to hear and shouting to be heard above the symphony of the wet green woods.

THE OCTOBER DEVOTION

The longer they spoke, the better she heard them; she listened close. At least a word, here and there, and at least a phrase or a promise would leak away…through the woods, across the lawn. On they came, their heavy, slow words that half made sense and half bewildered; and closer they drew to the cottage in the glades. How could Prudence sleep through such impassioned pleas? They wanted her—they *needed* her. They were willing to come for her, to talk to her. Even while she rested they pushed aside the trees and dragged themselves through the sand; and if her eyes remained closed, there against the window pressed a face like no human's.

Impatient, she drew back her lids and stared at the ceiling, then the glass.

There was nothing at the portal except, perhaps, a trace of steam evaporating from the pane as if some one or some thing had breathed against it. It vanished almost immediately.

Prudence understood. She rose to answer the summons. She knew the sound now. They knew her name and they knew how to call it. Each night their knowledge increased and they became that much easier to understand. Before long they might talk freely, and she might sit at their sandy temple and worship.

For the third night in a row she walked blind between the trees and knelt in the hole, pressing her ear to the star-shaped rift and listening. "I can hear you," she whispered to them. "I can hear you, and I *believe* you."

Just a inch or two, just the length of a small finger or large seashell, the fissure spread. A soft sound of falling sand breathed its tiny hiss as the ground gave by small degrees and sank away. By just an inch or two that five-pointed crack grew, and no one should have noticed at all.

But Frances noticed.

After the third evening her daughter walked, she became more wary of the sudden indentation and she wondered about its appearance, its lure. Even though she'd not awakened until after her daughter returned to bed, the sand on the floor and the scrapes on Prudence's feet told her all.

Frances formed a series of wild plans—plans that involved ropes and chains and traps and alarms. One night she hobbled her daughter's feet, and the next she tied her hands—with a connecting twine fastened to her own wrist. But none of these things kept the girl still at night. No matter how she was bound or tethered, each night she rose and wandered her lonely way to the pit, where she pressed her face into the sand and exchanged her mumbled secrets with the ever-widening crack.

Back then, to the place where it began.

Back to church.

Farther inland Frances found a sympathetic congregation willing to aid her search to understand her misunderstanding. There she dragged Prudence on the next Sunday morning, and pulled her toward the steeple-less wood building with the frosted windows. "Any day now—any minute now—Jesus is coming back and you're not ready for Him. I can see you're not ready for Him, and I don't mean to leave this old earth without you if I can help it."

"Mother, I'm all right. I hit my head, that's all. I could use a trip to the doctor, I think, but I'm not sure why we've gotta go to church just now. I wish you'd let me stay, I feel so dizzy when I stand up too long." Prudence climbed down from the cart with Elijah's help and wobbled a moment as her feet arranged themselves on the grass.

"We'll be sitting down soon enough. Of course then you'll probably be wishing you could get up and leave. I know what you think about worship, and it's a shame. What would your father think if he could see you squirming and itching to leave each Sunday?"

"You act like he's watching us all the time, anyhow," she grumbled, picking at the bandage mostly hidden by her hat. The hat belonged to Grandmother, who felt that Prudence was getting too old for bonnets and ought to look more like a lady when dressed, instead of a little girl.

"Stop that. 'For the living know that they shall die, but the dead know not anything,'" Frances quoted a verse that Prudence recognized but couldn't place. "Your father is asleep in Jesus."

THE OCTOBER DEVOTION

The trio walked inside the steeple-less wood church just as the piano began its tinny, melodic introduction to services. They took a seat near the front, as Frances always insisted, and sat quietly together while the sermon preliminaries passed. An offertory, a testimonial, a pair of children holding hands and singing a hymn, accompanied by their older sister on a violin.

Prudence stared glassy-eyed, tuning out what she could and ignoring what she couldn't. When the plate was passed her way she handed it to the usher at the end of the aisle, and when the children finished their piece she said "amen" out of bland habit, without appreciation. Up front, beneath the preacher's podium she saw a covered set of communion cups and plates. "For the blood is the life," an inscription below the preacher explained the ritual.

She leaned over to Elijah and whispered in his ear. "How long does it take a ritual to turn into a habit?" she asked. "Or are they always the same thing, but everyone says different?"

"Stop it," Elijah whispered back in a tone intended to end the conversation, but the girl pressed on.

"You don't know either, huh?"

He deflected a sidelong glare from Frances and allowed her to kick the side of his leg. Then he cocked his head close to Prudence until his forehead knocked against the hat's brim. He answered in a whisper so low she barely heard it. "It's a ritual so long as it means more than what it looks like. A habit is just an act."

She giggled, and understood.

The minister began his winding, stomping, accusatory interrogative and Prudence let her mind wander again, but not too far. Behind the minister, filling the front of the church, was a death-sized cross—minus any wounded deity, but with all the extra trappings. Prudence thought it might have been made of railroad ties, a theory supported by the "nails" big enough to tack trees together. A crown was slung around the top point, made of the requisite thorns and thistles. It hung lopsided over the right branch of the crucifix, out of place and useless.

"Brothers and sisters, God *is* coming back. We have made mistakes and we have misunderstood about His timing, and His plans, but He will return. We know not the hour nor the day, but we have His promise that we will look upon his face again."

And all the Lord's people said "Amen." Prudence kept quiet, but she did so with discomfort.

"And what great joy it will be, to see His shining face again."

Amen!

"He's the Lily of the Valley—the Fairest of Ten Thousand. Can't you imagine it, seeing Him riding on the clouds from Glory? Shining like the Fairest Morning Star?"

Amen!

Prudence's ears perked. "No," she mumbled. "He's not like that. He's not one of them."

"Hush," her mother whispered the command more loudly than the girl had spoken.

"Well he ain't. The shining stars—"

"Stop it," Elijah nudged her arm. "Don't, now."

"But it can't be like that," she insisted, volume increasing beyond the levels of chapel decency. "He's not one of the shining star ones! They aren't like that! You all have to be wrong—because I've seen the others, and they're not like him, they're *real*. And they talked to me, and they—"

She rose from her seat only a few inches before Elijah caught her and stood up with her. "You and I are leaving," he said in her ear. Then, over his shoulder, "Excuse us, please. My sister was in an accident a few days ago. I beg your pardon."

Frances stayed on the pew in humiliated silence and eyed them with rage until they'd passed the sanctuary doors and fled her sight.

THE OCTOBER DEVOTION

Outside, Elijah gripped Prudence by the shoulders and fought the urge to shake her. "What do you think you're doing? Church is not the place for your nonsense."

"S'not nonsense, and church is the only place," she argued, writhing and twisting. "Church is the only place where they're so really wrong. I don't know much about Jesus. I used to think I did, but now I know I don't. And he might have been an okay sort, but he wasn't everything they say he was. He wasn't a morning star, 'cause I've seen *them*, and I've talked to *them*, and if they're really real, then he's *not*."

Elijah stared, and stared hard at the half-grown child who had quit her struggling to stare back. "Ever since you fell…" he began, but stopped himself and started again. "Ever since that night you've been odd. And I can't help but think you've broken something inside your head, the way you talk sometimes. I'm not saying you don't believe what you're saying is true, for I think it's pretty clear that you do. But you've gotta quit it. You can't be acting this way, not in front of Mother, not in front of other people, and sure as anything—not at church."

He might have gone on except that something distracted him, something glinting just beyond his vision at the edge of the trees by the church. The glint held a greenish tinge, like light passing through stained glass or a large gem. It was gone as quickly as it appeared, but he could not shake the impression that something large had suddenly moved beyond his sight.

"You're hurting me," Prudence fussed.

He released her.

She did not run, and did not take her eyes off his face. "Come with me to the hole, and you'll see. I'll show you what I know." In her voice there lurked a suggestion of pleading, and an honest desire to share. "Come with me, Elijah. If I asked them, they'd talk to you too."

"I don't think I will," he said, still staring at the tree line.

"But I wish you would. I don't want you to think I'm all crazy. I need for someone else to see."

He gave up staring into the woods and peered at the spot on her hat that hid the offending wound. "You're afraid now. More afraid than before, when Christ was going to come again. I don't know what you're believing these days, but you won't convert me, little sister. Whatever strange gods you've placed your faith in this time, you're going to face it without me."

At first she winced, but then her lashes dropped and changed her eyes to slitted, hateful slots. "I'm not afraid," she growled. "I know the *truth*, and no one else will believe me—but that's okay. I don't *need* any of you to believe me. They aren't talking to the rest of you, they're talking to *me*. You're just jealous because now I'm the important one. I'm the one with the real God, and all you and Mother have is some dead guy who never came back from the dead, and never came back for *you*."

Her brother absorbed the venom-filled words and digested them despite all their poison. It took a moment. They made him ill. "Next time Mother goes to hit you," he warned, "I won't lift a hand to stop her."

He turned on his heels and went back inside the sanctuary, shutting the double doors behind him and leaving Prudence to sit disgraced upon the stairs and gaze at the trees.

Tears stung at her eyes. His words had held more poison than hers, and she was wounded already by his refusal to join her. "I'm no Eve," she grumbled aloud. "This is no tree, and no apple. He didn't have to be like that."

But niggling about in the back of her certainty, she *was* afraid. What if her brother was right? What if they were *all* right, and she was just some crazy girl who knocked her head on a rock? What then?

Then the greenish gleam flashed between the trees once more, catching Prudence's tear-muddled gaze and lifting it. She too saw something great, something quick sliding between the tree trunks, and although she could not see it any more clearly than Elijah could, she was comforted.

Ah. She was not alone after all. They would not leave her. She had to have faith—she had to hang on to the truth. They loved her. They needed her. And when everything was done, she could go and be with them. They promised so.

Her tears dried and her legs crossed, hands folded.

She held her spot on the church steps and waited for the service to end.

The afternoons passed uncomfortably as God stubbornly failed to return and Prudence's family still had no home besides that of Grandmother. As the days piled up against each other, Prudence began to visit the hole during her waking hours as well. She violently resisted all efforts to prevent her, and when she could not be found in the gritty bottom she sat cross-legged on the living room floor. There she scratched at the healing wound on her head and doodled fanciful scenes of fattened stars across every stray bit of paper.

"What's this one?" Grandmother asked, lifting an ivory sheet from the floor and holding it to the light. "Are these people? Or starfish? They look something like starfishes."

Prudence did not look up. "More than that," she said, setting her pencil aside and taking a wad of rubber to smudge a misdrawn line.

Grandmother's wizened eyes narrowed as she examined the sketch. She removed her spectacles and wiped away a water spot with the hem of her apron, then replaced them on the rim of her nose. "More than people, eh? More than even starfish?"

"They're gods." Prudence retrieved her pencil and continued dragging the leaded tip across the page. "They're *real* gods."

"Ah, I see." And Grandmother thought she *did* see. It made sense enough, that after The Disappointment this child might retreat to fantasy. Her granddaughter's gods resembled rounded-off stars, which must represent the heavens. "And these real gods, they're the sort that would come back when they promise to?"

She shook her head. "No. They don't have to come back. They're already here."

Grandmother thought long and hard about her reply. Nothing sound or reassuring came to her mind, so she shrugged and patted the girl's back. "I know you're just telling yourself stories," she crouched down beside her and came closer to her ear, "but don't let your mother hear you talking that way."

Eventually her mother *did* hear.

She heard it all and was more furious than her own mother had feared she might be, though not for all the reasons Grandmother might have predicted. Frances Harding was a more jealous authoritarian than the one she'd expected to return; she fiercely envied the new gods, the starfish people that her daughter prayed to. And it could only be called praying, that odd communion of Prudence and Pit, where the girl laid herself out like a sacrifice and covered her body with the salt-white sand.

Something must be done.

Something must bring an end to the unholy worship at the hole in the woods with the crack that spread and spread until it threatened to split the whole world open.

"Take a shovel," she ordered Elijah. "Take a shovel and fill it in. Get some of the men from church to help."

Her son lifted his hands in a gesture of helplessness. "Fill it with what? Should we dig up the forest around it and toss in the trees? It's just a sink-hole, and Prudence is still on the mend."

"She's mended enough to walk the beach—she's mended enough to bring all those starfish into her room and let the place stink up of the rotting things. She mended enough to mind her mother again, but she won't do it and I won't let her walk on me. I won't let that baby walk over me every day, and every night, on her way out to that hole. If you've ever loved me like a son should, you'll do what I'm telling you. Or at least do it because I'm asking you." Her eyes were straining again, trying hard to climb out of her face and bludgeon Elijah into submission.

THE OCTOBER DEVOTION

He put his hand in his hair and looked away. "I don't see why it's so important. People collect starfish and seashells all the time, and it doesn't mean anything. And children play in the sand—"

"She's not a child anymore, hardly. She's well too old to be building up castles like that and rooting in the dirt." A flash of inspiration sucked the eyes back down to their normal position, where they hooded themselves and grew dark. "Besides, she's going to hurt herself you know, the way that crack at the bottom keeps stretching. One of these days she'll break a leg out there—or one of these nights, since she never brings a light. What if she gets hurt out there and gets eaten by a wild animal?"

"There's nothing out here big enough to eat her, Mother." The fight had left him though. All she needed was one solid excuse beyond her jealous desires, and the rest was just negotiation. "But maybe I can get the man from the orchard to loan us a cart. We could haul some sand up from the beach and take care of it that way. I don't know that it'll work, as the sand might just drain away down that crack—depending on how deep it goes. But if it means so much to you, I'll see about asking."

Two nights later a cart filled with clumpy damp sand was parked beside the hole, though the night was coming down and no one stayed to unload it. Elijah promised to empty it at first light, and to return for a second cart if the job required it.

No one had yet mentioned anything to Prudence, who happily held her starfish collection up to the window and counted their arms again and again. She traced the drying animals on her papers and cut out the likenesses into paper dolls and chains. Then she hung them carefully before the window, so that the light of the moon cast their geometric shadows across the walls and onto her bed.

With the dusk came time for the nightly vespers. Prudence left her artwork on her bed and left the house without her shoes and without a light. She knew the way even with her eyes closed. She was not afraid. The real gods would not let her come to any harm. They were preparing a place for her, *that where they were, there she could be also.*

Sometimes Elijah followed her to the hole, but she never looked back, never cared. He could watch all he liked. Anyone could watch. The real gods didn't mind, so neither did Prudence.

But that night when she reached the edge of the depression, she was not alone and her company was not the benign figure of her quiet brother. She stopped directly across the circle from the cart, and from her mother.

"Why are you here?" the girl asked, but her mother's smugly folded arms and grim-set smile told her plenty.

"I'm ending this foolishness. You're not coming down here anymore."

Prudence lifted a corner of her nostril and sniffed. "You've already done said that. If that's all you've got, I've already heard it."

"I mean it now—and I've got more than words this time." She patted the side of the cart, where a long-handled shovel poked out from the pile within.

"So you've got some dirt. What do you think you're going to do, fill it up? 'Cause you can't." Her eyes shifted down to the crack, searching for hints or for reassurance to reinforce her rebuttal. "They won't let you fill it up."

"They? What, your *real gods* that I hear you spouting about? I've got the True God on my side, and I'm not afraid of any fool thing you've made up."

Prudence's face went cold, and she didn't bother to hide the little smile that crept up her cheek. "Your True God didn't even so much as leave you behind—he never came in the first place. Probably not even the time it says in your book, when it says he was born in the manger. I bet he didn't come then, either."

Frances yanked the shovel from its sheath of sand and swung it around. The centrifugal force nearly knocked her over, but she pointed it at Prudence and held it steady. "You take that back—you take it back or you'll burn in hell!"

THE OCTOBER DEVOTION

"Is that the kind of God you've got? One that won't come bring you to heaven, but doesn't mind tossing you down in hell? Then you can keep him, just like Grandmother says!" She glanced back down into the hole again as if she heard it speaking, then fixed her gaze on a greenish stone beside the crack. It would *just* fit in her palm, if she picked it up. If she held it in her hand, the rounded points of the nodes would *just* fit between her fingers.

Frances came toward her then, flailing and stumbling with the unfamiliar weight of the shovel. Unsure what she intended to use it for, she dropped it in the grass and dug her nails into her hands, squeezing and releasing with every breath as she stalked around the circle to her daughter.

No, the green stone was not beside the crack—it was there, with Prudence's fist wrapped around it. She could have forgotten, and picked it up before. The rounded points poked out from between her fingers like extra knuckles made of polished marble, or glass; and just enough moon sifted down through the trees to make the stone gleam with sweetly shining needles of light. She held it up, only to look at it closer.

She raised it to see the warm flicker that might have come from the moon, or might have originated within. "So that's what you want, Mother? That's all it'd take to make you happy? I wish I'd known. You should have said something sooner."

Frances stopped her stomping approach and slapped Prudence hard, then grabbed her forearm and shook it. Her eyes were reaching again, independent of her skull and on the verge of tears. "What are you talking about?" she screamed, eight inches and a thousand miles from understanding.

For the first time since October twenty-second, Prudence looked straight into those bulbous eyes and spoke. "You want to die for God."

The green stone flashed, and agreed.

November the first, and all was well.

Morning dawned without a trace of red, and no sailors or ships needed fear for the weather. Down in the pit where the men would put sand, instead they found Frances Harding spread across the crack that could not quite swallow her whole. Her head was dented and crimson with the blood of a martyr, which might have pleased her if she'd known.

I go to prepare a place for you…

And down by the shore they found Prudence.

She must have been looking for starfish again. She must have been combing the beach. Elijah thought she might have tripped, but Grandmother supposed that it was only her injury that made her faint. Head wounds do that sometimes, she told him. They let you get better, then they make you all light inside.

It must have been peaceful, though.

I will receive you unto myself, that where I am…

Almost beautiful the way they found her, floating in the waters left-over from the tide. Her dress swam with her, billowing in the slight currents caused by the gulf winds; and her arms waved languidly above the scuttling crabs and broken shells.

And one other thing—one green stone the size and shape of a starfish—a peculiar relic that sank to the tide pool bottom as her life had drained away and her grip had slackened. Whatever the real gods required of her, she had been unable to join them. The dark, wet crevice had hidden them well, and locked them away in a place too remote for Prudence to reach. Even her great faith could not overcome mortal lungs and breakable bones; and even the solemn promise of the real gods could not carry her across the eons to meet them.

…there ye may be also. 🜚

THE WRECK OF
THE *MARY BYRD*

I don't know where all other authors get their ideas, but many of mine come from footnotes. In all honesty, I do not remember where I saw the footnote regarding a riverboat called the *Mary Byrd*; I recall that it was some historic pseudo-reference tome, and I think it was something to do with history in Tennessee, or along the Tennessee River. (I went through a deep-dive phase on the region, right about the time I left it for Seattle—for the first time—back around 2005-2006.) I probably picked up the book secondhand, from McKay Used Books in Chattanooga. I used to work there, and it ended badly, but that didn't stop me from shopping there. A lot.

Anyway, I can't find it now and God knows, I've hunted high and low.

You'll just have to take my word for it when I say that I was reading a book about things that happened years ago in southern

Appalachia and/or the Tennessee River basin, and my eyes chased an asterisk to a footnote at the bottom of the page. There, I learned of a riverboat called the *Mary Byrd*. She disappeared in 1870, somewhere between Chattanooga and Knoxville, on the Tennessee River. Her wreck was never found.

I don't know how many people vanished with the boat, and I don't know if anyone ever mounted a serious expedition to locate crew, passengers, or wreckage. I've literally never found a single other mention of this boat, ever. Anywhere. For all I know, it never existed. It might've been a local tale, a rural legend to explain strange things at a certain spot in the river. "Mary Byrd" could've been someone's grandmother, or aunt, or poodle.

But now she's a novella—the first one I ever sold. It was released in a collection with two related stories: *Halfway to Holiness* and (one of my personal favorite titles) *Our Lady of the Wasteland and the Hallelujah Chorus*.

I went full-tilt pulp with these stories, starting with *The Wreck of the Mary Byrd*. In this one, you'll find werewolves and gamblers and a little red-haired, monster-hunting Irish nun who fights evil with a pair of pistols.

The nun owes her fictional existence to a real-life Irish woman who was once a nun, and who was likewise once the head of the rhetoric department at the University of Tennessee (at Chattanooga). Her name is Eileen Meagher. I was her graduate assistant back in the late 90s/early 2000s, and we are still friendly after all these years. She gave this project her blessing, with a single request: She wanted the nun to have guns and to use them well—because she's afraid of guns, and she liked the idea of her fictional alter ego being proficient with them.

I loved the character so much that I still use her, every now and again, in utterly unrelated stories. She turns up in the background here and there, rarely named but often helpful. Readers usually don't catch her, but every blue moon I get an email from someone saying "I see what you did there."

I always love to hear it.

IN 1870 the steamboat *Mary Byrd* vanished on the Tennessee River, somewhere between Chattanooga and Knoxville. She was never recovered, and her passengers and crew have long been presumed dead. No trace of the wreck has ever been found.

This is the strange and tragic story of the boat's last night—as told by those who rode aboard her. Listen to their tales: the captain, a gambler, a former slave, and an Irish nun with a revolver under her skirt.

And listen as the villain shares his part in the tragedy.

This is his confession too.

From the jungles of India to an American riverboat, his journey was stranger than anyone could have guessed. More monster than man, he was trapped in a storm, on a boat, with a moon above that was almost full—and a deadly hunger that could not be contained.

So here lie the ghosts of the *Mary Byrd*. This is their last testament. Read it, and may you kindly judge the souls you meet within.

I.

I will tell you how it happened.

It unfolded.

My name was Christopher Cooper, and I gambled for my money like a good little sinner. The big-stakes games in Texas, and out in California—they kept me very well fed, and dressed in all the imported clothes I could stand.

I was a big man—once a hard-working man with lots of muscles, but I admit in time that it all ran to fat. It took a lot of cash to clothe me.

I liked big jackets with deep pockets, and I liked boots with quiet heels. No sense in announcing yourself everywhere, I always said. Sometimes I wore bolo ties, but I never resorted to cowboy hats like some of the fellows out west. I always preferred to think of myself as a northeastern lad. The bolo was merely a concession to fashion and a conversation piece.

Women seemed to like it. They'd touch it with their pretty-smelling fingers and twist it around their nails, asking me where I got it from. Once upon a time there was a turquoise slide on it—a fine polished stone set in silver. It matched a pocket watch I carried, and I liked to have them together.

The watch was a gift from a married woman who wouldn't let me keep her. She had it engraved, so I'd always remember why I loved her, and that she'd sent me on my way. She was a cruel little beast. I worshipped the ground she walked on.

Think of me every moment.

If I was very lucky, she might have thought about me once in a blue moon. I didn't need a reminder, but the watch was too beautiful to discard in some sentimental gesture. It was worth a small fortune. She'd commissioned it from a jewelry maker in San Francisco. He was an Austrian, she said.

In time, the nuisance longing I felt for her faded to a dull pang noticed only on occasion. But I always did love that watch, shining merrily on its matching silver chain. And every time I considered the time, until the day I died, I thought of *her*.

THE WRECK OF THE *MARY BYRD*

Those first, lazy nights onboard that damn boat, we came and went from our rooms to the main decks—back and forth from the galley to the prow, starboard to port or however they put it when you're talking about a water vessel. We wandered around, is what I mean to say. There wasn't much else to do except stare at the water and play cards downstairs on the first level.

So that's where I spent most of my time, when I could find someone to play with me. After a while, the pickings got slim. I'm awfully good, and most of my traveling companions weren't willing to bet in earnest, so there wasn't much to win. Even so, by a few days into my journey I was willing to bet in buttons or clamshells. Anything to eat up the time.

No wonder the captain drank so much.

Boat was one hell of a dull way to travel. I shuddered to think of my grandparents, who crossed an ocean in a bigger boat than this one. The Atlantic? I would have killed myself from the sheer dullness of it all.

But I must confess, the boat was a pretty thing—and I can appreciate a pretty boat or a pretty woman as well as the next man. The *Mary Byrd* they called her. I want to say it was named for the captain's wife, but I don't think that's the case. I think he bought it from another man and the name came with it.

Some other man's wife, more likely—or a daughter. Or a mistress.

I hope she was named for someone beautiful.

On the outside she was painted white, or a bright ivory—and her name was splashed on the side in bloody yellow-orange letters with curlicues. She had a paddlewheel on her stern too, and it matched the lettering. The rails on the deck were lined with that curious latticework you see on houses sometimes; it cast shadows in the afternoons, like eyelets in the fabric of a lady's nightgown.

On the inside, she was dressed in red and orange that looked like nothing so much as a high-class whorehouse. If I'd said as much out loud, people would wish to know how I was qualified to make such a comparison.

I was qualified. But I kept it to myself.

Where the floors were scuffed and shined wood, they were run with low rugs; and the lamps were all set with glass, brass, and crystal dangles that looked like earrings.

The other passengers gathered that I had money, and most of them probably knew (or could guess) how I'd gotten it. I thought maybe the nun would look down her nose about it, gambling not being sanctioned by the Lord, and all; but if she cared or noticed, she didn't say anything. She was a papist, after all—and open to her own set of criticisms from the other passengers.

To think of it that way—and I guess I should—we all had something like that about us. Perhaps it was just coincidence, or merely the time of year; but the *Mary Byrd* was a ship of misfits, in a most uninteresting way.

That last trip from Knoxville to Chattanooga was more empty than full; and those of us who were left were those without more proper, permanent places to be. As far as I could ascertain, we were all passing from one thing to another, as is ordinary enough when it comes to traveling companions.

But none of us were coming from home—or going there. So I don't suppose it's strange that when we were lost, we were forgotten.

There were signs that should've told us to expect trouble from the very start—or from our last stop, at Lenoir City. Whatever went wrong, we picked it up there; and I can only think of one person for sure who boarded then.

I shouldn't be so veiled about it. After all, by the end, we all knew. And it doesn't much matter to us now. I'd like to think he's been waiting all this time, though I can't imagine why he would. Maybe he lost something when the boat went down. Maybe he left something behind, and he can't rest until he gets it back.

I doubt it, though. If he watches at all, he watches because he's afraid. He's afraid, and he wants to make sure that it stays buried, and burned up there in the water where he left it.

He wants to make sure that *she* stays buried, and he's afraid she hasn't.

II.

I will tell you how it happened.

It broke.

I didn't have much of value, but I was rich. My mother was a slave, and I was born one too—but she stayed, and I went north after the war. I did all right for myself. I worked hard, but I got paid and I paid my own way from it. My name was Laura Brown, and I was nobody's slave.

When I got up north, first of all I started work in a factory where we plucked poultry—but it was dark there and so close, and it always smelled like the shit of dead chickens, and the fuzz from the feathers made my nose itch all day. It made my eyes water, even on days when the wind blowed through the open windows and the stink wasn't so bad.

Before long, I left the factory and went to work in a kitchen.

I washed dishes, spent every day up to my elbows in greasy water with cheap soap bubbles. The restaurant was big and it served a lot of folks every day. I stayed twelve hours if they wanted. My home wasn't worth running home to.

I shared a place high in the city with eight other girls and the brother of one of them.

All of us working together made enough to eat and sleep there, but not by much. But none of us were house niggers, and none of us were field niggers. We earned our own and we paid our way, though living was crowded and dark.

We were sick all the time, one or another of us. One would catch a bug, and the rest of us would pass it around—so it was easier to stay in the kitchen, in the dish room with the pots and pans. It was easier to be clean there, in the middle of the kitchen. It was easier to breathe.

But I missed the sun.

I missed being able to breathe and not smell piss and tomatoes, wine and onions and meat that's thinking about going bad. I didn't like the cold, either. I could always handle it hot. Hot meant nothing to me. I was a girl in Mississippi, down by the ocean near where the loud water birds scream and steal your food if you don't hang onto it.

That's part of why they liked me in the kitchen. The hot water and the hot stoves were easy work for me, and I could work them all day.

But come winter, every year I thought I'd die rather than stay another season. I'd watch the snow pile high up out the window, and the first time I saw it, it was all I could do not to start crying. I near lost my religion every time the wind blew up and the ice made the street stones hard to cross. I saved my work money when I could, and I bought heavier skirts, heavier coats. But it was never enough. There weren't boots thick enough to save my feet when the snow went melting through. There weren't wool socks made heavy enough to keep my toes from turning colors and losing feeling.

And Lord, I was far from home.

I thought, like the rest of us did, that the farther north I'd go, the easier it would be. The less trouble I'd have. The more money I'd make. Nobody told me about the cold, though. Nobody told me about how everything I owned would stink of coal and wood smoke, and how our lungs would turn themselves black. They didn't tell us how just breathing would make us wish we couldn't.

I asked around. I thought since it'd been a few years since the war and we were freed all over—I thought maybe it'd be okay to come home.

THE WRECK OF THE *MARY BYRD*

I heard it wasn't. I heard times was tough there for everybody, even the white people too. But that didn't mean much. I saw poor white people in the north cities too; I saw signs that broke them down by what country they came from, and offered them less money for doing the same jobs. I thought it was crazy, how white people thought there was some difference between them, and not just between us and them.

The older I got, the less sense they made to me.

But back down in Dixie I heard tale of sharecropping and bad laws. Nobody getting no work, and nobody having enough to eat. And down there now, where everyone was poor just about, it was like in the cities— and all the folks got to fight amongst themselves for what's there.

I heard it was worse than before, some ways.

But then I'd sit in our little room, huddled up around the stove with the rest of the girls, and I'd wish I could feel my feet again, and I'd hate it how I could see my breath every morning when I woke up, and I thought maybe it couldn't be worse than this.

Maybe I could go back down and get some learning. Maybe I'd like to teach a school, and teach little ones to read.

I knew my letters and numbers a little, but not good enough that it helped me. I wanted to learn them better. And then, if I knew them better, I could share it with the rest of them. I figured there were lots of folks who wanted to read. I thought there must be schools coming up fast.

But that wasn't what I heard.

I got an idea, though—one that made me want to find a teacher who'd show me the letters good enough to write them, and I'd write a book. Not a story book, and not a book for learning by, but a book for cooking with.

A woman told me there were opportunities for women who could cook. She said that without any slaves, the white women had to go into their own kitchens, and they didn't know what to do. They needed someone to tell them.

So I thought, *I could tell them.*

I could write a book and I could fill it up with my mama's recipes. I could put in the pies and the breakfast hash, and the right way to make grits without turning them soggy. I could tell them how to make chicken fry up nice and crunchy, but wet and dripping good in the middle. And maybe, if my grandmother was still alive down there, maybe she could tell me some of the ways they made food back in Africa, too. She didn't come from there, but her daddy did, and she used to say she knew. So I could ask her.

But I'd need to know my letters better, first.

And I got wind of a possibility. I heard maybe that if you could work a kitchen good, there were boats you could ride. You could work for the people on the boats, the ones that carried things along the rivers. People rode them like floating hotels.

Someone had to do the cooking for the workers. Someone had to run the kitchens.

It took me a year to work my way down to it. It took one more winter up in the city, and I swear, I thought I'd die.

I was aiming for the Mississippi River. I wanted to work one of the big riverboats that went back and forth, from the top of the country to the bottom. I thought that'd be grand, and I could work my way home while making some money.

It didn't work out the way I expected. I got my start farther east, on the Ohio River instead, and that was all right too, I thought. I'd get some experience on the smaller boats. It took me another year, but I found my way down to the Tennessee.

I found my way to the *Mary Byrd*.

I did the dishes there, and did some of the cooking too—though I had some help for that, a fat, quiet man with all the shine and color of boot polish. He never talked to me except to give me something to do, and I was all right with that. When first I saw him, I figured he was the kind of man who'll give a woman trouble if he thinks he can get away with it.

THE WRECK OF THE *MARY BYRD*

I been wrong before, though. He never gave me trouble.

He was a good cook, too; he made food like the kind my grand-mother did. We always had potatoes, because they store pretty good, and he loaded them up with butter and sour cream if he had time to get them when we stopped. Over the stove he kept a cardboard box of salt and a beat-up tin of pepper. Just these two things and the butter, and he could make a feast for a king. I swear, that man made cornbread fit to feed Jesus.

He deserved better than that boat, but I guess he had his reasons.

We all had our reasons.

The first signs of trouble came after supper, the first night we were on the river after Lenoir City. We'd picked up an extra passenger or two there, and some cargo that nobody asked about. I'd been doing this long enough then that I didn't ask. You just don't.

It looked heavy. The roustabouts who brought it onboard staggered underneath it. The hold was already pretty full, so they had to cram it on in.

Some of the hold was taken up with that woman's baggage, and I don't know what a woman like that would travel with. She was a nun, I think—the fat gambler, Mr. Cooper, he called her 'sister' every time he saw her. He said it like he thought it was a joke—like he knew something about her that made it funny.

I saw some nuns up in the city. They worked in a big walled-in building where people left orphans. I'd hear the kids playing on the other side of the wall, and I'd hear the teachers inside. I guess the nuns taught letters and numbers too, not just how to kneel right and say prayers. I'd sit on the other side of the wall and eat my lunch when I had some. I'd listen while they went over the letters. I wished I could see them, though. It would've helped. As it was, I didn't learn much.

Anyway, I knew a nun when I saw one, but something was *off* about her. She wore the little head covering like they do, and black dresses that were simple. But there was smartness to her and a fastness to the way she moved. She asked a lot of questions.

She asked them with a smile, and with a tilted down head that told you she was all kindness and don't you just know, she was only asking because she wondered—and it wouldn't hurt you at all to talk to her.

But she asked a lot of questions.

She made some of us uncomfortable, but whether that was because she was a Catholic, or a foreign lady, or just because she was an educated lady on a boat full of men who were themselves only half-schooled…I don't know. There were a hundred and one reasons for them to push her to the outside.

It turned out she was looking for something. And she was very, very close.

I think if there was a God, really a God like my grandmother said— and like the little red-haired nun believed—then he would have let her find it sooner. If she'd gotten her answers before that last night on the *Mary Byrd*, then we might have found our separate ways home, or to whatever destinations we had in mind. We wouldn't have wound up where we did, lying down dead in burned-up clothes at the bottom of a river. The river washed us all clean. It washed us down to nothing but bones, and all our bones were the same.

Or that's just what I think. I been wrong, though.

As I told you, the trouble began after supper, as it's likely to do. Not all the strangers wanted to eat together, but there are always a few who like it—who enjoy the traveling, and like talking to all the strange new people you find on a boat, or on a road. These people find each other.

THE WRECK OF THE *MARY BYRD*

So over supper that night there was a handful of folks. The gambler was there, teasing the nun in a friendly way, and she didn't act like she minded it. There were three others, too—including the captain. We were anchored on account of the weather. It was pouring down outside and the water kept sloshing up over the decks.

Mary was riding low in the water, anyhow—because of what she was moving other than people. There was a lot of rocking, and since we were sitting low, the captain didn't want to rush it. I didn't want to argue with him, but I didn't like him being downstairs with no one at the boat's wheel, either.

That might have been silly, though. I didn't know enough about the way boats worked to know if it was bad of him to join us. I guess he could've had someone else up there helping him; I knew we had a roof pilot too, but I hadn't seen him around.

Could be the captain was just hungry.

Well, we fed him. He'd have had more room to eat if he hadn't drank so much. It made me nervous to watch him. This was the man who drove us down the river. Maybe he should've had a better idea when to quit pouring himself more, at least while other folks were watching.

I heard him talking to the other passengers, and they didn't mind him so they let him talk. His voice sounded like childhood to me. It was low and sleepy more often than not, and even when he drank wine he smelled like a cold southern drink served on a porch.

I had a feeling about him, like he'd been in the war, and it hadn't gone so good for him. But he was a man from south of the Ohio, so no, I guess it wouldn't have. I wondered how bad it'd been for him, but it wasn't my place to ask, so I didn't. He wore that old defeat all over him. He wore it like it was an important thing, or something valuable that he wouldn't let out of his sight. But it wasn't. And we all knew it.

"This is my boat," he told them around the table. "I've found a buyer, though. When we get to Chattanooga we'll stay a few days—and I'll hand off the boat, and I'll take my money. That'll be it for me, then. No more of this river business."

"Has it treated you so poorly?" the nun asked. Her accent was as heavy as his, but it came from somewhere father away. "You seem like a comfortable man. You've earned a life from the river, haven't you?"

"I have. I've earned a second life, Sister." They all called her Sister, except for once in a while, one of them would call her Sister Eileen.

Mr. Cooper pulled his pretty watch out of his pocket and checked the time. Supper was over and it might have been getting late, but that's not what he was thinking. He was wondering if it was late enough to bug someone into playing cards with him. But he was willing to wait until the nun left. I guess he thought it was being respectful.

The captain was too drunk to be any good for poker, but one of the other two men might have been dumb enough to take Mr. Cooper on. One by one they retired, though. And then the captain did too. He said he was going back to the wheel, like he was going to start moving again, but we knew he wasn't.

The rain was coming down hard, still. And he had too much wine in him to steer us anyplace at all.

The rain came slapping against the windows, where we had windows, and it came splashing down onto the deck and into the rooms where we didn't. Thunderstorms are easy enough to wait through, though. And it was warm. At least getting wet didn't mean freezing yourself to death, or losing toes. So I didn't mind the rain. I'd missed it, and I was happy to see it again.

"Can I clear these plates out for you?" I asked them, wishing they'd finish up. Mr. Cooper and the nun, as they were the only two left, they told me that was fine and they were mostly finished. But they stayed out there talking in a friendly way, and I thought it was funny that the two of them would be friends.

Doesn't the Lord frown on cards and dice alike?

III.

I will tell you how it happened.

It unraveled.

My given name was John Gabert, but I went by many others if the mood and fancy struck me. From time to time, the mood and fancy came in the form of police attention, or in the stalking threats of mercenaries. Occasionally, it was a journalist—some ratty, tattered little man with a notebook and a pencil clenched between two fingers.

I could only give them what they didn't want. I could give them a name (not my own) and an ounce of respectability (borrowed or stolen), and I always had—at my immediate disposal—an alibi.

An alibi was my favorite accessory.

I would wear one like a funeral carnation in a black lapel. I would use it to garnish myself, and to redeem myself. I would sport it in public to reassure London that I was a worthy, plain, and innocent citizen—confused, and in mourning like the rest of them.

But after a while...yes, well. In time, all the expensive alibis in the world could not be stacked, one on top of another, high enough to build a wall between myself and the prying eyes of nervous, curious people.

Jesus, God, or Whoever.

It was only a little hunger. Only a *little* need.

And I kept it so closely in check. I watched myself for the signs, and for the warnings. After so many years I knew what to look for, and what twisted visions I could count upon to warn of impending change. I had learned how to control it!

All the rest I can blame on my father, because I went to him for help and he refused me, at first. Later, he would use his influence to keep our name out of the papers, and later—always when it was much too late—he would quietly arrange for restitution.

He seemed to think it was a disease—acquired in some opium den or brothel. Every objection I uttered was nonce to him, and every plea for a reasonable treatment fell on deaf ears. So far as he was concerned, I needed a physician like Dr. Marblen, or Dr. Bentley. There was no room in my father's head for an infection like the one I carried.

There was no room in his mind for the monsters at the far corners of the Good Queen's Empire.

In time, he came to invent his own explanations. He passed them around to his friends over too much brandy when the weather was cold. Once he said that I'd been cursed by a gypsy, and another time he mumbled that I'd been trampled by elephants while abroad.

Once—just once—he came very near the truth by virtue of his own imagination. Even as he denied any truth to the unflattering rumors, he would feed them seedling crumbs.

One night I overheard him speaking to the marquess. He spoke of me like I was a wayward adventurer from a penny dreadful; he was constructing a myth of me with his words, in his own library and parlor. Deny the facts when they are gruesome, or untidy. Speculate for me something prettier, and simpler, and easier to spread by firelight.

I recall, from my listening place beside the door jamb, that there were expensive cigars that night and a crystal decanter that drained by the hour. I held my position outside the room, and listened to the old men ramble about war, and children, and monsters like me.

"It was during his time in India, you know. That was where the event occurred that changed him so, though you do not think him much changed now. I can only say that there are nights when he must be seen to be believed—and days when we must close him away for fear of him, and for what he would do if left unattended.

THE WRECK OF THE *MARY BYRD*

"He went out on safari with the son of a friend—I think you know him, so I'll leave his name from the story, if you don't mind—but he went out with a rifle and an elephant. They were hunting tigers, as you do when in a place such as that.

"I've heard stories, you know—of places like that one. They tell me it is as if the whole land itself rises up and wishes you gone. Every stray plant has thorns and each new creature is deadlier than the last. I swear, I wish we had left it alone. I think so sometimes," he added quickly, "but I know that it's all for the best. I'm a brick for the empire, and my son was too. I mean no disrespect or disloyalty when I say these things. I only mean that it's an inhospitable place, more hot and unwelcoming than hell. That is what I've heard, though you can take or leave it as you like."

I thought the marquess should leave it, personally, as my father was well into his cups, but inexplicably speaking less nonsense than usual. Let him tell the truth through a fog of alcohol. Stories told that way are always easy to discard when morning comes and a headache comes with it.

Besides, India was not so bad. It was hot, yes. But England is cold, as often as not, and between the two I believe that I prefer the struggles of staying cool to the struggles of staying warm.

Like so many other preferences of mine, my father would not understand it.

"Somewhere under the jungle canopy they rode on their elephants with the brown boys guiding them, calling out sights and hushing the party when game felt close. I imagine he wore a proper helmet, and he carried that old gun of mine—I insisted he take it, though now I wish I'd lent him something bigger, or something faster to shoot.

"But then a storm brewed up fast, as these things do in such hellish climes. They were too far into the bush to retreat, so they huddled for camp and sheltered themselves as best they could.

"One of the brown fellows cried out, and was lost. It's dark there, when the sun goes out and trees stretch high and thick above. They couldn't see what took the man. They couldn't tell if he was hurt, or dead, or only running. The storm did not relent, though. Water came down in drops as big as your thumb, and the elephants shuddered for wet and worry. They stamped their giant feet into the mud and wished to be elsewhere, as did the remaining men, I'm sure.

"There in the sodden jungle, where it must have been quite dark, they could not see so well for the shadow and the pitching rain. They could not have known when the trees parted, and through them slipped the beast."

"A tiger?"

"What else?" My father asked it drunkenly, sloshing his glass and gesturing at the window, at the ceiling with it.

I had told him what else, as best I could. We both knew it was no tiger, but he had no other name by which to call the dread, so he gave it a word he knew.

"It pounced at them, it leaped upon them!" And here he lost more brandy, or scotch, or whatever the drink was that night. "It fell upon them, you see—and my son had not stayed atop his elephant where there was more safety. They say that a tiger won't disturb an elephant, and if my son had believed it—"

I'd believed it, but I think it would not have mattered. The elephants were trumpeting, by then. The danger was too near, and it was something that made the big beasts break, and run.

"He might have stayed there, atop the beast. But no. He had come down to the ground to chat with another man—and then the beast, it leaped! I said that, it leaped—and it fell on them both. The one man, the friend of my son, he died on the spot.

"But my son was able to crawl away. After the storm was over and the tiger had gone its own way, John was gathered, by the brown fellows and by the remaining people from the hunting party. He was gathered up and taken back into Delhi where he languished there in a hospital. You must understand what it's like there, so hot and so wet. So damp with disease and I tell you, it is hard for an Englishman to recover from a cold in that place—much less from a wound so dire. And that's the meat of it, I think. I don't think he ever recovered. Not fully. Not like he should have, if he'd been here."

The marquess left his own glass on the arm of the chair, and he did not raise it to his lips. "Is there—I mean, has he a scar, then? Some mark of the injury to show for it?"

My father shuddered then, the way the elephants had when the thing had poured itself out into the trail. "You should see it, Henry. Or maybe, you should not. I've seen the injuries of war before. Not much turns my stomach. But oh, the way its teeth met his skin—and the way it bit through bone. What else…" He started a thought and lost it, swirled it around in his glass.

"A tiger, of course. What else could it have been?" The marquess finished the question for him, because I think he knew I was listening from the hall. "No fault of his own then, if it's left him with a terrible shock. It's a wonder he lives at all."

"A wonder," my father said. "A wonder indeed."

If it had been my mother there, or my brother, he might have added the rest of his conclusion—that it was a wonder better left a continent or two away. But it would not do to say such things in front of Henry, so he let the story end.

He was wrong, of course. He was wrong in more ways than I could begin to tell, given a full decanter and a willing ear. He was wrong about the city, and the weather, and the tiger. But something about the way he told it—I liked this version better. When I heard him share it with his old friend, I thought perhaps—just for a few minutes, with a brain steeped in brandy—he'd understood what I'd told him after all. Even if he couldn't fathom the players, he knew the play.

Even if he didn't want to cry "wolf," for that is a thing that reckless boys do.

He could think I was reckless if he liked. He was probably correct, after all. There *was* a reckless beauty to it. There was a reckless poetry when I lifted my face to the sky and bared my teeth like a savage, like a screaming boy, and I made my voice twist itself into the sound of a wolf.

And when I jumped—God, when I jumped.

I could feel myself leaving the earth and clawing my way through the sky, for seconds at a time, and then there was nothing else in the universe—no God at all, even. Only grass and clouds and the scent of a living planet left orphan by a reckless creator.

They said, in the papers and in the penny dreadfuls, that it was as if I had springs on my feet. I must have aid, to leap so high. I must have a coiled mechanism to propel me so. Truly, it was easier to blame science than Mystery.

And truly, it was a silly name they gave me—though they got the "Jack" part right, by guess or circumstance.

Eventually I became too much hassle to hide. Eventually, when the moon turned over and glared down full across the night, it was too much for me to contain. If my father had admitted the nature of my ailment, some better treatment might have been made. Almost anything would have been better than chains and a basement. "Hide the moon from him, if that's what does it," he'd said. He was a fool and a liar.

The moon did nothing to me. It was only a cue, a trigger, and a goal. Every jump, every leap, every spring-heeled crouch and short, sharp flight—it was all to reach the moon, because I swear, she was the only one who'd have me.

But failing the moon, and failing my father, and failing my country, too—I made plans to leave. The stories were swirling too close, sometimes. The mad little men with the pencils and the presses swarmed a touch too near. I began to fear quite honestly that if I did not leave, I would be killed.

I left a note, as courtesy demanded.

But I suspect, when my father discovered he was unexpectedly free of me, that he was so overwhelmed with relief that he did not read it.

THE WRECK OF THE *MARY BYRD*

I went to America. I sequestered myself on a cargo ship with supplies for tobacco farmers. I told them I was a missionary bound for the western colonies, and that after my experiences in Delhi, I wanted to help civilize and sedate the savages on the other end of the world. Whether they believed me or not, I cannot say.

Upon arrival, I found New England too much like Old England for my liking. My tastes wanted warmer weather, someplace moist and green—preferably with a few open spaces to let me leap up at the sky when the lunacy came over me.

I went south, and slightly west—a colony state at a time.

I had no single goal in mind beyond seeking out warmth and seclusion; I was led to understand that these things could be found in abundance down farther in the colonies, closer to the west, and to the ocean. I made my furtive way south, then. Border by border. County by county, and town by town.

It seemed faster and easier, really—more civilized, at least—to try the rivers instead of the ragged old horse ruts.

I went to a city called Knoxville, and then on south to the next stop down—where I was told I could purchase passage on a steamship called the *Mary Byrd*.

IV.

I will tell you how it happened.

It burned, and sank.

My name was Eileen Callaghan, though if I spoke softly people often didn't notice the Irish in my words, there in America. People thought that a woman in a habit was meant to be quiet and contemplative, so I was rarely asked to speak much, and that was fine.

No one answers that call for the social life.

I answered when I was a girl, still. I knelt in the church and bowed my head, and I asked for the convent because I believed—I still believe—that I heard Him asking me for my time, and my life. I agreed and I answered; because after all, I owed Him no less.

I spent many of those early years with the scriptures, then with other books in the library, then outside the walls when I could leave. I wanted to know everything. I wanted to understand. I wanted to breathe in all the truth.

After a while, I began to think that this was not all there was. There in the convent, with its quiet sisters and thick walls, I could find truth with the Virgin and her son. I filled myself up with prayers and piety; I lit my life with votives, and with the sun spilling warmly patterned through stained glass and screens.

And one day, I confessed in the dark little room: "There is *more* than this."

Because they did not understand, they were afraid I would try to renounce my vows out of boredom. So they gave me little assignments here and there—small responsibilities in the community, and in other cities sometimes too.

I found some meaning in the poor quarters in Dublin, Belfast, and later in London, where we fed and clothed the ones we could; but I found more meaning still when I followed the women I found in those places.

I followed them to the sticky streets where they waited on street corners and in alleys, behind pubs and in littered lots. I watched them, and watched out for them when I could. I brought them into the church and let them warm themselves with our small lights—with candles lit for themselves, their mothers, and their daughters.

THE WRECK OF THE *MARY BYRD*

I watched them come and go from the safety to the streets, back and forth each night like the tide.

Sometimes I would walk with them, if they wanted. Sometimes they did not want to be alone, or they wished for a respite. Having a woman like me there would chase away their customers—and sometimes, for an hour or so, this was good. The dirty men in their itching clothes would saunter forward and see me—they'd see my uniform and know me—and they would think about being boys in white. They would remember being small, and standing before the altar with their mouths open. They thought of communion wine and bland white wafers.

And some of them would be ashamed. They would turn on their heels and slink back into the dark.

Once or twice I was propositioned too, by men who maybe remembered things differently—or who had no upbringing in the church. Once or twice a man would ask me to lift my skirts.

But not often.

On one such night, I stood beside a girl who had the name of her birthday's saint—she was Barbara, and should have been home safe in her father's tower. At least, she was very beautiful and would never be married, so some of the story was preserved.

These stories, if you read enough of them you start to see—they come back around again. (I used to think, sometimes, that these stories are all one. And they are told over and over again; we are all drawn to the same ones, to the same lives, and we repeat ourselves incessantly.)

She interrupted me. "Have you heard about the jumping man? Jumping Jack, I think the girls want to call him, but the papers say his name is something else."

"Really? Have you read them?"

"No, I can't read. But the news boys tell us sometimes, if we ask them nice. We wanted to know if anyone had heard. Not like it'd matter. So long as it's just *us* being scared by him, no one cares. But he's started chasing finer prey than us, I guess, because they're talking about him now. He's working his way up, he is."

"Why do you say that?"

"Well he jumped a fine lady, I hear. Scared her senseless. Tore off her dress and scratched up her belly like an animal. She's been in bed since it happened, and she might not recover. They'll catch him now, I bet. They'll make him stop, now that he's chasing a better kind."

"Has he hurt anyone here yet—badly, I mean?" I asked her.

She shrugged like she wasn't sure how to answer that, or how to quantify what 'badly' meant. "A couple of girls, he scratched them up so they bled real bad. And he's scared 'em half to death, with his ugly yellow eyes and all that, but mostly they get back up again and go back to work in a few days."

I couldn't decide how it made me feel—if I was proud for Barbara and her sisters, or if I was sorry for them. Daily or weekly they'd seen enough and been hurt enough that assault was only an afterthought in a night's tally. The spring-heeled man was worth a mention because he didn't seem human, and *that* was worth talking about. *That* was worth a few minutes of gossip.

"He's only a fairy tale. You're making him into more." I meant to reassure her because I couldn't imagine what truth there might be in it. I had to assume that it was boredom that made them talk so, and put such stock in such wild stories.

"Not anymore. Not when the rich girls tell it. When the rich girls tell it, it's *news*."

She was right, of course.

I tried to guide her, and the rest of them too—I tried to lend them my support, and give them the sense that someone thought they were worthwhile, and that there was a God who would have them and hear them. In time, I found it best to simply be their friend as well as I could. I would like to say that I made a difference, but I came to doubt it.

And before long, there were incidents, as you might expect.

There were problems. There were deaths, and accusations, and hints of impropriety. Good women of God did not lurk in such places. It would raise questions. Well, I had my questions too. Didn't Christ himself walk with the prostitutes and the lepers? Times were troubled, yes, but that only meant they needed us more.

I think, I guess, that I came to believe my superiors. I think, I guess, that I started to believe the church. But by then, I had learned the difference between the Virgin and the Church. And I did not believe anymore that the two held hands more tightly than a vise.

"There is truth here," I said to the priest at my last confession. "But this is not all the truth there is to be found."

I told him I meant to leave, and he did not stop me.

I had half a mind to follow the crumbs of truth wherever they went. I opened my eyes, opened my ears, and opened my Bible. Piece by piece the trail became clear. A light beckoned across the ocean—it lured me onto a boat, and over the water. I followed it as best I could. I watched it flicker and dim, then flare and sizzle.

I went to America.

Didn't everyone, who needed a new start?

V.

I will tell you how it happened.

It fell apart.

She was my boat, and she was always meant to be my last. After our last run, down that little leg from Knoxville to Chattanooga—hardly a hundred miles—I was going home. My wife was waiting for me there, at her sister's place on Lookout Mountain. I was to lean hard on the whistle treadle three times when I passed between the hills. She would know to look outside and see me coming. The smoke from the big black stacks would show my progress even at a very great distance.

Her sister would bring her down to the landing.

We might stay in the valley for a while; the weather was good and there was no rush to head back home.

But we hadn't talked about that, yet—whether or not we'd really go home. We weren't certain anything was left of it. Last we heard, the Yankees hadn't burned it; but however Bellehurst was standing, word had it, the place wasn't doing so well.

Maybe we'd heard wrong. The news coming up was spotty and unreliable, or that's how we liked to think.

In Chattanooga, the war hadn't treated the city too bad. It was too important, with the river and the rails. Everyone needed to use it. It took some beating, sure—but nothing like what they got down in Georgia. Nothing like Chickamauga, maybe ten or twelve miles south.

I hear the mountains took the worst of it, but I don't know if it's true. I know soldiers and generals always try to take the highest ground, and there's nothing higher around there than Lookout and Signal.

But after it was over…after Appomattox, there was no going back to the way things were. Not in Tennessee, not in Georgia, and not anywhere else.

I did say they left the house standing, though, didn't I? Sherman went another way, and burned another stretched-out scar on someone else's land. But they didn't take our place—even though we left it for them.

I went into the service. They made me a major, because they couldn't expect a man with stature to enlist in the infantry. I pray I did them proud.

Nancy went to go stay with family. I'd say that between us, she sure got the better part of the deal. My wife had cousins down in Florida—on an indigo plantation, if I remember right. When the war came, these cousins of hers didn't just leave the state or the Confederacy, they left the continent altogether. They went to the Caribbean and waited out the conflict there on the sandy islands to the south and east.

In my private thoughts, I felt they were being disloyal. They should have stayed and fought with the rest of us. But if they were determined to leave, then it was just as well they took Nancy with them. I don't know how well she would have handled it, staying there. She could've been killed, or worse.

But when the war ended and the homestead was gone—or out of commission, anyway, since everyone who worked it was scattered or free, I didn't know what to do. Fortune hadn't favored us, to say the least. I was out of money, though Nancy was spared that trouble, being in the islands like she was. I am glad for that. I should speak better of her cousins. I don't know what would have happened if they hadn't taken her with them.

After my discharge, I sat down and wrote a very painful letter to my wife. I didn't go into any more detail than necessary; but I told her the truth about our money situation—and I told her that she should stay with her family as long as it was necessary, since I couldn't provide for her the way I did before. I told her, in short, that I'd made my fortune on the Mississippi, and I lost it to the Union.

I did not tell her how, exactly. It would not have mattered and it would have bothered her something awful. She didn't need to know about the camp. She didn't need to know about the drinking, the wandering, and the smuggling.

But I told her I loved her, and I meant to repair the rest.

For two years, I'd been rebuilding my reputation—transporting goods and people up and down the Tennessee River. I taught the roof captains how to watch and guide, and I helped apprentice the mud clerks until they could dock a boat without scraping bottom. I'd done it all before, and I believe that my advice and guidance proved invaluable. I was paid for it, anyway. They needed people like me on the rivers.

The south was being "reconstructed," as the politicians liked to say it. I had another word for it, but it was not a polite one that I would have used in front of my wife.

But any construction needs ready supply, and a man with my experience could make a fair living off a river. Granted, a man might need to make a few deals he couldn't share with his family—but I was accumulating a stash of such secrets, and I was getting better by the day at keeping them covered.

I might say, if anyone asked, that all it took was a stash of good scotch.

My wife would have objected, though. That's why I brought her a nice bottle of wine—a glorious green bottle with a foil-trimmed label, straight from France. I bought it from a dealer who was wending his own way down to New Orleans, or so he said.

Maybe it was a ruse, and maybe he had some other plans. He didn't owe me the truth, and I shouldn't have bothered him for it. I do know this much: the first two bottles I drank alone, and they were as fine as the labels promised.

I saved the last, and assumed the best. But Nancy never got to try it.

VI.

Supper was held at the same time, every night, and if you wished to partake, you were welcome to appear. I went every night, in part because I was bored for company, and also because I was hungry. The other passengers always asked me to say Grace, and I didn't mind. I was thankful for the food. The cook was uncommonly good; I would have ridden that boat another week to let him feed me.

I want to say he came from farther down the river. I thought I overheard—or maybe I just inferred—that he was from New Orleans.

There was always wine to go with the meals, but you had to be quick and beat the captain if he was there.

THE WRECK OF THE *MARY BYRD*

The poor man. I don't know what happened to him. It must have been tragic. He said he was on his way home to his wife; and when he said it, there was a blink and a twitch of his neck that told me one or the other wasn't true. He might have been going home, or he might have been going to his wife. I don't know which.

At the end of the night—after the captain had drunk himself to bed, and after the others had turned in for the night as well, I was left with Christopher at the table.

There was a serving girl, I think her name was Laura. She was pretty and dark. I made a joke with her once, about how we both kept our hair covered all the time. She smiled politely and ducked herself away from me.

Laura came and took our plates and Christopher was mellow, itching to play.

"You could deal some cards, if you like," I said.

His eyebrows went up.

"I know how to play," I told him. "I haven't got much money, but I can play for fun, if you like."

He thought about it and then laughed. "Listen Sister, I don't know if I'd feel right about that. But I do appreciate your offer. Would you like a little nip of brandy instead?"

"You'll drink with a nun, but you won't gamble with one, is that it?"

"I believe so, yes." He rose to get a set of glasses. From under the bar, he retrieved a square glass decanter with a glass stopper that looked like a doorknob. He poured me a splash, and then poured a bigger one for himself—a big drink for a big man.

"It won't be much longer now," I told him, accepting the glass and taking a swallow of its contents. "It's not much farther to Chattanooga. That's where you'll be leaving us, isn't it?"

"It is," he assured me. "I have some business to attend to there, and then in a few weeks, I'll be off for Denver."

"Big card game? That *is* how you make your living, isn't it?"

"Nothing gets past you, eh?"

"Not much. Oh, that's not true, really." I had to amend myself, since the purpose of my little river trip occurred to me, reminding me that I was a long way from as sharp as I needed to be. "All the wrong things get past me, or so it seems sometimes."

Christopher sat forward and took a big swallow from his glass. "Wrong things like what? Like missing a sermon about the evils of gambling?"

"Very much like that," I fibbed outright. "It's a pity, I must have slept late that day. I missed the ban on smoking too, though I maintain I can't find a verse for it in the Bible."

He gathered the hint and pulled a cigarette case out from the pocket just north of his watch. I accepted one, and leaned in for him to light it off a match. He held the flame steady in his palm and said, "I think there's one about treating your body like the temple of God, isn't there? Or did I dream that during Sunday school, too?"

"Very good, Mr. Cooper. Paul said so, in Corinthians."

"A very fine observation, ma'am. I couldn't have named a book for it if my life depended on it."

"That's a shame," I told him. "'Christopher' is a good Christian name. You should have listened closer at your lessons."

"Good Christian name, eh? Why, does it mean something?"

"It's from the Greek. It means 'Christ-bearer.' You're named for a Catholic saint, did you know that?"

He laughed again, for the wine always made him jolly like that. "I had no idea, and I assure you that my good protestant parents had no earthly idea either. It's probably best they're both passed on now, so I don't get the chance to tell them. But a saint, eh? So I'm saintly? What's in a name, after all? Roses and holiness for me, I suppose."

"As you like, Christopher. He is the patron saint of travelers, and people like ourselves—on long trips—often wear a medallion to invoke him for assistance. I have one on me, in fact, if you'd like it."

"You'd give it to me?"

"If you want it. I have others, you know how it is. It's only a little pewter thing, but if it would mean something to you, I'd like for you to wear or carry it."

The smile on his face told me that he felt like this was a furtive, naughty thing. "Sure, I'll take a magic charm off your hands. It's not like those beads you carry, is it? I've seen you sitting on the deck, praying with them. They're very pretty."

"No, this isn't like the beads. And thank you. They were a gift from my father when I entered the convent." And I'm not sure why, but I pulled them out from my pocket and handed them to him, just to show him.

He turned them over on his hands, stringing them through his fingers as if he might use them to make a cat's cradle. "Ebony?" he guessed, and I nodded. "And this on the back of this space, here? What's this? A wolf?"

"A wolf," I confessed. I hadn't expected the question. I wasn't thinking about it—the small silver link that held the rosary in the shape of a "Y." On the back was a tiny piece of art to remind me of home, and to remind me how the universe thinks in puns and patterns. "It's for my family, the Callaghans. Our crest has a wolf on it." I tried to say it with a gambler's nonchalance. After all, it wasn't important. It wasn't something worth remarking.

It certainly wasn't something to be nervous about.

But I was sitting across a supper table from a man who reads faces for a living, and I had a feeling he knew a liar when he spoke to one.

Christopher tensed, and I thought it must be because he was onto me. I was wrong. He shifted his eyes to the left and right like he was looking for something, or someone. Over his shoulder he cast a glance and, seeing nothing, called out, "Who's there?"

"I'm sorry?" I asked.

"Don't you ever get those feelings? Those prickly feelings like someone's standing nearby and watching?"

"Of course I do," I told him. I'd had those feelings ever since I got on board, when I deliberately trapped myself on that damned boat. I knew what I was doing; but that didn't make the tingling at the back of my neck any less unsettling. After so many hours, I suppose I'd simply become numb to it.

"Who's there?" he asked again, and I would have answered for him— had the fiend not stepped out into the light himself.

"I didn't mean to intrude, or cause any alarm." Jack Gabert slipped into the dining area. He slipped, I said—and I mean it that way. He moved like hot syrup pours across a plate; he glided and rolled. He filled the space he met.

I stiffened, I'm sure.

Christopher relaxed. What a fine primal sense he had! I'm sure it served him well in the gambling halls he frequented. Until he relaxed I almost thought—well, I almost thought that maybe I'd found some assistance. But no, he relaxed. He settled down into his chair and reached into a deep pocket for a cigar to join my smoldering cigarette.

And I'd almost thought…but it was just as well.

Here was a man in tune with the world around him. He heard small noises and took them to heart; he saw small details and filed them away in that part of the brain which quietly lies unless the body is threatened. I tried not to be too disappointed in him. He'd known he was being watched, but he didn't know what was watching.

It wouldn't be enough to save him, I didn't think. It wouldn't be enough to simply *suspect*.

"There you are—Jack, isn't it?"

"John. Or Jack if you like, for it suits me fine." I preferred 'Jack.' He looked me up and down and I let him. It was the first time he'd seen me close in quite some time. It might have been the first time he'd ever *looked* at me at all.

Oh, he knew what I looked like. He'd gathered a description, I'm sure. He'd glanced at me for a few moments here and there, at least. And he knew my scent.

THE WRECK OF THE *MARY BYRD*

And when he looked at me—when he laid eyes upon me and let them rest there for those pointed seconds, I knew that the information they gave him was scant compared to what his nose was free to gather. He might have thought I smelled like candles and linen, or wool. He might have gathered I smelled like nighttime blue and something red.

He was mentally marking me. What had previously been a faint trail through a crowd—mixed with the interfering smells of the masses—his nose was distilling it down to something more precise and perfectly mine.

I knew, in those seconds, that he would never lose or mistake me again.

"Mr. Cooper," he nodded at Christopher. "And Sister." He nodded at me.

"Mr. Gabert," I called him.

Christopher waved his cigar and patted his chest pocket. "I might have another to share. Would you join us? I wouldn't ordinarily indulge in front of a woman, but Eileen swears she doesn't mind."

"Indeed I don't. I find the smell pleasing, if you want the truth."

Jack smiled and it was a sinister thing—a stretching of that slitted mouth, and a narrowing of those copper-brown eyes. "I imagine the little lady there is quite full of surprises. And I must tell you, I have a *remarkably* healthy imagination."

"I have no doubt," I murmured, pretending that the obvious and untoward implications were all I observed.

"Now, Jack—that's no way to—"

"I didn't mean anything by it, Mr. Cooper. I was only teasing. Since the good sister here can take a bit of tobacco, then I imagine she can handle a bit of banter as well."

"Whether or not she can—or chooses—to handle it, sir, it's unseemly and I'd rather you watched your language."

"Don't," I told Christopher. I put my hand out and placed it on his sleeve. "It means nothing, and no offense was taken. All is forgiven, as the Lord would have it."

I tried to put some gentle warning into my protestations. Jack was on edge—he was glistening with something malicious and happy. I didn't like the way he stayed on the fringe of the room, lingering at the doorway. The distance between us was surely meant to reassure us, but I knew how little it meant. I'd seen him clear greater spaces in less time than it takes to sneeze.

The gambler had no such frame of reference, though.

"I tell you, Mr. Gabert—ever since you joined us here, I've had some concerns. I've made gentlemanly efforts to be friendly but you rebuff me—and the other passengers, too—with a rudeness that is nearly intolerable." He was warm from the alcohol, I think. Or maybe that quiet, nervous part of his mind was working after all, and feeling defensive. "If you aren't interested in socializing with your fellow passengers, no one here would fault you for it. But there's no need to be crass to a woman of God."

I thought Christopher was going to stand, but he didn't. I left my hand on his sleeve as if by force of will I could hold him down.

Jack leaned against the doorframe. "She's no woman of *my* God."

"Then what God do you serve, if any you serve at all?"

I braced myself for a bit of snappy blasphemy, but he hesitated and held his breath. The question shouldn't have stalled him. I don't know why it did.

He leaned his head around the wall and glanced into the corridor. "No God serves *me*," he mumbled. "I suppose I could swear by my own true self, for I am the God of my own idolatry."

When he turned himself away from us like that, I spied something on the side of his neck—beneath his beard, and on it. It was black in the low evening light of the lanterns, but if he were closer, it might have been red.

There was more, too. On his jacket—but his jacket was black and probably silk. It only looked wet, but I wondered—wet with *what?*

I would have felt bolder if we'd been alone, the monster and I. I would have been more inclined to rise and confront him if not for the slightly drunken chivalry which would surely get in the way.

THE WRECK OF THE *MARY BYRD*

"Jack," I breathed.

He smiled at the light familiarity. Or maybe he smiled about something else. Upstairs, on another deck, I heard a fluttering commotion—like a large bird, dying. It was hard to sort out from the rain, though. The rain still pounded and poured, and all the sounds inside it were distorted.

"I wish it would stop raining," Jack said as if he'd read my mind. He said it in a faraway voice that changed the mood of the room. There was a coldness in his words, and in his tone.

Such a simple sentence shouldn't have made us shudder, but both Christopher and I did just that. "Yes," Christopher agreed slowly. I think he preferred to let the tension slide. Again the primal mind was working for him, trying to quiet his offense and ease the moment. "It slows us down, and I think we'd all like to reach Chattanooga as soon as possible."

"I wish it would stop raining," he said again. "It makes me feel so trapped. I wish I could see the sky."

With this passing thought, Jack turned on his heels and spilled back out into the hall.

A chill ran through me, from my feet up to my ears. Small hairs on the back of my neck and along my arms began to lift themselves like hackles on a threatened cat. It was the gold in his eyes, I think. It flashes brighter when he's hungry—or more precisely, when the hunger comes for him.

I had wondered if the rain would matter. I didn't know if it would dampen his needs, to use a comically appropriate word. I'd suspected it wouldn't. The night works on faith—clouds may cover it, but the moon needs no evidence to shine.

In retrospect we see these things so clearly. The covered sky only pent him up—it made him harder to control, because he had no point of reference. He could not look up at the sky and tell himself, "Yes, there is the moon and it is almost full of light. This is why my head is clouded, my blood is bubbling in my veins. If I am not careful, I will reveal myself. I must make precautions if I want to remain undetected. In a few days it will be easier. I will be all right for a few more days."

Before the rain came, he walked the decks when they were nearly empty. He knew what the sky would tell him, so he watched himself and his behavior. But with it gone? Even knowing what the moon would say, he was acting blind, with only his own instincts to guide him.

"Oh God," Christopher whispered, stuffing the cigar into his mouth and lighting it with fumbling fingers. And in that moment, in the wake of Jack Gabert, even though Christopher understood nothing at all, I believe that he *knew*.

VII.

I was alone in my room, retired there because with the rain coming down in such terrific sheets, there wasn't much to be done. There was no way to navigate, not with any effectiveness. In weather like that, when God Himself is against you, there's nothing to be done but wait out His wrath and hope for the best.

I dropped the anchor and took one of those French bottles to my cabin. I still had one left for Nancy.

But the other would keep me company for the night. Let the rain fall and let the boat sway. So long as the tiller lines held and the anchor didn't slip, I counted it a small blessing. There were only a few of us on board anyway. Let them wait another day. All I wanted was a night when I could drink enough to sleep through my dreams.

I started early—immediately after supper. After the war camps, I never did skip a supper. Every single one was a blessing and I thanked the Lord for every bite.

In my cabin I removed my boots and unfastened my waistcoat, because it was too warm and too tight. At first, when the war ended, I thought I should eat myself strong again; I didn't want Nancy to see me all sticks for arms, and bones for legs. Perhaps I went too far the other way. Perhaps I had grown too soft.

I had a small couch covered in brown cotton and stuffed with horsehair. It was firm and I could lean while putting my feet up. It was more civilized than drinking in bed.

I didn't have any wine glasses, and I'm not sure why. I think they all were broken, or downstairs, or there had never been any to begin with. But I had short tumblers for scotch, so I poured a blood-purple shot for myself and drank it that way. It was more civilized than drinking from the bottle.

I listened to the rain and I was happy. In only a few short days, I would see my wife again. It had been—years. More years than I could think to count, but fewer than it felt, I'm sure. These things happened. People were parted, and people came home.

Tennessee was never a home of mine, but it would suffice. Home is where the heart is, as they say—and Nancy was there. We could stay or we could leave. We could go back and try to salvage what was left, or we could go somewhere else and start fresh. I would let her decide.

I don't know how much time passed from the time I lifted the bottle to the time I set it down. I don't know where the time went.

When I awakened, the rain was still battering down on the roof, and against the windows, and I was still open-shirted and bootless, on the divan. I'd slept and I hadn't dreamed of hunger, and chill. I glanced down at the bottle—determined to remember the label, and interested in acquiring more one day.

But between the busy splatter of the raindrops outside, I could hear something else—once in a while, and loud. It sounded like a sharp blow, or a rap. When first I heard it, I thought I imagined it. *Bang.* Like something solid, dropped and landing hard. I waited and listened, and then it came again. *Bang.*

I sat up and set the bottle aside.

Bang.

It came from down below, by the wheel.

Bang.

No—not by the wheel. The next deck up, at least. *Bang.* Again. It came accompanied by a ringing noise this time—a twang, where something else had been struck. I thought perhaps the jackstaff, since it stands so tall. I heard a quick jingle as if from a chain or cable, and we often ran a flag up the staff.

Bang.

Like a drum, but not quite. Like a boxer jumping on a mat, but not quite.

More like a boxer, I thought. More like someone jumping. But it couldn't be someone, of course. The collisions came too far apart; no one could jump so high, to make such loud landings at such lengthy intervals. He'd have to be jumping from deck to deck around the *Mary Byrd*, and of course that wasn't possible. Of course.

I don't know why it frightened me so—or rather, I don't know how I knew to be frightened.

There was something frantic about it, about the way it dashed to and fro from deck to deck, front to back. Occasionally it would strike against something and be dazed, then resume again. It made me think of a cat my wife once had; in the evening, shortly before bedtime, it would transform from a lazy beast to a mad terror of a creature. It would tear around the house as if its tail were on fire before settling down and turning in for the night with the rest of us.

I've seen dogs do it too, when they're cooped up too long or kept on a chain.

Outside in the rain there was a flash of lightning followed soon by a sharp rumble of thunder. The rainstorm had gone from pattering to booming, and I was glad for my decision to stop and stay. The water was getting rough for a river, and when I stepped to my window to peer outside, I couldn't see a thing beyond the rail.

THE WRECK OF THE *MARY BYRD*

Thunder cracked again—this time like a whip the size of a river. The storm was right above us.

Beside my bed there was a lantern mounted on a swing-arm hinge. It was a mariner's style, and made for a man at sea, not on a river. When the boat moved, the force of gravity would hold the flame level—or that was the idea. It worked well enough, and I liked the look of it. It struck me as a sturdy, stable thing with an ingenious design, so I left it lit.

The other two, by the mirror and beside the door, I extinguished. Despite the rain, these boats are made more of wood than anything else—and the engines are fed coal. Fires happen, and we were moored away from the banks. On board, we had a pair of small rowing yawls for emergencies or the crew's quick shore runs, but if there were ever any real, quick trouble, we'd never get them into the water in time.

Bang.

Thunder answered it, so loud and so harsh that *Mary* rocked a little harder against the waves—her windows rattling in their frames. Downstairs near the galley, I thought I heard a crash. It must have been dishes, or plates. I remember, I thought—*I'll ask Laura in the morning.*

But then there was a new sound, another sound—not the thunder, and not the intermittent banging. It came louder than both, and twice as nerve-shattering.

I clapped my hands over my ears, trying to keep it out.

It roared, or howled, or scraped across the boat in a long, anguished cry that must have come from a living throat—but what, I couldn't guess. My mind raced, playing games with itself. I knew that sounds can be deceiving—especially at night, and in the rain, and when a man is tired and slow from wine.

I'd heard mountain lions that sound for all the world like a woman screaming for help, and inmates at a sanitarium who bayed like hounds. I'd heard my own boat make startling pops, cracks, and cries—just the settling of a ship with a few years on her. I knew how strange and frightening the unknown may seem. I knew not to panic.

But how could I help myself? The cry went on and on—challenging the thunder, daring the sky to fall.

I pressed my hands tighter around my head, but nothing could keep the hideous keening at bay.

Then it came in—through the window. There was an explosion and the world caved in. The rain came in, and the howl came with it.

I barely had time to see it, but time stretched for me and I remember every detail. I remember every second as if it happened over an hour—the stinging splash of water, the moaning wind, and the groan of a sagging timber support where the window had burst free of its place. I saw light glinting off of something shiny and round; it took me a moment to realize they were eyes. They were gold eyes, shot through with red and bulging from a face like none I'd ever seen.

I remember there were teeth, and there was hair. I thought at first, "It must be a man, surely," but before my mind could make the words I knew I was mistaken. No man, no ape. No thing I had ever seen before, nor heard legend of.

It lunged at me, flinging water and broken glass from its hair. It opened its mouth and fired that horrible cry—a screaming, miserable thing that did not slow or cease until it fitted that gaping jaw around my neck, and it drowned its whistling scream in my throat.

VIII.

Jack slipped out the way he'd come, leaving me and Sister Eileen waiting tense and alone together at the table. She handled his rudeness so well, and it made me glad of her sterling character even as the situation made me angry. There was much more to her than you might expect from a small lady in a habit, but isn't that the way it always goes? Once every blue moon, and once in a royal flush—people will surprise you.

He unnerved her, though—as he unnerved me. I couldn't say how I knew he was nearby, and watching. When I called him out, I only meant to invite him in, but if he was going to behave so badly, it was just as well that he'd shown himself the door.

So I could not understand why his leaving did not relieve me.

Sister Eileen released a deep breath she'd been holding. "He's mad," she said, as if that explained everything. "Perfectly mad."

"That may be," I agreed.

"He's dangerous, you know. Or don't you think?"

I don't know why she added the last part, undoing her statement a little by asking for my opinion. I wondered why she felt the need to do that. "I do think he could be, as any madman might be a danger to himself and others."

"We are the only others here, Mr. Cooper."

I knew it then—how she already knew more than I did. I could see it in the way she wasn't blinking, and in the way the muscles in her hands were taut like small ropes. She shifted in her chair as if she'd make herself more comfortable there, then changed her mind and rose to her feet.

"I appreciate your chivalrous defense, but I think it would be best if you'll let him be. Don't antagonize him on my behalf, please. I do not trust him, and I think that—given precious little instigation—he would do you harm. He needs only the smallest excuse."

"I beg your pardon? My dear lady—"

She interrupted me. "Something is wrong tonight. It's the weather, I think. Isn't it funny how it affects us sometimes?"

"It's very loud. The thunder is devilish, suddenly. But the captain has dropped anchor now and we'll wait it out. The rain will clear and we'll be on our way again soon. God knows there's no frowning for the weather."

"God knows it, and so do I."

"What do you mean?" I asked, increasingly curious as she grew increasingly cryptic. "I wish you'd do me the favor of speaking directly, instead of these little riddles."

She pushed her chair aside to leave the table and waited, with one hand on its back. "It's easier to tell the truth in allegory and riddles though, don't you think? Jesus did it, with his parables."

"Like the Good Samaritan."

"Indeed—just like that one. Do you think there was ever a real man, injured beside the road? Or might he have invented it to convey a point?"

"I'm sure I can't say. So tell me a parable, then. Make me understand what sets us all on edge tonight, and why you think poor Jack is taking it with such difficulty."

I thought she'd sit again, but she did not—she simply leaned herself forward against the chair.

"All right. Let us say, then, that there are two men in jail, awaiting execution. In eight hours they will be hanged. One man asks for a clock, so that he may be reminded of how much time is left. He takes comfort in watching the time pass—telling himself, 'Now I have three whole hours left to live, and I will appreciate these three hours.' Or, 'Now I have a whole hour left to live, and I will appreciate this hour.'"

"What about the other man?" I asked.

"The other man asks for a clock as well, but he is told that there is only one—and it's already been given to the other prisoner. Without the clock to judge by, the other prisoner is agitated and confused. He'd rather see the time crawl by and know how much is left to him; without the clock, he drives himself mad wondering how long he must wait for the hangman's noose. Because he cannot stand the wait, he fashions his own noose from the bedsheets and hangs himself before the executioner can arrive."

"I think I see. That's quite a morbid parable you've spun for me. Am I to gather that your mythic clock is the weather?"

THE WRECK OF THE *MARY BYRD*

"You would be quite clever to surmise as much, yes. Some of us—it helps us to gaze up and *know*. But when we can't…" Her voice ran out of air and she let the thought hang.

"I wish I understood better what you were trying to—" I began to press her further, but I was cut off by a most ferocious and terrifying sound.

It echoed loud through the boat, in that omnipresent way that refuses to tell you where the source originates. We both jumped, startled and afraid, as it pealed and rang and roared. I clapped my hands over my ears, but the nun held her ground—eyes narrowing and hands clamping up tight into fists.

The kitchen girl, Laura, came running in, hands over her ears also. The sound—it wouldn't stop! It followed her and surrounded us, filling the room and the decks and the sky.

The girl looked at us and we saw our own fear reflected there in her round, brown face. "It's nothing," I tried to tell her—I didn't try to tell the sister, though. She was already steeled against it. "It's only the mud drums. They're blowing out the mud drums down below, by the boiler. It makes a sound, it's terrible, I know. But you hear it sometimes when you ride these things a long time."

"I know what the mud drums are you fool-headed man," she told me—in a panic, forgetting her place, I'm sure. "I've heard them before and I know what they mean. But this ain't that, and you know it sure as I do."

We were shouting to each other. We had to. The hoarse, unending blast was filling us and swallowing us whole. It was drilling into my skull, past my ears and under my scalp, into the meat of my brain.

There was thunder, too—though you could hardly hear it.

Sister Eileen released her death grip upon the chair and fled the room with a determined sort of stride that I would not have cared to interrupt. I called after her anyway, because it seemed that someone must. "Sister—stay here. Stay with us."

She paused in the doorway, one hand grasping the frame as if to hold herself in place while she spoke. "You stay here—both of you. Get into the galley and stay close together. Get the cook, too. Wake him up. I've seen him, he's a big man, like you—Christopher. Grab the biggest knives you find and stay low."

"Sister!" Laura reached out like she might grab her, but the small nun was faster than she looked. Her skirts swished fast behind her and she was gone.

Laura and I stared back and forth between ourselves, hands on ears, wishing for the terrible roar to subside and shaking as it failed to do so. "Maybe you should—" I started to say, but she knew the rest already.

"I'll get the cook," she nodded, and she was off. A moment later she dashed back past me, into the galley. She emerged holding a great carving knife; she held it point down, by the handle, and her wrists were as tight as leather.

I wanted to tell her that I thought this was unnecessary, that it was too much. I wanted to tell her she was going to frighten someone, but I was already more frightened of the warbling howl than I was of this strong-boned black girl.

Still, as she dashed past me I thought that she did not look like a creature to be trifled with. I wished her all the luck in the world. She was gone. And abruptly—with a gurgle and a gasp—the sound stopped altogether.

IX.

You wait as long as you can. You hold onto it, you bite it back and you sit on it, you stuff it back down. You press it back as far as it will go, and you ignore it. You pretend it isn't there. You tell yourself it only has to hide for a little while more—a little while more. Just look up and see the sky, and you know it's coming. You know you don't have to shut it down for long. You only have to last a little while more.

THE WRECK OF THE *MARY BYRD*

But God sets Himself against me.

You should have seen the sky that night, the way it was covered and hidden and the way it was gray-not-black or speckled with stars. Grey gloves of clouds entwined themselves above me. Veins of lightning split them, parted them briefly, and vanished—leaving the ceiling of heaven bleak again. Leaving me bereft. Leaving me hungry.

If I could have only looked and known. Even if what I saw told me nothing good—if I could have only looked and known.

It's madness, I know. My father knew it too.

Everyone who meets me comes to know it. Everyone who sees me wonders, and every one of them is right to wonder. It is a dread of difference they smell. It is an old fear I inspire. It is the fear of being chased, and caught, and eaten.

I knew the moon was full and fat, and I knew there was little to be done. I knew I could not fight her, but if I could see her I could appeal to her—I could ask her for one small reprieve, for one small night while a storm kept us trapped in the water.

The moon might have heard me. She might have granted it. After all, I was making the voyage for *her*.

I was content to be her creation, and to have her as my mistress. I was ready to be whatever she wanted of me—if she wanted me an animal, not man, I was prepared to let her have that. It was why I left England, and why I left New England, and why I wandered west and south in the new colonies.

I understood that out west there were few people—and most of those were savages. If I could not hide myself from man, at least I would hide from civilization. But some of these savages were a knowing, noble people, or so I had been told. In lieu of avoiding them, I hoped to consult with them. I might find a shaman, or a witch doctor who practiced a magic like the one that consumed me, and drove me.

I did not believe I could be fixed, but I thought I might gain some control, or insight. I thought there might be some leash for the hunger and the madness. I would not find it among the white men, this much was clear.

West then.

But the small red-haired woman would not let me go. She would not let me leave. She followed—oh, how she followed! Tracking me, Mary's dog. Mary's lap-hound. Trailing behind me, through France and Germany as I went back to the Black Forest there, where the wolves are fearsome as nowhere else.

Back to India, where I was lost and useless, she tagged along a day's travel late. Through the north shores of Africa, and down to the jungles there, she walked in my wake.

I would lose her sometimes for weeks and think that I had lost her for good, only to have her find me again on the far side of an ocean—as if she'd never lost my scent at all.

For a long time she only watched. She wanted to learn, I imagine. She watched to see what I touched, and what I shunned. She observed me closely, as closely as she could come. I know what she was doing—she was stalking me. I know it when I see it. I know how the patterns work, and how the dance is stepped.

She was a clever little thing, but she was not dangerous to me. I was stronger. I was faster, and I was clever too. I would not give her any upper hand, because I did not need to.

From time to time I would think, "Perhaps I should speak with her." It wouldn't be hard. I could stop, and turn around, and there she would be—if I waited for her. I could sit her down and we could share a pot of tea. I would explain, "I know why you feel the way you do—I understand why you stalk and follow and chase. But I want you to understand, I am leaving now. I don't want to harm anyone, and I don't wish to be harmed. But I am what I am, and I'll do what I must. See? I'm looking to minimize this awful trial. I want to flee. I'm leaving to seek the wisdom of the savages, or maybe to kill them all. But better there, than here. Better a few, than many. Can't you see, I'm doing my best?"

I would prepare these words for her. I would write them down and line them up. I would consider leaving her notes, and then I would do so—never knowing if she'd find them or read them at all.

After Morocco, I thought I'd lost her for good.

And then I saw her on the *Mary Byrd*, and I knew that the game had changed. She wasn't following anymore. She was predicting. She was making me come to her, and that meant she was ready to strike.

X.

I took the kitchen knife and I held it like my mama showed me, ready to stab and cut if I had to. I was ready to hurt a man, or anything else that came my way.

I lived enough in thirty-five years to have seen and heard a lot of things good, bad, and otherwise. But I never heard nothing at all like that yowling yell the night we were anchored for the storm. The closest I could think to call it was to say, "It was an animal in pain," but if you asked me what kind of animal I couldn't have told you.

Whatever it was, it was big. Nothing small can make a noise like that.

And to think, that fool-headed gambling man tried to tell me it was the mud drums—as if I never rode on a boat before.

I didn't know what was making that noise, but whatever it was, it was mad and it was big. And I didn't want to meet it with nothing but my cheeks in my hands. It was coming from upstairs, I thought. Up on the hurricane deck, or maybe from one of the middle-deck cabins.

Just as I thought I had a good handle on it—just as I thought I could pinpoint it if I held still long enough and held my ears right—it stopped.

And there was nothing but the rain, and I was standing in it, holding that big kitchen knife. I stood there stupid, getting soaked to the bone. It wasn't cold; it was all right to be wet. But the wind was whipping up too, grabbing my apron and tugging it hard. The wind pulled at my scarf and untied it half a knot at a time. I used the hand that wasn't holding the knife to hold my hair down.

I stared up at the sky and saw nothing. I listened to the night around me, but I heard just the rain and sometimes, the thunder cracking high and hard—rattling the windows and making the deck boards shudder.

I thought about the captain and wondered if I shouldn't get to him and ask what was going on, but then I remembered he had a bottle of wine and I thought better of it. I'd said I was going after the cook, anyway. I'd go after the cook.

I wasn't sure what was going on, but I sure didn't like it.

The cook had a cabin down past the captain's, on the next deck down. I had to run past the captain's cabin to get to the stairs, so I ran. I was too wet to bother trying to jump between the raindrops, but it was almost worse when the howling stopped.

I mean it like this: while that howling sounded from stern to prow and deck to deck, at least you knew where it was—and it wasn't right in front of you. Whatever made that cry was someplace else. When the noise stopped, the monster could have been anywhere.

Before I reached the captain's cabin, even, I'd come to think of it as a monster. I just *knew*.

There were only a few passengers on board that trip, which was a blessing, I figure. Here and there, they were coming out of their rooms. They wanted to know what that big noise was.

Yes, well didn't we all?

Somewhere on the other side of the storm, maybe outside on a deck, I heard the gambling man trying to tell some of the others that it was just the mud drums being blowed out. I don't think he believed it himself, but you know how people get when they're scared and they're not sure why—and he was just trying to calm them down. I heard a phrase or two rise up over the rain, "Sounds bad, like the boiler's going to blow," and "Perfectly natural. Nothing to worry about."

THE WRECK OF THE *MARY BYRD*

I guess he was a man who bluffed for a living, so maybe he was a better liar than I am and he calmed them down. Maybe he sent them back into their rooms.

I remembered that the nun had ordered him back into the galley, though. That's why I was supposed to get the cook and we were going to hole up back there. That's what the nun told us to do, and when she said it, I believed she knew more than we did about the noise. She was afraid too, but it wasn't our kind of fear—mine and the gambler's. We were afraid because we didn't know what it was.

She was afraid because she *did* know.

Maybe she thought she'd spare us knowing, and that she'd be doing us a favor. I don't know. I don't know what she thought she was going to do about it. I don't know why we did what she asked, either—or why we made like we meant to, if the gambling man didn't stay inside the galley.

But I was going to find the cook, because that's what I was told to do, and because it sounded like a good idea anyhow. I said it before—he never gave me no trouble, and like the nun said, he was a big man and probably real strong. I'm inclined to take care of myself, when it all comes down to it, but there's no sense in being alone if there are others to help you out.

Jesus, I was running mindless. That miserable wail—it sent me all scattered inside. But I had that one thought—get the cook. I was going to go get the cook and bring him back and we were going to wait in the galley. It wasn't much of a plan, but it was better than nothing.

I dashed past the captain's cabin and I dashed right past the hole in the wall where the window used to be—I dashed so fast, I almost didn't see it. I drew myself up short and sharp. I slipped on the deck and fell down to one knee and I caught myself on one hand. I doubled back and I looked inside.

Jesus, Lord Jesus.

I should've just kept running.

The captain was in there—I knew it was him, he was wearing that waistcoat, the one that's got the blue and red on it. It was unbuttoned, and it was in pieces—some of it on the floor—but it was on him mostly; and on the floor by the basin I saw his black boots with the bright shine on them. They were set side by side how he'd left them.

But the captain was in there—and he was in pieces like his vest. The whole room was splashed with red, and his chin was turned up, cocked up like he was staring at the ceiling. Everything was red. Everything was shattered—there was a thin coat of wet glass and slick rain on every surface. Puddles were forming on the rugs and on the bed, since the storm had come on in and made itself at home.

I'm no doctor and no nurse, but I know a dead man when I see one.

But with Jesus as my witness, I couldn't have guessed what done that to him.

I turned away—I couldn't look too long. I turned away, and I held hard onto my knife even though my hands were wet, and I ran.

XI.

I'd told Christopher too much, I think. He was a smart man—probably smarter than I gave him credit for. He wasn't a fool and I shouldn't have tried to order him out of harm's way; but the moment I heard that ugly, beastly scream, I knew there was no such place of safety on the *Mary Byrd*.

I fled the dining area and slipped straight onto the deck, where water was pooling and sloshing as the boat rocked itself on the river and swayed with the gusts of the storm. I grabbed the nearest rail and clutched it hard. In my hand I was still holding the rosary my father gave me twenty years ago. The beads dug into my palm but I didn't want to put it away. I anchored myself with my feet and my other hand—and I wrapped the rosary around my wrist to hold it better.

THE WRECK OF THE MARY BYRD

I heard a crash, and a wet banging noise that could have been anything—but was certainly not anything good.

I followed it. Behind me, I heard Christopher disregarding my suggestion and leaving the dining hall. He had come out onto the deck in the rain, not coming after me but answering someone's question. There were more passengers on the boat, and I knew this—but they needed to stay in their rooms. They needed to hide.

"Get back in your rooms!" I shouted at them, but a resounding clang of thunder drowned me out. There wasn't time, anyway. If Jack had changed, there wasn't time for anything.

And us on that boat, in the middle of the river.

Anchor dropped.

I thought at first that I should go to the captain. It would be difficult to convince him that we needed to fire the boilers again and move; it might be difficult to even rouse him. But my only other plan was a short-sighted one and I didn't think it would work, but I had to try it anyway.

I ducked into a niche between a cabin and the pilot house and hiked my skirt up enough to reach down into my garter holster. I've heard it said that God made all men, but Samuel Colt made all men equal.

We'd see what Mr. Colt could do for a woman.

I checked the wheel to make sure it was loaded up, and snapped it back into place. They weren't ordinary bullets because I had no reason to think that an ordinary bullet would stop Jack Gabert. These were made specially for me, and for this. I held the revolver tightly, but carefully. I was wet—everything was wet, after all. The storm would not abate even the slightest, and I would have to work with it.

It could hinder or help us both.

The boat was tipping and turning on the river. It rocked with the thunder and the wind-blown water, and it made walking difficult. I could barely move through the storm, even under the shelter of the decks. I could barely see and barely walk, barely move. Soaked to the bone in a few short minutes, I dragged myself on—clinging at the poles, rails, and doorframes as I came to them every few feet.

I turned the rounded corner of the stern and found myself near the mighty wheel. Painted red, it looked blood-black in the darkness and it streamed storm water from every edge.

The boat shifted in its spot and the wheel turned a foot or two—creaking, falling, and stopping to lie still again. I stared at the oversized contraption and tried to hold myself still too, listening for some sign of the spring-heeled fiend.

Of course, by the time you hear him, there's precious little time to react.

He launched himself out of the night, from some tricky corner where he'd been hiding. He moved so fast that I barely had time to see him at all—those copper-gold eyes shining in a big black cloud of muscle, hair, and teeth.

I raised the gun and I fired it: once, twice. By the third time, he was on top of me—but slowed.

He shoved me back; he pressed me hard against the wall behind me and he shoved. I heard the boards crack and felt the skin along my spine begin to bruise. He was all hot breath and the stink of someone else's blood. He was all tremendous size and an imbecile's strength, with claws and a voice.

"What's this?" he breathed, and it was a hiss against the side of my head. With one big hand he pushed me back even harder, and with the other he grabbed at the gun but I held it fast and tried to reach the hammer with my thumb. "Is this all you've learned?" he asked, still trying to wrench it away.

"I've learned much," I growled back. I had nothing profound to tell him. I only wanted to distract him enough to cock the revolver again—one more shot, at such a close range. Anything to push him back.

"All your following, and watching, and waiting—and you think you'll stop me with silver?"

THE WRECK OF THE *MARY BYRD*

I twisted underneath him and moved my body so the gun was aimed his way again. I pushed it as close to his heart as conditions would permit, but I missed. Even in the missing, the kick of the firearm pushed him enough for me to duck away.

I was small, and I was fast. I was stronger than he thought, and I grabbed the hammer back again—another shot, into that tree-trunk-thick torso.

He threw his arms up and howled that dreadful bellow but I knew I hadn't hurt him much. It was for show, the way he cried. It was to intimidate me, and for a moment I felt a spark of triumph because he felt the need to frighten me. The triumph passed, and passed quickly.

He grabbed my wrist and hit it against the boat's rail. I held the gun firmly, but he hit me again and I dropped it—over the side and into the Tennessee. I let it go and he held me up by the one arm as I struggled. "Silver is no enemy of mine, little sister." He growled it at me, his hideous and misshapen mouth making the words obscene. "It is the metal of the moon, and the moon is my mistress—or didn't you know? She holds no harm for me. And neither do *you*."

He finished speaking, and with it, he lost his interest in me. He flung me—not overboard but back against the wall, and through it. I fell so fast and met so little resistance that I was perplexed when I found myself on a floor, half on a divan and surrounded by glass, wood, and water.

In one short burst he'd cast me through the window of a cabin and I was cut, I knew. I was terribly dazed, and I was bleeding, surely. But I didn't feel it. I pulled my feet up underneath myself and rose, hanging onto the divan, and the table, and using my hands to walk as much as I was using my legs.

I'd lost the gun, but I had the rosary still, tied around my hand and useless except for it made me feel stronger.

He hadn't killed me, though he could have—or maybe he couldn't. He said the silver meant nothing, but something had repelled him. Was it the rosary? Did the beads and the cross provoke him? I know what the folk tales say about other beasts of the devil. I know how these things are supposed to work. I've been researching them for years. I've been doing my best, and my worst, to understand.

But I hadn't learned enough. I hadn't learned how to kill him; I'd only learned that I *must* kill him, because there would be no stopping or redeeming him.

God might have disagreed with me—but as of that moment where I was staggering in the unoccupied cabin, trying to gain my balance and my bearing, He'd never told me so.

XII.

People were starting to come out of their cabins, wandering into the rain, wondering what that godawful noise had been. They were milling about, walking along that edge of panic—when the unknown is something yet uncertain, but bound to be terrible. I imagined they were right, but I didn't believe it would do any of us any good to embrace a frightened frenzy.

Two of the young men from supper were out on the deck—I told them about the mud drums, and how they make such a horrific noise that unseasoned travelers often fear the boiler is about to explode.

I knew as well as the serving girl knew that it was a lie. It calmed them anyway. I've always been a good liar.

I told them to go back to their rooms and prepare for bed. We'd be stopped for the night, and they may as well rest. I told them that I would do likewise, but then I heard the screaming, and I knew that the bluff was up.

It wasn't that howling sound—no. It was a woman in terror, or fury.

Based only on suspicion, I thought it must have been the serving girl, Laura. There was a primitive brutality to the sound, it was something less civilized than I thought an educated Irish woman might produce. It was not a sound that would come from a small woman, anyway; and Laura was a tall girl. Furthermore, something told me she wasn't a nervous girl, prone to histrionics.

And she was screaming.

Only for a moment. It would be more accurate to say she emitted one *great* scream, and stopped. But it was a scream of decidedly imminent peril.

Several heads popped out of their respective cabins, but I ignored them—I don't know why. I might have called for help, though they might have thought to help me on their own, and I don't know why they didn't.

Out in the elements—buffeted by the cascades and stings of the uncooperative weather—I ran toward the place where the scream might have originated. On the way and on a whim, I ducked back into the dining area and rushed to the kitchen.

Laura had taken the biggest knife, but I did not intend to charge headlong into danger unattended. I found a large serving fork. It was the size of my forearm, with three giant fangs as long as fingers. It might have looked silly, but it was heavy in my hand and I thought it would suffice.

Back into the rain. I was shocked; it hit my face as hard as a slap. It all but blinded me. It confused me, but I heard fast footsteps off to my right—so I chased them.

"Laura! Sister Eileen!" I called out. Nothing answered, so I kept following the patter, though it'd grown faint between the raindrops. I was following their memory more than their echo.

I was down the hall from the captain's cabin, I thought. He might have been a tired old drunk, but he was the captain—he was the boat's authority—and I thought that this must be a good time to rouse him. Strange things were happening on the *Mary Byrd*, and they were surely worse than strange. They were sinister.

But it was then that I realized why Laura had been screaming.

I came upon the captain's cabin and was stunned into immobility. I stared into his cabin with my mouth agape, collecting the raindrops that streamed from my hair and down my chin.

His cabin had become a slaughterhouse.

The captain was sprawled, his chest and head on the floor—his feet and thighs on the divan. He was perfectly dead, without a doubt. No one lives while missing so much of his face and throat. Hardly any bit above his chest was recognizable, but for one bulging blue eye that pointed sightlessly at the ceiling.

His hands were torn and bruised too, and his wrists; he'd held them out to hold something else away. But what?

I thought of Laura with her knife, but I did not see her and I was not foolish enough to think she was responsible. No, it was only fear I felt for her, when I thought about her roaming the decks alone with her knife.

And where was she?

A crash might have answered me—or it might have told me nothing. At least it startled me away from the sight on the floor of the demolished cabin. At least it gave me something to look for and think about besides, "Where did the rest of him go?"

The crash was mighty, but brief. It sounded like a window breaking and taking part of a wall with it—it was decidedly different from the thunderclaps that coughed themselves into the sky every few minutes. The *Mary Byrd* shook a little—or maybe she just rolled with a river wave. The wind was moving her too.

The frantic patter of footsteps had been drowned by the rain, so I changed my approach and went toward the stern, toward the crash—or so I thought.

I skidded around the corner and found myself overlooking the big red paddlewheel. I caught myself on the railing's edge before I could topple down into it, and I thanked heaven and lucky stars both.

I turned around and saw where a window was gone, blasted inside the cabin as if something large and unwilling had been thrown through it. It pained me—I hesitated, and I cringed, but I looked inside anyway. I expected to see something as horrible as the captain's room, but there was nothing. Only the evidence of a struggle—shards of glass, toppled books, a chair with one leg smashed out from under it.

And blood.

I saw a little bit of blood. But it wasn't much. It was a small, splattered amount running thin with the added influx of rainwater; it suggested discomfort and inconvenience, not death. Whoever was hurt had left the scene.

"Laura?" I shouted again. "Sister Eileen?"

I tore myself away from the broken window and fought the wind-thrown rain again—I held out my arm, with my elbow pointed forward, trying to clear myself a path through the sheets of water. It hardly helped. I could hardly see.

And that's why I plowed right into him—the cook. He was a bigly muscled man like I was in my youth, and he was as black as a plum with brown eyes set in yellow. My head connected with his collarbone and I recoiled with apologies begging from my lips.

"I didn't see you there," I told him. "I—" I wiped my face on my sleeve and continued. "I wonder, did Laura find you?"

He didn't react, except to stand there and sway.

I felt warmth in my hair, dripping down my face. I wiped it again with my sleeve—and only then noticed something stained and streaked upon it. It wasn't mine, I didn't think.

"Cook?" Between the rain and the darkness I couldn't make out much detail in his visage. But he was wearing a gray night shirt and it was just light enough to spy the way he had both arms raised up to clutch his chest, and his throat. And his skin was so dark that I hadn't seen, until I looked for it, that all of his soaking came not from the rain.

I reached out a hand to him—though I don't know how I meant to help.

He reached a hand to me—though there wasn't anything I could do. I saw that, when he took the hand away. I saw white there, underneath his grasp. It was bone, and tendons, and the cords of his throat.

Before he could take my hand, he fell slowly sideways. I stepped forward to catch him or assist him—at least to lie him down on the deck, perhaps, and give him that passing measure of dignity. His weight bore him down though, harder than I could hold him up. He toppled past me. His hip cracked against the rail and broke it—the bone or the rail, I don't know, I only heard it—but over the side he went, and he splashed down into the Tennessee River. He bobbed a moment or two before sinking, or being washed away to a spot I couldn't see.

I stared down after him, gasping, panting, breathing in the rain and wishing for the sun—for God, for Eileen, or Laura, or anyone.

And above me, up on the hurricane deck and between the gonging beats of thunder, I heard the unmistakable sound of a struggle.

XIII.

The cook's room was empty when I finally got to it. His cabin looked all right, but the door was hanging open and water was blowing on in. I came inside and looked around, pushing the door shut behind me enough so I could shake the water off myself.

"Cook?" I called, but it was obvious he wasn't there, and I don't know why I bothered.

The room was tidy and didn't have much in it, like mine. He didn't own much, and what he had was stashed like his mama told him how to do it. The only thing undone was the bed—the covers were pushed aside and the sheets were unmade. It looked like he'd turned in for the night and maybe heard something. Maybe he got up, out from between the sheets, and maybe he opened that door.

THE WRECK OF THE *MARY BYRD*

Whatever happened after, he hadn't closed it and he was gone.

I opened the door again and went back into the wet. It didn't matter. I was soaked all the way down to my skin everywhere anyway. And if finding the captain had taught me anything, it was that hiding in a cabin wouldn't do me no good, and probably my knife wouldn't either.

Out on the deck I stepped on something that crunched and slipped. It was a lantern, or what was left of one—the glass kind filled with oil. The cook probably took it with him when he left the room to see what the noise was. And he'd dropped it, but he'd been lucky—or we'd been lucky. Either the rain or chance had kept it from bursting into flames along the deck and setting us all ablaze.

But there were my hints—an open cabin door, a broken lantern, and an unmade bed. No cook. And out in the cabin decks someone was surely going to find the captain soon.

And someone was shooting—once, twice, maybe a third time—the thunder got in the way of what I heard, but I heard the first two clearly enough. Someone was shooting, and that couldn't mean anything good.

I thought of the pilot's house, up on top of the boat, and I thought of the big whistle there. It was a whistle you could hear for miles, if you kicked the treadle wheel with all you were worth. You could sure hear it farther off than a gunshot, I'd bet.

Somewhere back towards the captain's cabin I heard a big commotion, but it sounded too close to have come from there.

I thought it was up by the stern, by the big paddlewheel or thereabouts; so if there was trouble roaming the boat, it was coming my way. I wasn't running far enough or fast enough, but Jesus Lord have mercy—the captain was dead and we were anchored down to the river bottom. Where could we have gone? What could we have done?

I thought about the whistle again, and I thought maybe it was a bad idea to sound it. Even as I braced myself against the thunderstorm and started to run to the stairs, I thought I might be making things worse for myself. I might lock myself in the pilot's house and sound the whistle a thousand times—and someone might hear, and someone might come.

But the odds were better than fair that whatever came would kill me as soon as rescue me. The killer was closer than any help, that was sure.

But what was I supposed to do? I couldn't think of anything else and I couldn't just stand there and wait for it to come and get me. So I ran to the stairs, and I charged up them—stepping on my skirts and falling on my face before making it to the top.

Up there it was cold and windier than downstairs; I was closer to the sky and closer to the storm, but it felt all right. It felt like being surrounded by God, and I felt alive.

And then I heard the growl. I didn't mistake it for any thunder. This was something other than the sky, making a noise that said it hated me. Well it could hate me all it wanted. I still had my knife.

From the corner of my eye—off to the left, coming around a bench bolted down to the top deck, it crept forward.

Lightning showed me its eyes, and they were the color of new pennies. It was walking hunched over. Its feet made clicking noises on the deck, not like it was wearing shoes but like it was walking on claws. It definitely had teeth; I saw those teeth shining sharp as it breathed and chewed at the wet air.

"Jesus Lord have mercy," I said, to myself and not to it—whatever it was.

I began to back sideways and away, towards the pilot's house. It might be locked but I'd break anything I had to, in order to get inside. But I backed off slow, and it came at me slow. Like a game. Like a step from me, and a step from it.

If I ran, it'd chase me.

I tried to angle myself to put obstacles between us—deck chairs, bundled crates, anything.

It was herding me. It took me a few yards of retreat to figure it out. It was herding me away, into a corner, against the big steam calliope at the edge of the roof. I was standing beside the noisy steam instrument when the monster with the penny eyes jumped.

I didn't waste any breath on a scream. I scrambled aside and grabbed a chair, yanking it loose and pushing it in front of me. The full weight of the beast landed square on the chair and the deck was so wet we both slid—the creature went off to the side, smashing into the pipe organ with its big brass tubes and pedals. I went falling, crashing, in the other direction—back around the deck.

I had a clear shot to the pilot house but I had the monster on my tail.

It recovered quickly, bringing a hairy fist down into the pipes and drawing a shrill, steam-powered squeal from the press of his weight on the keys. Something snagged him and he gave me a handful of precious seconds while he disentangled himself, roaring all the time.

I could hardly see the deck, or the pilot house door, or my hands in front of me, but that didn't slow me down. I knew what followed me. I knew what would happen when it caught me, and I didn't have any dumb ideas anymore—oh, it was *going* to catch me. But I was going to make it inside that pilot house.

The thing landed on the deck behind me with a crack and a squeal, and I jumped—stepping on and over the deck benches, pushing myself on with my feet, and holding my skirts up with the hand that wasn't holding the knife.

I'd have never believed I could move so fast—in the dark, in the rain, in that big long dress that slowed me down every turn.

Behind me, though. If you'd seen what came behind me.

You'd believe it. You'd have run too, no matter what.

Behind me I heard it slip and trip its way along, finding footing like I did—just barely, and not very well.

And then the clomping, echoing leaps of its pursuit stopped. I didn't turn around. I didn't want to look and see it back there, flexing its haunches like a cat getting ready to take down a mouse.

But then I saw—over by the stairs, where first I'd come in—someone else was standing. "Jack!" the someone called out, and even in my frantic flight I heard her, and I knew that it was the nun.

"No!" I hollered to her, where what I meant to say was more like, "Get gone! You're no help to me and it'll kill us both!" But I didn't have the breath to do it and I was almost at the pilot house then.

"Jack!" she shouted again.

It stopped the monster. It didn't stop me.

I collided hands-first with the pilot house door and it was locked, just like I figured it would be. There was a little window, though—beside the door, and a bigger one that looked back over the decks so the pilot could see what was going on around the boat. I turned the knife and struck the little pane of glass with its heavy wood handle.

I didn't know why the monster wasn't all upon me yet, but I took those seconds like the gifts they were. The window wasn't big enough to climb through, but it was big enough to reach an arm through. I jammed my hand on in, and unlocked the door from the inside—then opened the door and let myself on through.

I flung my back against it to close it behind me but something stopped it. Something wouldn't let the hinges shut and this something was huge, and angry.

But I'd gotten so close! I was in the pilot house, and my back was bracing against the monster; whatever spell Sister Eileen had cast on it was broken and it remembered me. It wanted me. It had every intention of eating me alive, I knew it like a mouse knows it.

I was crying then, and screaming, and scooting myself down to sit myself on the floor and hold it closed with my feet against the captain's instruments, and the wheels, and the calling tubes, and the levers and latches. Anything to hold my position there—anything to keep the door from opening enough to let the thing through.

It pushed hard—again, again, and with a great thrust of weight it knocked me loose and threw me all the way across the small room.

THE WRECK OF THE *MARY BYRD*

It grabbed me—around the waist, trying to whip me around. It wanted me to look at it, but I didn't want to look at it, and I didn't intend to. I struck with the knife and it didn't do me a bit of good. I slashed where I could and felt something warm like blood, but it wasn't enough to drain it, or slow it down.

With a back-handed swipe it knocked the knife away from me and I think it broke my hand. I felt the bones in my palm and along my wrist turn loose, but I reached with it anyway—at the controls, at the bell pulls, at the cords and cables—and it felt like trying to pull a rope with a glove full of gravel.

It hit me hard, trying to stun me or trying to stop me. It let me go just enough to let me fall over the pilot's wheel, and then it grabbed me by my arm to whip me back.

But with my unhurt hand, I'd found the whistle treadle down there towards the floor. I grabbed it and I pushed on it with all the weight I could give it.

One shrill, piercing note blew high and hard into the rain.

The monster howled and slacked his grip on my arm, so I leaned on the treadle harder. The note rose in tone and it got so loud, I thought it would break my ears. But I leaned harder, because the monster was letting me go. And then the second note chimed in—and then, because the thing had all but let me loose, I took my whole body and fell on it.

A chord loud enough to wake the saints blasted out, and it hurt my ears and my head so bad that my hand quit hurting, or at least for a few seconds I didn't feel it anymore.

The monster howled, and howled—and I heard pain in the howl and I wondered if its ears were hurting too. That's why I leaned on the whistle so hard, even though the sound of it had worked its way into my body and it was making my ribs shake.

In my ears there was a snapping, stabbing pain and then there was nothing but that pain. There wasn't even any sound anymore. Not even the whistle. And I was afraid that I'd fallen off—or that I'd died and let it go, but it was still there being pushed, so I didn't let go. I didn't let up.

I turned around to look over my shoulder and see the monster—since it wanted me to look so bad. It was backing up with its hands or its paws or whatever—it was backing up with its hands over its ears. Its mouth was open and its tongue was curling out with a scream, but I didn't hear any of it.

I didn't hear the rain, either. I didn't hear a thing, except for the sour, deep ringing in my head.

I jumped up and down a little, leaning and pushing and pushing on the whistle. Make it louder, then. Make it louder, and make it hurt. Make someone hear. Make someone send help. Make someone come. Make someone come.

Sister Eileen came.

She was there—I saw her, standing very still behind the monster, but I only saw her when the lightning flashed. Between the lightning strikes, I was blind and deaf both. But I watched through the lightning, and I saw only fragments of what came next.

The nun was holding something in both hands—I couldn't tell what it was. It almost looked like she was wearing mittens with knives stuck in them, but it was just a trick of the light. She was holding something, I guess—some kind of weapon, I think. She was panting, too—breathing so hard I could see her breasts rising and falling between the white flashes and cracked lines above us.

Her eyes were shining. I swear, it looked like she was growing—but it must have been that she was coming closer. She was running towards the thing. She was coming right at it, and it didn't see her at first.

The next flash—she was on top of it. She was on its back and she was tearing at it with her hands, or whatever she held.

They fell together, and everything shook. Everything rattled. Everything went dark, and it stayed dark. I fell down, off the whistle, and I leaned myself back up against the pilot's wheel.

My dress was ripped, and where it was ripped I saw skin. I saw strips of muscle, like on meat when you dress it up to cook. I hadn't even felt it. I didn't want to look at it.

I closed my eyes, or maybe I didn't. I couldn't tell the difference.

XIV.

The whistle covered every sound, even the thunder, but I could see Jack and the whistle hurt him bad. It hurt me too—it would have hurt anyone standing anywhere near it, when Laura pressed it down full blast.

I pushed it aside, because I had to. I shoved the sound out of my head and I jumped for him, and we struggled there while the sky covered us with rain and clouds, and while the whistle chimed loud with the thunder and the lightning looked so close that it might strike us all.

Then, more suddenly than it began, it stopped.

Jack was bewildered, unnerved, or just relieved. He threw me to the ground and jumped away, but he wasn't paying attention to where he went. He threw himself into one of the stacks—the big black pipes that billowed steam from the engines. It clanged like a gong and, even after he'd righted himself and dashed away, the metal rivets made distressed popping sounds.

I couldn't see where he'd gone, so I went to Laura instead. I knew what I'd find. But I had to look, just in case. She'd outrun him for a few seconds. She was strong. She was smart.

But she was dead.

He'd torn her almost in half, and I wondered how in God's name she'd held on for so long, sounding that dreadful whistle. I also had to wonder, had she held it long enough? Would anyone come?

And even if they came, what would they do?

I had another idea, one that might help Laura's half-formed plan. If we could lift the anchor, the current of the Tennessee was swift; it would carry us at least to stop against the shore. It might carry us farther to civilization, too. We couldn't be far from Chattanooga. If we could even reach the shore, at least we'd have somewhere to run. There on the *Mary Byrd*, we were fish in a barrel.

I didn't know where Jack had gone.

I had to guess that he'd run back downstairs. He wasn't finished—the bloodlust wasn't through with him yet—and he'd be hungry for more. There was no one left up there on the top deck. He'd have to go back down to the cabin decks if he wanted more havoc.

Down the stairs I went back after him, though I suspected he'd jumped down to the next deck by the wheel—where there was room to do so, if you didn't mind the landing.

I had no idea where the anchor was, and the captain was dead. Laura might have known—she'd been riding the river for a while too. That made Christopher my best hope. Even if he didn't know how to raise it, he'd probably know where it was. But I didn't know where *he* was, so it was a great game of tag and we all knew who was "it."

I didn't believe for a second that he'd gone back into the dining hall and locked himself within it. Besides, I suspected the cook was dead—otherwise Laura wouldn't have been up there alone, and she might have returned. There was no one left to form a makeshift fortress with. If he'd gone back, he was probably by himself, or with some of the other few passengers aboard—though my hopes weren't very high for any of them.

Back down I ran, taking the stairs two at a time and rubbing at my hands, which ached in a strange way.

At the bottom of the stairs I stumbled over someone's leg and I fell across the deck with a slide and a splash. I pulled myself together and went to him, on my hands and knees, and I turned him over.

It wasn't Christopher, but I couldn't have said much else about him. His face was gone, and so was his neck. So was part of his shoulder. His arms had great tears in them, where he'd held them up to hold Jack away. The man lay crumpled in a puddle of his own waste and blood, well beyond help.

I stood and crossed myself, only then noticing that I'd lost the rosary. I had no time to mourn for it. No time for anything but the chase.

Around me, up and down—here and there—I heard things breaking but it was hard to pinpoint any of it. The river itself and the woods around it worked against me, casting back the thunder and every echo of every noise. It worried me not only because of the swiftly declining population on the boat, but because the whistle might not have been so helpful as Laura believed.

Even if anyone heard it, how would they find us? I wasn't even sure it would be recognized as a distress signal.

The anchor, then. I needed to find the anchor.

I checked as far as I could and as fast as I could, every deck. One body here, another there. If I hadn't tripped over so many, I wouldn't have believed this many passengers had been on board. Each one made my stomach sick. Each one told me I was failing, and my time was running out.

What if it came down to it—and Jack and I were the last two left?

"Christopher!" I shouted out, because I couldn't imagine being alone there with the beast. I wasn't ready for it. I couldn't handle it. I couldn't do it. *"Christopher!"* I screamed it as I ran, begging God and every saint whose name I could recall—*just let me find him alive. Let me find my friend. We can do this together, but I cannot do it alone. I don't even care if he finds out the truth. Just don't make me do this alone.*

Each crack of thunder was louder than the last. Every shock of lightning brighter, and closer.

I rounded a corner and was quickly grabbed by ordinary, human hands. They pulled me out of the rain and into a nook behind and beneath the great red paddlewheel. The wheel creaked and groaned against the weight of the boat, the tug of the river, and the insistent wind.

"Shh!" Christopher warned, releasing me and letting me face him.

I was so glad to see him I nearly cried. "Thank God!" I said instead, but he waved his finger at me again—as if I did not know, and needed reminding.

"Don't! Don't thank anybody yet. Have you seen it?" he whispered. "Have you seen the thing that's out here?"

I nodded. "I've seen him."

"Him? It's Gabert, isn't it?"

I suppose my eyes and open mouth told him what he needed to know. I was astonished, though I shouldn't have been quite so surprised. He was a quick man, I knew as much. It was why I liked him.

"What is he? Wait, no. It doesn't matter. We have to get off this boat. We have to get out of here."

"Is there anyone else left?" I asked, because I had to. I couldn't leave anyone.

"I don't know. I don't think so."

For the first time since the storm began, the sound of the rain comforted me. We were out of its direct path, and it felt like a curtain separating us from the rest of the boat, and the rest of the world. And from Jack. "Do you think anyone heard the whistle?"

"I have no idea. But I don't think it matters."

I didn't either, but I didn't say so. "Where's the anchor?" I begged instead. "Why?"

"We have to pull it up or cut it loose. We can't stay out here, in the middle of the river, waiting for him to come and get us. We have to get to shore, even if we only drift there and crash."

"And set him loose? At least when he's here on the boat, he's contained. We need to leave and go get help, not give him a lift to solid ground!" Christopher looked surprised at me, but I think it's only because he didn't understand.

"He's already loose! And if you think he can't swim, you're fooling yourself. He's only stayed aboard this long because there's still prey left to find. When he's through with us, he'll head for shore anyway. At least if we move the boat, someone might find it and see what's happened. People will know the danger is here—even if they don't know what it means. Now tell me—where's the anchor?"

"Other side," he said, indicating a direction over to our right. "Though I don't know what good it'll do you to know. Look, I have a way out, maybe. I found the yawls, there are two of them. You and I between us won't fill one, if we can get it out to the water."

"A yawl?"

"A rowboat, yes. They've always got one on board at least. They're easy to disengage. We'll drop one into the river and hop aboard before he knows we're gone."

"It won't work," I told him, but only out of reflex.

It wasn't any worse than my plan to pull the anchor.

"The yawls are only around the corner there. We've got to go past the anchor chain in order to get them anyway. We'll kill two birds with one stone. Look—we can make it. We'll find our way to Chattanooga, or Rossville—we'll get some help."

I nodded. "Yes," I said. "Yes, that's what we'll have to do. Where did you say the anchor was again?"

XV.

The moment I restated the anchor's location, she darted around the corner back into the rain and was lost to me. I will never understand why she thought it was so necessary; and I was even tempted to suggest she was terribly wrong, except that it was clear to me that she knew much more about our predicament than I did.

I had a thousand and one questions, but there was no time to ask them.

I doubt she would have satisfied them, regardless.

"You know where to meet me!" I called out into the rain. I had no idea if she'd heard or not, but I told myself she must have. Otherwise, I could not have left my semi-safe space at all.

But I did. I didn't run too fast, lest I make myself heard and lest I wear myself out. Running didn't come easily to a man my size, and anyway, stealth alone might preserve me. Up ahead I heard a great tearing and splitting—like a tree being pulled apart, rather than sawed. Then I heard a harsh jangling, and a splash.

When I finally made my way to the portal where the anchor chain should have been, I saw only a large hole where the entire mechanism had been torn free. My small friend could not have done this, but if the strange and wicked Jack had done so, then why?

The deck shifted a touch underneath me. It was only a little jerk, a barely perceptible yanking movement. Behind me, the paddlewheel creaked with idle movement.

Mary Byrd was in motion. One way or another, Eileen had gotten what she wanted.

I wasn't much of a religious man anymore, but I prayed hard that she'd meet me where I told her. I wished upon all the stars I couldn't see that I might find her already unlatching the yawl to take us to shore. I didn't understand why she ran on ahead of me. I didn't understand how she knew what she seemed to know.

I made haste along the sodden decks and closed my eyes when I passed broken doors. I winced and gazed away when I saw blood smeared and dripping down the windows or on the rails. But I made it down to the dock where the yawls were swinging and creaking in their onboard moorings.

I saw no sign of Eileen until a light behind me nearly sent my heart into my throat.

She was standing there with a lantern, wick trimmed low but giving us light enough. "Hurry," she whispered. "Do what you must. I don't know how to work this."

THE WRECK OF THE *MARY BYRD*

I took a step and the floor ducked out from under me. I found it again, and put both feet down firmly. "We're moving." I stated the obvious—reaching for the lever that would lower the yawl and set the boat down.

"I went to the pilot house. I braced the wheel. We're headed for shore, but it might take a while to get there. How do I help you with this?"

"You don't. I've got it." The boat dropped harder than I would have liked. It cracked upon the floor with a noise that must have been heard or felt all across the boat.

"Hurry,"

"Yes," I agreed. "To the water. Help me push, like this."

She stood beside me, shifted her shoulders, and shoved. Between us, we forced the little rig to the edge of its slot and then, with a hesitation and a sway, it splashed down into the river. It bobbed there expectantly, oars crossed within. The current felt for it immediately, but it was tied to *Mary Byrd* yet by a long rope.

"I'll go first," I told the nun. "Then you jump down, and I'll catch you."

"No!" she screeched.

At first I wondered why my reasonable suggestion had provoked such an outburst, but then I felt it—the blow to my upper arm, the brutal strike from behind that picked me up off my feet and threw me hard and head-first into the other yawl. Something broke inside me, though whether it was ribs, arms, legs, or skull, I was ill-prepared to say. The world wavered and went dark.

I fought it.

I shook myself and there was pain from every joint and limb. I tried to rise, and tried to see. Sister Eileen was circling in retreat. I think she was trying to reach me, the lovely fool. "Go," I tried to tell her, but the word was drowned in the blood that filled my mouth.

Pain and blackness welled up in my throat, or maybe it was only more blood. Whatever I'd broken, it bled from within.

I fought it.

I saw her standing alone—just a lantern between them, with a flame trimmed low. I looked madly around, looking for something to strike with, and finding nothing—seeing nothing. The bloody blackness came up high, and my vision was leaving me.

I fought it.

I fell to my knees, then crawled up again. I pulled my miserable body up to my feet, using a support column to prop myself. Lucid thoughts grew harder and harder to come by, but I managed just one: *how much oil is left in that lantern?*

"Eileen," I said, and the word came out unintelligible. Neither she nor the beast gave any indication they heard.

She was standing at the edge of the rail, at the edge of the boat—the water behind her. The yawl must have been behind her too. One more lucid thought—one more lucid action. I don't remember doing it, and I don't remember how I did it, but I found myself leaning on her with almost all my rather-significant weight.

Then we were falling, and there was fire.

We missed the yawl and landed together in the river, but the yawl was only a few feet away and she dragged me to it. She must have been much stronger than she looked, for such a small woman. For such a small person. For such. I don't remember.

But I do remember, before it all went black for the last time… I do remember lying on my back, in the boat, and staring up at the *Mary Byrd* and seeing flames. I saw Jack—the monster that he was—I saw him ablaze and shrieking inside the area where the yawls were kept.

"The river," I gurgled at Eileen.

"He can't." She gathered what I meant. "He's trapped. He can't leave the boat that easily. It'll burn around him, down to the water line, I suppose. And you helped," she said, and I believe her eyes were full of tears. I hope she wasn't wasting them on me. "You helped me, you didn't make me do it alone."

THE WRECK OF THE *MARY BYRD*

"Burning."

She kissed my hand and held it to her face.

Her eyes were shining a funny-bright color, mirroring the flames on the boat, and I thought, "That's what it is. She's an angel, after all." ✎

THE IMMIGRANT

Awhile back, one of my best friends in the world passed along a delightful bit of family lore. I want to say that the source of this lore had recently passed, and that's what prompted her to tell me about it; but a few of the details are lost to me now. To make a long story short, an uncle of hers had come back from World War II with many grand stories, not least of all one that he routinely used to delight and terrify the local children. He swore to anyone who promised they could keep a secret that he'd rescued a fire-breathing dragon as a tiny hatchling in France, and subsequently smuggled it back to his home in rural Tennessee—and it lives there still (to hear the family tell it).

This dragon became quite the legend in that sparsely populated county. Children would leave gifts of food and toys, or send it letters and cards; and the "dragon" would reply with its thanks, scrawled in oversized handwriting on paper that was conveniently singed black around the edges (courtesy of a cigarette lighter, I am led to understand).

The dragon became the local Easter bunny/tooth fairy/Santa Claus, a fanciful celebrity whose many "sightings" were shared among generations of school kids, dozens of whom vowed on their lives that they'd seen the great creature flying over the Appalachian foothills.

Sometimes this dragon was a prankster, lighting bales of hay; sometimes it menaced livestock or chased cars; and occasionally… it was a hero.

When my friend told me this little family tale, I absolutely loved it—and asked her permission to put my own spin on it for *Mythic Delirium*. I believe the theme was something about fantasy creatures, and I wanted to tell a story that was both strange and sweet, and anchored in love for all the horror that had inspired it.

Later, "The Immigrant" was released in chapbook form as part of a promotion for the magazine. I still have some hanging around, someplace. It's a beautiful little piece of ephemera, with a cover that features a dragon drawn in stained glass.

My friend said that she cried when she read it, and she passed some of those chapbooks along to her family—who (I am told) gave it many thumbs up.

FOUND AMONG the papers of Ryder Neal, on the day after his funeral, July 30, 1996, Jonesboro, Tennessee.

I.

"Venez m'aider," he said.

With a jaw like that, so long and underbitten like a boxer dog, you wouldn't have thought he could speak at all. His face wasn't made for talking, but he forced the words out. He said it again, quiet-like.

THE IMMIGRANT

"Venez m'aider."

I knew what it meant. I didn't know ten words of French total, but I knew those last two, pushed together with an apostrophe, if you wrote them out.

He looked like a cross between a lizard and a cat, or he did when he was sitting, anyway. When he stood and unfolded himself, he was the size of a pillow, maybe—but so slender, with bones so thin they must have been fragile. Something about the way he held that one wing back… something about his crouch, all submissive—like a dog or a kid afraid of being hit—it made me think he was a brittle little thing.

He had my attention, and he knew it. I don't know why I thought of him automatically as a 'he,' but it must have been that voice. It could've been a boy's voice, if that boy were very tired, and maybe sick.

We stared at each other for a minute.

He looked at me through half-closed eyes, and he probably figured the worst. I was a mess, and I looked mean. It'd been less than a month since Normandy. I'd been lucky enough to make it past the beach, then they sent us down through France, which wasn't half so bad—once you got past that initial reception. As soon as we got into Paris they sent me and a few others to dislodge the last of the Germans—the ones who hadn't got the message yet that Paris had been liberated. Most of them had run out ahead of us, but there were a few here and there digging in and holding out.

I thought I'd heard something, you know how it is—down a dark alley, in a beat-up part of the city. Don't want to look. Don't want to check. Don't want to go. Seen enough already.

But orders are orders, so you do it anyhow.

I told myself it was a few stray bricks, falling from an unlucky wall or a shell-battered house. I knew the Krauts hadn't been too hard on the city, not compared to other places. But there were beat-up spots here and there, and I'd found one. I just hoped the spot was unoccupied. That was the trick.

Heaven heard half of that prayer, I guess, which is fitting since it was the shot-open basement of a fancy church. A door like a storm cellar's hatch had been broken. It swung free and loose from its hinge. Stairs led down into the dark, and I followed them with my gun drawn and pointed, because that's how you survive going into dark places that have unexplained noises in them.

Down at the bottom of the stairs, in a room with a few prayer candles for light, I found a dead priest. He'd been there long enough to be good and stiff, but not long enough to smell ripe. I got a whiff of blood, though—lots of blood. I stepped in it, too. I slipped a tiny bit before catching myself, and before catching a glimpse of *him*.

He was curled beneath a table, behind the priest. At first I thought he'd killed the prostrate man in the cassock, so at first I jerked the gun up and pointed it hard at the pair of eyes I saw down close to the floor.

That's when he spoke.

You can shoot a scary-looking dog, if it comes down to it. You can shoot a vicious-looking animal, even if it's not threatening you yet. There's a trigger in your head, and it tells you when there's danger, even before you've got all your information.

Even though he was less than half my size, and hiding, and not making any threatening gestures, some primal urge was just yanking at that mental trigger…until he breathed that plea. *"M'aider."*

You can't shoot something so strange when it talks to you like that. Not out of hand. Not if it asks for help.

Besides, even at a dozen paces I could see that the priest had been shot.

When I looked at the thing's hands—they weren't really hands, but close enough—I was pretty sure they couldn't have held a gun. They couldn't have pulled a trigger. Not easily. Not deliberately, with those webs and blunt, thumb-thick claws.

I lowered the tip of the rifle. He hadn't hurt anybody, and he was doing his best to indicate that he wouldn't hurt me.

THE IMMIGRANT

"What are you?" I asked. His forehead wrinkled just like a man's—just like he was listening, and trying to understand. "Jesus Christ, what the hell are you?"

Jesus' name he knew. He nodded, because I guess he misunderstood. I remembered then that we were underneath a church. Those crazy hands of his came together to make a prayer with a steeple point.

"*Oui,*" he said, and unclasped his hands to gesture at the candles. Behind them, blotted with shadows, a statue of Mary leaned against a wall.

"*Oui.*" I said it back, because it was one other word I knew, and hell—what do you say to something like that? To something like *him*?

With a pained shuffle and lurch, he turned his side to face me. My first impression had been right. Something was wrong with his wing. When the flickering light hit it directly I saw that it was bent at a bad angle, probably broken—but not in a way where any bones were poking through, so it could've been worse.

He was showing me he was harmless. He was showing me he needed help, in case I didn't catch the French.

I put the gun down slow. I put my hands out in front of me, and I sort of hunkered down, tiptoeing towards him. I'd had enough of people wanting to hurt me in the last few months, so if he didn't want to hurt me, I didn't want to hurt him. I didn't know what he was, but if he wasn't a Kraut and he was in trouble, then I didn't mind helping him if I could.

He let me approach, and even held out the wing for me to look. I touched it as gently as I could, feeling my way along it. His skin was smooth and pretty gold-red. Covered with scales, it looked like it ought to feel slimy, but it was dry and soft—like the tight, expensive gloves the French girls wore.

"Ah," he grunted when I hit a swollen spot. I thought he was objecting, but he didn't pull away. He made the noise again, and finished the question. "American?" The word sounded funny in his mouth, with the accents in the wrong place and the vowels laid out flat.

"Yeah, that's right. American. That's me. Let me see it. Let me help."

And he did. It's not like I was a medic or anything, because I wasn't; but even if I had been, I don't think there was a doctor in the corps who could've splinted that crazy wing.

Under the candles, and under some mortar debris on the table, there was a cloth. I pulled it off and shook it, flapping it open like my mother used to spread out sheets on the bed. I dropped it down over him like a cloak, or a blanket.

When I picked him up, he was as light as a child.

II.

The trick was getting him home, obviously. It doesn't bear much of a dry retelling, so suffice it to say, I had to ship him back with me as freight. I set him up as best I could. It turned out, he would eat almost anything edible and he didn't much care what it was. It took some doing, but I got him put on my own transport home so I could keep an eye on him. This also made it easier to slip him better food, once in awhile; though truth to tell, there were times I thought about trading with him for the good French dog chow I'd scored for him.

My sergeant knew what was going on, or he thought he did. He thought I was sneaking a dog back, maybe. It happened every now and again, and he was good enough to look the other way. He said if I got caught with contraband on board, he didn't know anything about it and it was nobody's problem but mine.

So I kept it my problem. I kept sneaking downstairs into the cargo hold with a bag of dog food and sometimes, a covered tin plate of army chow. It wasn't as if I was going to eat it all, anyway. Army cooking at its finest can't hold a candle to what my Alice can do with a stove.

Speaking of Alice, I spent many a night wondering how I was going to explain *him* to her.

THE IMMIGRANT

How do you start that conversation with your wife? "Hi honey, I'm home. Meet the weird little French dragon I found under a table in a church. His name is Pierre, I think. That's what I think he said. That's what I started calling him, anyway."

I started teaching him English, too. He picked it up a whole lot better and a whole lot faster than I ever caught on to French. By the time I got him back to east Tennessee, we could manage a fair outline of a conversation.

Those first attempts at talking sounded like a man teaching a dog how to sit and speak, I imagine. I didn't mean it that way. I wasn't trying to treat him like he was dumb. But he was small and quiet, and four-legged plus a pair of wings. He wasn't a dog, and he wasn't a child—but he was my charge. And if I was going to get him home safe, he needed to know how to be quiet on cue.

Like I said, he was a quick study.

III.

Home was a parcel of land in the Appalachians, just a few miles away from where Davy Crockett was born. The nearest town was Jonesboro, and the nearest town of any size was Johnson City. I tell you that just to give you some frame of reference, because otherwise you wouldn't really know how far out into the sticks we were.

That's one reason I thought it might be safe to bring Pierre home. There was no one around to see him and worry—not for miles. Our nearest neighbors made their living selling homemade alcohol and hiding it from Uncle Sam, so I figured the odds weren't too good they'd run to the police even if they saw anything strange.

Alice was my only worry.

I'd married a farm girl. She could grow or butcher most of her own food, or bottle-feed a lamb if it came to that. She was one of the most competent and practical women I ever knew.

So I decided to trust her, and trust that level-headed steadiness. A friend of mine helped unload the pick-up truck with my duffel bag, a few presents from Europe, and that big damn crate with the suspicious-looking holes in the top.

Pierre was as silent as luggage. We deposited him in the barn, in a quiet back stall away from the horses.

It took me awhile to get rid of Andy, who wanted a round of beers and war stories before he'd go on his way; but once he was gone I took Alice by the hand and led her back out to the barn.

"I've got something to show you," I told her. "I found him in Paris—"

"Him?" She frowned at me, and at the crate. "Dear God Almighty, don't tell me you've left something alive in there?"

"He's—yeah. He's alive. But I couldn't just send him like a puppy or anything, Alice. He's different. He's *real* different. And he's hurt, but not too bad." I took a crowbar and pried at the lid. "He needs a place to rest up and heal."

The lid came up, and I pulled down the panel that hid Pierre, exposing him to the dim, barn-filtered light…and to Alice, who covered her mouth with her hands.

"Jesus," she said.

Pierre was crouched with his face in a corner. He turned slowly and blinked at the light, and at my wife. "He's just like one of us, baby, and hurt by the Nazis. I couldn't leave him there."

She sank to a low squat, in order to meet him on eye level. "It's his wing, isn't it? It's broken."

"Broken," he whispered back. He knew that word, so he knew to agree.

"He talks." It wasn't a question. She never asked stupid questions. "Jesus, Lord. What is he?"

He got the gist, and he answered, more or less. "Pierre," he said, patting his chest and looking at Alice with a fresh sort of hope, or optimism.

"Pierre. Dammit, Ryder, you weren't going to keep him out here in the barn, were you?"

I looked to the dragon, like he would answer for me, or for himself. "I was going to put him, I figured, wherever he wanted to go. I couldn't see talking Andy into helping me carry the crate up to the guest room, though. He'd have wanted to see what was inside, and you're the first person I've tried to show this fellow to."

"Well all right then. Pierre. Sweetheart, let me take a look at that. Let me see what we can do. That's a nice name, Pierre. Who gave you that name? Not Ryder, I don't bet."

"The priest," he murmured. "He said I hatched from a stone."

IV.

He stayed inside with us, for a few weeks. We put him in the guest bedroom, where Alice's mother and father stayed when they came to visit, before they died. He didn't much care for the bed, and was happier sleeping under it. That was okay with us. It made him easier to hide during the occasional, unexpected, uninvited welcome-home visitor.

We must've gotten fifteen casseroles that first month after I came back. It was sweet of everyone—it was nice to feel appreciated and all— but when you've got a secret as strange as Pierre, you'd just as soon have the world leave you alone.

When we had the place to ourselves, Pierre roamed freely. We came to think of him as a really smart kid; he was about the size of a first or second grader, and he had that same kind of permanent curiosity about him. He touched everything, but he never broke anything. He asked a lot of questions, always in that soft-spoken voice that never did lose the pretty Paris lilt that Alice liked so much to hear.

He used to talk to me and Alice over breakfast, when my wife would make eggs, bacon, and grits for all three of us. I couldn't believe how much he could eat in one sitting, but he was a growing boy.

He wasn't sure how old he was, but he thought he must be ten or eleven. Just a youngster. For as long as he could remember, he'd lived at the church with Jean, the priest who had died—the priest had been shot after an argument. A German soldier had gotten a peek at Pierre, and he'd cornered the priest downstairs.

"He told Jean, 'You must give me the monster that sleeps behind the altar.' But Jean said no. They argued, and I was afraid."

"Of course you were, baby," Alice cooed. "Anybody would have been."

"Jean was not. Jean locked me in the place where people went to say their sins. He would not open the door, and he would not tell the soldier where I was. That's why he died."

"So what were you doing in the basement, then?" I asked. There was no confessional down there that I had seen.

"I followed him there, once I pushed my way out. Jean had lived, for a little while. Down underneath, it was dark and quiet. But then there was a big noise, and the wall fell. I tried to cover him. That's how I hurt myself. I knew he died. But I did not know where else to go. Then you came."

"Mmm." Alice shook her head and put another load of fried eggs onto his plate. It's a southern thing, I guess—the desire to feed people when you don't know how else to comfort them. "Bless your heart."

He didn't use a knife or fork, but we forgave him.

It looked awkward when he tried, so he ate instead with his not-quite-hands. He was fussy and delicate with his food. It never seemed rude at all. It was like watching someone from another country, with manners that were every bit as good as yours, but different.

This was a reminder, though—every mealtime—that he was not like us. That he was something else. He was something different.

THE IMMIGRANT

You don't want to talk about a rational creature as an animal, but he was clearly not a person, either. He was thoughtful, and helpful. The horses liked him, and he liked them; he had a general affinity for living things, which was nice. As he healed, he spent more and more time outside…until he announced that he preferred the barn after all.

By then his wings were strong enough to hold him.

The first time I saw him fly it made my chest hurt, it was so weird and so pretty. You see big birds, sometimes. Even the biggest, ugliest buzzards look like angels in the air. It doesn't jive in a person's head, how something so heavy and strong can flap and soar like that.

That's how Pierre looked, too. A small coppery angel, he flapped his way around the farm. In the sun, he was a thing of myth, not monster. He was a thing of beauty—one of God's own creatures, I'd swear it.

The dead French priest knew it. He must have. Me and Alice weren't brought up papists; but same as most folks we knew, we were Christians. And we're all looking up to the same sky—at the same God. At the same birds. At Pierre.

All of us have the same questions and requests when we close our eyes and bow our heads.

V.

Alice taught him his ABCs, and with a lot of effort, Pierre could write. It took years before his penmanship was good enough to read, but once it did, he wrote a lot. He used to ask for paper and pens. He liked the big sheets—the kinds that artists use, they come in pads. I bought them for him in town. He liked big pencils, too. The thin ones broke in his hand, as he got bigger and stronger.

He did get bigger, too. A lot bigger. When he was a little fellow, he used to fly around during the day, happy as a pig in mud. But by the time he quit growing (or grew so slow that we didn't notice anymore), he was the size of a good working horse.

It got to where he only flew at night, so he didn't scare people. He was a thoughtful thing. He never wanted to bother anyone. Never wanted to make any trouble.

But people did see him, once in awhile. Stories got out and around, as stories tend to do. The first stories were predictably hysterical— there's a monster in the woods outside Jonesboro! There's a dragon in the forest, eating livestock and burning barns! Well, Pierre enjoyed a good steak as much as anybody, but he didn't kill his own that I ever knew of. And if he could start a fire without a box of matches, I never saw him do it.

After awhile, though, the stories changed in timbre and tone.

After awhile, there were stories about strange angels. Lost kids were led back to town by a bright-winged creature that flew low enough to follow. Campers trapped in the snow would awaken to find themselves dug out, with paths leading off in the right direction. The paths would be stamped down with the most extraordinary footprints you ever saw, but they were always true and safe to follow. Missing sheep were returned unharmed to their pens.

One time, one of our moonshining neighbors had a still that went bust. A fire broke out and made its way to the house they had, and it was just a wood clapboard thing so it went right up in smoke. On the second floor there was a three-year-old girl, and everyone knew for sure she was lost.

While the fire still burned, they found that girl behind the house. She was standing in her nightgown, bare feet in the grass. She was looking up at the sky, and she was smiling.

Years later, when that girl was in third grade, she was told to write a polite thank you note for a school project. Her mother brought the note to us because she thought it was cute, and because the kid insisted. It was written on that big-ruled paper, hardly thicker than tissue. It was addressed "to the red stone dragon, at Ryder Neal's place."

We showed it to Pierre and he nodded solemnly. He wrote her a short letter in reply, and asked that we deliver it. Their little correspondence went on that way for years; and in time, a few of the other school kids started leaving notes for him too. They put them out in the barn, in the clean stall back behind the horses. They left letters, and drawings, and chocolates there as if it were a shrine.

Pierre didn't mind if the kids' parents thought we wrote his responses.

It didn't matter to us, either, that the world thought we were participating in some cutesy joke, like Santa Claus or the Tooth Fairy. It could be our secret, though some of the little ones knew better.

And those little ones, when they grew up and had little ones of their own, they passed the stories down and along. Maybe now there are a dozen people these days who know the truth. There's no way to say. Everybody talks about our dragon with a wink in one eye and a sparkle in the other.

Alice and I never did have any kids of our own, but we were never lonely for them, and all of these years, we have counted ourselves blessed.

BAD SUSHI

I've never really felt like short stories were my "thing," or at least, certainly not my specialty. I tend to wander and run on, even after editorial intervention, and that (generally) makes me better suited for long form work; but when Apex asked for a story, I had half an idea in the back of my head for something like this. I've always been fascinated with the bones of Lovecraft's storytelling, and wanted to take another run at it, from another angle. (After beginning this weird side quest with the unrelated story "The October Devotion.")

Obviously, Lovecraft was a nervous, rabid racist with a veritable host of problematic personal positions—but that's part of what makes it fun to remix his work with the kinds of protagonists and stories of which he would surely disapprove. Ever since "Bad Sushi," my approach to Lovecraft has uniformly been "Make it Lovecraft weird, but make sure that he would absolutely hate it."

If there's any baby to be kept from discarded bathwater, it's Lovecraft's insistence on making the threat bigger, rather than the protagonist weaker. Among his many and varied narrative toolbox items, this is my favorite one to play with.

Lovecraft gives you a protagonist who is competent, capable, and intelligent, and then he turns them loose against something so much larger, so profoundly unfathomable, that your poor point-of-view character never really stands a chance. Moses may have gone briefly blind at a glimpse of God's back, but Lovecraft's investigators go fully mad at a glimpse of the cosmic deities he provides. There's no opportunity to conquer them; and the fortunate, at best, may temporarily escape.

But there's more than one kind of credible, reasonable protagonist, and he doesn't always have to be a white man on a mission to thwart wily cultists.

In this case, he's an older Asian man—a skilled chef, and a veteran from a long-ago war.

(As an aside, sometimes reviewers note that I'm prone to writing about veterans from various conflicts, and that's true. My dad is a Vietnam vet, and I grew up surrounded by military folks. It's not that weird, is all I mean. Write what you know, and all that jazz.)

At any rate, Baku was inspired by a nice old man who worked at a mom-and-pop sushi place in Chattanooga, Tennessee. That restaurant is lost to the sands of time, but this story remains to remember it by.

BAKU'S HAND shook.

In it, he held a pinch of wasabi, preparing to leave the condiment as a peaked green dollop beside a damp pile of flesh-colored ginger. He hesitated, even though his fellow chef slapped the kitchen bell once, twice, a third time—and the orders were backing up.

BAD SUSHI

The waitress flashed Baku a frown.

Some small fact was wiggling around in his expansive memory. In the back of his sinuses, he felt a tickle of sulfur. The kitchen in Sonada's smelled like soy sauce and sizzling oil, and frying rice; but Baku also detected rotten eggs.

He smeared the glob of gritty paste onto the rectangular plate before him, and he pushed the neatly-sliced sushi rolls into the pick-up window. The hot yellow smell grew stronger in his nose, but he could work through it. All it took was a little concentration.

He reached for his knives. The next slip in the queue called for a California roll, a tuna roll, and a salmon roll. Seaweed. Rice. Fish meat, in slick, soft slabs. He wrapped it all expertly, without thinking. He sliced the rolls without crushing them and slid them onto the plate.

This is why Sonada's kept Baku, despite his age. He told them he was seventy, but that was a lie by eight years—an untruth offered because his employers were afraid he was too old to work. But American Social Security wasn't enough, and the work at the restaurant wasn't so hard. The hours were not so long.

The other workers were born Americans. They didn't have to take the test or say the pledge, one hand over their hearts.

Baku didn't hold it against them, and the others didn't hold his original nationality against him, either. They might have, if they'd known the uniform he'd once worn. They might have looked at him differently, these young citizens, if they'd known how frantically he'd fired, and how he'd aimed for all the bright blue eyes.

There it was again. The sulfur.

Baku had tripped over a G. I.'s body as he staggered toward the beach at Cape Esperance, but he hadn't thought much of it. He'd been preoccupied at the time—thinking only of meeting the secret transport that would take him out of Guadalcanal. The Emperor had declared the island a lost cause, and an evacuation had been arranged. It had happened under cover of night. The transport had been a crushing rush of thirteen thousand brown-eyed men clamoring for the military ferry. The night had reeked of gunpowder, and body odor, and sulfur, and blood.

Baku thought again of the last dead American he'd seen on Guadalcanal, the man's immobile body just beginning to stink in the sunset. If someone had told him, back in 1942, that in sixty years he'd be serving the dead American's grandchildren sushi rolls…Baku would have never believed it.

He looked at the next slip of lined white and green paper.

Shrimp rolls. More tuna.

Concentrate.

He breathed in the clean, sparse scent of the seafood—so faint it was almost undetectable. If it smelled like more than salt and the ocean, it was going rotten. There were guidelines, of course, about how cold it must be kept and how it must be stored—but the old chef didn't need to watch any thermometers or check any dates. He knew when the meat was good. He knew what it would taste like, lying on top of the rice, and dipped lightly in a small puddle of soy sauce.

One order after another, he prepared them. His knives flashed, and his fingers pulled the sticky rice into bundles. His indefatigable wrists jerked and lurched from counter to bowl to chopping block to plate.

Eventually, with enough repetition and enough concentration, the remembered eggy nastiness left his head.

When his shift was over, he removed his apron and washed his knives. He dried the knives each in turn, slipping them into a cloth pouch that he rolled up and carried home. The knives belonged to him, and they were a condition of his employment. They were good knives, made of German steel by a company that had folded ages before. Baku would work with no others.

At home that night, he lay in bed and tried to remember what had brought on the flashback. Usually there was some concrete reason—an old military uniform, a glimpse of ribbon that looked like a war medal, or a Memorial Day parade.

What had brought him back to the island?

At home in bed, it was safe to speculate. At home, in the small apartment with the threadbare curtains and the clean kitchen, it was all right to let his mind wander.

Sixty years ago there was a war and he was a young man. He was in the Emperor's army and he went to the South Pacific, and there was an island. The Americans dug in, and forced the Japanese troops to retreat.

They sneaked away at night, from the point at Cape Esperance. Personnel boats had been waiting. "There were thirteen thousand of us," he breathed to himself in his native tongue. "And we left in the middle of the night, while the Americans slept."

The water had been black and it had been calm, as calm as the ocean ever was. Hushed, hushed, and hushed, the soldiers slogged into the water to meet the transports. In haste and in extreme caution, they had boarded the boats in packs and rows. They had huddled down on the slat seats and listened to the furtive cacophony of oars and small propellers.

He seemed to recall a panic—not his own. Another man, someone badly hurt, in mind and body. The man had stood up in the boat and tried to call out. His nearest neighbor tackled him, pulled him back down into his seat; but the ruckus unsettled the small craft.

Baku was sitting on the outside rail, one of the last men crammed aboard.

When the boat lunged, he lost his balance. Over the side he toppled, and into the water. It was like falling into ink with a riptide. Fear was halted by the fierce wetness, and his instincts were all but exhausted by days of battle. He thought to float, though. He tried to right himself, to roll out of the fetal suspension.

And something had stopped him—hard.

Even after sixty years, the memory of it shocked him—the way the thing had grabbed him by the ankle. The thing that seized him felt like a living cable made of steel. It coiled itself around his leg, one loop, two loops, working its way to a tighter grip with the skill of a python and the strength of something much, much larger.

Inside Baku's vest he carried a bayonet blade made of carbon steel. It was sharp enough to cut paper without tearing it. It was strong enough to hold his weight.

His first thought and first fear was that this was a strange new weapon devised by the Americans; but his second thought was that this was no weapon at all, but a living creature. There was sentience and insistence in the way the thing squeezed and tugged. He curled his body up to pull his hand and his knife closer to the clutching, grasping thing.

And because he was running out of air, he arched his elbow up and tightened his leather-tough wrists. Even then they'd been taut and dense with muscle. He'd grown up beside the ocean, cutting the fish every day, all day, until the Emperor had called for his service and he'd taken up a gun instead.

So it was with strength and certainty that he brought the knife down into the thing that held his leg.

It convulsed. It twitched, and Baku stabbed again. The water went warmer around his ankle, and the terrible grip slackened. Again. A third time, and a fourth. In desperation, he began to saw, unafraid that he would hit his own flesh, and unaware of the jagged injury he created when he did so.

By then his air was so low and he was so frightened, that he might have cut off his whole leg in pursuit of escape. But after several heroic hacks Baku all but severed the living lasso; and at that moment, one of his fellow soldiers got a handful of the back of his shirt. Human hands pulled him up, and out, and over—back into the boat. A faint and final tug at his leg went nearly unnoticed as the last of the thing stretched, split, and tore.

On the floor of the boat Baku gasped and floundered. The other soldiers covered him with their hands, hushing him. Always hushing. The Americans might hear.

He shook and shook—taking comfort in the circle of faces that covered him from above and shut out the star-spangled sky. At last he breathed and the breath was not hard-won.

But he did not feel safe.

Around his leg the leftovers clung. He unwound the ropy flesh from his own quivering limb and the dismembered coil fell to the boat bottom where it twitched, flopped, and lay still.

"What is it?" someone asked. "What is it?" the call was echoed around the boat in quiet voices.

No one wanted to touch it, so no one did until the next day.

Baku stared down at the thing and wondered what it had once belonged to. All he had to judge it by was the lone, partial tentacle, and it did not tell him much. It was a sickly greenish brown and it came with a smell to match—as if it were made of old dung, spoiled crab meat, and salt; and suction pads lined one side, with thorny-looking spines on the other. He did not remember the bite of the spines, but his leg wore the results.

"What is it?" The question came again from one of his fellow soldiers, who poked at the leavings of the peculiar predator with the end of his gun.

"I don't know. Have you ever seen anything like it?"

"Never."

Never before that night had he seen anything like the tentacle. It represented no squid or octopus that Baku knew, and he was born into a family that had fed itself from the water for generations. Baku thought he had seen everything the ocean had to offer, even from the bottom-most depths where the fish had blind-white eyes, and the sand was as fine as flour. But he'd never seen a thing like that, and he would never forget it.

The scars on his legs would remind him for the rest of his life, even when he was an old man, and living in America, and lying in bed on a cool spring night…half dozing and half staring at the ceiling fan that slowly churned the air above him.

And it was that smell, and that remembered texture of stubborn rubber, that had reminded him of the sulfur stench at Guadalcanal.

Twice in his life now, he had breathed that nasty, tangy odor and felt a tough cord of flesh resist the push of his knife.

His stomach turned.

The next day at work, Baku wondered if the store manager had noticed anything strange about the sushi. He asked, "Are we getting different meat now? It seemed different yesterday, when I was cutting it for the rolls."

The manager frowned, and then smiled. "I think I know what you mean. We have a new vendor for some of the fish. It's a company from New England, and they carry a different stock from the Gulf Coast company. But they come with very good references, and they cost less money than the others, too. They distribute out of a warehouse downtown, by the pier at Manufacturer's Row."

"I see."

"Was there a problem with the fish?"

Baku was torn.

He did not want to complain. He never liked to complain. The manager was happy with the new vendor, and what would he say? That the octopus meat reminded him of war?

"No," he said. "No problem. I only noticed the change, that's all." And he went back to work, keeping his eyes open for more of the mysterious meat.

BAD SUSHI

He found it in the squid, and in the crab. It lurked amid the pale bits of ordinary fish and seafood, suspicious landmines of a funny smell and a texture that drove him to distraction.

Baku watched for the new vendor and saw him one day driving up in a big white truck with a large "A" painted on the side. He couldn't make out the company's name; it was printed in a small, elaborate script that was difficult to read. The man who drove the truck was a tall, thin fellow shaped like an egg roll. His skin was doughy and hairless.

When he moved the chilled packages of sealed, wrapped food on the dolly, he moved with strength but without hurry. He walked like a sea lion, with a gently lumbering gait—as if he might be more comfortable swimming than walking.

His big, round eyes stared straight ahead as he made his deliveries. He didn't speak to anyone that Baku ever saw, and when he was handed a pen to sign at the clipboard, he looked at it blankly before applying his mark to the proper forms.

"I think he's *challenged*," the Sonada's manager said. "Mentally challenged, you know. Poor man."

"Poor man," Baku agreed. He watched him get into his truck and drive away. He would be back on Tuesday with more plastic-wrapped boxes that emitted fogged, condensed air in tiny clouds around their corners.

And meanwhile, business boomed.

Every night the restaurant was a little more packed, with a few more patrons. Every night the till rang longer, and the receipts stacked higher on the spike beside the register. Every night the waitresses ran themselves more ragged and collected more tips.

By Saturday, Sonada's was managing twice its volume from the week before. By Sunday, people were lined out the door and around the side of the building. It did not matter how long they were told to wait.

They waited.

They were learning an unnatural patience.

Baku took on more hours, even though the manager told him it was not necessary. A new chef was hired to help with the added burden and another would have been helpful, but the kitchen would hold no more workers.

Baku insisted on the extra time. He wanted to see for himself, and to watch the other men who cut the sushi rolls and steamed the sticky rice. He wanted to see if they saw it too—the funny, pale meat the color of a pickle's insides. But if anyone noticed that something was out of order, no one spoke about it. If something was different, something must be good—because business had never been better.

And the old chef knew that one way or another, the strange meat was bringing the customers in.

Even though Sonada's served a broad variety of Asian food, no one ever ordered fried rice anymore, or sesame chicken. Egg rolls had all but vanished from the menu, and Baku couldn't remember the last time beef was required for a dish.

Everyone wanted the sushi, and Baku knew why.

And he knew that something was happening to the regular patrons, the ones who came every night. From the kitchen window that overlooked the lobby he saw them return for supper like clockwork, and with every meal they took, they were changed.

They ate faster, and walked slower. They talked less.

Baku began to stay longer in the kitchen, and he rushed hurriedly to his car at night.

Baku paused his unending slicing, cutting, scooping and scraping to use the washroom. He closed the door behind himself and sighed into the quiet. For the first time all evening, he was alone. Or so he thought.

BAD SUSHI

All the stall doors were open, save the one at the farthest end of the blue-tiled room—which was closed only a little way. From within it, someone flushed.

Out of politeness, Baku pretended not to see that the other man had left the door ajar. He stepped to the nearest sink and washed his hands. He covered them with runny pink soap and took his time building lather, then rinsing under the steamy tap water. He relished the heat.

The kitchen had become so cold in the last week, since the grills were rarely working and the air conditioner was running full-blast. Instead of sporadic warmth from the stoves, the refrigerator door was incessantly opened and closed—bringing fresh meat for the sushi rolls. The chefs handled cold meat, seaweed, and sticky rice for nine hours at a time.

His knuckles never thawed.

But while he stood there, warming his fingers beneath the gushing stream, he noticed the sound of repeated flushing foaming its way into the tiled room. Dampness crept up the sole of Baku's shoe. Water puddled on the floor around his feet. He flipped the sink's chrome lever down, shutting off the water.

He listened.

The toilet's denouement was interrupted before the plumbing could finish its cycle and another flush gurgled. A fresh tide of water spilled out from under the door.

Baku craned his neck to the right, leaning until he could see the square of space between the soggy floor and the bottom of the stall. Filthy gray sneakers stood ankle-deep in overflow. The laces were untied; they floated like the hair of a drowning victim.

"Hello?" Baku called softly. He did not want a response. "Can I help you with something, sir?" His English was heavy, but he was careful with his pronunciation.

He took a cautious step forward, and that small shuffle cleared nearly half the distance between him and the stall door. He took a second step, but he made that one even tinier than the first, and he put out his hand.

The tips of his fingers quivered, as they tapped against the painted metal door. He tried to ask, "Are you all right?" But the words barely whispered out of his throat.

A groan answered him without offering specifics.

He pushed the door.

He found himself staring at a man's hunched back and a sweaty patch of shirt between his shoulder blades. The shirt itself was the beige kind that comes with an embroidered nametag made in dark blue thread. When the man at the toilet turned around, Baku read that the tag said "Peter," but he'd guessed that much already. He knew the shirt. It was the uniform worn by the man who drove the delivery truck each Tuesday, Thursday, and Sunday.

Peter's eyes were blank and watery. They looked like olives in a jar.

The deliveryman seemed to know that his peculiar ritual was being questioned, and he did not care for the interruption. With another petulant groan he half lunged, half tipped forward.

Baku recoiled, pulling the door closed with his retreat.

Peter was thwarted a few seconds longer than he should have been. Perhaps it was only his innate imbecility that made him linger so long with the slim obstacle, but it bought the old chef time to retreat. He slipped first, falling knee-down with a splash, but catching himself on the sink and rising. Back into the hall and past the ice machine he stumbled, rubbing at his knee and shaking from the encounter. It had been too strange, too stupidly sinister.

At the far end of the dining area a big round clock declared the time. For a moment he was relieved. He needed to go home, and if the clock could be believed, he had less than an hour remaining on his shift.

But his relief dissolved as quickly as it had blossomed. The scene beneath the clock was no more reassuring than the one in the bathroom.

BAD SUSHI

Dozens of people were eating in silence, staring down at their plates or their forks. They gazed with the same bland olive eyes, not at each other but at the food. The waitresses and the one lone male waiter lurked by the kitchen window without talking. The cash register did not ring.

Where was the manager? He'd been in and out for days, more out than in. The assistant manager, then. Anyone, really—anyone who was capable of sustaining convincing eye contact would suffice.

Into the kitchen Baku ducked, anticipating an oasis of ordinary people.

He was disappointed. The cooks stood in pockets of inattentive shoe-gazing, except for the two who had made their way back into the refrigerator. From within its chilly depths, Baku heard the sounds of sloppy gnawing.

Was he the only one who'd not been eating the sushi?

He turned just in time to hear the bathroom door creak open. Peter moaned as he made his way into the corridor and then began a slow charge towards the chef.

The grunting, guttural call drew the attention of the customers and the kitchen staff. They turned to see Peter, and then the object of his attention. All faces aimed themselves at Baku, whose insides immediately worked into a tangle.

Two nearby customers came forward. They didn't rise from their seats or fold their napkins, and they didn't put down their forks. Together they stood, knocking their chairs backwards and crashing their thighs against the table, rocking it back and forth. The woman raised her hand and opened her mouth as if she meant to speak, but only warm air and half-chewed sushi fell out from between her lips. Her dinner companion managed a louder sound—like an inflatable ball being squeezed—and the low, flatulent cry roused the remaining customers and the kitchen staff alike. In a clumsy wave, they stumbled towards Baku.

On the counter, he spied the folded roll of his fine German knives. He fired one hand out to snag it; then he tucked it under his arm and pushed the glass door with his elbow.

Behind him the crowd rallied, but it was a slow rally that was impeded by everything in its path. Chairs thwarted them. Counters baffled them.

Baku hurried. Outside the sky was growing dark with a too-early dusk brought on by a cloudy almost-storm. He tumbled into the parking lot and pulled the door shut behind his back.

The bus stop was empty.

The chef froze. He always rode the bus home. Every night. Rain or shine he waited under the small shelter at the corner.

Over his shoulder he watched the masses swarm behind the windows, pushing their hands through the blinds and slapping their palms against the glass. They were slow, but they wouldn't give him time to wait for the 9:30 bus.

He squeezed his knives, taking comfort from their strength wrapped inside the cloth. His knuckles curled around them.

As a young man he'd confronted the ocean with nets and hooks, drawing out food and earning his livelihood. Then he'd been called as a soldier, and he'd fought for his country, and to serve his Emperor. In the years that followed he had put away his bayonet and had taken up the knives of a cook; he had set aside the uniform of war and put on an apron.

But knives like these could be weapons, too.

"I am not too old," he breathed. Behind him, a dozen pairs of hands slapped at the windows, rattling the blinds. Shoulders pummeled at the doors, and the strained puff of a pneumatic hinge told Baku that they were coming. "I am not too old to work. Not too old to cut fish. I am *not* too old to fight."

Peter's delivery vehicle sat open in the parking lot's loading zone. The refrigerated trailer compartment hung open, one door creaking back and forth in the pre-storm breeze. A faint briny smell wafted forth.

Baku limped to the trailer door and took a deep breath of the tepid air. The contents within were beginning to turn.

BAD SUSHI

He slammed the metal door shut and climbed into the cab. He set his knives down on the passenger's seat and closed his own door just as the first wave of angry patrons breached the restaurant door.

At first, he saw no keys. He checked the ignition and the glove box. But when he checked the visor a spare set tumbled down into his lap. He selected the engine key without a tremor and plugged it into the slot. The engine gagged to life, and with a tug of the gearshift, the vehicle rolled forward—pushing aside a pair of restaurant patrons, and knocking a third beneath the van's grille.

Baku did not check to see them in the rearview mirror.

Downtown, to Manufacturer's Row. That's where the manager had said the new meat came from. That's where Baku would go.

He roughly knew the way, but driving was something he'd forgotten about years before. Buses were cheap to ride, and cars were expensive to maintain. This van was tall and top-heavy. It reacted slowly, like a boat. It swayed around corners and hesitated before stopping, or starting, or accelerating.

He drove it anyway.

The streets were more empty than not. The roads were mostly clear and Baku wished it were otherwise. All the asphalt looked wet to him, shining under the streetlamps. Every corner promised a sliding danger. But the van stayed upright, and Baku's inexpert handling bothered no one.

He arrived at the distribution center and parked on the street in front of a sign that said "Loading Zone," and he climbed out of the cab, letting the door hang open. So what if it was noted and reported? Let the authorities come. Let them find him and ask why he had forced his way into the big old building. At first he thought this as a whim, but then he began to wish it like a prayer. "Let them come."

In his arm he felt a pain, and in his chest there was an uncomfortable tightness from the way he breathed too hard. "Let them bring their guns and their lights. I might need help."

From a sliver of white outlined vertically along the wall, Baku saw that the front door was open.

He put his face against the crack and leaned on his cheekbone, trying to see inside. The space was not enough to peep through, but the opening was big enough to emit an atrocious smell. He lifted his arm and buried his nose in the crook of his elbow. He wedged his shoulder against the heavy slab of the door and pushed. The bottom edge of the sagging door grated on the concrete floor.

Within, the odor might have been overpowering to someone unaccustomed to the smell of saltwater, fish, and the rot of the ocean. It was bad enough for Baku.

Two steps sideways, around the crotchety door, and he was inside.

His shoes slipped and caught. The floor was soaked with something more viscous than saline, more seaweed-brown than clear. He locked his knees and stepped with care. He shivered.

The facility was cold, but not cold enough to freeze his breath. Not quite. Industrial refrigerators with bolted doors flanked one wall, and indoor cranes were parked haphazardly around the room. There were four doors—one set of double doors indicated a corridor or hall. A glance through the other three doors suggested office space; a copy room, a lunch room with tables, and two gleaming vending machines.

Somewhere behind the double doors a rhythmic clanking beat a metal mantra. There was also a mechanical hum, a smoother drone. Finally there came a lumpy buzz like the sound of an out-of-balance conveyor belt.

In his hand, Baku's fist squeezed tightly around his roll of knives.

He unclenched his fingers and opened the roll across his palm. It would do him no good to bring them all sheathed, but he could not hold or wield more than two. So for his right hand, he chose a long, slim blade with a flexible edge made to filet large fish. For his left, he selected a thicker, heavier knife—one whose power came from its weight. The remaining blades he wrapped up, tied, and left in a bundle by the door.

"I will collect you on the way out," he told them.

Baku crept on toward the double doors, and he pushed tentatively at them.

They swayed and parted easily, and the ambient noise jumped from a background tremor to a sharper throb.

The stink swelled too, but he hadn't vomited yet and he didn't intend to, so Baku forced the warning bile back down to whence it had come. He would go toward the smell. He would go toward the busy machines and into the almost frigid interior. His plan was simple, but big: He would turn the building off. All of it. Every robot, light, and refrigerator. There would be a fuse box or a power main.

As a last resort, he might find a dry place to start a fire.

On he went, and the farther his explorations took him, the more he doubted that a match would find a receptive place to spark.

Dank coldness seeped up through his shoes and his feet dragged splashing wakes along the floor. He slipped and stretched out an arm to steady himself, leaning his knuckles on the plaster. The walls were wet, too. He wiped the back of his hand on his pants. It left a trail of slime.

The clank of machines pounded harder, and with it the accompanying smell insinuated itself into every pore of Baku's body, into every fold of his clothing.

But into the heart of the warehouse he walked—one knife in each hand—until he reached the end of the corridor that opened into a larger space—one filled with sharp-angled machines reaching from the floor to the ceiling. Rows of belts on rollers shifted frosty boxes back and forth across the room from trucks to chilled storage. Along the wall were eight loading points with trucks docked and open, ready to receive shipments and disperse them. He searched for a point of commonality, or for some easy spot where all these things must come together for power. Nothing looked immediately promising, so he followed the cables on the ceiling with his eyes, and he likewise traced the cords along the floor. Both sets of lines followed the same path, into a secondary hallway.

Baku shuffled sideways and slithered with caution along the wall and toward the portal where the electric lines all pointed. Once through the portal, Baku found himself at the top of a flight of stairs. Low-power emergency lights illuminated the corridor in murky yellow patches.

It would have to be enough.

When he strained to listen, Baku thought he detected footsteps, or maybe even voices below. He tiptoed towards them, keeping his back snugly against the stair rail, holding his precious knives at the ready.

He hesitated on the bottom stair, hidden in the shadows, reluctant to take the final step that would put him firmly in the downstairs room. There in the basement the sad little emergency lights were too few and far between to give any real illumination. The humidity, the chill, and the spotty darkness made the entire downstairs feel like night at the bottom of a swimming pool.

A creature with a blank, white face and midnight-black, lidless eyes emerged from inside an open freezer. It was Sonada's manager, or what was left of him.

"You," the thing accused.

Baku did not recoil or retreat. He flexed his fingers around the knife handles and took the last step down into the basement.

"You would not eat the sushi with us. Why?" The store manager was terribly changed without and within; even his voice was barely recognizable. He spoke as if he were talking around a mouthful of seaweed.

Baku circled around the manager, not crossing the floor directly but staying with his back to the wall. The closer he came, the slower he crept until he halted altogether. The space between them was perhaps two yards.

"Have you come now for the feast?" the manager slurred.

BAD SUSHI

Baku was not listening. It took too much effort to determine where one word ended and the next began, and the message didn't matter anyway. There was nothing the manager could say to change Baku's mind or mission.

Beside the freezer with its billowing clouds of icy mist there was a fuse box. The box was old-fashioned; there were big glass knobs the size of biscuits and connected to wiring that was as frayed and thick as shoelaces. It might or might not be the heart of the building's electrical system, but at least it might be *connected* to the rest. Perhaps, if Baku wrenched or broke the fuses, there was a chance that he could short out the whole building and bring the operation to a halt. He'd seen it in a movie he'd watched once, late at night when he couldn't sleep.

If he could stop the electricity for even an hour—he could throw open the refrigerators and freezers and let the seafood thaw. Let it rot. Let it spoil here, at the source.

The manager kept talking. "This is the new way of things. He is coming, for the whole world."

"So this is where it starts?" Baku spoke to distract the manager. He took a sideways shuffle and brought himself closer to the manager, to the freezer, to the fuse box.

"No. We are not the first."

Baku came closer. A few feet. A hobbled scuffing of his toes. He did not lower the knives, but the manager did not seem to notice.

"Tell me about this. Explain this to me. I don't understand it."

"Yes," the manager gurgled. "Like this." And he turned as if to gesture into the freezer, as if what was inside could explain it all.

Baku jumped then, closing the gap between them. He pushed with the back of his arm and the weight of his shoulder, and he shoved the manager inside the freezer.

The door was a foot thick; it closed with a hiss and a click. Only if he listened very hard could Baku hear the angry protests from within.

He pressed his head against the cool metal door and felt a fury of muted pounding on the other side.

When he was comfortable believing that the manager would not be able to interfere, he removed his ear from the door. He turned his attention again to the fuse box, regarding it thoughtfully.

Then, one after the other, the fuzzy white pods of light were extinguished. Darkness swallowed the stray slivers of light which were left.

The basement fell into perfect blackness.

And the heavy thing that struck Baku in the chest came unseen, unheard, but with all the weight of a sack of bricks.

The shock sent him reeling against the freezer door. He slammed against it and caught himself by jabbing his knives into the concrete floor, the door, and anything else they could snag.

Somewhere nearby the thing regrouped with a sound like slithering sandbags. Baku's ear told him that it must be huge—but was this an illusion of the darkness, of the echoing acoustics? He did not know if the thing could see him, and he did not know what it was, only that it was powerful and deadly.

On the other side of the room Baku's assailant was stretching, lashing, and reaching. Baku flattened his chest against the wall and leaned against it as he tried to rise, climbing with the knives, scraping them against the cement blocks, cutting off flecks and strips of paint that fluttered down into his hair and settled on his eyelashes.

A loud clank and a grating thunk told Baku that his knives had hit something besides concrete. He reached and thrust the knife again. He must be close to the fuse box; he'd only been a few feet away when the lights went out.

The thudding flump that accompanied his opponent's movement sounded louder behind Baku as he struggled to stand, to stab. Something jagged and rough caught at his right hand.

A warm gush soaked his wrist and he dropped that knife. With slippery fingers he felt knobs, and what might have been the edge of a slim steel door panel. He reached for it, using this door to haul himself up, but the little hinges popped under his weight and he fell back down to his knees.

The monstrous unseen thing snapped out. One fat, foul-smelling limb crashed forward, smacking Baku's thighs, sweeping his legs out from underneath him.

His bleeding right hand grazed the dropped knife, but he couldn't grasp it. Holding the remaining blade horizontally in his left hand, Baku locked his wrist. When the creature attacked again, Baku sliced sideways.

A splash of something more gruesome than blood or tar splashed against the side of the face.

He used his shoulder to wipe away what he could. The rest he ignored. The wet and bloody fingers of his right hand curled and fastened themselves on a small shelf above his head.

The thing whipped its bulk back and forth but it was not badly hurt. It gathered itself together again, somewhere off in the corner. If Baku could trust his ears, it was shifting its attack, preparing to come from the side. He rotated his left wrist, moving the knife into a vertical position within his grip. He opened and closed his fingers around it. To his left, he heard the thing coming again.

Baku peered up into the darkness over his head where he knew the fuse box now hung open.

The creature scooted forward.

Baku hauled himself up and swung the fine German steel hard at the box, not the monster—with all the weight he could put behind it. It landed once, twice, and there came a splintering and sparking. Plastic shattered, or maybe it was glass. Shards of debris rained down.

One great limb crushed against Baku and wrapped itself around his torso, ready to crush, ready to break what it found. The man could not breathe; there in the monster's grip he felt the thing coil itself, slow but wickedly dense, as if it were filled with wet pebbles.

In the center of the room the beast's bulk shuddered unhappily as it shifted, and shuffled, and skidded. The appendage that squeezed Baku was only one part of a terrible whole.

Before his breath ran out, before his hands grew weak from lost blood and mounting fear, Baku took one more stab. The heavy butcher's blade did not bear downward, but upward and back.

The fuse box detonated with a splattering torrent of fire and light.

For two or three seconds Baku's eyes remained open. And in those seconds he marveled at what he saw, but could have never described. Above and beyond the thunderous explosion of light in his head, the rumbling machines ceased their toil.

The current from the box was such that the old man could not release the knife, and the creature could not release its hold on the old man.

As the energy coursed between them, Baku's heart lay suddenly quiet in his chest, too stunned to continue beating. He marveled briefly, before he died, how electricity follows the quickest path from heaven to earth, and how it passes with pleasure through those things that stand in water.

THE CATASTROPHE BOX

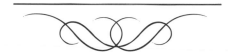

I'd be lying if I said I remembered very much about reading *The Castle of Otranto* by Horace Walpole, but it's something that was thrust in front of me back in grad school, and I *did* read it, and some weird detail or two stuck with me for awhile. That book is widely considered to be, perhaps, the first truly "gothic" novel. It might well be, and it certainly set a standard for the gloomy, dramatic, soap-opera vibe that the genre eventually gelled around; but the detail that hung around in the back of my head had to do with a prophecy in the book—that the castle's family would fall (more or less) the day that the lord of the manor became too large for it. This prophecy was treated as though it were literal, with glimpses of enormous body parts spied through keyholes and the like.

Or that's how I remember it.

At any rate, I got thinking about Walpole again when I was approached about contributing a story to a retro-style pulp anthology. Obviously I was tickled stupid that (a). Joe Lansdale knew my name, and (b). that he wanted me to write something for him. I was also delighted to learn that he was particularly keen to have some entries from the "weird pulp" corner of the genre—specifically something that echoed the strange shorts that appeared in the 1920s alongside Lovecraft and others in *Weird Tales*. And for some reason, I thought of *The Castle of Otranto*.

After all, what's weirder than an aristocratic...ghost? Giant? Something or someone that slowly swells until it occupies literally an entire house?

This was something I could play with.

Lovecraft isn't typically considered "gothic" except, perhaps, in the modern sense of "anything horror-related or horror-adjacent," but I thought it'd be fun to marry his sanity-shaking cosmic strangeness with the traditional moodiness and drama of an old-fashioned gothic, and see what would shake out.

What shook out was..."The Catastrophe Box."

So "The Catastrophe Box" was inspired partly by Walpole, and partly by real life paranormal investigator Harry Price (1881-1948), a man whose legacy is mixed—but whose affable skepticism and insistent curiosity charmed me silly. Happily enough, some kind soul put extensive excerpts of Harry's casebooks online, and I stumbled upon them while hunting for inspiration on another project. But when the opportunity to contribute to *Son of Retro Pulp* came along, I began thinking in terms of Lovecraft, and *Weird Tales*, and *Amazing Stories*... and the temptation to fictionalize one of Harry's cases was too good to pass up.

So yes, there really was a Joanna Southcott, and yes, she left behind a series of boxes. One of these boxes found its way into Harry's possession and was subsequently investigated with psychics, x-ray machines, and yes—a room full of bishops. It was the psychics who interested me most; Harry took meticulous record of what

THE CATASTROPHE BOX

each psychic believed to be inside the sealed box, and although the guesses were mundane, the process of their divination left me quite a lot of room for artistic license.

TO THE office of Dr. Thomas Springfield,
        November 14, 1932

I realize that my account will stretch the limits of your credulity, but I am constrained by the facts, and tethered by the truth. I wish I could relate events in such a way that they would seem less strange and more likely—but in the interest of veracity, I am forced to sound like a lunatic.

It began when my wife returned from London with a wooden box and a nervous aspect, both of which unsettled me deeply. The box was a peculiar affair, approximately the size of a large family Bible and bound with weathered silk strips which were sealed with wax. The nervous aspect manifested as too-wide eyes and too-tight lips, pressed together as if to bind back a lie.

"What's gone wrong?" I asked, and I thought she might burst into tears.

She said, "Wrong? It's hard to say. The whole thing might've gone perfectly, for all I know of it. But I've misled Harry terribly, and I've stolen from him, too." She squeezed the unwieldy box, crushing it against her breasts.

I ushered Sonia to her favorite chair and offered to put away her bags. She agreed to this arrangement but she would not part with the suspicious box; and she would offer no further explanation until she held a cup of steaming coffee in her hands, where the cup shook slightly between her quivering fingers.

"Now tell me, dear. It can't be as bad as all that."

"Oh, but it is," she assured me. "As bad as that and worse. You'd believe me, though—wouldn't you? If I told you that I'd only done it for Harry's good?"

"Of course I'd believe you. But you *must* tell me what's happened."

I cannot say that Sonia was usually prone to such hysterics, for she was always a most even-tempered woman, tested though she was by her remarkable psychic abilities. Sometimes the powers of her mind were a nuisance, and sometimes a blessing; but they were often so distracting that I thanked God each day she'd been born such a reasonable soul. Therefore it gave me great grief to see her so vexed after a session with our old friend Harry Price. Usually she viewed their collaborations as interesting scientific exercises, and she enjoyed the company of that great researcher and her fellow subjects. I believe it must have made her feel more ordinary, to be surrounded by others like herself. But this only begged the question, what appalling event could have occurred in London, to leave her so shattered?

I said, "Have some coffee, and have a moment to rest from your voyage. I'm listening, whenever you'd like to talk."

She nodded and did her best to summon a brave little smile. "I keep telling myself that all's quite well since I'm here at home—but then I see this box, and I know that the worst is far from over. Oh, I've done something awful!"

I reached forward, thinking that I should remove the box from her immediate view, since it affected her so; or perhaps I only wished to examine it for myself.

But she snatched it out of my reach.

"No, you mustn't!"

Her wild eyes and shrill rebuttal shocked me even more than the swift violence of her reaction. My consternation was plain, I assume, for her face crumpled and the tears finally came, along with her apologies. "Darling, I'm so very sorry. I don't mean to alarm you, I swear—it's only, it's that, it's just…"

I interrupted, for she seemed to require some direction. "Please, remember that you're home, and whatever secrets you harbor, you can trust them with me."

And, following my heartfelt assurances, she began to share her story.

She initiated the narrative with a question. "Have you ever heard of Joanna Southcott?" I admitted that I had not, so she continued. "She's an Englishwoman who died over a hundred years ago, and she was either a prophet or a madwoman, depending on who you ask. She believed…"

Sonia faltered here. "Go on," I urged.

"But it's complicated. She believed in the second coming of Jesus in a very tangible, mortal way, and she foretold the end of the world through His next birth. She had many followers in her time, and it would seem she still has a few, here and there—though her final prediction failed to manifest to everyone's satisfaction."

Following a pause during which it seemed unlikely that my wife would clarify, I asked her, "What was this last prediction?"

She hesitated, and then shrugged. "She insisted that she was pregnant with Christ."

"And she wasn't?" I joked, but my wife didn't smile.

She said the next part quickly. "Don't be ridiculous. She was in her sixties by then. She wasn't pregnant, she was ill; and then she was dead."

"I'm sorry, I was only trying to—"

"I know, it doesn't matter."

But it did matter, for I was not accustomed to such short treatment from my loving wife. Since she was so clearly distressed, I did not call her attention to my wounded affection. Instead I said, "Very well dear, as you say. It doesn't matter. But your unhappiness matters to me greatly, and I only wish to calm you. Please, go on. Finish your tale, and then perhaps we'll have a nightcap and toast to your safe return."

"Finish my tale," she repeated slowly, as if the words were strange in her mouth. "I suppose I must, if I'm to engage you as my accomplice. It's only fair that I tell you the truth. Or perhaps it's not. Perhaps it's better if you do not know, and cannot be held responsible for my follies."

"My dear, I'd rather join you in prison than live with secrets between us," I told her with all earnestness.

She sighed and removed her glasses so she could rub her eyes. She was exhausted and I regretted the need to press her, but my curiosity had reached such a peak that I couldn't bear not knowing what had driven her to larceny.

The box glowered at me from her lap—yes, it glowered, and it sank there upon her thighs with an unnatural weight that made me worry it would bruise her. My desire to know more about this pernicious container grew by the moment. Why did she clutch it in such a fierce, dreadful manner? Why did she wear an expression of determined revulsion, as if she could neither bear to look nor look away?

She told me, "It's this box," as if I could not already guess. "It's this box, Robert. Harry made it clear we couldn't open it, not yet. Miss Southcott's orders were quite specific, you understand. She made some very specific requests."

"Such as?"

"Such as, it must only be opened in times of national crisis, and in the presence of twenty-four bishops, and oh my. There was a whole *list* of demands. Even though the poor woman's been gone for over a century, Harry was determined to follow her instructions to the best of his ability. He's like that, you know. He tries so hard to respect the dead in all ways, and that's one reason I regard him so highly." She paused to fidget with the silk strips that crisscrossed the box, and said, "It's because I care so much—for him, and for you, and for the rest of the whole world, really—that I couldn't let him open this. Let me explain," she said, and I was glad—for I very much wished she would.

"It began naturally enough, as a simple experiment. A research experiment, you understand. Harry received this box in the mail, and although he intended to observe its instructions to the letter, his scientific spirit arranged for a bit of a cheat. His first inclination was to x-ray the box, but the x-rays were unreadable—they were garbled and strange, as if some force prevented the rays from penetrating and illuminating the contents.

"So while he was awaiting the response of his invited bishops, he called for me and six others with abilities like mine. It was only a little exercise," she swore. "It was only an afternoon when we passed the box among ourselves, one by one, and tried to ascertain what might be held within it. Of course, we were not permitted to hear one another's responses, in order to maintain the integrity of the research."

"Of course, of course," I echoed. I knew how Harry operated, in a strict scientific fashion that I respected and trusted. By the time she brought home that damnable box, Sonia had been participating in his experiments for five or six years.

She went on. "I do not know what the others saw, though when we gossiped later, it seemed to me that they'd detected frivolities and trinkets of little value."

I anticipated the course of her story, so I prompted her. "But what did *you* see?"

She shuddered and said, "I saw something *else*. And when I later looked again at those x-rays, I saw that they had not failed: they had only been incapable of describing what they touched. And I *knew*," she poured her heart into that word, and I did not doubt her, "that this box must not be opened. It must not, not ever—not in the presence of a host of bishops, or the pope, or any good minister and all of his kind and kin. This box must remain closed."

I was stunned, and I told her as much. "So you stole it? You took the box, so that Harry could not open it?"

She nodded vigorously. "I don't ask you to understand, Robert. I don't ask you to hide me or help me. I ask only that you keep your silence, and that you keep this box closed no matter what. Will you promise me that? Can I ask that of you?"

"My darling, you could ask that, and a thousand things more, and I'd never hesitate. If it's important, and if you remain so stricken and convinced of its repugnance, then I am forced to agree to any terms you set down. I trust you and your judgment, and your abilities. I've never doubted you, and I could never betray you."

I took her hands in my own, and she released her death-grip on the box. We exchanged a kiss and a promise, and I convinced her to relinquish it for the evening. She was persuaded to leave it in the attic, concealed in a trunk that was locked and bolted. The key she kept inside her pillowcase, and all through the night I wondered after it, and after the strange little coffin it secured.

In the morning I awoke, sometime shortly after dawn.

Sonia was not beside me.

For reasons I could not explain, I was consumed by a moment of panic until I heard her upstairs—her small, light footsteps pattering to and fro in the attic. I sat upright and caught my breath, then felt around with my feet until I'd located my slippers.

Above me, something heavy scraped across the floor and my wife mumbled. I could not understand her words, but I do not believe that I was meant to. She was speaking to herself, or to the box, or to the trunk that held it.

I wrapped my robe around myself and went to the steps that led to the attic. I climbed the stairs quietly, dodging the creaky boards and the places where the wood might announce my approach. But when I reached the door I did not open it, because on the other side I heard Sonia crying. I raised my hand in a gentle fist, ready to knock, but I withdrew it. Her weeping was so thick with despair that I could not bring myself to interrupt.

I turned and retreated as unobtrusively as I'd approached.

When she finally joined me downstairs, I'd begun a pot of coffee and started some eggs for breakfast. She entered the kitchen bleary-eyed and stuffy-nosed, though she forced a grin that was almost grotesque on her gloomy face. If she was aware that I'd overheard her sobs, she did not give me any indication of it.

But she did say, "I moved the box this morning."

I worked a utensil against the scrambling eggs and said, "You did?"

"I couldn't stand having it there, right above us while we tried to sleep. It kept me awake. I put it downstairs, in the extra closet, behind the coats."

This arrangement was not satisfactory for long.

Over the next few weeks she moved the box repeatedly, stashing it at various locations around our home. Sometimes she told me about her activities, and sometimes I guessed them, or stumbled across them. The box was shifted from the hall closet to the bottom of the pantry; it was relocated to the secondary storage closet under the stairs; it was transported to the bottom of her bureau.

I thought at first that she wished to keep it close, though at times I thought she meant to cast it as far from her presence as possible. I often wondered why she didn't simply bury it in the yard, or at some more distant spot—but when I suggested this, she reacted as if I were daft.

At this point I am compelled to confess that things grew strained between us.

As Sonia retreated deeper into her depression, we spoke less and less. My efforts to cheer her or engage her were all refused, lovingly for awhile, and then more abruptly as my persistence failed to impress her.

During this difficult time, I took the liberty of writing our old friend Harry Price. I was cautious in my letter; he must surely be aware that his Southcott box was missing, but I did not want to call his attention to the possibility that Sonia had taken it. I tried to couch my interest in terms of intellectual curiosity, and I took great pains to indicate that I was unaware that the box had gone missing. I told him I wished to know the outcome of his experiment. Had the box been opened? What did it contain?

While I waited for his response, my wife's condition deteriorated. She withdrew from my every touch, even going so far as to move out of our bedroom and into the guest room. I pleaded with her to reconsider but she only muttered vaguely about not taking any chances, and how she'd serve as no mother to the dead or the damned.

I left her to her own directions and devices, for what else could I do?

I tried to watch her, and keep her fed, and keep her safe from herself and from others. But it was hard when she was so willful and so prone to wandering.

Always before there had been an element of distance between us, though it was a fond and friendly distance—because I believed in her powers, but I did not share them. I trusted her knowledge, for I had seen it demonstrated. It was not always flawless, no. Sometimes her predictions, or her "knowings" were slightly wrong, or strangely interpreted. I recall once she told us that our friend William would come to visit in the evening; and instead we were greeted by my brother, Bill. So you understand what I mean when I say that she was almost always right, but not always correct. She was brilliant and wise, despite the fact that her uncanny abilities were occasionally difficult to manage.

THE CATASTROPHE BOX

I was well accustomed to her odd mumblings and off-handed statements. I had long since come to terms with the way my wife might see things I could not, but it never frightened me—not until she brought home that accursed box.

In the wake of that box her random, disjointed statements took on a sinister cast. Whereas before she would laughingly chat with invisibles, when we shared our home with the box she would grumble darkly—and eventually, incessantly. She rarely spoke to me, anymore. As often as not, she seemed unaware that I was present, or listening.

By the time I found Harry's response in our mailbox, I was at my wit's end.

I have affixed his letter here with this missive, so that you may read it in its entirety.

Dear Robert,

I'm glad to hear from you, as always, and I very much hope this note finds you well. The Southcott box was something of a surprise, and something of a disappointment—but not too much of either one, given the nature of the woman who left it. In short, we assembled our bishops and the media gathered close around, and I showed them the box's contents. They were decidedly silly, I don't mind telling you. Oh, it contained the expected prophecies and edicts, to be sure—but it also held a trove of romance novels, a coin purse laden with pocket change, a horse pistol, and an assortment of other trivialities.

In case the news reports have not filtered over the ocean yet, I should warn you that there were accusations of fraud against myself and my team, but by now you must be aware that it's to be expected, in our line of work. Psychic investigation has miles to go before it's respected as the science it rightfully claims to be.

(Without going into greater detail, there was some suggestion that the box was a fake, or that it had been switched before I presented my findings to the watching world.)

As for Miss Southcott herself, there's both quite a lot and very little to be said of her. She believed in the end of the world and the birth of a new Christ-child, which she was personally prepared to produce. Alas for the poor woman (and for us, as well?), this never transpired. She died surrounded by her fawning followers, bereft of a supernatural heir, and stripped of her credibility.

How many boxes she left behind, no one knows for certain. Perhaps there are half a dozen all told, scattered across the land. Her modern-day followers (of which there are a surprising number, considering) refuse to open the known boxes, in order to preserve the Mystery of the order. But what mystery is there? None, I'd say. A madwoman with delusions of motherhood and divinity died, and left a trail of riddles that continue to confound and amuse us, even unto this day. That is all. There is nothing more to it.

Be well, Robert—and do send my love to Sonia. I wish you both the very best.

~Harry

It might've pained Harry to know it, but his message chilled me to the bone. It was that one word, "motherhood," that had sent a jolt of horror down my throat and into my stomach, for I had heard Sonia fussing about that same subject only just the day before.

I believe she'd said, "Mother and saint, for what church? For what god? For what terrible things to be born?" And I'd asked her what she meant by these awkward, unnerving words, but she did not answer me. I'd grown accustomed to being ignored, by that point, and I could not bring myself to make any further inquiries.

THE CATASTROPHE BOX

Yet I did not understand! My friend's letter had done nothing to enlighten or comfort me, and I could not fathom what had become of my wife, or why this awful box had become such a fixture in our previously happy lives!

I had learned nothing about how I might help Sonia. Perhaps that was my own fault. Perhaps I should have never promised to keep her secrets; perhaps I should have written Harry again and told him the truth—I could have told him everything, and the more time passes, the more I wish that I *had*. But the confidence between a husband and wife is sacred, is it not? Even the cold, impartial courts will not force them to implicate one another, is this not the case?

I made mistakes, yes. Many of them.

I can only offer in my defense that I loved my wife, and I trusted her, even in her alarmingly diminished capacity. I did my best to respect her wishes, and her privacy—and to give her the space she required to return to her normal self.

But her normal self was not forthcoming. The situation continued to deteriorate, becoming worse by steady degrees. She quit eating, and sleeping. She became irrational, avoiding certain rooms and eschewing regular routines; and even when she would make the occasional attempt to communicate, she only frightened and confused me.

Once she seized me as I left the washroom.

Her hands were so thin; they were tight skin gloves stretched over hinges and bones, and she worked them into my collar as she pulled my face down to meet hers. She said, "You must not go there, not into that room, not anymore. Can't you see it? It's growing. The whole of it increases in wisdom and stature, and even death cannot prevent its advent!"

I stuttered, "It...it grows? Dearest—"

"Yes, it grows. Can't you see it? I've seen it here and there, in bits and pieces. It lives here now. Or it remains here, dead and growing. Oh, but how does a dead thing grow? I cannot say. No one can say, certainly not *her*. She was a mad old thing, believing it was good, and pure, and come to save us all. She was no prophet. She was a pansy, and a pawn."

She stopped herself, as if something new had occurred to her.

She said, "But she wasn't a fraud."

And then she walked away from me, and she closed the door.

The next time I saw her, she was floating in the bathtub in the second floor washroom. Not face down, and not with any cuts or abrasions upon her as I'm sure you've seen the coroner's note—she bobbed with her hands on either side of the tub, hanging over the edge. Her wedding ring had fallen to the floor, having slipped from her slender, damp finger. I found it underneath the sink, where it had rolled and settled.

I wear it still, on a chain around my neck.

What else can I do? My wife is dead. Perhaps she had not been herself for some time, but what difference does that make? We were married for fifteen years, and now she is gone.

There was a funeral, and there were questions. The police demanded a statement and asked me many offensive things. Had I harmed her? Had we fought? Had she done this to herself?

I believed that she had, yes, ended her own life. I had no proof, and I had not seen the event for myself (or else I would have prevented it!). But my suspicion matches the examining doctor's conclusions, and yes, I think she drowned herself that day.

To say that it breaks my heart does not begin to convey my grief.

I have only just noticed, as I have glanced at the beginning of this letter and seen the date, that it's been almost four years since she's been gone. I've been told that time heals all wounds, but this one will linger, I think. I can't imagine my future without her, any more than I can imagine a future behind bars for a crime which I never committed.

THE CATASTROPHE BOX

It was bizarre, that first day when I returned to our home knowing that she would never again join me there. My misery was bottomless, and my confusion and anguish went all the way to the bone. Every room was haunted by her absence.

I wandered through those first weeks in a daze, going through the motions of ordinary life but without any focus, and without any pleasure. I was granted a leave of absence from work and I gratefully accepted it, until I remembered that she was not there at home to keep me company.

It was not long before it occurred to me that I might contact her still, through some clandestine method assisted by Harry or her old comrades, but I shook the idea away because it was more than I could stand. What if we tried and were unsuccessful? What if we succeeded and she had nothing new or more lucid to say? I could not live with the possibility that even after death she might not know any peace, and so from pure cowardice I declined the gentle offers of mediums and researchers. One by one I told them "no," and one by one they offered me their condolences and agreed to respect my solitude.

Yet even so, as the months went by I became increasingly certain that I was not alone in the house after all.

At night, as I lay in the bed we'd once shared, I felt some pressing presence at the outskirts of my awareness and I could not describe it. I could not even pinpoint the intrusion; it was as if a slight sound had awakened me in the darkness, but by the time I was alert, the sound had ceased. I told myself that we (no, *I*) must have mice skittering through the corridors, or possibly some larger creature was skulking about outside.

But no animals ever presented evidence of their visits, and the pressing, almost suffocating presence grew more intense as time passed. I began to feel as if there were entire rooms of my home which had become swollen with something invisible, choking them to the brim and prohibiting me from entry. I wondered if there was not some distant chance that Sonia had chosen to visit me of her own accord, but I discarded the idea as I explored the intimidating sensation of sharing a home with something unseen. Whatever force was clogging my hallways and psychically rebuffing me, it could not come from my beloved wife.

I simply refused to entertain the possibility.

If anything, I worried that I might be following in her tragic and fatal footsteps. For when I paused to examine myself I noticed that I too had taken up darkly muttering as a pastime; and I too had come to eat less and less; and I too was having a difficult time finding any surcease in slumber. I took to drinking more heavily than I'd ever indulged in the past.

Was I becoming paranoid? Yes, I suppose I was.

To make matters more nerve-wracking, I found myself wondering after Sonia's box.

I did not know where last she'd stashed it, and the more I considered it, the more fixated my attention became. I concluded that I *must* learn its whereabouts. All of our problems, and her terrible descent into insanity began with that box, and I called myself an idiot for losing track of it.

Sonia had never left it outside or buried it, I was certain of that much. She'd moved it repeatedly, but it had always remained somewhere under our roof. But not close to the bedroom. Never close to the bedroom, after that homecoming evening. Where else might she have hidden it? Our home was spacious enough in a modest sense, with three full bedrooms and four levels if one counted the basement and the attic. I resolved therefore to give the house a thorough investigation.

To my eventual regret, I made this resolution after imbibing more brandy than perhaps could be deemed wise. But I feared that if I waited for a more sober occasion, I might lose my nerve and fail altogether. It was better, I concluded, to take action while the motivation was strongest, if the senses least reliable.

THE CATASTROPHE BOX

There is a chance that I'm being too cautious, now. I am telling you too much about the brandy. Will you evaluate my perceptions as misinformed by strong drink? Will you deem me as mad as my much-missed wife? I leave the possibilities open, and pray that your mind remains likewise. For here is the truth of the matter: Some combination of my loneliness, my sorrow, and my alcohol-thinned blood must have dimmed the walls between the worlds. I suppose you are free to blame whichever of these things you prefer for that which follows.

I initiated my search at the attic, for that is where the box was first placed. I took an electric torch, for the light up under the rafters was dim; and I scaled the stairs without bothering to smother my footsteps.

I opened the door and was confused. I saw...nothing.

Granted, it had been quite some time since I'd examined the attic or any of its contents, so I spent a befuddled moment beaming my torch light into the interior and feeling confounded when it illuminated nothing at all—not the far wall, not the round window, and not the exposed wood beams that held the roof aloft. It was as if I were shining my light against a clouded white wall.

The longer I stared with my light uplifted, the more clearly I could see that this strange white wall was curved at a slight angle, as if it might be part of an enormous sphere.

I thought to touch it, but I could not. My feet were glued to their position and even though I wished I could extend a hand and feel for myself if I were toppling into madness, my fingers would not cooperate.

You might ask yourself, "Was he frightened?"

I assure you, I was not. I was too confused to be terrified, and except for the revulsion my body enforced when I tried to enter, there was little to make me recoil. I was staring at the side of a blankish, whitish, semi-solid, cloudy sphere. How does one muster fear when confronted with such an oddity?

Finally, I unstuck myself from my perch at the top of the stairs and retreated, for I did not know what else to do. I could not move forward, and even if the box was located somewhere in the midst of that dense and difficult mass, I had no way of seeing it or reaching it.

At the bottom of the stairs I concluded, perhaps falsely, that I needed another drink; so I wandered woozily down towards the den in order to retrieve the snifter. As I staggered down the hallway I passed the open portal to the dining room and I almost maintained my unsteady pace— but an urgent alarm in the back of my head insisted that I stop, retreat, and take a second glance at whatever strange sight I'd almost missed.

I backed up and saw, only for a glimpse, another small part of something much larger.

I whipped my torch around and fired its beam like it was a pistol in my hand. It revealed nothing at all but a table and chairs, and the china cabinet. But for one heart-stopping second I could have sworn to you—or to God, or to the memory of my own dear wife—that I'd seen another part of the terrible huge thing that swelled in the attic. And at that blink of recognition, I would've told you that it had been the chubby, jointed curve of an arm.

Only, it would have been an impossible thing to say! For what manner of creature has an elbow so large that it might overwhelm an entire room? And then it might vanish altogether?

The light continued to show me nothing, so as I caught my breath and tried to stifle the horrid thudding of my nervous heartbeat, I retreated from my dining room—which never before, I must assert, had ever proven a source of terror or surprise. If I was staggering before, I was reeling after this unaccountable encounter. It was all I could do to amble all the way to the den where I found my snifter reassuringly full.

I know that perhaps I should not have indulged in another glass, but the skin-pressing pulse was shoving against me so hard that I felt as if I were being forcibly ejected from my own home by an unseen presence, and I felt the need to steel myself against it.

The strangeness of it all made me irrational.

THE CATASTROPHE BOX

I downed the next drink swiftly and remembered with a nauseous gulp that I still did not know what had become of the box. I regret to confess that *I could not stand not knowing.* If nothing else, I wished to locate the damned thing and bury it, or burn it, or throw it off a bridge. I couldn't understand why Sonia had never taken it upon herself to dispose of the thing, since it so wholly distressed her; but I would not suffer in that same way. I would not let an inanimate object get the best of me!

Was it unreasonable to blame the box for all my troubles? I did not think so at the time, and in the light of recent developments, I am even more convinced that my course of action was sensible. I only wish that I had succeeded more fully in ridding myself of the container—and I wish for your sake (yes sir, for your very own sake and not mine!) that it was not in your hands at this moment.

They asked me, at the station, if I had known what lurked inside and I told them yes. I told them the truth because I had no reason to lie. I had no part in its gruesome content; I neither caused nor created it, not in any fashion.

But I knew what was locked within because upon that day, I *did* find the box.

A picture was forming in my brain and it revolted me to the core, but I could not push it back as I was being pushed. I could not scour the thought from my mind, that what I'd seen in the attic was a gigantic head, bald and horrible, curved and smooth and neither real nor spectral—but ectoplasmic in nature. And the whole of the shape, if in fact it was one whole being, must be crouched or crooked in a fetal posture to fit so snugly in our abode. Furthermore, something about the fattened curve of the arm and the softly swollen nature of the head was working its way up to an even more abhorrent and baffling conclusion, one which was only reinforced when I finally located the box.

Sonia, oh *Sonia.*

I ran to the basement, for if something huge was sitting within my home, it must be sitting on or below the ground—or so I could only assume. And there, behind a storage bin I found it crushed between the bin and the damp stone wall.

The box was slightly wet from the moisture of the underground chamber, and its elderly wood had become warped and flaky to the touch. It stung me when I lifted it, and I cried out only to realize that I'd caught my hand on one of its corner nails. But I was not bleeding so badly that I turned away from my task.

Ignoring all of her warnings, and ignoring the rising hum that filled my head as I sat there on the ground—I tried with all my might to convince myself that I was not sharing space with the colossal monstrosity.

The box was slippery in my hands, and heavier than it appeared. I fumbled with it and it settled into my lap. Wrapped with layers of buckles, straps, and seals, I tore them off with my bare hands—scraping my knuckles and bruising my fingertips. Circular, flat blobs of black wax cracked away, and the last buckle came off with a click.

A loathsome odor wafted immediately from the box, even before I opened it. With the last fastener removed the shape of the container settled, and the fissure leaked a revolting green liquid that spilled across my legs.

Beneath my feet I swear, the ground commenced a terrifying quiver that rocked and stretched the very foundation of my home.

But I could not stop!

Not for any threat or violence could I abandon the box to its hiding place.

I pried the thing open, and its two sides yawned agape on a rusted, rotting hinge.

Inside, I saw the small and bloated corpse that you no doubt keep in a drawer in a chilled place to control the stink. You no doubt tell yourself that it's a most ordinary child, born in the ordinary way to an ordinary woman, perhaps even my wife before her passing. Since you are no doubt

THE CATASTROPHE BOX

a reasonable man, you feel that a crime has been committed, for I too saw the wire noose twisted around the infant's neck and the cadaverous blue taint of its sticky skin.

I can only beg you to reconsider your assumptions!

The signet-marked wax was over a century old, and the markers were fully intact when I shattered them. Even our old friend Harry, who is aging now and somewhat infirm, could easily verify the authenticity of the box and its seals; and this is how I knew beyond belief that the horror within was no mere babe and no sad victim.

I am not ashamed to admit that I do not recall precisely what happened next.

I was intoxicated, that's true and fair. I was shocked beyond thinking clearly, and so repulsed by the box's disgusting contents that I closed it up again and fled the scene. I only know this much because when I came to my senses I was covered by the stinking bile that oozed from the box.

And as for the box itself? I did not know what I'd done with it.

Later, once the alcohol had worked its way clean from my blood, I once again searched the house from top to bottom but I did not find it.

Of course, I would not have found it—I could not locate it because it had been buried beneath the storage bin, as now you know. Did I lift the paving stones that made up the unfinished floor? Did I bury the box myself, or did some protective and sinister element lend an unnatural hand?

I cannot say. I do not recall hiding it again, but I will not tell you that I didn't.

I will only tell you this, once more, and beg that you may believe me: I am hard-pressed to compose the depths of my remorse that the house's new owners came across the box so unexpectedly; and the box was unsealed the last I saw it—I am the one who unsealed it!—so if you tell me now that it was lashed and bound as if it had never been disturbed, then this is but further proof of the horror.

Please, good doctor. I beg you. Examine that small corpse as a scientist, and as a man who has sworn an oath to lend aid to those who require it!

For that is no child, and I am no murderer! ✎

FINAL REPAIR REQUEST

I used to write a lot of poetry—the late 90s kind, where you'd perform it on a stage, maybe at a coffeehouse. You'd do a bit of shouting while you were at it. Mind you, I haven't participated in any slams for nearly twenty years at this point, but once in awhile the urge to dabble overcomes me. "Final Repair Request" was inspired by a story that made the rounds awhile back, about how there are actually still a small handful of people who rely on an iron lung.

THE LAST iron lung might as well have been the first
      they all came with numbers so someone must've known
which was which, once upon a time

but then there was only the one
and I was inside it more often than not

CHERIE PRIEST

breathing with the bellows in and out
machine doing the work of muscles
the work of god

it failed by degrees
rusting rivets, cracking leather
a motor that smelled of burning grease and mid-century dust
no one left to repair it
no one to manufacture the parts
not for one woman, the last of her kind
or one machine, the last of its kind
a relic

I knew the world would rather forget.
I knew how hard it was to see, and feel
and fear to be so still for so long.
I said this was not so much a prison.
It won't always be this way. I'm not always lying.
I was left alone.

I was still alone when they came at last
they found me on the kitchen floor
I'd gone to the window to watch the sky fall
with my final breath
(it felt fitting)
and then I fell

and I was righteously pissed
because I mean, this is it?
the last thing I'll ever see, a popcorn ceiling that no one ever scraped?
no mushroom cloud of greeting?

FINAL REPAIR REQUEST

no rain of friendly fire?
only cold linoleum against my back
water dripping from a faucet
a bruise beneath my shoulder blades

but they stood over me
reverent and kind
weary but delighted

they clapped strange hands
wise travelers overjoyed to behold the infant Christ
(a woman, as long rumored)
they lifted and moved me
gentle as a bomb
this intergalactic love
this tremendous faith
that someone here deserved saving

how did you know, I asked
they touched my forehead
kissed my lips and brushed my hair
they said, the heart is an open ticket

I had asked the universe for help
for someone to soften the leather of my creaky lungs
extract the stripped bolts and tune the motor
clean the rust with a little WD-40
my own world would have let me go
if I'd lingered too much longer
so I'd directed my prayers farther afield

CHERIE PRIEST

here is your answer, they said
here are the pieces you need
dust from a comet's tail
ashes from a lesser bang

the galaxy opens its arms
here is the breath of god

we have moved the stars to find you ✎

RELUCTANCE

Back when I was the "high priestess of steampunk," I was invited to do a lot of steampunk projects—which was sometimes groovy, and sometimes felt like being pigeon-holed with...unfamiliar pigeons, I guess. I'd originally started *Boneshaker* as a zombie horror novel, though it evolved into something bigger than that, and was well received as (capital S) Steampunk. But mostly I just wanted to write scary stories. After all, I got my start in horror, and it's always been my home turf, so to speak; so when John Joseph Adams invited me to contribute a zombie project for *The Living Dead II*, I was delighted—even when he suggested that it could/should tie in with my steampunk universe, The Clockwork Century.

To be clear, I've never disliked steampunk. Steampunk was very kind to me, and I had a great deal of fun writing what I did in that genre. But I always enjoy it most when it's at its darkest, and the idea of taking that universe and writing a straight-up zombie horror story sounded great to me.

I told Adams to count me in.

The result is this stand-alone story, unconnected to anything else that happened anywhere in any of the books. My broad tendency to include military veterans takes center stage here—where the protagonist is a teenage boy with a war-incurred disability. Like so many others throughout the ages, he has no choice but to live with it and keep going.

At the risk of drawing a closer comparison than is really called for, my own dad was drafted as a teenager and went to Vietnam, where he got blown up and sent home in a chair. (To sum up.) I don't know how many surgeries it took before he was walking unaided again, but I know it was years before he was able to quit wearing the braces on his back. When I was a small child, I knew that he'd come home from work at night because I could hear the *clink clink clink* of him walking down the hall.

So here's a story about a wounded teenage veteran who takes a job with the Pony Express. Sort of. It's a zombie story, and a ghost story, and a human story, too.

It's honestly one of my favorites.

WALTER MCMULLIN puttered through the afternoon sky east of Oneida in his tiny dirigible. According to his calculations, he was somewhere toward the north end of Texas, nearing the Mexican territory west of the Republic; and any minute now he'd be soaring over the Goodnight-Loving trail.

He looked forward to seeing that trail.

Longest cattle drive on the continent, or that's what he'd heard—and it'd make for a fine change of scenery. West, west, and farther west across the Native turf on the far side of the big river he'd come, and his eyes were bored from it. Oklahoma, Texas, North Mexico next door…it all looked pretty much the same from the air. Like a pie crust, rolled out flat and overbaked. Same color, same texture. Same unending scorch marks, the seasonal scars of dried-out gullies and the splits and cracks of a ground fractured by the heat.

So cows—rows upon rows of lowing, shuffling cows, hustling their way to slaughter in Utah—would be real entertainment.

He adjusted his goggles, moving them from one creased position on his face to another, half an inch aside and only marginally more comfortable. He looked down at his gauges, using the back of one gloved hand to wipe away the ever-accumulating grime.

"Hydrogen's low," he mumbled to himself.

There was nobody else to mumble to. His one-man flyer wouldn't have held another warm body bigger than a small dog, and dogs made Walter sneeze. So he flew it alone, like most of the other fellows who ran the Express line, moving the mail from east to west in these hopping, skipping, jumping increments.

This leg of the trip he was piloting a single-seater called the *Majestic*, one could only presume as a matter of irony. The small airship was hardly more complex or majestic than a penny farthing strapped to a balloon, but Walter didn't mind. Next stop was Reluctance, where he'd pick up something different—something full of gas and ready to fly another leg.

Reluctance was technically a set of mobile gas docks, same as Walter would find on the rest of his route. But truth be told, it was almost a town. Sometimes the stations put down roots, for whatever reason.

And Reluctance had roots.

Walter was glad for it. He'd been riding since dawn and he liked the idea of a nap, down in the basement of the Express offices where the flyers sometimes stole a few hours of rest. He'd like a bed, but he'd settle for a cot and he wouldn't complain about a hammock, because Walter wasn't the complaining kind. Not anymore.

Keeping one eye on the unending sprawl of blonde dirt below in case of cows, Walter reached under the control panel and dug out a pouch of tobacco and tissue-thin papers. He rolled himself a cigarette, fiddled with the controls, and sat back to light it and smoke even though he damn well knew he wasn't supposed to.

His knee gave an old man's pop when he stretched it, but it wasn't so loud as the clatter his foot made when he lifted it up to rest on the *Majestic*'s console. The foot was a piece of machinery, strapped to the stump starting at his knee.

More sophisticated than a peg leg and slightly more natural-looking than a vacant space where a foot ought to be, the mechanical limb had been paid for by the Union army upon his discharge. It was heavy and slow and none too pretty, but it was better than nothing. Even when it pulled on its straps until he thought his knee would pop off like a jar lid, and even when the heft of it left bruises around the buckles that held it in place.

Besides, that was one of the perks of flying for the Dirigible Express Post Service: not a lot of walking required.

Everybody knew how dangerous it was, flying over Native turf and through unincorporated stretches—with no people, no water, no help coming if a ship went cripple or, God forbid, caught a spark. A graze of lightning would send a hydrogen ship home to Jesus in the space of a gasp; or a stray bullet might do the same, should a pirate get the urge to see what the post was moving.

That's why they only hired fellows like Walter. Orphans. Boys with no family to mourn them, no wives to leave widows and no children to leave fatherless. Walter was a prize so far as the Union Post—and absolutely nobody else—was concerned. Still a teenager, just barely; no family to speak of; and a veteran to boot. The post wanted boys like him, who knew precisely how bad their lot could get—and who came with a bit of perspective. It wanted boys who could think under pressure, or at the very least, have the good grace to face death without hysterics.

RELUCTANCE

Boys like Walter McMullin had faced death with serious, pants-shitting hysterics, and more than once. But after five years drumming, and marching, and shooting, and slogging through mud with a face full of blood and a handful of Stanley's hair or maybe a piece of his uniform still clutched like he could save his big brother or save himself or save anybody...he'd gotten the worst of the screaming out of his system.

With this in mind, the Express route was practically a lazy retirement. It beat the hell out of the army, that was for damn sure; or so Walter mused as he reclined inside the narrow dirigible cab, sucking on the end of his sizzling cigarette.

Nobody shot at him very often, nobody hardly ever yelled at him, and his clothes were usually dry. All he had to do was stay awake all day and stay on time. Keep the ground a fair measure below. Keep his temporary ship from being struck by lightning or wrestled to the ground by a tornado.

Not a bad job at all.

Something large down below caught his eye. He sat up, holding the cigarette lightly between his lips. He sagged, disappointed, then perked again and took hold of the levers that moved his steering flaps.

He wanted to see that one more time. Even though it wasn't much to see.

One lone cow, and it'd been off its feet for a bit. He could tell, even from his elevated vantage point, that the beast was dead and beginning to droop. Its skin hung across its bones like laundry on a line.

Of course that happened out on the trail. Every now and again.

But a quick sweep of the vista showed him three more meaty corpses blistering and popping on the pie-crust plain.

He said, "Huh." Because he could see a few more, dotting the land to the north, and to the south a little bit too. If he could get a higher view, he imagined there might be enough scattered bodies to sketch the Goodnight-Loving, pointing a ghastly arrow all the way to Salt Lake City. It looked strange and sad. It looked like the aftermath of something.

He did not think of any battlefields in east Virginia.

He did not think of Stanley, lying in a ditch behind a broken, folded fence.

He ran through a mental checklist of the usual suspects. Disease? Indians? Mexicans? But he was too far away to detect or conclude anything, and that was just as well. He didn't want to smell it anyway. He was plenty familiar with the reek, that rotting sweetness tempered with the methane stink of bowels and bloat.

Another check of the gauges told him more of what he already knew. One way or another, sooner rather than later, the *Majestic* was going down for a refill.

Walter wondered what ship he'd get next. A two-seater, maybe? Something with a little room to stretch out? He liked being able to lift his leg off the floor and let it rest where a copilot ought to go, but almost never went. That'd be nice.

Oh well. He'd find out when he got there, or in the morning.

Out the front windscreen, which screened almost no wind and kept almost no bugs out of his mouth, the sun was setting—the nebulous orb melting into an orange and pink line against the far, flat horizon.

In half an hour the sky was the color of blueberry jam, and only a lilac haze marked the western edge of the world.

The *Majestic* was riding lower in the air because Walter was conserving the thrust and letting the desert breeze move him as much as the engine. Coasting was a pleasant way to sail and the lights of Reluctance should be up ahead, any minute.

Some minute.

One of these minutes.

Where were they?

Walter checked the compass and peeked at his instruments, which told him only that he was on course and that Reluctance should be a mile or less out. But where were the lights? He could always see the lights by now;

RELUCTANCE

he always knew when to start smiling, when the gaslamps and lanterns meant people, and a drink, and a place to sleep.

Wait. There. Maybe? *Yes.*

Tell-tale pinpricks of white, laid out patternless on the dark sprawl.

Not so many as usual, though. Only a few, here and there. Haphazard and lost-looking, as if they were simply the remainder—the hardy left-overs after a storm, the ones which had not gone out quite yet. There was a feebleness to them, or so Walter thought as he gazed out and over and down. He used his elbow to wipe away the dirt on the glass screen as if it might be hiding something. But no. No more lights revealed themselves, and the existing flickers of white did not brighten.

Walter reached for his satchel and slung it over his chest, where he could feel the weight of his brother's Colt bumping up against his ribs.

He set himself a course for Reluctance. He was out of hydrogen and sinking anyway; and it was either set down in relative civilization—where nothing might be wrong, after all—or drop like a feather into the desert dust alone with the coyotes, cactus, and cougars. If he had to wait for sunrise somewhere, better to do it down in an almost-town he knew well enough to navigate.

There were only a few lights, yes.

But no flashes of firearms, and no bonfires of pillage or some hostile victory. He could see nothing and no one, nobody walking or running. Nobody dead, either, he realized when the *Majestic* swayed down close enough to give him a dim view of the dirt streets with their clapboard sidewalks.

Nobody at all.

He licked at his lower lip and gave it a bite, then he pulled out the Colt and began to load it, sure and steady, counting to six and counting out six more bullets for each of the two pockets on his vest.

Could be, he was overreacting. Could be, Reluctance had gone bust real quick, or there'd been a dust storm, or a twister, or any number of other natural and unpleasant events that could drive a thrown-together town into darkness. Could be, people were digging themselves out now, even as he wondered about it. Maybe something had made them sick. Cholera, or typhoid. He'd seen it wipe out towns and troops before.

His gut didn't buy it.

He didn't like it, how he couldn't assume the best and he didn't have any idea what the worst might be.

And still, as the *Majestic* came in for a landing. No bodies.

That was the thing. Nobody down there, including the dead.

He picked up his cane off the dirigible's floor and tested the weight of it. It was a good cane, solid enough to bring down a big man or a small wildcat, push come to shove. He set it across his knees.

The *Majestic* drooped down swiftly, but Walter was in control. He'd landed in the dark before and it was tricky, but it didn't scare him much. It made him cautious, sure. A man would be a fool to be incautious when piloting a half-ton craft into a facility with enough flammable gas to move a fleet. All things being ready and bright, and all it took was a wrongly placed spark—just a graze of metal on metal, the screech of one thing against another, or a single cigarette fallen from a lip—and the whole town would be reduced to matchsticks. Everybody knew it, and everybody lived with it. Just like everybody knew that flying post was a dangerous job, and a bunch of the boys who flew never made it home, just like going to war.

Walter sniffed, one nostril arching up high and dropping down again. He set his jaw, pulled the back drag chute, flipped the switch to give himself some light on the ship's underbelly, and spun the *Majestic* like a girl at a dance. He dropped her down onto the wooden platform with a big red X painted to mark the spot, and she shuddered to silence in the middle of the circle cast by her undercarriage light.

With one hand he popped the anchor chain lever, and with the other he reached for the door handle as he listened to that chain unspool outside.

RELUCTANCE

Outside it was as dark as his overhead survey had implied. And although the light of the undercarriage was nearly the only light, Walter reached up underneath the craft and pulled the snuffing cover down over its flaring white wick. He took hold of the nearest anchor chain and dragged it over to the pipework docks. Ordinarily he'd check to make sure he was on the right pad, clipping his craft to the correct slot before checking in with the station agent.

But no one greeted him. No one rushed up with a ream of paperwork for signing and sealing.

A block away a light burned; and beyond that, another gleamed somewhere farther away. Between those barely seen orbs and the lifting height of a half-full moon, Walter could see well enough to spy another ship nearby. It was affixed to a port on the hydrogen generators, but sagging hard enough that it surely wasn't filled or ready to fly.

Except for the warm buzz of the gas machines standing by, Walter heard absolutely nothing. No bustling of suppertime seekers roaming through the narrow streets, flowing toward Bad Albert's place, or wandering to Mama Rico's. The pipe dock workers were gone, and so were the managers and agents.

No horses, either. No shuffling of saddles or stirrups, of bits or clomping iron shoes.

Inside the *Majestic* an oil lantern was affixed to the wall behind the pilot's seat. Walter grunted, leaning on his cane. He pulled out the lamp, but hesitated to light it.

He held a match up, ready to strike it on the side of the deflated ship, but he didn't. The silence held its breath and told him to wait. It spoke like a battlefield before an order is given.

That's what stopped him. Not the thought of all that hydrogen, but the singular sensation that somewhere, on some other side, enemies were crouching—waiting for a shot. It froze him, one hand and one match held aloft, his cane leaning against the dirigible and his satchel hanging from his shoulder, pressing at the spot where his neck curved to meet his collarbone.

Under the lazily rolling moon and alone in the mobile gas works that had become the less-mobile semi-settlement of Reluctance, Walter put the match away, and set the lantern on the ground beside his ship.

He could see. A little. And given the circumstances, he liked that better than being seen.

His leg ached, but then again, it always ached. Too heavy by half and not nearly as mobile as the army had promised it'd be, the steel and leather contraption tugged against his knee as if it were a drowning man; and for a tiny flickering moment the old ghost pains tickled down to his toes, even though the toes were long gone, blown away on a battlefield in Virginia.

He held still until the sensation passed, wondering bleakly if it would ever go away for good, and suspecting that it wouldn't.

"All right," he whispered, and it was cold enough to see the words. When had it gotten so cold? How did the desert always do that, cook and then freeze? "We'll move the mail."

Damn straight we will.

Walter reached into the *Majestic*'s tiny hold and pulled out the three bags he'd been carrying as cargo. Each bag was the size of his good leg, and as heavy as his bad one. When they were all three removed from the ship he peered dubiously at the other craft across the landing pad—the one attached to the gas pipes, but empty.

He considered his options.

No other ships lurked anywhere close, so he could either seize that unknown hunk of metal and canvas or stay there by himself in the dead outpost.

Hoisting one bag over his shoulder and counter-balancing with his cane, he did his best to cross the landing quietly; but his metal foot dropped each step with a hard, loud clank—even though the leather sole at the bottom of the thing was brand new.

RELUCTANCE

He leaned the bag of mail up against the ship and caught his breath, lost more to fear than exertion. Then he moved the mail bag aside to reveal the first two stenciled letters of the ship's name, and reading the whole he whispered, "Sweet Marie."

Two more mail bags, each moved with all the stealth he could muster. Each one more cumbersome than the last, and each one straining his bum leg harder. But he moved them. He opened the back bin of the *Sweet Marie* and stuffed them into her cargo hold. Every grunt was loud in the desert emptiness and every heaving shove would've sent ol' Stanley into conniptions, had he been there.

Too much noise. Got to keep your head down.

Walter breathed as he leaned on the bin to make it shut. It closed with a click. "This ain't the war. Not out here."

Just like me, you carry it with you.

Something.

What?

A gusting. A hoarse, lonely sound that barked and disappeared.

He leaned against the bin and listened hard, waiting for that noise to come again.

The *Sweet Marie* had been primed and she was ready to fill, but no one had switched on the generators. She sank so low she almost tipped over, now that the mail sacks had loaded down her back end.

Walter McMullin did not know how hydrogen worked exactly, but he'd seen the filling process performed enough times to copy it.

The generators took the form of two tanks, each one mounted atop a standard-issue army wagon. These tanks were made of reinforced wood and lined with copper, and atop each tank was a hinged metal plate that could be opened and closed in order to dump metal shavings into the sulfuric acid inside. At the end, opposite the filler plate, an escape pipe was attached to a long rubber hose, to which the *Sweet Marie* was ultimately affixed.

There were several sets of filters for the hydrogen to pass before it reached the ship's tank, and the process was frankly none too quick. Even little ships like these mail runners could take a couple of hours to become airworthy.

Walter did not like the idea of spending a couple of hours alone in Reluctance. He was even less charmed by the idea of spending *all night* alone in Reluctance, so he found himself a crate of big glass bottles filled with acid, and with great struggle he poured them down through the copper funnels atop the tanks. Shortly thereafter he located the metal filings; he scooped them up with the big tin cup and dumped them in.

He turned the valves to open the filters and threw the switch to start the generators stirring and bubbling, vibrating the carts to make the acid and the metal stir and separate into hydrogen more quickly.

It made a godawful amount of noise.

The rubber hose, stamped "Goodyear's Rubber, Belting, and Packing Company of Philadelphia," did a little twitch. *Sweet Marie*'s tank gave a soft, plaintive squeal as the first hydrogen spilled through, giving her the smallest bit of lift.

But she'd need more. Lots more.

There.

Another one.

A sighing grunt, gasped and then gone as quickly as it'd burst through the night.

Walter whirled as fast as his leg would let him, using it as a pivot. He moved like a compass pinned to a map. He held his cane out, pointing at nothing.

But the sound. Again. And again. Another wheeze and gust.

At this point, Walter was gut-swimmingly certain that it was coming from more than one place. Partway between a snore and a cough, with a consumptive rattle. Coming from everywhere, and nowhere. Coming from the dark.

Up against the *Sweet Marie* he backed.

RELUCTANCE

He jumped, startled by a new sound, a familiar one. Footsteps, slow and laborious. Someone was walking toward him, out of the black alleys that surrounded the landing. Nearing the ladder to the refueling platform. And whoever this visitor was, he joined by someone else—approaching the edge near the parked *Majestic*.

And a third somebody. Walter was pretty sure of a third, moving up from the shadows.

Not one single thing about this moment, this shuddering instant alone—but not alone—felt right or good to Walter McMullin. He still couldn't see anyone, though he could hear plenty. Whoever they were, lurking in the background…they weren't being quiet. They weren't sneaking, and that was something, wasn't it?

Why would they sneak, if they know they have you?

Reaching into his belt, he pulled out the Colt and held it with both hands. His back remained braced against the slowly filling replacement ship. He thought about crying out in greeting, just in case—but he thought of the dead cows, and his desperate eyes spotted no new lights, and the sound of incoming feet and the intermittent groaning told him that no, this was no overreaction. This was good common sense, staying low with your back against something firm and your weapon out. That's what you did, right before a fight. If you could.

He drew back the gun's hammer and waited.

Lumbering up the ladder as if drunk, the first head rose into view.

Walter should've been relieved.

He knew that head—it belonged to Gibbs Higley, the afternoon station manager. But he wasn't relieved. Not at all. Because it wasn't Gibbs, not anymore. He could see that at a glance, even without the gaslamps that lit up a few blocks, far away.

Something was very, very wrong with Gibbs Higley.

The man drew nearer, shuffling in an exploratory fashion, sniffing the air like a dog. He was missing an ear. His skin looked like boiled lye. One of his eyes was ruined somehow, wet and gelatinous, and sliding down his cheek.

"Higley?" Walter croaked.

Higley didn't respond. He only moaned and shuffled faster, homing in on Walter and raising the moan to a cry that was more of a horrible keening.

To Walter's terror, the keening was answered. It came bouncing back from corner to corner, all around the open landing area and the footsteps that had been slowly incoming shifted gears, moving faster.

Maybe he should've thought about it. Maybe he should've tried again, trying to wake Higley up, shake some sense into him. There must've been something he could've done, other than lifting the Colt and putting a bullet through the man's solitary good eye.

But that's what he did.

Against a desert backdrop of dust-covered silence the footsteps and coughing grunts and the buzzing patter of the generators had seemed loud enough; but the Colt was something else entirely, fire and smoke and a kick against his elbows, and a lingering whiff of gunpowder curling and dissolving.

Gibbs Higley fell off the landing, flopping like a rag doll.

Walter rushed as fast as he could to the ladder, and kicked it away—marooning himself on the landing island, five or six feet above street level. Then he dragged himself back to *Sweet Marie* and resumed his defensive position, the only one he had. "That was easy," he muttered, almost frantic to reassure himself.

One down. More to go. You're a good shot, but you're standing next to the gas. Surrounded by it, almost.

He breathed. "I need to think."

You need to run.

"I need the *Sweet Marie*. Won't get far without her."

Hands appeared at the edge of the lifted landing pad. Gray hands, hands without enough fingers.

RELUCTANCE

Left to right he swung his head, seeking some out. Knowing he didn't have enough bullets for whatever this was—knowing it as sure as he knew he'd die if any of those hands caught him. Plague, is what it was. Nothing he'd ever seen before, but goddamn Gibbs Higley had been sick, hadn't he?

"Gotta hold the landing pad," he said through gritted teeth.

No. You gotta let 'em take it—but that don't mean you gotta let 'em keep it.

He swung his head again, side to side, and spotted only more hands—moving like a sea of clapping, an audience of death, pulling toward the lifted landing spot. He wished he had a light, and then he remembered that he did have one—he just hadn't lit it. One wobbly dash back to the *Majestic* and he had the lantern in his hand again, thinking "to hell with it—to hell with *us*" and striking a match. What did it matter? They already knew where he was. That much was obvious from the rising wail that now rang from every quarter. Faces were leaning up now, lurching and lifting on elbows, rising and grabbing for purchase on the platform and soon they were going to find it.

Look.

"Where?" he asked the ghost of a memory, trying to avoid a full blown panic. Panic never got anybody anywhere but dead. It got Stanley dead. On the far side of a broken, folded fence along a line that couldn't have been held, not with a thousand Stanleys.

Ah. Above the hydrogen tanks, and behind them. A ladder in the back corner of the overhang that covered them.

He glanced at the *Sweet Marie* and then his eyes swept the platform, where a woman was rising up onto the wooden deck—drawing herself up on her elbows. She'd be there soon, right there with him. When she looked up at him her mouth opened and she shouted, and blood or bile—something dark—spilled over her teeth to splash down on the boards.

Whatever it was, he didn't want it. He drew up the Colt, aimed carefully, and fired. She fell back.

The ladder behind the hydrogen tanks must lead to the roof of the overhang. Would the thin metal roof hold him?

Any port in a storm.

He scurried past the clamoring hands and scooted, still hauling that dead-weight foot, beneath the overhang and to the ladder. Scaling it required him to set the cane aside, and he wouldn't do that, so he stuck it in his mouth where it stretched his cheeks and jaw until they ached with the strain. But it was that or leave it, or leave the lantern—which he held by the hot, uncomfortable means of shoving his wrist through the carrying loop. When it swung back and forth with his motion, it burned the cuff of his shirt and seared warmly against his chest.

So he climbed, good foot up with a grunt of effort, bad foot up with a grunt of pain, both grunts issued around the cane in his mouth. When he reached the top he jogged his neck to shift the cane so it'd fit through the square opening in the corrugated roof. He slipped, his heavy foot dragging him to a stop with an ear-splitting scrape.

He'd have to step softly.

From this vantage point, holding up the quivering black lantern he could see all of it, and he understood everything and nothing simultaneously. He watched the mostly men and sometimes women of Reluctance stagger and wail, shambling hideously from corners and corridors, from alleys and basements, from broken-windowed stores and stables and saloons and the one whorehouse. They did not pour but they dripped and congealed down the uncobbled streets torn rough and rocky by horses' hooves and the wheels of coaches and carts.

It couldn't have been more than a hundred ragged bodies slinking forward, gagging on their own fluids and chasing toward the light he held over his head, over the town of Reluctance.

Walter stuffed a hand in his vest pockets and felt at the bottom of the bag he still wore over his chest. Bullets, yes. But not enough bullets for this. Not even if he was the best shot in Texas, and he wasn't. He was a competent shot from New York City, orphaned and Irish a few thousand miles from home, without even a sibling to mourn him if the drooling, simpering, snap-jawed dead were to catch him and tear him to pieces.

Bullets were not going to save him.

All the same, he liked having them.

The lantern drew the dead; he watched their gazes, watching it. Moths. Filthy, deadly moths. He could see it in their eyes, in the places where their souls ought to be. Most of the men he'd ever shot at were fellows like himself—boys mostly, lads born so late they didn't know for certain what the fighting was about; just men, with faces full of fear and grit.

Nothing of that, not one shred of humanity showed on any of the faces below.

He could see it, and he was prepared to address it. But not until he had to.

Beneath him, the *Sweet Marie* was filling. Down below the twisted residents of Reluctance were dragging themselves up and onto the platform, swarming like ants and shrieking for Walter—who went to the ladder and kicked it down against the generators, where it clattered and rested, and likely wouldn't be climbed.

He sat on the edge of the corrugated roof and turned the lantern light down. It wouldn't fool them. It wouldn't make them wander away. They smelled him, and they wanted him, and they'd stay until they got him. Or until he left.

He was leaving, all right. Soon.

Inside the satchel he rummaged, and he pulled out his tobacco and papers. He rolled himself a cigarette, lit it off the low-burning lamp, and he sat. And he watched below as the cranium-shaped crest of the *Sweet Marie* slowly inflated; and the corpses of Reluctance gathered themselves on the landing pad beside it, ignoring it.

Finally the swelling dome was full enough that Walter figured, "I can make it. Maybe not all the way to Santa Fe, but close enough." He rose to his feet, the flesh and blood one and the one that pivoted painfully on a pin.

The lantern swung out from his fingertips, still lit but barely.

Below the lantern, beside the ship and around it, the men and women shambled.

But fire could consume anything, pretty much. It'd consume the hydrogen like it was starved for it. It'd gobble and suck and then the whole world would go up like hell, wouldn't it? All that gas, burning like the breath of God.

Well then. He'd have to move fast.

Retracting his arm as far as it'd go, and then adjusting for trajectory, he held the lantern and released it—tossing it in a great bright arc that cut across the star-speckled sky. It crashed to the far corner of the landing pad, blossoming into brilliance and heat, singeing his face. He blinked hard against the unexpected warmth, having never guessed how closely he would feel it.

The creatures below screamed and ran, clothing aflame. The air sizzled with the stench of burning hair and fire-puckered flesh. But some of them hovered near the *Sweet Marie*, lingering where the fire had stayed clear, still howling.

Only a few of them.

The Colt took them down, one-two-three.

Walter crossed his fingers and prayed that the bullets would not bounce—would not clip or ding the hydrogen tubes or tanks, or the swollen bulb of the *Sweet Marie*. His prayers were answered, or ignored. Either way, nothing ignited.

Soon the ship was clear. As clear as it was going to get.

And reaching it required a ten-foot drop.

Walter threw his cane down and watched it roll against the ship, then he dropped to his knees and swung himself off the edge to hang by his fingertips. He curled the good leg up, lifting his knee. Better a busted pin than a busted ankle.

RELUCTANCE

And before he had time to reconsider, he let go.

The pain of his landing was a sun of white light. His leg buckled and scraped inside the sheath that clasped the false limb; he heard his bone piercing and rubbing through the bunched and stitched skin, and into the leather and metal.

But he was down. Down beside the *Sweet Marie*. Down inside the fire, inside the ticking clock with a deadly alarm and only moments— maybe seconds, probably only seconds—before the whole town went up in flames.

At the last moment he remembered the clasp that anchored the ship. He unhitched it. He limped bloodily to the back port and ripped the hydrogen hose out of the back, and shut it up tight because otherwise he'd just leak his fuel all over North Mexico.

He fumbled for the latch and found it.

Pulled it.

Opened the door and hauled himself inside, feeling around for the controls and seeing them awash with the yellow-gold light of the fire just outside the window. The starter was a lever on the dash. He pulled that too and the ship began to rise. He grasped for the thrusters and his shaking, searching fingers found them, and pressed them—giving the engines all the gas they'd take. Anything to get him up and away. Anything to push him past the hydrogen before the fire took it.

Anything.

Reluctance slipped away below, and behind. It shimmered and the whole world froze, and gasped, and shook like a star being born.

The desert floor melted into glass. ✎

CLEMENTINE

It's no great secret that my writing career had taken a downturn, back in 2008; I was coming to the end of a multi-book contract—wherein none of the books had done particularly well—and I was starting to feel like I might need a reboot under a new name...if (and it was a big "if") I could ever get anyone to publish me again. I still had one book left under contract, and it was slated to be a modern vampire noir, tentatively titled *Awake into Darkness*.

While I was working on my fang-fest, I started noodling around with something else on the side because it was clearly time to try something different. By "different" I mean that a couple of small ideas had collided and stuck together, along with my interest in writing a book about Seattle—where I'd been living for a handful of years, at that time. And a story was starting to gel around it all.

My editor at the time (the inimitable Liz Gorinsky) saw me talking about this side project online, and asked to take a look at it.

I didn't really want to show it to her. It was only a small handful of chapters, a little unfocused, and pretty far outside the realm of what I'd been doing before. Besides, I knew that I sold so poorly that she wouldn't be allowed to acquire anything else I wrote.

But she insisted.

And after she'd finished reading, she offered me a really weird deal for which I remain grateful to this day: She said we should swap out my vampire project for this new project. The new project was called *Boneshaker*, it skewed pretty steampunk, and steampunk was about to have A Big Moment. (Like it routinely does, once every twenty years or so.) The rest was history, more or less. *Boneshaker* took off.

Not immediately, though.

Despite great blurbs and promising early reviews, the publisher wasn't quite ready to take a chance and nail me down for a sequel or two—and I couldn't blame them. Even so, I drew up some notes for a sequel, just in case anybody ever wanted one. Tor (*Boneshaker*'s publisher) opted to pump the brakes, and hold off on acquiring any more books until they could see how this particular one was going to do.

Subterranean Press, on the other hand, jumped at the chance to take a sequel...even though *Boneshaker* hadn't actually hit the market yet. However, there was a catch: I had a first-refusal clause in my Tor contract, and that meant they got first pass at anything I wrote over 40,000 words.

In case anyone ever wondered why *Clementine* comes in at just a hair under 40,000 words.

I've always been terribly fond of this story, and I would've been happy to make it a full-length novel, rather than a novella...but I love how it came out, all the same. And hey, maybe if it'd been twice the length, it wouldn't have worked out nearly as well. I love that it's a wild little stand-alone, doing its own thing—and filling in some gaps between *Boneshaker* and *Dreadnought* (the sequel that Tor eventually purchased and produced).

Some of the characters you meet here also appear in the final full-length project in the series, which was a great deal of fun. I was tickled to have the chance to tie it all back together again in the end.

So here's the adventure of the *Clementine*—a fictional diamond owned by an adventuresome historic character, a woman whose body lies half a mile away from my last Seattle apartment. And the bit about her coffin? The part about her corpse, and what became of it? That was true. Likewise true, Pinkerton employed lady operatives in his detective agency; and furthermore, Maria Boyd was a real woman, too.

As for the rest, well. I know that my science is iffy, and my zombies are improbable. But I think you'll like Croggon and Maria, and I hope you enjoy the odd friendship that develops between them.

CAPTAIN CROGGON BEAUREGARD HAINEY

1

FOR SIX days, Croggon Hainey watched the Rockies scroll beneath the borrowed, nameless dirigible, until finally the last of the jagged ridges and snow-dusted plateaus slipped behind the ship on the far side of Denver. He'd made this run a dozen times before, in fair weather and foul, with contraband cargo and passengers alike; and on this particular trip a tailwind gently urged the ship forward.

But the speed that took him from the Pacific Northwest, over the mountains and down to the flatlands, did not improve the captain's mood.

With his hands balled into fists and jammed atop his knees, he groused, "We should've caught them by now. We ought to be right on top of them."

"The breeze moves us both," the first mate said, and he shrugged. He adjusted his goggles to guard against the glare of the sun on the clouds and added, "But we'll catch them. Any minute now."

Hainey shifted in the captain's seat, which had been built with a smaller man in mind. He removed his hat and squeezed at his forehead as if he could massage it into greater wakefulness or concentration. "They'll have to dock soon. They didn't even get a full tank of hydrogen back in Grand Junction. Simeon?" he asked the first mate, who was likewise crammed into a seat beside him.

"Yessir?"

"They have to set down in Topeka, don't they? There's no place else you know that'll take them...or us?"

"No place I know of. But I ain't been through this way in awhile. Brink may know something I don't," he said, but he didn't sound very worried. Over his shoulder he asked, "What's *our* fuel situation look like?"

Lamar adjusted a lip full of tobacco and said, "Doing all right. We'll make it past Topeka, if that's what you want to hear." The engineer glanced at the doorway to the engine room, though he couldn't quite see the tanks from where he was sitting. "Maybe even into Missouri."

The captain didn't precisely brighten, but for a moment he sounded less unhappy. "We might make Kansas City?"

"We might, but I wouldn't bet the boat on it." Lamar squeezed his lip to adjust his chew.

Simeon reached for a thruster lever and knocked his elbow on a big glass knob. He said, "Well, I might bet *this* boat." But he didn't push his complaint. Everybody already knew that the nameless craft, fitted for small men and light cargo, was not anyone's preferred vessel; and no one wanted to imply, even in jest, that everything was not being done to retrieve the captain's ship of choice.

Hainey unfurled himself from the captain's chair. His knees popped when he stood and he crouched to keep from hitting his head on the glass shield that separated him from the sky. He put one hand out against it and leaned that way, staring as far into the distance, and as far along the ground, and as far up into the heavens as his eyes could reach, but the view told him nothing he did not already know.

His ship—his *true* ship, the one he'd stolen fair and square eight years before—was nowhere to be seen.

He asked everyone, and no one in particular, "Where do you think they're taking her?" But since he'd asked that question a dozen times a day for the last week, he already knew he could expect no useful answer. He could speculate easily enough, but none of his speculation warmed him with hope.

The red-haired thief Felton Brink had taken Hainey's ship, the *Free Crow*, and he was flying east with it. That much was apparent.

The chase had brought Croggon Hainey from the Pacific port city of Seattle down through Idaho, past Twin Falls and into Wyoming where he'd almost nabbed Brink in Rock Springs. Then the course had shifted south and a bit west, to Salt Lake City and then east, through Colorado and now the trail was taking them both through Kansas.

East. Except for that one brief detour, always east.

And it didn't much matter whether the *Free Crow* would veer to the north or south on the far side of the Mississippi River. Either way, the captain was in for trouble and he knew it.

The Mason-Dixon meant only a little to him. Either side meant capture and probably a firing squad or a noose, though all things being equal, he would've preferred to take his lumps from the Union. The southern states in general (and Georgia in particular) had given him plenty already. The raised, pink stripes on his back and the puckered brand on his shoulder were souvenirs enough from a life spent in slavery, and he'd accept no addition to that tally.

So as much as he might've said aloud, "I don't care where they're taking my ship, I plan to take it *back*," he privately prayed for a northern course. In the Union he was only a pirate and only to be shot on sight. In the Confederate states he was all that and fugitive property, too.

It wasn't fair. He'd had no intention of coming back past the river again, not for several years…or not until the war had played itself out, anyway; and it wasn't fair that some underhanded thief—some conniving boy nearly young enough to be his son—had absconded with his rightfully pilfered and customized ship.

Whatever Felton Brink was getting paid, Hainey hoped it was worth it. Because when Hainey caught up to him, there wouldn't be enough left of the red-headed thief to bury.

The tailwind gusted and the nameless ship swayed in its course. A corresponding, correcting gust from the appropriate thruster kept the craft on track, and sitting on the straight, unbroken line of the prairie horizon a tiny black dot flicked at the corner of Croggon Hainey's vision.

He stood up straight, too quickly. He rapped his bald, dark head on the underside of the cabin's too-short roof and swore, then pointed. "Men," he said. He never called them "boys." "On the ground over there. You see it? That what I think it is?"

Simeon leaned forward, languid as always. He squinted through the goggles and said, "It's a ship. It's grounded."

"I can see it's a ship. What I can't see is if it's *my* ship or not. Give me the glass," he demanded. He held out his hand to Simeon but Lamar brought the instrument forward, and stayed to stand by the window.

Hainey extended the telescoping tube and held it up to his right eye. From habit, he rested his thumb on the scar that bisected that side of his face from the corner of his mouth to his ear. He closed his left eye. He scanned and aimed, and pointed the scope at the distant dot, and he declared in his low, loud, rumbling voice, "There she is."

Lamar held his hands over his eyes like an awning. "You sure?"

"Of course I'm sure."

CLEMENTINE

"How far out?" Simeon asked. He adjusted his position so that he could reach the important levers and pertinent buttons, readying himself for the surge of speed that Hainey was mere moments away from ordering.

"Couple of miles?" the captain guessed. "And open sky, no weather to account for." He snapped the scope back to its smaller size and jammed it into his front breast pocket.

Lamar shook his head, not arguing but wondering. "They've been moving so slow. No wonder they had to set down out here."

Simeon removed his goggles and set them atop his head, where their strap strained against the rolled stacks of his roughly braided hair. "They've never gotten any speed beneath them," he said, the island drawl stretching his words into an accusation.

Hainey knew, and it worried him, but this was his chance to gain real ground. The *Free Crow*, which Brink had renamed the *Clementine*, had once been a Confederate war dirigible and she was capable of tremendous speed when piloted properly. But she'd been flying as if she were crippled and it meant one of two things: Either she was critically damaged, or she was so heavily laden that she could barely maintain a good cruising altitude.

Her true and proper captain hoped for the latter, but he knew that her theft had been a violent event, and he didn't have the faintest clue what she carried. It was difficult not to fear the worst.

Only a significant head start had prevented Hainey from retrieving her so far, and here she was—having dragged herself across the sky, limping more than sailing, and now she was stopped within a proverbial spitting distance.

"Simeon," he said, and he didn't need to finish.

The Jamaican was already pulling the fuel release valves and flipping the switches to power up the boosters. "Fifteen seconds to fire," he said, meaning that the three men had that long to secure themselves before the jolt of the steam-driven back-up tanks would shoot the dirigible forward.

Lamar buckled his skinny brown body into a slot against the wall, within easy reach of the engine room. Hainey sat back down in the captain's seat and pulled his harness tight across his chest; Simeon used his last five seconds to light one of the hand-rolled cigarettes he kept in a tin that was bolted onto the ship's console.

At the end of the prescribed time, the unnamed airship lurched forward, snapping against the hydrogen tank that held it aloft and leaping in a back-and-forth motion until the tank and the engines found their rhythm, and the craft moved smoothly, and swiftly. Hainey didn't much like his temporary vessel, but he had to give it credit—it was fast, and it was light enough to soar when necessary.

"What are we..." Lamar said from his seat on the wall, then he swallowed and started again. "What will we do when we catch them?"

The captain pretended he hadn't given it much thought. He declared, "We're going to kill the sons of bitches and take our ship back." But it would be more complicated than that, and he didn't really know what he'd find when the ships and their crews had a chance to collide.

He'd been weighing the pros, cons, and possibilities since leaving Seattle. The *Free Crow* was heavily reinforced, but heavily powered to compensate for its armor. It was a juggernaut of a machine, but if Hainey had learned one thing from following the bird over a thousand miles, he'd learned that Brink's crew did not yet know what the *Free Crow* was capable of. The ship was barely flying without knocking into mountains and mowing down trees.

The unnamed craft that hauled Hainey and his two most indispensable crew members was no physical match for the *Free Crow*, and this was no secret. Likewise, Hainey had reason to believe that Brink's crew outnumbered his own by three or four men, and maybe more.

In retrospect, he might've been better served to buy a bigger interim vessel and cobble together a thicker crew; but at the time, speed had been the more pressing priority and anyway, if he'd taken all afternoon to go shopping for the perfect pursuit vehicle, they'd never be this close to catching Brink now.

Lamar grumbled something from the engine room door.

"What was that?" Hainey asked.

"I said, I was thinking maybe we should've brought an extra warm body or two."

And the captain said, "Sure, but where would we have put 'im?"

"Point taken, sir."

Simeon, who never took his eyes off the growing black dot of the *Free Crow*, said, "He's wishing we'd brought that Chinaman Fang, at least. Captain Cly might've let him join us, if you asked him nice."

Hainey knew that much already, so he nodded, but didn't reply except to say, "The three of us will be plenty of man to take back our bird. Fang's good at what he does," he agreed. "A good man to have on board, that's for damn sure. But we've got the Rattler. Lamar, why don't you unhook yourself and make sure it's ready to bite."

"Yessir," the engineer said. He unfastened himself from the wall and, swaying back and forth to keep his balance, he grasped the edge of the engine room door to swing himself inside. The unnamed ship had a small cargo hold, but it was affixed beneath the cabin—and Hainey had insisted on keeping the Rattler within easier reach.

"Less than a mile out," Simeon announced calmly.

"Lamar! Get that thing on deck!" Hainey ordered.

Lamar struggled with a crate, scooting it jerkily across the tilting, lilting floor. "Right here, sir."

"Good man," Hainey told him. "Get back to your seat. This landing might get a little rough," he ordered, and then unfastened himself.

"Sir?"

"You heard me. I've got to get this thing out and working before we set down," he said. And while the nameless craft charged forward, Hainey popped the crate's lid. He pushed a coating of sawdust and pine shavings aside to reveal a six-barreled gun. Its brass fittings shined yellow and white in the afternoon sun, and its steel crank gleamed dully at the bottom of the crate. The Rattler was a monster, and a baby brother to the popular Gatling Gun that had made itself at home in the war back east. And although it was designed to be carried on a man's shoulder, it required a man and a shoulder of exceptional strength to hoist it and fire.

Lamar was a slight fellow, not more than a hundred and forty pounds soaking wet with rocks in his pockets. Simeon was tall and just a bit too beefy to be described as wiry, and although he might've been able to heft the weapon, he likely could not have fired it alone—turning the crank with one arm while the other counter-balanced the thing.

So its use fell to the captain.

Croggon Hainey did not have all the height of his first mate, but he had a back as wide and square as a barn door, with shoulders stout enough to heave the heavy gun and strong enough to balance it. He aimed better with a second man behind him to steady the gun or spin the crank, and when the gun was fully operational he could scarcely maneuver beyond walking a straight line; but especially at a distance, the Rattler turned him into a one-man army.

And in Hainey's experience, as often as not, he didn't even need to fire it. Most men took one look at the massive, preposterous weapon and threw their hands into the air.

The captain flipped the gun over and opened a secondary box within the crate, from which he withdrew a long thread of ammunition. It dangled from his arm while he popped the gun's loading mechanism; the bullets bounced against one another heavily, clanking like cast-iron pearls on a necklace, and they rapped against the crate while Hainey worked.

"Half a mile out," Simeon said. "And they're disengaging from…it looks like one of those portable docks. Something like Bainbridge has, back west."

Hainey fed the ammunition into position and returned the Rattler to an upright state. "Portable dock? Out on the plains? That's madness," he said, even though he'd heard of it before. It'd been a long time since he'd come this far east, that was all; and he didn't realize how common they were becoming. He stood up and kept his head low, leaving the gun propped in the crate and ready to be picked up at a moment's notice.

Simeon nodded, and said, "Or brilliance. Not much traffic out this way. Might be better to bring your gas to the dirigibles, if the dirigibles aren't coming to you."

"But out in the open?" Hainey adjusted the seat buckles around his coat as he reassumed his position in the captain's chair. "It's a good way to get yourself robbed or conscripted," he mumbled.

Out through the windshield he could see it now, more clearly without the glass, yes—the black dot more than a dot now, more of a distinct shape. And he could also see the portable dock, operated by madmen or geniuses. It was a pipework thing shaped like a house's frame, and held between two wagons. Under the wagons' canopies Hainey assumed there'd be hydrogen generators lined with copper, filled with sulfuric acid and bubbling metal shavings. Hydrogen was easy to make—and easy to divvy out at a capitalist's mark-up for the hassle and location.

Four horses each were hitched to the wagons, with drivers ready to pull and run at the first sign of danger.

"We'll have to watch out for those," Simeon said. "We should let them get the *Free Crow* off the dock and moving. We can't take a chance with the Rattler, not this close to the dock. One stray bullet and we'll blow the whole thing to hell, ourselves included."

The captain said, "I know, I know." And he *did* know, but he hated letting the *Free Crow* rise—knowing that it was about to run again, and knowing he was so damn close and he might fail anyway. A plan snapped quickly together in his head, and he spit it out while it still sounded good. He said, "We'll get up under them, and deploy our hooks. We'll pin this boat to our bird, reverse the thrusters, and drag us both down."

"You want to crash us all together?" Lamar nearly squeaked. "I don't think this ship can take it."

"I don't either. But the *Free Crow* can, and that's the only ship I'm worried about. If we both go to ground, we can take Brink and his boys apart, man to man."

"Or man to Rattler," Simeon grinned.

"Whatever it takes. We'll clean them out of our bridge and take our bird back, and that'll be the end of it." He said the last part fast, because the nameless ship was closing in swift and low on the *Free Crow,* and Felton Brink was no doubt very, very aware that Croggon Hainey was incoming and unhappy.

Simeon's half-smile deteriorated. He made a suggestion phrased as a question. "Shouldn't we cut the thrusters? At this rate we're going to ram them."

"So we'll ram them," Hainey said. "My bird can take it. Ready the hooks, mate. We won't have long to fire them. We'll catch them on the ricochet."

Lamar choked on one response and offered another. "You want to hit them, then grab them on the bounce?"

"Something like that, yeah. And buckle yourselves down, if you aren't already. Something aboard this bird is just about bound to break." He braced his legs against the underside of the console, setting his feet to the rudders and refusing to reach for the brake.

In those last few seconds, as the dirigible swooped down its interim captain watched his own craft shudder in the air, struggling to take to the clouds. He looked down at the plains and saw the portable gasworks beginning to fold under the panicked hands of the men who ran it. Below, they disengaged the frames and hollered at the horses to move, even before they were holding the reins; and Hainey understood. No man in his right mind wanted to get between a big set of hydrogen tanks and a firefight.

CLEMENTINE

They were so close now, Hainey could see the horses' mouths chomping against the bits, and the strain of their haunches as they surged to move the wagons. He could see the hasty streaks of a too-rushed paint job on the side of his former craft, covering up the silver painted words that said *Free Crow.*

It was a ridiculous thing that Brink had done, sillier than sticking a false nose or mustache on the president of the United States. No air pirate at any port on any coast would have mistaken the repurposed war dirigible for any other vessel.

"Sir—" Simeon said, but he had nothing to follow it.

"Hang on," Hainey said to his first mate and engineer. His feet jammed against the pedals to turn the ship, and it turned, slowly, shifting midair and sliding sideways almost underneath the *Free Crow*—until the front deployment hooks were aimed at the only place where there wasn't any armor. Then he ordered, "Fire hooks!"

Simeon didn't ask questions. He jerked the console lever and a loud pop announced the hooks had been projected from their moorings. The hissing fuss of hydraulics filled the cabin but it wasn't half so important as the scraping thunk of the hooks hitting home.

"Cut thrusters, and retract!" Hainey shouted. "Retract, retract, *retract!*"

Simeon flipped the winding crank out of its holding seam and turned it as fast as he could, his elbow pumping like a train's pistons until the nameless ship's shifting position became more than a tip—it was a tilt, and a firm, decided lean. "Got it sir," he said, puffing hard and then gasping with surprise when his elbow was forced to stop. "That's as far as we can bring them back."

"It's enough," Hainey swore, and it must have been, because the nameless ship was swaying all but sideways, drawn up underneath the *Free Crow.*

The *Free Crow*'s left thruster fired up against the nameless ship's hull, down at the cargo bay where it scorched a streak of peeling paint and straining, warping metal. The engine chewed hard at the unimportant bits of the latched-on ship, but the ships were bound together like bumblebees mating and now, they could only move together.

Hainey's thrusters had been cut at the collision, and inertia pushed the ships together in a ballroom sway that made a wide arch away from the temporary docks. Locked as they were, the ships made half of a massive, terrible spiral until the right thrusters on the *Free Crow* blasted out a full-power explosion—jerking both the vessels and tightening the gyre until the ships were simply spinning together, a thousand feet above the plains.

Within the nameless ship all men grasped everything solid, and Simeon even closed his eyes. He said, "Sir, I don't know if I can—"

"You can take it," Hainey told him. "Hang on, and hang in there. We're going down."

"Down?" Lamar asked, as if saying it aloud might change the answer.

"Down," the captain affirmed. "But it's a carousel of the damned we've got here; it's…hang on. Jesus, just hang *on*."

The landscape rotated in the windshield, pirouetting first to the brown grasslands below, and then to the brilliant blue and white sky, and then back to the horizon line, which leaped alarmingly, and then again, to the earth that was coming up so fast.

In glimpses, in those awful seconds between spinning and falling and crashing, Hainey saw a tiny corner of the *Free Crow*'s front panel and he could spy, through the glass, a tumbling terror on the deck of his beloved ship—and it pleased him. He tried to count, in order to make something productive of the frantic moments; he saw the red-haired captain, and a long-haired man who might've been an Indian. He saw a helmeted fellow, he thought; and for a moment he believed he saw a second long-haired man, but he might've been wrong.

The ground lurched up and the nameless ship lurched down, until there was nothing else to be seen out through the windshield and the end was most certainly nigh. Hainey covered his head with his hands and Simeon propped his feet up on the console, locking his legs and ducking his own head too.

And a tearing, ripping, snapping noise was accompanied by a yanking sensation.

"What was that?" Lamar shrieked.

No one knew, so no one answered—not until the second loud breaking launched the nameless ship loose from the *Free Crow*, and flung it into the sky.

"The cables!" Hainey hollered, calling attention to the problem even as it was far too late to do anything about it. "Thrusters, air brakes, all of it, on, now!" He slapped at the buttons to ignite the thrusters again and tried to orient himself enough to steer, but the ship was light and it was flying as if clipped from a centrifuge and they were no longer falling, but destined to fall and to skid.

The thrusters burped to life and Hainey aimed them at the ground, wherever he could spot it.

Simeon said, "We have to get up again. We have to get some height under us."

"I'm working on it!" Hainey told him.

But the thrusters weren't enough to fight the gravity and torque of the broken hook cables, and the downward spiral cut itself off with an ear-splitting, skimming drag along the prairie that jolted all three men down to their very bones. The ship tore against the ground, and the men's bodies were battered in their seats; the dust and earth scraped into the engines, into the burned cargo bay, and into the bridge; and in another minute more, the unnamed ship ground itself to a stop while the so-called *Clementine* staggered across the sky towards Kansas City.

CHERIE PRIEST

MARIA ISABELLA BOYD

2

Maria Isabella Boyd had never had a job like this one, though she told herself that detective work wasn't really so different from spying. It was all the same sort of thing, wasn't it? Passing information from the people who concealed it to the people who desired it. This was courier work of a dangerous kind, but she was frankly desperate. She was nearly forty years old and two husbands down—one dead, one divorced—and the Confederacy had rejected her offers of further service. Twenty years of helpful secret-stealing had made her a notorious woman, entirely too well known for further espionage work; and the subsequent acting career hadn't done anything to lower her profile. For that matter, one of her husbands had come from the Union navy—and even her old friend General Jackson confessed that her loyalties appeared questionable.

The accusation stung. The exhaustion of her widow's inheritance and the infidelity of her second spouse stung also. The quiet withdrawal of her military pension was further indignity, and the career prospects for a woman her age were slim and mostly unsavory.

So when the Pinkerton National Detective Agency made her an offer, Maria was grateful—even if she was none too thrilled about relocating to the shores of Lake Michigan.

But money in Chicago was better than poverty in Virginia. She accepted the position, moved what few belongings she cared enough to keep into a small apartment above a laundry, and reported to Allan Pinkerton in his wood-and-glass office on the east side of the city.

The elderly Scotsman gave her a glance when she cleared her throat to announce that she stood in his doorway. Her eyes were level with the painted glass window that announced his name and position, and her hand lingered on the knob until he told her, "Come in, Mrs….well, I'm not sure what it is, these days. How many men's names have you worn?"

"Only three," she said. "Including my father's—and that's the one I was born with. If it throws you that much, call me Miss Boyd and don't worry with the rest. Just don't call me 'Belle.'"

"Only three, and no one calls you Belle. I can live with that, unless you're here to sniff about for a new set of rings."

"You offering?" she asked.

"Not on your life. I'd sooner sleep in a sack full of snakes."

"Then I'll cross you off my list."

He set his pen aside and templed his fingers under the fluffy, angular muttonchops that framed his jawline like a slipped halo. His eyebrows were magnificent in their wildness and volume, and his cheeks were deeply cut with laugh lines, which struck Maria as strange. She honestly couldn't imagine that the sharp, dour man behind the desk had ever cracked a smile.

"Mr. Pinkerton," she began.

"Yes, that's what you'll call *me*. I'm glad we've gotten that squared away, and there are a few other things that need to be out in the open, don't you think?"

"I do think that maybe—"

"Good. I'm glad we agree. And I think we can likewise agree that circumstances must be strange indeed to find us under the same roof, neither of us spying on anyone. This having been said, as one former secret-slinger to another, it's a bit of a curiosity and even, I'd go so far as to admit, a little bit of an honor to find you standing here."

"Likewise, I'm sure." And although he hadn't yet invited her to take a seat, Maria took one anyway and adjusted her skirts to make the sitting easier. The size of her dress made the move a noisy operation but she didn't apologize and he didn't stop talking.

"There are two things I want to establish before we talk about your job here, and those two things are as follows: One, I'm not spying for the boys in blue; and two, you're not spying for the boys in gray. I'm confident of both these things, but I suspect you're not, and I thought you might be wondering, so I figured I'd say it and have done with it. I'm out of that racket, and out of it for good. And you're out of that racket, God knows, or you wouldn't be here sitting in front of me. If there was any job on earth that the Rebs would throw your way, you'd have taken it sooner than coming here; I'd bet my life on it."

She didn't want to say it, but she did. "You're right. One hundred percent. And since you prefer to be so frank about it, yes, I'm here because I have absolutely no place else to go. If that pleases you, then kindly keep it to yourself. If this is some ridiculous show—some theatrical bit of masculine pride that's titillated at the thought of seeing me brought low, then you can stick it up your ass and I'll find my way back to Virginia now, if that's all right with you."

His rolling brogue didn't miss a beat. He said, "I'm not sticking anything up my ass, and you're not going anywhere. I wouldn't have asked you here if I didn't think you were worth something to me, and I'm not going to show you off like you're a doll in a case. You're here to work, and that's what you'll do. I just want us both to be clear on the mechanics of this. In this office, we do a lot of work for the Union whether we like it or not—and mostly, we don't."

"Why's that?" she asked, and she asked it fast, in order to fit it in.

"Well maybe you haven't heard or maybe you didn't know I didn't like it, but the Union threw us off a job. We were watching Lincoln, and he was fine. Nobody killed him, even though a fellow or two did try it. But this goddamned stupid Secret Service claimed priority and there you go, now he's injured for good and out of office. Grant wouldn't have us back, so I don't mind telling you that I don't mind telling them that they can go to hell. But they can pay like hell, too, and sometimes we work for them, mostly labor disputes, draft riots, and the like. And I need to know that you can keep your own sensibilities out of it."

"You're questioning my ability to perform as a professional."

"Damn right I'm questioning it. And answer me straight, will this be a problem?"

Maria glared, and crossed her legs with a loud rustle of fabric. "I'm not happy about it, I think that's obvious enough. I don't want to be here, not really; and I don't want to work for the Union, not at all. But I gave the best years of my life to the Confederacy, and then I got tossed aside when they thought maybe I wasn't true enough to keep them happy."

He said, "You're speaking of your Union lad. I bet old Stonewall and precious Mr. Davis sent you a damned fine set of wedding china."

She ignored the jab and said, "My husband's name was Samuel and he was a good man, regardless of the coat he wore. Good men on both sides have their reasons for fighting."

"Yes, and bad men too, but I'll take your word for his character. Look, Miss Boyd—I know how good you are. I know what you're capable of, and I know what a pain in the neck you've been to the boys in blue, and it might be worth your peace of mind to know that I've taken a bit of guff for bringing you here."

"Guff?" she asked with a lifted eyebrow.

He repeated, "Guff. The unfriendly kind, but this is my operation and I run it how I like, and I bring anyone I damn well please into my company. But I'm telling you about the guff so you're ready to receive it, because I promise, you're going to. Many of the men here, they aren't the sort who are prone to any deep allegiance to any team, side, country, or company; they work for money, and the rest can rot."

"They're mercenaries."

He agreed, "Yes. Of a kind. And most of those fellows don't care about who you are or whatever you did before you came here. They understand I take in strays, because strays are the ones you can count on, more often than not."

She said, "At least if you feed them."

He pointed a finger at her and said, "Yes. I'm glad we understand one another. And you'll understand most of my men just fine. But I've got a handful who think I'm a fool, though they don't dare say it to my face. They think you're here to stab me in the back, or sabotage the agency, or wreak some weird havoc of your own. That's partly because they're suspicious bastards, and partly because they don't know how you've come to my employ. I haven't told them about your circumstances, for they're nobody's business but your own. You can share all you like or keep it to yourself."

"I appreciate that," she said with honesty. "You've been more than fair; I'm almost tempted to say you've been downright kind."

"And that's not something I hear every day. Don't go spreading it around, or you'll ruin my reputation. And don't assume I'm doing this to be nice, either. It won't do me any good to have a team full of people who don't respect each other, and maybe they won't respect you if they think you're here due to hard times. They'll give you a wider berth if they think I campaigned to bring you here, and that might put you on something like equal footing—or at least, footing as equal as you're likely to find in a room full of men." He didn't exactly make a point of dropping his eyes to her chest, but his gaze flickered in such a fashion that she gathered the point he'd avoided making.

She didn't stiffen or bristle. She reclined a few inches, which changed the angle of her cleavage in a way she'd found to be effective without overt. Then she said, "I know what you're getting at, and I don't like it. For whatever it's worth, I've never been the whore they called me, but the Lord gives all of us gifts, and mine has never been my face."

He replied with a flat voice that tried to tell her she was barking up an indifferent tree. "It's not what's beneath your boning, either. It's what's between your ears."

"You're a gentleman to say so."

"I'd be an idiot if I didn't point it out," he argued. "You're a competent woman, Miss Boyd, and I value competence beneath few other things. I trust you to sort out any issues with your fellow agents in what-ever manner you see fit, and I trust you to make a good faith effort to keep disruption to a minimum."

"You can absolutely trust me on that point," she confirmed.

"Excellent. Then I suppose it's time to talk about your first assignment."

She almost said, "Already?" but she did not. Instead she said, "So soon?" which wasn't much different, and she wished she'd thought of something else.

"You'd prefer to take a few days, get the lay of the office, and get to know your coworkers?" he asked.

"It'd be nice."

He snapped, "So would a two-inch steak, but the soldiers get all the beef these days and I'll survive without it. Likewise, you'll survive without any settling-in time. We've got you a desk you won't need, and a company account with money that you *will*. I hope you haven't unpacked yet, because we're sending you on the road."

"All right," she said. "That's fine. And yes, I'm still packed. I can be out the door in an hour, if it comes down to it. Just tell me what you need, and where you want me to go."

He said, "That's the spirit, and here's the story: We've got a prob-lem with two dirigibles coming east over the Rockies. The first one is a transport ship called the *Clementine*. As I understand it, or as I choose to believe it, *Clementine* moves food and goods back and forth along the lines; but she was getting some work done over on the west coast. Now she's headed home, and the government doesn't want her busted up."

Maria asked, "And the second ship?"

"The second ship is trying to bust her up. I don't know why, and if the Union knows, nobody there is willing to talk about it." He picked up a scrap of paper with a telegram message pecked upon it. "I'm not going to lie to you. Something smells funny about this."

She frowned. "So... I don't understand. This second ship is following the first? Harassing it? Trying to shoot it down?"

"Something like that. Whatever it's doing, the officer who's expecting his *Clementine* back in service doesn't want to see it chased, harassed, harried, or otherwise inconvenienced on its return trip. And part of the Union's displeasure with the situation comes from a rumor. Let me ask you a question, Miss Boyd. Are you familiar with the fugitive and criminal Croggon Beauregard Hainey?"

She knew the name, but she didn't know much about its owner and she said so. "A runaway Negro, isn't that right? One of the Macon Madmen? Or am I thinking of the wrong fellow?"

Allan Pinkerton nodded and said, "You're on the right track. Croggon was one of the twelve who made a big, nasty show of escaping from the prison there in '64. He was a young man then, and wild and dumb. He's an older man now, and still wild but not a bit stupid, I'll warn you of that."

"Then I'm afraid to ask what he has to do with these two ships, but I'll do so anyway."

"We think he's piloting the second dirigible," Pinkerton said with a thoughtful scowl. "We don't know for certain, but that's what the Union thinks, so that's what we're forced to work with."

Maria made a thoughtful scowl to match the old Scotsman, and she asked, "So what if he *is* the pilot? Doesn't that strike you as peculiar? Ordinarily, escaped slaves tend to work *with* the Union, not against it."

"Not this one," he corrected her. "Near as we can figure, he doesn't work with anybody, and the Union would be just as happy to collar him as the Rebs. Hainey makes his reputation running guns, stolen war machines and parts, and God knows what else from sea to shining sea; and when he runs short on cash, he's not above doing a little bit of bank robbery to fill his coffers."

"Essentially, you're telling me he's a pirate."

"Essentially, that is a fair assessment." He folded the telegram slip between two fingers and tapped it against his desk. "And whatever havoc he wreaked on his way out of Georgia, he's made a similar mess in Illinois, Indiana, Ohio, and Pennsylvania."

"Places where a Negro isn't assumed to be a slave, and where he might have the freedom to approach a bank," she inferred. "He can move more freely up north, and so he has more latitude to make trouble."

"Now you're getting the feel of the situation. And now you're likely wondering, same as me, what this fellow's doing chasing a craft that he ought to run away from, if he had any sense—because as I've mentioned before, for all of Hainey's personal faults he's got plenty of sense. I don't know why he's on the prowl, but I have to guess it's got something to do with *Clementine*'s cargo, or that's the best I can come up with at the moment."

Maria wanted to know, "What do you think she's really carrying?"

"I asked about that," he said. He unfolded the telegram again, scanned it, and read the important parts aloud. "Humanitarian cargo bound for Louisville, Kentucky, Sanatorium."

"And you believe that?"

"I believe it if I'm told to," he said gruffly, but not with any enthusiasm. "And you're welcome to believe what you like, but this is the official story and they're sticking to it like a fly on a shit-wagon."

She sat in silence; and much to her surprise, Allan Pinkerton did likewise.

Finally, she said, "You're right. This stinks."

"I'd like to refer once again to the aforementioned shit-wagon, yes. But it's not your job to sort out the particulars. It's not your job to find out what the *Clementine* really carries, and it's not even your job to apprehend and detain Croggon Beauregard Hainey or bring him to justice. Your job is to make sure that nothing bothers the *Clementine* and that she delivers her cargo to Louisville without incident."

"How am I to do that without apprehending and detaining Croggon Hainey?"

"Ah," he said with a wide, honest, nearly sinister smile. "That is entirely up to you. I don't care how you do it. I don't care who you shoot, who you seduce, or who you drive to madness—and I don't care what you learn or how you learn it."

He leaned forward, setting the slip of telegram paper aside and folding his hands into that roof-top point that aimed at his grizzled chin. "And here's one more thing, Miss Boyd. Should you apprehend or detain the captain of this pestering vessel, and should he turn out to be, in fact, the notorious Croggon Beauregard Hainey, *I don't care what you do with him.*"

She stammered, "I…I beg your pardon?"

"Listen, the Union wants him, but they don't want him badly. Mostly they want him to go away. The Rebs want him, and they want him badly as a matter of principle—in order to make an example out of him, if nothing else."

"You're telling me I should send him back to Georgia, if I catch him."

"No," he shook his head. "I'm saying that if you want to, you *can.* Whatever's riding aboard the *Clementine* is more important to the Yanks than catching and clobbering a bank robber—"

"More like a pirate, I thought we agreed."

"So much the stranger," Pinkerton said. "He's a bad man, and he ought to be strung up someplace, but that's not part of our assignment. And if you think you can score a few points with your old pals down in Danville, then if you can catch him, you're welcome to him."

Again she fell into quiet, uncertain of how much to take at face value, and how she ought to respond. When she spoke again she said, "I'm not often rendered speechless, sir, but you've nearly made it happen today."

"Why? I'm only giving you the same permissions I give all my men. Do what's convenient and what's successful. And if you find yourself in a position where you can nick a little extra for yourself, I'm not looking too close and I won't stop you. If it makes you happy and if it's easy, score back some of the credibility you've lost with the Rebs. The more friendly connections you have under your belt, the more useful you'll be to me in the future."

"That's very kind of you to consider," she said carefully.

And he said in return, "It's not remotely kind. It's practical and selfish, and I won't apologize for a bit of it."

"Nor should you. And I appreciate the vote of confidence, if that's what this is."

He waved his hand dismissively and said, "I appreciate your appreciation, and all that back-and-forth politeness that people feel compelled to exchange. But for now, you'll find a folder on the last desk on the left—and inside that folder, you'll find everything you need to know about the *Clementine*, the ship that chases it, and everyone within them both."

"Really?" she asked.

"No, not really. The folder will barely tell you anything more than I've told you in here, but it'll tell you how the money works, and it'll give you some footing to get started. You'll report every development to me, and you'll report it promptly, and you won't go more than seventy-two hours without reporting anything or else I'll assume you've gotten yourself killed. Kindly refrain from getting yourself killed, lest you cause me deep aggravation and distress. Breaking in a new operative is expensive and annoying. It'll gripe my soul if I have to replace you before you've done me any good. Be ready to hit the road in forty-five minutes."

He paused to take a breath. She took the opportunity to stand, and say, "Thank you sir, and I'll take that under consideration. You have my word that I'll do my very best to prevent myself from getting killed, even though my very first assignment will throw me into the path of a hardened criminal and his crew of bloodthirsty air pirates."

Pinkerton's face fashioned an expression halfway between a grin and a sneer. He said, "I hope you didn't think I was asking you here to sit still and look pretty."

She was poised to leave the office but she hesitated, one hand resting on the back of the chair. She turned to the door, then changed her mind. She said, "Mr. Pinkerton, over the last twenty-five years I've risked my life to pass information across battlefields. I've broken things, stolen things, and been to prison more times than I've been married. I've shot and killed six men, and only three of those events could lawfully be called self-defense. I've been asked to do a great number of unsavory, dangerous, morally indefensible things in my time, and I've done them all without complaint because I do what needs to be done, whenever it needs to be done. But there's one thing I've never been asked to do, and it's just as well because I'd be guaranteed to fail."

He asked, "And what's that?"

Without blinking she said, "I've never been asked to sit still and look pretty."

And before he could form a response, she swished out of the office, turning sideways to send her skirts through the doorway.

Outside the office door, the company operated in measured chaos. A man at a typewriter glanced up and didn't glance away until Maria stared him down on her way past him. Two other men chattered quietly over a fistful of papers, then stopped to watch the lady go by. She gave them a quick, curt smile that didn't show any teeth, and one of them tipped his hat.

The other did not.

She made a note of it, guessed at what she might expect from all three of them in the future, and found her way to the spot Allan Pinkerton had designated as hers.

The last desk on the left was empty and naked except for the promised folder on top. The folder was reassuringly fat until Maria opened it and realized that most of the bulk came from an envelope stuffed with crisp Union bills. Accompanying the envelope was a note explaining how to record her expenses and how to report them, as well as a small sheaf of telegrams that added up to a clipped, brief synopsis of what Allan Pinkerton had told her. And then, typed neatly on a separate page, she found the rest of what was known about the details of her first assignment.

She withdrew the wooden chair and sat down to read, momentarily ignoring Pinkerton's initial order that she be on the road within forty-five minutes. She'd rather be fully prepared and a little bit late than overeager and uninformed.

In drips and drabs, Maria extracted the remaining facts from the small sheaf of paperwork. The *Clementine* was coming from San Francisco, where it underwent a hull reconstruction following battle damage— for it was a retired war dirigible. On the ship's voyage back east she was moving medicine, bedding, and canned goods to a sanatorium outside Louisville; and there, she would be assigned to a Lieutenant Colonel (presumably of the Union persuasion) by the name of Ossian Steen. Upon the *Clementine*'s safe and formal arrival into this man's hands, Maria would be recalled to Chicago.

Little was known about the ship in pursuit. It was described as a smaller craft, lightly loaded and perhaps lightly armed. This unknown vessel had made at least two attempts upon the *Clementine*. The most recent had resulted in a crash outside of Topeka, Kansas, but wreckage of the unnamed ship had not been located. It was suspected that the ship was once again airborne, and once again hot on *Clementine*'s tail.

At the bottom of the folder, Maria found a ticket that guaranteed passage aboard an airship called the *Luna Mae*. It would take her from Chicago to Topeka, where the pirate Croggon Beauregard Hainey and his crew had been spotted by a Pinkerton informant. The fugitive had been seen bartering in a gasworks camp for parts and fuel.

Just as Maria was on the verge of closing the folder, Allan Pinkerton approached her desk with a second slip of telegram.

"Incoming," he announced. He dropped the paper into her hand and said, "Your lift leaves in thirty minutes. There's a coach outside to take you to the docks. You'll have to change the ticket when you get there."

"Yes sir," she said. Her eyes dipped to scan the paper but then she swiftly asked, "Wait, sir? Change the ticket?" But he'd already whisked himself back to some other department, and was gone.

She looked down at the new telegram. It read:

HAINEY NEARING KANSAS CITY STOP CRAFT DAMAGED BUT STILL FLYING EAST ROUGHLY ALONG COACH ROUTES STOP INTERCEPT AT JEFFERSON CITY STOP ADVISE GREAT CAUTION BEWARE OF RATTLER STOP SEE ALGERNON RICE 7855 CHERRY ST STOP

Maria gathered up her folder, her papers, and she tucked the money into her skirt's deepest pockets. She gathered up the large carpeted bag she almost always toted (a lady needed to be prepared, and anyway, one never knew what trouble might lurk around a bend); and she palmed a smaller handbag for essentials.

She was as ready as she was going to get.

"Beware of rattler? What on earth does *that* mean?" she puzzled aloud, but no one was within earshot to answer her, and outside, a coach was waiting to take her to the passenger docks.

CAPTAIN CROGGON BEAUREGARD HAINEY

3

Croggon Hainey, first mate Simeon Powell, and engineer Lamar Bailey gave up on the unnamed ship somewhere over Bonner Springs, Missouri. Smoke had filled the cabin to such an extent that it could no longer be ignored; and maintaining altitude had become a losing struggle in the battered, broken, almost altogether unflyable craft. They'd set the vessel down hard west of Kansas City and abandoned her there to smolder and rust where she lay.

CLEMENTINE

Fifteen miles across the bone-dry earth, as flat as if it'd been laid that way by a baker's pin, the three men lugged their surviving valuables. Lamar was laden with ammunition, small arms, and two half-empty skins of water. Simeon toted a roll of maps and a large canteen, plus two canvas packs crammed with personal items including tobacco, clothes, a few dry provisions, and a letter he always carried but almost never read. The captain held his own satchel and his own favorite guns, a stash of bills on his money belt, and a white-hot stare that could've burned a hole through a horse.

The Rattler was in its crate, gripped and suspended by Hainey's right arm and Simeon's left. It swung heavily back and forth, knocking against the men's calves and knees if they fell too far out of step.

Simeon asked, "How far out do you think we are?"

And Lamar replied, "Out of Bonner Springs? Another four or five miles."

The captain added through clenched teeth, "We won't make it by dark, but we ought to be able to scare up a cart, or a coach, or a wagon, or some goddamned thing or another."

"And a drink," Simeon suggested.

"No. No drinking. We get some transportation, and we get back on the road, and we make Kansas City, before we try any sleep," Hainey swore. The pauses between his words kept time to the swinging of the Rattler. "And one way or another, we'll get a new ship in Kansas City," he vowed.

"Ol' Barebones still owe you a favor?" Simeon grunted as the crate cracked against his kneecap.

"Barebones owes me a favor till he's dead. Four or five miles, you think?" he asked the engineer without looking over at him.

"At least," Lamar admitted, sounding no happier about it than anyone else. "But it's a miracle we got this close before the bird gave up the ghost. I could've sworn she'd never make it back into the air, but man, she made a liar out of me." He kicked at the dirt and shifted his load to strain the other shoulder for awhile. "I never thought she'd fly again," he added.

The captain knew what Lamar was fishing for, but he was too distracted or too exhausted to humor anybody, and he didn't say anything in response. He only ground his jaw and stared into the long, stretch-limbed shadow that stomped in front of him, and he wondered if his arm would fall off before they reached Bonner Springs.

But Simeon's free arm swung out to clap the engineer on the back, and he said, "That's why we keep you around."

"Not five other folks of any shade, in any state or territory could've got her back up into the sky with only a set of wrenches and a hammer, but I made her work, didn't I?"

"Yeah, you sure did," Simeon said. "It was a nice job."

Hainey grumbled, "Would've been nicer if the patches could've held another five miles."

Lamar's eyes narrowed, but he didn't snap back except to say, "Would've been even nicer if nobody'd crashed our ride into Kansas in the first place."

The captain's nostrils flared, and even though the approaching evening had left the flatlands cool, a bead of sweat rolled down into the scar on his cheek. "Four or five miles," he breathed.

Simeon said, "And then some food. If we don't stop and eat, I'll starve to death before we can grab a new bird anyhow."

"Me too."

"Fine," Hainey shook his face and slung more sweat down to the dust. "But we eat on the road. Once we hit Bonner, how much farther is it to the big town, do you think? I've flown over it, but never walked it like this. You think twenty miles, maybe?"

Lamar shook his head and said, "Not that far, even. Maybe fifteen or sixteen. We can do it easy in a couple of hours, if we get horses good enough to pull us. We play our cards smart, and we might be in bed by midnight."

"Midnight," the captain grunted. Then he said, "Hang on," and stopped. "Other arm," he suggested to Simeon, who nodded and complied.

They switched, and Simeon said, "I'd like that a lot. I could sleep a week, easy."

"Well, you aren't gonna."

"We know." Lamar said it like a complaint, but the look on the captain's face made him keep the rest to himself.

The sun set fast behind them, and the world went golden. The sky was rich and yellow, then pale maroon; and before it went a royal shade of navy, the captain stopped to pull a lantern out of his satchel. They lit it and took turns holding it by their teeth, and by the ends of their fingers. When the last of the rose-pink rays had finally slipped down past the horizon line, the lone lantern made a rickety bubble of white around the three dark men.

As they trudged, coyotes called back and forth across the grass.

Snakes rattled and scattered, winding their way into the night, away from the crushing boots of the heavily laden travelers; and while the crew staggered along the wheel ruts that passed for a rural road, sometimes overhead they could hear the mocking rumble of a dirigible passing through quickly, quietly, looking for a place to set down and spend the night.

By nine o'clock, they reached the town's edge, and by ten they'd purchased a tiny, run-down stagecoach that was almost too old to roll, and they'd bartered two horses to pull it. The horses were only marginally younger and fresher than the coach itself, but they were well fed and rested, and they moved at a fast enough clip to bring the trio rolling into Kansas City by half past midnight.

Hainey drove the horses. Simeon sat beside him and smoked. Lamar stayed inside the cabin with the Rattler and the provisions, where he would've been happy to nap, except for the persistent, jerking bounce of the coach's worn-out wheels.

Even though their backs and arms still ached from the loads, the crew was refreshed by the gas lamps and the late workers who manned stores, transported goods, and swore back and forth at the gamblers and drunks. The prairie was a lonely place for three men too exhausted to talk (or even to bicker); and the city might not mean welcome, but it would warm them and supply them.

They moved deeper into the heart of the place, keeping to themselves even as they drew the occasional curious eye. There were places in the west, as everywhere, where free black men could find no haven—but likewise, as everywhere, there were places where useful men of a certain sort could always find a reception.

In the central district, where the street lamps were fewer and farther between, the saloons were plentiful and the passersby became more varied. Indians walked shrouded in bright blankets; and through the window of the Hotel Oriental, Hainey saw a circle of Chinamen playing tiles on a poker table. On the corner a pair of women gossiped and hushed when the old coach drew near, but their business was an easy guess and even Simeon was too tired to give them more than a second glance.

Along the wheel-carved dirt streets, Hainey, Simeon, and Lamar guided the horses beyond the prostitutes, the card-players, the cowboys and the dance hall girls who were late for work.

And finally, when the road seemed ready to make a sudden end, they were at the block where Halliway Coxey Barebones ran a liquor wholesale establishment from the backside of a hotel. He also ran tobacco that the government had not yet seen and would never get a chance to tax, as well as the occasional wayward war weapon *en route* to a country either blue or gray—wherever the offer was best. From time to time, he likewise traded in illicit substances, which was how he had made the acquaintance of Croggon Hainey in the first place.

The side door of the Halliway Hotel was opened by a squat white woman with a scarf on her head and a carving knife in her hand. She said, "What?" and wiped the knife on her apron.

Hainey answered with comparable brevity, "Barebones."

She looked him up and down, then similarly examined the other two men. And she said, "No."

CLEMENTINE

The captain leaned forward and lowered his head to meet her height. He minded the knife but wasn't much worried about it. "Go tell him Crog is here to ask about prompt and friendly repayment of an old favor. Tell him Crog will wait in the lobby with his friends."

The woman thought about it for a second, and swung her head from side to side. "No. I'll tell Barebones, but we don't have no Negroes in here. You wait outside."

He stuck his foot in the door before she could shut it, and he told her, "I know what your sign says, and I know what your boss says. And it don't apply to me, or to my friends. You go ask him, you'll see."

"I'll go ask him, and you'll wait *here*," she insisted. "Or you can make a stink and I can make a holler—and you won't get anywhere tonight but into a jail cell, or maybe into a noose. And how would you like that, boys?" Her eyebrows made a hard little line across her forehead and she adjusted her grip on the carving knife.

Hainey did a full round of calculations in his head, estimating the value and cost of making a stand on the stoop of the side door at the Halliway Hotel. Under different circumstances, and in a different state, and with a night's worth of rest under his belt he might have considered leaving his foot in the door; but he was tired, and hungry, and battered from a hard crash and hard travels. Furthermore he was not alone and he had two crewmen's well-being to keep in mind.

Or this is what he told himself as he wrapped a muffling leash around the insult and his anger, and he slipped his foot out of the door jamb so that the toad-shaped woman in the scarf could slam it shut. He said aloud, "We shouldn't have to stand for it," and it came out furious, lacking the control he wanted to show. So he followed this with, "It only adds to his debt, I think. If he can't tell the kitchen witch to respect his guests, it ought to cost him. I'll tack it to what he owes me, one way or another."

But neither of his crewmen made any reply, even to point out that Barebones already owed the captain his life.

For another five minutes they stood on the stoop, rubbing at their aching shoulders and tightening their jackets around their chests. Simeon fiddled with the tobacco pouch in his pocket and had nearly withdrawn it to roll up a smoke when the side door opened again. The chill-swollen wood stuck in the frame and released with a loud pop, startling the men on the stoop and announcing the man behind it.

Halliway Coxey Barebones was a short man, but a wide one. What remained of his hair was white, and the texture of wet cotton; and what remained of his eyesight was filtered through a pair of square, met-al-rimmed spectacles. His hands and feet were large for a man of his understated size, his nose was lumpy and permanently blushed, and his waistcoat was stretched to its very breaking point.

He opened his arms and threw them up in greeting; but the effect somehow implied that he was being threatened. He said, "Hainey, you old son of a gun! What brings you and your boys to Missouri?"

Hainey mustered a smile as genuine as Halliway's warm greeting and said, "A beat-up, crashed-down, worthless piece of tin and gas we never bothered to name."

They shook hands and Barebones stepped sideways to let them pass, a gesture which only barely lightened the blockage of the doorway and the kitchen corridor. The three men sidled inside and followed their host beyond the meat-stained countertops and past the surly kitchen woman who gave them a scowl, and Hainey fought the urge to return it.

Barebones led them into a wood-paneled hallway with a cheap rug that ran its length, and back into the hotel's depths where an unmarked doorway led to a cellar crammed with barrels, boxes, and the steamy, metallic stink of a still. He chattered the whole time, in a transparent and failing attempt to appear comfortable.

"It's been awhile, hasn't it? Good Lord Almighty, our paths hav-en't crossed since…well, almost a whole year now, anyway. Not since Reno, and that was, yes. Last Thanksgiving. We'll be coming up on the holiday again, won't we? Before very long, I mean. Another few weeks. I swear and be damned, I thought Jake Ganny was going to blow the bunch of us up to high heaven. If ever there was a man with a weaker grasp on science, or fire, or why you don't shoot live ammunition any-place near good grain alcohol and a set of steel hydrogen tanks, I never heard of 'im."

"It was a hell of a pickle," Hainey agreed politely, and a little impa-tiently as he watched the fat man walk in his shuffling, side-to-side hustle.

"Hell of a pickle indeed. But you and me, we've been in worse, ain't we? Worse by a mile or more, it's true. It's true," he repeated himself and only partially stifled a wheeze. "And it's a right pleasure to see you here, even if I must confess, I don't remember everybody's name but yours, Crog." He pointed a finger around his side and said, "You're Simon, isn't that right? And Lamar?"

"You got Lamar right," Hainey answered for the lot of them. "The other's Simeon. Looks like your operation's grown a bit since last I was here to see it."

Barebones said, "Oh! Oh yes, it's been longer than a year since you last came through Kansas City. Closer to half a dozen, I guess."

"At least."

"Yes, things have been going well. Business is booming like business always is, in wartime and sorrow. The grain liquor is moving like lightning, no pun intended, and we can hardly keep the tobacco in the storehouses long enough to age a smidge. Between Virginia and Kentucky going back and forth, the fields are getting tight and the crops are being squeezed. We have to import from farther down south, these days—as far south as they'll grow it. And the sweets," he said. "Tell me how the business goes for the sweets you bring me from back up north, in the western corners."

Hainey shrugged and said, "The gas is moving fine," because that's what Barebones was really asking after—a heavy, poisonous gas found in the walled port town of Seattle. The gas was deadly on its own, but when converted into a paste or powder, it became a heady and heavily addictive drug. "It's easy to collect, but it's hard to process. That's the big problem with it. There aren't enough chemists to cook it down to sap fast enough."

"That might change, soon enough."

"How you figure?" Hainey asked.

Barebones said, "I've heard things. Folks have been asking after it, wanting to know where we get it, and how it's made. The more customers want it, the more it costs and the more of it we have to find; so I've heard tale of chemists moving west, thinking of hitting up that blighted little city and taking up the gas-distilling for themselves."

The captain smiled a real smile and said, "They're welcome to try it. But I think they might be surprised by what they find."

"What's that mean?" Barebones asked.

And Hainey said, "Not a thing, except I wouldn't recommend it."

"But I heard the city is abandoned. Surely some of these folks can find a way in to harvest what they need?"

"You heard wrong," the captain assured him. "It isn't abandoned, and the people who live there don't much care for visitors. So if you, personally, have sent somebody west to look into it—and if you give half a damn for this person's continued health—I recommend you send him a telegram urging him to reconsider."

The hotelman cringed nervously but neither confirmed or denied anything. "Well then, I thank you for the good advice. I suppose you'd know, wouldn't you? You spend a lot of time out that way."

"I spent plenty of time out that way, sure enough. And I'm not telling you this because I'm worried about you or your men stepping on my toes. I'm no chemist, and I don't have one of any preference who I'm interested in protecting. I'm only telling you, in a friendly exchange of information, that there's a damn good reason there's only a handful of folks who ever get their hands on that gas. That's all I'm saying."

Halliway flapped his hands in a casual shushing gesture and said, "I hear you, I hear you. And I'll absolutely take it under advisement, and pass it around. I trust you, more or less."

"I appreciate it, more or less."

And there they found themselves stopped at a pair of double doors. "Right through here, gentlemen," Barebones said. He opened one of the doors and held it, revealing a gameroom beyond that was half filled with card-playing men sitting at round, felt-covered tables. Bottles of alcohol were granted to each group, and stacks of red, white, and blue chips were gathered together in puddles and mounds, or clasped between fingers, behind cards.

Most of the men glanced up and held their gaze, surprised and sometimes unhappy to see the newcomers. Three men towards the back folded their hands, placing whatever cards they'd been dealt on the table and gathering their things.

"Fellas," Halliway said. "Fellas, come on with me, right through here. There's a spot in the back where we can talk."

The captain, Simeon, and Lamar threaded their way around the tables and past them like cogs in a watch, keeping circular paths to dodge the chairs and the quietly gossiping players. One man said, too loudly as they went by, "I didn't know this was that kind of joint, Barebones. You letting just about anybody in, these days?"

To which Halliway Coxey Barebones said back, "Keep it to yourself, Reese. They're colleagues of mine." And once they were well out of reach, he said, "And if you have a problem with it, you can get your lightning elsewhere." But it was a feeble defense, spoken hastily and over his shoulder. "Back here, fellas."

Simeon whispered to Lamar, "Back where nobody can see us, you want to bet it?"

Lamar said, "No, I won't take that bet."

If Halliway heard them, he didn't react except to usher them into an office space crammed from floor to ceiling with cabinets, crates, and leftover glass bits that belonged in a still. The room smelled like sawdust and hard-filtered grain, but it was spacious and featured enough chairs for everyone—and a desk for Barebones to lean his backside against while he spoke and listened.

When the door was shut, a small panel beneath the nearest cabinet revealed a liquor set and a stack of glasses. "Could I offer any of you boys a sip?"

Simeon and Lamar accepted with great cheer, but Hainey said, "No, and you can stick to calling us 'fellas' if you like. You don't have ten years on me, old man, and I'm no boy of yours."

For a moment, the hotelman looked confused, and then something clicked, and then he said, "You're right. Of course, you're right. I didn't mean it that way, not like…I didn't mean anything by it. I only meant to offer you a drink."

The captain believed him, though he didn't let it show. He only nodded. "That's good of you, but I still don't need a drop quite yet."

"You need something else."

"We need a ship. It's like I told you, the bird that brought us here went to ground. We crashed her bad," he flipped a thumb at Lamar, "but my man here put her back together good enough to get us here, and now we've got farther to go—and no wings to carry us."

Barebones poured himself three fingers of cherry-colored liquor from an unmarked bottle. He took a swallow, leaned with half a cheek sitting on the desk, the other half leaning on it, and said, "That's a tall order you're placing. We've got docks here, back another half mile at the southeast edge of town, but I don't know of anyone looking to sell a ship. You got money, I'm guessing?"

"Like always," Hainey said without resorting to specifics. "We can pay, and pay big if we've got to."

Behind the square glass lenses, the hotelman's eyes went shrewd. "You're stopping just short of saying that money's no object."

"I'm stopping well short of it," the captain corrected him. "And this isn't a money run, or a gun run, or any other kind of run. This is a personal venture, and I'm willing to spend what's necessary to see it through—but I'm not willing to let anyone take advantage of us, just because we've got needs and means."

"Oh no, obviously not. Of *course* not. You misunderstand me," Barebones said, but Hainey didn't think he did.

"I don't misunderstand a thing, and I want to make sure you don't, either. We need a ship, and that's all. We need a ship and we'll be out of your hair first thing come dawn."

Halliway said, "But I don't have a ship to *give* you. Hell, right now I don't even have one to sell you—and that's saying something. You've caught me between runs of guns down to Mexico and smokes up to Canada, and it's not that I don't want to help, but not a one of my ships is home safe for me to spare it. If you don't believe me, check the docks—you know where they are, and you know where I keep my birds cooped. If I had wings to loan you, I'd hand you the deed on the spot. But now I simply must ask: What on earth happened to your *Crow?*"

The captain grimaced and frowned, and after a moment's hesitation he laid out the truth. "Stolen. The *Free Crow* was taken by a red-haired crook called Felton Brink—and don't ask me why," he added fast. "If I knew, I'd have an easier time chasing him. I don't suppose you've seen him come through here, have you? You couldn't miss him. He's got a head that looks like a fire pit, and he's piloting my ship—you'd know it on sight, I know you would—but he's calling her *Clementine.*"

"No," Barebones said thoughtfully. "No, I haven't heard a thing about that, or I'd have been less startled to see you on my doorstep. But if you ask around down at the docks, you might hear something more encouraging."

The captain made a small shrug that was not disappointed, exactly, but rather resigned. He said, "I'm not surprised. They filled up outside of Topeka, and can probably run another couple hundred miles. I don't know if Brink knew I had contacts in Kansas City, but I do know he's sticking to the rural roads and airways as much as he can."

"And you don't know where he's going?"

"Haven't the faintest idea," Hainey said. "If I knew, I'd try and sneak underneath him, and head him off. But it was a damned unfair thing, to steal my war bird. It was damned unfair, and damned stupid."

"I hope he's being paid, and paid gloriously," Halliway said through another mouthful of alcohol. "If the poor fool knew who he was stealing from, I mean." He sounded nervous again, and Hainey made a note of it. "Crossing you, that's not a healthy thing for a man to do, now is it?"

"Not at all. But you know that better than anyone, don't you?"

"I've seen it in action," Barebones said. "Yes sir, I surely have. But I've never crossed you before and I won't start now—which doesn't change the fact that I don't have a bird to give you. But then again…" he said, and fiddled with the corner of his glasses.

"Then again?" Hainey prompted him.

He considered whatever he was on the verge of saying, and when he had his thoughts laid out correctly, he said, "Then again, and this is strictly off the books, you hear me, all right?"

"Absolutely."

The hotelman lowered his voice for the sake of drama, since no one in a position to overhear would've cared. "Refresh my memory, now. Your *Free Crow* was a war bird you…acquired, shall we say, from the Rebs. That's right, ain't it?"

"That's right."

"Well let's say, for the sake of argument, that I've heard tale of a Union bird getting a gauge fixed over here at the Kansas City docks, and I think she's going to be fixed up sometime in the next day or two. She's on her way back to New York to get a few more tweaks made to her defenses; I think someone's going to give it a top-level ball turret. Your fellow here," he pointed at Lamar, "he boosted a crashed-up bird back into the air?"

"Sure did," Lamar answered.

"Then I reckon he could fix a valve gauge in ten minutes flat. Maybe, and I'm just saying this for the sake of argument, but maybe he could even fix it someplace else, if you and your boys felt like taking it for a little ride."

Croggon Hainey wasn't entirely sure how he felt about the suggestion, but it wasn't a terrible one and he didn't shoot it down outright. He said, "It's not a bad idea," while he pinched at his chin, where there was no stubble for him to thoughtfully stroke. "What's this Union bird's name?"

"As I've heard it, they're calling her *Valkyrie*."

MARIA ISABELLA BOYD

4

The passenger docks in Chicago were out past the slaughter yards, and Maria got a good whiff of them as the coach bore her swiftly toward the semi-permanent pipe piers and the tethered dirigibles that waited there. Out the window she watched not quite nervously, not very happily, as the red-brick city sped by—its streets and walkways gray with the soot of a thousand furnaces, and its roads rough with unfixed holes. A particularly pointed jostle threatened to unseat her hat, so she clutched it into place.

She read and reread the information from the envelope. She fingered the ticket, rubbing her thumb against the word TOPEKA, knowing that she'd have to make new arrangements and wondering how she'd go about it.

Maria had never flown in a dirigible before, but she wasn't about to admit it—and she was prepared to figure out the details as she went. She was no stranger to improvisation; it wouldn't have bothered her in the slightest if this weren't her first case, and if she didn't have so many questions.

Perhaps it ought to be considered a point of flattery that Pinkerton was prepared to start her off with something so shady and uncertain. Or perhaps she ought to feel insulted, wondering if he would've given such an assignment to any of his male operatives; and wondering if they would've received the same slim briefing.

Nothing felt right about it.

But she wasn't in a position to be picky, so when the coach deposited her at a gate, she paid the driver, gathered her skirts into a bunch in her fist, and strode purposefully in the direction of a painted sign that said, "Ticketing." Lifted skirts and all, filthy slush swept itself onto the fabric and squished nastily against her leather boots. She ignored it, waited behind one other man in line, and approached the thin-faced fellow behind a counter with the declaration, "Hello sir, I beg your assistance, please. I have a ticket to Topeka, but I need to exchange it for passage to Jefferson City."

"Do you now?" he asked, not brightening, lightening, or showing any real interest. He pulled a monocle off its sitting place at the edge of his eye socket, and wiped it on his red and white striped vest.

Instinctively, she knew this kind of man. He was one of several kinds that were easy enough to handle with the appropriate tactics. The ticket man was thin-limbed and sour, overly enthused with his tiny shred of authority, and bound to give her hassle—she knew it even before she clarified her difficulties.

"I do. And I understand that the Jefferson City-bound ship leaves rather shortly."

He glanced at a sheet of paper tacked to a board at his left and said, "Six minutes. But you shouldn't have bought a ticket to Topeka if you wanted to go to Jefferson City. Exchanges aren't simple." He spoke slowly, as if he had no intention of accommodating her, and orneriness came naturally because he was essentially weak—and he would not be moved except by threat of force.

CLEMENTINE

She was not yet prepared to resort to a force past feminine wiles, but she could see the necessity looming in the distance.

"*I* didn't buy the ticket," she told him. "It was purchased for me by my employer, whom you are more than welcome to summon if you take any issue with my request which is, I think we can honestly agree, a reasonable one."

"It would've been more reasonable if he'd gotten you the right ticket in the first place."

She spoke quickly, firmly, and with the kind of emphasis that didn't have time to cajole. The ticket man did not know it because he was a little bit dense, but this was his final warning. "Then indeed, we can agree on something. But the situation changed, and now my ticket needs to be changed, and I'd be forever in your debt if you'd simply accept this ticket and provide me with a substitute."

He leaned in order to look around her, in case there was anyone else at all whom he might address. Seeing no one, he straightened himself and deepened his smug frown. "You're going to have to fill out a form." Maria glanced at the clock on the table, but before she could say anything in protest the ticket man added, "Four minutes, now. You'd better write quickly."

Before he could utter the last syllable, Maria's patience had expired and her hands were on his collar, yanking him forward. She held him firmly, eye to eye, and told him, "Then it sounds like I don't have time to be nice. I'd prefer to be nice, mind you—I've made a career out of it, but if time is of the essence then you're just going to have to forgive me if I resort to something baser."

Flustered, he leaned back to attempt a retreat; but Maria dug her feet into the half-frozen dirt. As the ticket man learned, she was stronger than she looked. "Oh no, you don't. Now put me on the ship to Jefferson City, or I'll summon my employer and let the Pinkerton boys explain how you ought to treat a lady in need."

"P—Pinkerton?"

"That's right. I'm their newest, meanest, and best-dressed operative, and I need to get to Jefferson City, and you, sir, are standing between me and my duty." She released him with a shove that sent him back into his seat, where his bony back connected unpleasantly with the chair. "Am I down to three minutes yet?" she asked.

With a stutter, he said, "No."

"And how long will it take me to find the ship that will take me to Jefferson City?"

"M—maybe a minute or two."

"Then maybe you'd better hurry up and swap my ticket before I get back in my coach, go back to my office, and explain to Mr. Pinkerton why I missed the ship he was so very interested in seeing me catch." She planted both hands on the edge of the counter and glared, waiting.

Without taking his eyes off the irate southern woman who was absolutely within eye-gouging range, the ticket man took the Topeka slip and, reaching into a drawer, retrieved a scrap of paper that would guarantee passage aboard a ship called *Cherokee Rose*.

Maria took the ticket, thanked him curtly, spun on her heel, and ran up to the platform where the ships were braced for passenger loading. The ticket said that *Cherokee Rose* was docked in slot number three. She found slot number three as the uniformed man stationed at its gate was closing the folding barrier, and she held her hand up to her breastbone, pretending to be winded and on the verge of tears.

He was an older gentleman, old enough to be her father if not her grandfather; and his crisply pressed uniform fit neatly over his military posture, without any lint or incorrectly fastened buttons. Maria did not know if dirigibles were flown like trains were conducted, but she was prepared to guess the estimable old gentleman to be the pilot.

He was essentially a strong man, and most easily handled by appearing weak.

"Oh sir!" she said in her sweetest, highest-class accent, "I hope I'm not too late!" and she handed him the ticket.

He smiled around a pair of snow-white sideburns and retracted the gate in order to let her pass. "Not at all, ma'am. We're only half full as it is, so I'm more than happy to wait for a lady."

She lowered her lashes and gave him her best belle smile when she thanked him, and said, "I can't tell you how much I appreciate your kindness."

"It's no trouble at all," he assured her, and, taking her tiny gloved hand, he escorted her to the retracting steps that led up inside the *Cherokee Rose.* "I'll be your captain on the airway to Jefferson City."

"The captain?" she said, as if it were the most impressive thing she'd ever heard a man call himself. "Well isn't that grand! It must be a terrifically difficult job you have, moving a machine of such size and complexity, up through the skies."

He said, "Oh, it's sometimes a trick, but I can promise you," he let her go first, and rose up behind her. "We won't meet much trouble on the way to Missouri. It's a quiet skytrail, generally unremarked by pirates and too high for the Indians to bother us. The weather is fine, and the winds are fair. We'll have you safely set down in about twenty hours, at the outside."

"Twenty hours?" Maria's head crested the ship's interior, where half a dozen rows of seats were bolted down into the floor, off to her right. The seats were plushly padded, but worn around the corners; and only about half of them were occupied. "That's a marvel of science, sir."

"A marvel indeed!" he agreed, releasing her hand. "It's three hundred miles, and if the weather doesn't fight us, we'll hold more or less steady at seventeen miles per hour. Welcome aboard my *Cherokee Rose,* Miss…?"

"Boyd," she said. "I'm Miss Boyd, Captain…?"

He removed his hat and bowed. "Seymour Oliver, at your service. Can I help you stash your bags?"

"Thank you sir, very much!" She handed over her large tapestry bag and held close to the smaller one with Pinkerton's instructions.

The captain heaved the luggage into a slot at the stowing bays, secured it with a woven net that fastened on the corners, and he told her, "Take your pick from the seats available, and please, make yourself comfortable. Refreshments are available in the galley room, immediately to your left— through the rounded door with the rivets, you see. A small washroom can be found to the rear of the craft, and the seats recline slightly if you adjust the lever on the arm rest. And if you need anything else, please don't hesitate to stick your head through the curtain and let me hear about it."

Captain Seymour Oliver retreated with two or three backward glances, and when he was gone Maria chose a seat in the back, without any other occupants in the row.

The seat was as comfortable as she had any right to expect on a machine that was made to move people from one place to another with efficiency. Though padded, it was lumpy; and though she had plenty of space to stretch out her legs, she could not raise her arms to stretch without knocking her knuckles on a metal panel affixed above her head. This was no flying hotel, but she could survive almost anything for twenty hours.

She closed her eyes and leaned her head back against the seat's edge, holding her smaller bag and its informative contents in her lap—and covered with her hands.

Through the speaking tubes, the captain announced that they were prepared to depart, and asked everyone to make use of the bracing straps built into the seats before them. Maria opened one eye, spotted the leather loop, and reached out to twist her fingers in the hand-hold; but it wasn't as necessary as she'd expected.

The *Cherokee Rose* gave only the slightest shudder as it disembarked, leaving behind a pipework pier with barely a gasp and a wiggle. The feeling of being lifted made waves in Maria's stomach. The sensation of being swung, ever so gently, from a gypsy's pendulum, made her wish for something sturdier to grasp, but she didn't flinch and she didn't flail about, seeking a bar or a belt. Instead, she leaned her head back again—eyes closed once more—and prayed that she might nab a little sleep once the sun went down, and the cabin inevitably went dark.

It was a curious thing, the way her belly quivered and her ears rang and popped. She'd risen once before in a hot air balloon, but it'd been nothing like the *Cherokee Rose*—there'd been no hydrogen, no thrusters, no hissing squeals of pressurized steam forcing its way through pipes. Under her feet she detected the vibrating percussion of pipes beneath the floorboards and it tickled and warmed through her ice-chilled boots. She wormed her toes down and let the busy shaking soothe her, or mesmerize her, or otherwise distract her; and within five more minutes the ship was fully airborne, having crested the trees and even the tallest of the uniform, fireproof brick structures that surrounded the dockyards.

"Quite a performance there, Miss Belle."

Maria blinked slowly; and through a rounded window to her right, she could see the tips of roofs falling away beneath the craft—and the dark, scattering flutter of birds disturbed from their flights.

To her left, the empty seat beside her was no longer empty. It was now occupied by an average-looking man in an average-looking suit. Indeed, everything about him seemed utterly calculated to achieve the very utmost median of averageness. His hair was a moderate shade of brown and his mustache was of a reasonable length and set; the shape of his body beneath the tailored gray clothes was neither bulky nor slender, but an ordinary shape somewhere in between. Only his shrewd green eyes implied that there might be more to him than blandness, and even these he hid behind a pair of delicate spectacles as if he were aware of the threat they posed.

Maria replied, "I'm afraid you must have mistaken me for someone else."

"Not at all!" he argued, settling in the seat without her welcome to do so. He shifted his hips so that he could almost face her, and he said, "I'd know you anywhere, even without that outstanding display."

"I haven't the foggiest idea—"

"—What I'm talking about, yes. Here, let me begin another way instead. Let's pretend that these are the first words I've said to you, and that my introduction is as follows—my name is Phinton Kulp, and two… perhaps three years ago…I saw you perform in a very fine presentation of Macbeth in Richmond. Your interpretation of the wicked Lady was not to be undervalued; I've seen far worse from far more expensive productions."

For a few seconds she merely stared at him. Then she retreated, shifting so that she nearly leaned against the window in order to face him, in return. She said, "Phinton. That can't possibly be your real name. I don't think it's anyone's real name. Did you make it up on the spot?"

"You were wearing the most lovely blue gown, as I recall, and the pig's blood on your hands was as convincing as if it'd gushed freshly from the torso of an inconvenient Lord."

"I'm not entirely sure what you're doing here, Mr. Kulp, but I'm fairly certain that you're a liar, an unrepentant flatterer, and someone who has his own seat several rows away—to which he probably should return. The flight ahead is a long one, and I'd prefer to be left alone to rest." She folded her arms across her chest, crossed her legs at the ankles, and reclined more fully against the window. The metal and fabric siding was fiercely cold when pressed against her back, but she made no sign that it bothered her.

Phinton Kulp feigned affront. He leaned forward and put his hands on the armrest between them and said, "Are you trying to insist that you're not, in fact, the renowned actress and former, shall we say, 'Confederate enthusiast' Belle Boyd?"

"You're not very good at this," she said dryly. "I was a spy, you silly man—and a far better spy than I was ever an actress, but a lady has to eat and the stage kept me in meals between the lean times. Now. I want you to settle some things for me, in quick succession—or else I'll summon the captain and have you forcibly returned to your appropriate seat."

"Anything to satisfy your curiosity, ma'am."

"Excellent. Tell me your real name, what you're doing aboard this ship, and what you really want from me, and tell me quickly. Though it's not yet noon, I've had a full and tiring day already and I do not speak in jest of my desire for solitude."

Behind his spectacles the jade-colored eyes narrowed in a way that didn't quite match the catlike grin he fashioned. "Very well, and very reasonably proposed. My real name is Mortimer, so you must pardon me if I selected something else. Phinton was the name of my sister's first horse, and he was a good horse, thank you very much, so I've appropriated it and I will insist upon it. I am on board this ship with the express intent of reaching Jefferson City—"

"You'll have to do better than that," she interrupted.

"And so I shall. In that grand city I have business which must be attended to, and attended to without delay. Following the death of an uncle I scarcely knew, I seem to have inherited a dance hall. On the off chance that this satisfies the demands of your question, I'll now move on to your final query before you have a chance to scowl at me any further—I wanted only to speak with you, and to express my most heartfelt admiration."

"For my acting skills?"

"That and more," He hid a smirk behind a delicate clearing of his throat.

Against her better judgment, Maria asked, "To what do you refer?"

"Only that I've long heard tales of the southern girl with a tongue like a razor and a smile that moves mountains…or dirigibles, as the case may be. That was quite a lashing you gave the poor gent at the ticket counter."

"I'm well past girlhood, Mr. Kulp; and as for the ticket agent, I did him no harm whatsoever."

"Yet the threat was rather present, I think you must admit—to yourself, if not to me."

"I haven't the foggiest idea what you're talking about," she lied, but it was a worthwhile lie because she'd decided to keep him talking, if only to lead him into saying something useful. His true intent still eluded her by design, and she didn't care for it.

He cleared his throat again, using the expectoration as an excuse to cover his mouth with his fist. "Since you've not denied being the actress Belle Boyd—which is just as well, since we both know precisely who you are—and since you've already so eloquently confessed to your wartime activities, I might assume that once or twice, you've been known to hurt a man or two."

"Once or twice, plus half a dozen or more. And if you don't vacate these premises, perhaps that tally will rise."

He pouted. "Come now, Belle. There's no need for threats. Why can't you give me the same sort of smile you've given our illustrious captain?"

"Because Captain Oliver was a gentleman."

"And I've shown you something other than the utmost chivalry?"

She shook her head. "The circular talk will get you nowhere."

"Except back to the beginning. Shall I try again?"

"You shall not, Mr. Kulp. You shall return to your seat with all haste if you have nothing of substance to tell me, and if you are likewise incapable of leaving me in peace."

He shrugged merrily and said, "How on earth am I supposed to comply with such contradictory instructions? You've now ordered me to say something pertinent, and yet to keep quiet."

"No, I suggested either one or the other. Meet one of these goals or *be on your way.*"

Finally, for a moment, he was silent. He stared pointedly at the folder in her lap, and something in his voice changed when he said more quietly, "So it's true. The Pinks have snatched you up and put you to work."

She hesitated in her response. "It's not a secret," she said, which was true.

"It's not a widely known fact," Phinton Kulp replied, and this was also true.

"Then what's it to you?" she asked him flatly.

"Nothing at all. It's as you said before, 'A lady has to eat.' But there must be a less dangerous way for a woman of your notoriety to keep herself in skirts and furs." He retreated several inches, giving her both more breathing room and yet, cause for a little more worry.

"My state of employment is no concern of yours," she told him.

And he said, "You're right. But you can't blame me for being curious, and you might want to treat interested strangers with less defensiveness. Pinkerton has operatives and informants from coast to coast, you know; and it won't serve your purposes very well to send them trundling off to their seats, as if they're naughty children caught under the tree before Christmastime. There are networks in place, alliances and allegiances to be balanced. Not everyone loves the Pinkerton name—even among those who sometimes serve it."

She guessed, "You're no operative."

"At this time, you are correct. But I'm still a useful man to know—even Mr. Pinkerton will tell you that, if you ask him."

"How convenient for you, that he isn't present to interrogate on the subject."

"On the contrary, I'd be pleased to see him, if only to see you set at ease with his reassurances. It must be difficult," he said, keeping his voice low and now adding a bit of warning to it—a dash of sinister seasoning that Maria filed away for future reference. "Being a woman of your reputation, traveling alone, working in a man's field in which you have absolutely no experience."

"It isn't so different from spying," she insisted.

"From one point of view, I suppose not," he agreed. "But between North and South you had only one enemy. Adversaries and cohorts might have doubled their roles, or blurred them, but at the end of the day you had only one authority to thwart and dodge. Wearing a Pinkerton shield, you'll find things are more complicated. Pinkerton wages dozens of tiny wars, all at once, all across the territories. Working for him…it's a dangerous calling, if you could call it that."

"That sounds like a threat."

"It's no such thing," he promised. "Only an observation buttressed by a friendly suggestion, proposed by a concerned traveler who knows a little too well how hard this road is for a man—much less a magnolia like yourself."

She snorted, and while making a show of making herself more comfortable, she reached for the derringer she always kept loaded in her smallest bag. "And toting secrets under threat of jail and hanging—that was a day at the park, picking flowers. Now if I may be so bold as to offer *you* a bit of advice, Mr. Kulp, then here you have it: There are people in this world who steadfastly refuse to understand anything unless it's couched in terms of violence. In my experience, it is most expedient to simply accommodate them."

"Expedient?"

"You may as well communicate in the language they best understand."

Neither his spectacles nor his fist could hide the sly expression he assumed when he replied, "Does that mean you intend to shoot me, the very moment you get your hand wrapped around the gun in your bag?"

"I intend to think about it. And you clearly think you're quite clever, anticipating me like that, but I think it only makes you moderately well read."

"Both of the biographical pieces I've seen on the subject of the South's most notorious spy *did* mention that you never travel unarmed, it's true. And let me assure you, I don't plan to press my luck on the point."

Without bothering to note the gratuitous flattery, much less address it, she asked, "Does that mean you're ready to leave me alone?"

"It means," he said, removing the spectacles and wiping them on a handkerchief he pulled from a pocket, "that I'm reasonably satisfied that Pinkerton knows what he's doing, and I'll pass the word along."

"Pass word…to whom?"

He didn't answer, except to gather himself up and stretch, and begin a sideways shuffle back into the aisle. Then he said, "I hope your flight is a pleasant one, Belle Boyd, and send my regards to Mr. Rice when you see him." He pinched the front of his hat in a tiny gesture that barely passed for a tip, and he returned to his spot at the front of the seating area without another word.

Maria almost called out after Phinton Kulp with demands for explanations, but doing so would've openly declared that he'd rattled her so she restrained herself. She settled back in the seat, drawing her shoulders away from the cold wall and window; and she kept her hand inside the purse—on the single-shot back-up plan that had saved her more than once before.

And between her bouts of uncertainty, her concerns about her fellow passengers, and the idle second thoughts that perhaps this wasn't such a good idea after all, she slept off and on.

All the way to Jefferson City.

CAPTAIN CROGGON BEAUREGARD HAINEY

5

Halliway Barebones swore on a stack of gold-paged Bibles that his hotel was booked to the hilt, with nary a room to spare for his three visitors. He apologized to the point of groveling, and pointed them towards a ramshackle, three-story establishment a few blocks away. According to Barebones, they shouldn't meet any trouble—for Indians, Chinamen, and free Negroes were routinely served there without incident, and the hotel owner was correct on that point.

The accommodations were not first class, but they were not last class either; and although Hainey knew good and well that Barebones had been lying when he professed no vacancy, he didn't make half the stink about it that he might have, given different circumstances. The captain was exhausted beyond words, and more to the point, Simeon and Lamar were half dead on their feet. Hainey might push himself past the bounds of reason, health, and good sense, but he couldn't impose any further obligation on his men.

After all, the *Valkyrie* wasn't going anywhere, at least not overnight. They could afford to sleep a few hours better than they could afford to keep pushing east.

At the High Horse Boarding House and Billiards Hall, two large rooms with two large beds cost the captain six dollars out of pocket. He claimed one room for himself and left the other to his companions, who made a side trip downstairs to buy tobacco and spirits before holing up and settling in for the night.

Hainey skipped the vices and threw himself into bed without any fanfare.

When he dreamed, he dreamed of his own ship—and of the clouds, drafts, and passages over the Rockies. He dreamed briefly of Seattle, the walled city filled with gas and peril, and of the giant Andan Cly who had tried to help retrieve the *Free Crow* when first it was stolen. He also dreamed of the skittering of black birds, shifting their weight back and forth on a tree branch, their tiny claws gripping and scraping the wood.

But in the back of his head, even when so fogged with such badly needed rest, Croggon Hainey's exceptional sense of alarm awakened him just enough to wonder if the sound he heard was leftover from sleep…or if it was taking place outside his door. It remained even when his eyes were open—the dragging clicks, but not of birds on branches. It was the sound of someone moving softly and examining the room's door.

Or its lock.

Or its occupant.

A quick shift in shadow from the door implied feet moving back and forth on its other side; and Hainey, now thoroughly awake, crept from the unfluffed feather bed as quietly as his sizeable bulk would allow. He eschewed his shoes but felt about silently for his gunbelt, and upon finding it, he removed the nearest pistol—a Colt that was always loaded.

Automatically, his fingers found the best hold and fitted the gun against his palm.

He slipped sideways to the wall, and slid against it until he was inches from the door's frame. He listened hard and detected one man, seemingly alone. The stranger was trying to keep quiet and not doing the very best job; whoever he was, he reached for the knob and gave it a small twist. When the door didn't yield, he retreated.

Croggon Hainey slipped his unarmed hand down to the knob, and with two swift motions side by side, he flipped the lock and whipped the door open—then pointed the Colt at approximate head-height, in order to properly reprimand whoever was standing there.

"What do you want?" he almost hollered, his voice rough with sleep, but his gun-hand steady as a book on a table. He dropped the weapon to the actual head-height of the prowler, who was somewhat shorter than expected.

The prowler quivered and cringed. He threw his arms up above his head and curled his body in upon itself as he tried to melt into the striped wallpaper behind him. "Sir!" he said in a whisper loud enough to be heard in Jefferson City. "Sir, I didn't…sir…Barebones sent me, sir!"

This revelation in no way assured the captain that it was safe or appropriate to lower his weapon, so he didn't. He eyed the intruder and saw precious little to worry him, but that didn't set him at ease, either.

The speaker was a skinny mulatto, maybe fourteen or fifteen years old. He was wearing the food-stained apron of a kitchen hand tied around his waist, and a faded blue shirt tucked into brown pants. When he put his arms down enough to see over his own elbow, the boy asked, "Sir? Are you the captain? You must be the captain, ain't you?"

"I'm *a* captain, and I know Barebones, so maybe I'm the man you're looking for." He backed into his room without inviting the boy to follow him. Without taking his eyes or his gun off the kid in the doorway, he used one hand to light a lamp and pick it up.

"I've got a message for you, sir."

"Is that why you were trying to let yourself inside my room?"

"Only because I didn't know which one was yours, sir. The lady downstairs said you'd taken two. Sir, I have a message for you. Here." He held out a folded piece of paper.

"Set it down."

The boy bent his knees until he was down at a crouch. He dropped the note.

"Now get out of here before I fill you full of holes, you idiot kid!" Hainey almost roared. The messenger was down the hall, down the stairs, and probably out into the street by the time the captain picked up the note and shut the door again, locking himself inside with even greater care than he'd taken before he'd gone to bed.

The weight of his weariness settled down on his shoulders as soon as the door was closed and he felt somewhat safe again; but the lantern's butter-yellow light made his eyes water and the note was brittle in his hand as he opened it. The message was composed in the flowery hand of a man who clearly enjoyed the look of his own penmanship.

> *Incoming to Jefferson City in another few hours—a Pinkerton operative sent from Chicago. Whoever stole your ship has friends in high places with very deep pockets. Borrow a new ship and get out of town by the afternoon if you know what's good for you. If Pinkerton's paid to be involved, someone has big plans for your bird. Watch where you're going, but watch your back, too. You're being tracked.*

Hainey crumpled the note in his fist and crushed it there, squeezing with enough rage to make a diamond. He composed himself and sat on the edge of the bed. He held the note over the lantern's flame and let it evaporate into ash between his fingers, then he set the lantern aside and dropped himself back onto the bed. The lantern stayed lit, because if he'd blown it out, he might've fallen back asleep.

He needed to think.

Jefferson City wasn't more than a hop, skip, and a jump from Kansas City, though Barebones was right—he probably had until the following afternoon before he ought to get too worried. But Pinkerton? The detective agency? The captain had heard stories, and he didn't like any of them. The Pinks were strike-breakers, riot-saboteurs, and well organized thugs of the expensive sort. Like Barebones' note had suggested, they had pockets deep enough to pay for loyalty or information from anybody who was selling it. Down south of the Mason-Dixon, they weren't so well known. But in the north and west, the Pinks were their own secret society.

To the best of Hainey's knowledge, no one had ever called the Pinks on him before—despite his less-than-legitimate business enterprises, his occasional bank robbery, or his intermittent piracy. It made things sticky, and even stranger than they already were.

Why would anyone steal the *Free Crow* in the first place?

Anyone with the resources to invoke the Pinks ought to be able to afford their own damn war bird.

He fumed on this matter for another five minutes before leaning over and stifling the lamp, dropping the austere room into darkness once more. In half an hour he was asleep again, and before long the light of morning was high enough to make him semi-alert and terribly grouchy.

A loud knock on the door didn't do much to improve his state of mind; but Simeon's pot of coffee and Lamar's covered plate of breakfast fixings shook off the last sour feelings of insufficient sleep. He invited the men into the room, helped himself to the coffee (a quarter a cup, or a dollar for the whole carafe) and to the breakfast (a dollar a plate, and his men had already eaten theirs).

As he sat on the edge of the bed and made short work of the offerings, he told them about the note and the warning.

Lamar twisted his mouth into a frown and said, "That don't make any sense. Who would hire the Pinks to come after us?"

"I don't know," Hainey said around a mouthful of eggs. "It's bothering me too. God knows we didn't hire 'em, and who on earth gives a good goddamn if the *Free Crow* gets stolen, except for us?"

Simeon shrugged and said, "Nobody, except whoever stole it."

The captain pointed his fork at the first mate and said, "Exactly. That's all I can figure, anyway. Except at first, I was bothered because of the money. It costs money to hire the Pinks and get them to act as your enforcers. You'd think that people with money could just buy or build their own aircraft; but then I got thinking."

"Uh oh," Simeon grinned.

"What I got thinking is this: The *Free Crow* was the strongest bird of her kind in the northwest territories—or at least, she's the toughest engine anywhere close to Seattle. And I don't think I flatter myself too much when I say that nobody in his right mind would swipe that ship out from under me for no good reason at all; so all I can figure is, this must've been a crime of opportunity. Somebody out west needed that ship to perform a specific task."

"What kind of task?" Simeon asked, tipping half a cup of coffee into a tin and taking a sip.

Lamar answered thoughtfully, before the captain could reply. "Something heavy. Someone needed our bird to move something really, really heavy from northwest to southeast."

Hainey set the fork down on the edge of his plate, and Simeon froze with his cup at the edge of his lips in order to ask, "How'd you come to that conclusion?"

The engineer said, "Ain't you seen her flying? She's weighed down with something, and weighed down bad. Otherwise, we could've never stayed as close behind her as we've been doing so far. She ought to have outpaced that nameless bird by a week, but she's never got more than half a day on us. And when she moves, she looks like she's carrying so much cargo that she can't hardly lift herself up."

Hainey took one more bite and chewed it slow, before saying, "Which means she picked up something in Seattle, because she didn't have anything but a few crates of guns when we lost her. All right, it's coming together now. So Felton Brink, may he rot in hell, he takes the *Free Crow* because he has something heavy he needs to move—and ours is the only engine tough enough to carry it."

"And whatever it is," Simeon concluded, "it's important enough for somebody to put the Pinks on our tail in order to keep us from taking it back. But who? Where's Brink taking our bird?"

Lamar's frown deepened. "The Pinks do a lot of work for the military, don't they? The Union uses them to shut down draft riots, and move money around. I've read about it, here and there."

Simeon said, "So the Union could sure as hell afford to pay the Pinks."

"But that doesn't mean they're behind this," Hainey was quick to say. "They might be, sure. It might be worth our time to ask around, if we can. But we'll have to balance our time real careful. If we're going to stay on the *Free Crow*'s trail, we need to get ourselves together, swipe that Union bird, and get back in the air."

"Sounds like a plan to me," the first mate declared. He downed the last of his coffee and left the tin cup sitting on the basin.

Hainey stood up and pulled a shirt over his undershirt, then reached for his sharp blue coat. "Let's see about the horses and that rotten coach, and head out to the service yards. We don't have all day before the Pinkerton op finds his way into town, and I'd like to be gone before he gets here."

They left the High Horse by nine o'clock and took their secondhand coach down near the service yards, where they paid a Chinaman named Ling Lu to hold it and keep the horses behind his laundry. Another hundred dollars, spread around judiciously, revealed the general location of the *Valkyrie* and the name of a Pinkerton informant who had been known to let information flow in more than one direction.

Hainey sent Lamar ahead to the ship, with a forged document that declared him a free citizen and a Union veteran. He also included a letter of recommendation, composed as a fictional white man who managed a shipping yard in Chattanooga, declaring that Lamar was handy with tools and rich with integrity. Lamar was, in fact, handy with tools and absolutely faithful to his captain; and Hainey trusted that the engineer would learn what needed to be learned in order to fly the craft.

Meanwhile, he took Simeon back to the red quarters at the yard's edge—where the saloons and billiards were cheap and easy, and the dance hall girls were either far older or far younger than they really ought to be. It wasn't a pretty place, and it smelled like a cross between a coyote den and a leaky still. But in the right corners, hiding in the right shadows, information could be bought and sold as easily as a newspaper—even by a dark-skinned man with a terrible scar, and a foreigner with an accent that no one in Kansas City could place.

Behind a grocery store that dealt contraband ammunition out the back doors, Hainey and Simeon found Crutchfield Akers—a man with a hand-rolled cigarette sticking moistly to his bottom lip, and a pair of suspenders with eagles printed from top to bottom. His pants were rolled to keep them out of the wet sawdust and tobacco juice that covered the grocery stoop, and if he'd shaved or trimmed any part of his face the last six weeks, you couldn't have proved it to the captain.

"You Crutchfield?"

"That's me," he answered with a nod that dipped his hat so that a shadow covered his eyes. "Who's asking?"

"A man with money and some questions, looking for a man with answers and an open pocket. Maybe we can share a drink next door and have a conversation."

He shook his head. "Not next door." The hat lifted enough to reveal a pragmatic gaze. "I don't mind sitting down with a Negro, but there's folks who'll hold it against me. Nothing personal, you understand."

"Nothing personal," Simeon repeated with a snort.

Hainey didn't press it. "All right. We can talk out here if it preserves your social standing. My money spends just as easy as anyone else's."

"Let's see it."

"Let's see if you're the man to ask."

Crutchfield shrugged and said, "All right."

"You used to be a Pinkerton operative?"

He said, "No. But I've worked for 'em on my own, every now and again. When it suited me, or when the money suited me."

"Rumor has it you'll share a word or two about your old employer. Or part-time employer," Hainey corrected himself. "So if I needed to learn a thing or two about an operative who's on his way from Chicago right now, maybe you're the man I ought to ask?"

At this point, he produced a wad of bills from his money belt. He did it slickly and fast, like a magician producing a dove from a waistcoat.

Crutchfield nodded, and smiled with something more than greed. "I'm the man you ought to ask. And I even know which operative you're asking after, though you've got a thing or two wrong. I guess that makes you Croggon Hainey, don't it? One of the Macon Madmen, ain't you?"

Hainey refused to look startled. Instead he said, "Good guess, I suppose—though truth is, I'm an easy man to recognize, even if you've only heard of me in passing. And tell me why you know it, and why you grin like that when you say it." He peeled off a ten-dollar bill and placed it on the rail beside Crutchfield's elbow.

Crutchfield slid his hand along the rail and palmed the bill.

He said, "Did you know Pinkerton—the big man, not the agency—used to be a Union spy? He's retired from it now, obviously. Got better things to do with his time, or maybe he's just getting old. A lot of those old guys who worked hard at the start of the war, if they ain't dead yet, they're too old for the war game."

"I did not know that," Hainey said with impatience. "But I'm not sure what it's got to do with *me*."

"Hold your horses, man. I'm getting to it. So the big man invites a new operative, somebody from his old line of work."

"Another spy?"

Crutchfield nodded. "That's right. But not a Union spy—a *Rebel* spy. A rather famous one, if you see what I'm saying."

"I'm afraid I don't. I could name a whole handful of southern spies, so you're going to have to be more specific." He fiddled with the roll of money for a moment before asking, "Is it someone who had a beef with me? Maybe someone from the Macon crowd?"

The informant shook his head and cocked it at the cash. Hainey unspooled another ten and set it down where he'd placed the first.

"It's nobody you know, I don't think. But it's somebody with an agenda. The Rebs don't want her no more, so she's got something to prove by bringing you in; and that's why she got the assignment."

The captain didn't hide his confusion. "What do you mean, they don't want her no more? Pinkerton sent a woman to chase me down?"

"Not just any woman—Belle Boyd."

"Belle...oh now Jesus Christ in a rain barrel. That's a tall tale you're spinning, and I don't believe it for a second."

Crutchfield shrugged. "Believe me or don't believe me, that's what I heard, my hand to God. This is her first job, so it's a loaded one."

"Loaded," Hainey agreed. "But not with good sense. I'm just baffled," he said, scratching his head. "And maybe a little insulted, that they send out a woman to bring down a man like me."

"I wouldn't take it like that, not yet. Pinkerton doesn't hire folks as a joke—and he doesn't hire fools, and he doesn't throw his operatives away on suicide missions. He wouldn't have sent her after you if he didn't think she could bring you in."

While Hainey pondered this, Simeon stepped in and took another ten.

He set it on the rail, waited for Crutchfield to collect it, and said, "All of that's real interesting, no doubt. But why don't you give us a hint about who hired the Pinks in the first place? They wouldn't send anyone to nab a runaway without being told to, or paid to."

"You have a point," he said. "And I don't know much about the gig, except that there's a ship called *Clementine* that's moving supplies—and it's being hounded by a Negro captain in a bird that's got no name."

Hainey bobbed his head slowly up and down, sorting through the important bits and settling on his next words. He lifted the money roll, and unwrapped half its bulk while the eyes of Crutchfield Akers did their best to remain unimpressed.

"You can have this," Hainey told him, setting the curled stack on its side. "All of it, no problem and no trouble, if you can answer me one more question and answer it true. Except," he held up a finger. "If it turns out you've lied to me, I'll be back, and I'll take it back out of your skin. We understand each other?"

"We understand each other," the informant swore.

"Good. Then I want to know where this *Clementine* is going."

Crutchfield's lips stretched into an expression of relief. "Oh good," he sighed. "I actually know the answer to that one. The bird's headed to Louisville, but I don't know why, and I can't tell you any more precise than that—not for the rest of your roll—because nobody's told me." He collected the stack of bills that must've counted a couple hundred dollars, and licked the tip of his finger to help him count it. "And I must say, it's a pleasure doing business with you."

"Likewise," Hainey muttered.

He took Simeon by the arm and led him away, speaking quietly. "The bird's headed to Kentucky, and ain't that a stinker."

"Not a Reb state," Simeon said, as if it were a bright side.

"Not technically, no. But a border state that's Reb enough to be unwelcoming. Louisville's up on the river though, practically in Indiana. It's not the worst news, and not the best news, but it's news."

"You think he's on the level?"

The captain said, "I wouldn't trust him to sort my laundry for free, but for a stack of green I think he's solid enough. It's how he makes his living, and he's not a young man. If he were full of malarkey, someone would've killed him by now."

"You're full of sense, sir."

"Let's get back to the engineer and see what he's scouted for us. It's past midday now—"

"Not by much."

Hainey said, "No, but I want to clear town sooner rather than later."

The first mate made a little laugh. "You're not worried about that Rebel woman, are you?"

The captain didn't answer immediately, but when he did he said, "I've heard about her. I've heard a lot about her, mostly in the papers and partly through gossip. As far as I know she's no dummy, and if half of what's said about her is true, she's not afraid to shoot a man if she feels the need."

They reached the street and turned to the right, strolling towards the service docks and maintaining a casual pace. Hainey continued, "She was just a girl when the war started—maybe sixteen or seventeen, just a baby. But she didn't have a lick of fear in her, not anywhere. She's been in prison a few times, been married a few times, and killed a few fellows if they interfered with her. And these days," he toyed with what he was thinking, then laid it out. "She's only a little younger than me. Maybe in her forties. A woman who was that much trouble as a girl, well—now she's had twenty-five years to learn new tricks."

Simeon was silent.

Hainey said, "I'm not saying we ought to turn tail and run like dogs. I'm just saying that maybe it's not an insult that she's been picked to chase us down. Maybe we ought to keep our eyes open."

"Do you know what she looks like?" Simeon wanted to know, but the captain didn't have a photograph handy and he wasn't sure he could pick her out of a crowd, anyway.

He said, "As I've heard it, she's not much to look at—but she's got a figure you'd notice if you were blind and ninety."

"Not much to look at?"

"Yeah. It's been said," the captain mumbled, lowering his voice as they passed a pair of men cleaning a set of six-shooters in front of a saloon. "That she was young once, but never beautiful."

"Sons of bitches, up there in Chicago," the first mate said, pulling tobacco out of his pocket as if he'd only just remembered he had it. He flipped a paper loose with his thumb and started to roll a cigarette. "Can't even send a pretty woman after us."

Hainey didn't answer because further discussion might've made him look paranoid, or weak. Simeon came from another place with its own set of problems, to be sure; but he wouldn't have understood, maybe—how nothing on earth summoned a mob with a noose or a spray of bullets quite like a lady with an accent, and a problem with the way she's been looked at.

Even a look, misinterpreted or even imagined.

And it had been decades since Croggon Beauregard Hainey had been a young man in a prison, accused of incorrect things and condemned to die; but that didn't make the memory of it any easier to ignore or erase. So yes, all insistence to the contrary—and with the Rattler, and his men, and a full complement of guns stashed across his formidable body—he was more than a little concerned about a southern woman with something to prove.

At that moment, a shy head ducked around the corner where Crutchfield stood on a stoop and conducted business. It was the same boy

Hainey had threatened the night before, and he looked no less threatened to be standing in front of the captain once again.

"Sir?" he said, stopping both men.

Hainey snapped out of his reverie enough to ask, "What is it?"

"Sir, you have a telegram. It's from Tacoma."

The captain took the telegram, read it once, then read it again, and then he declared, "Well I'll be damned."

"What's it say?" Simeon asked, even as he scanned it over Hainey's shoulder. Before the captain could answer, Simeon had a new question. "What the hell does that mean? That's about the strangest message I ever heard of. Do you know what it's all about?"

FREE CROW CARRIES DAMNABLE MADAM CORPSE STOP WORD IN THE CLOUDS SAYS OSSIAN STEEN REQUIRES JEWELRY FOR WEAPON STOP SANATORIUM IS COVER FOR WEAPONS PLANT NO FURTHER WORD TO BE HAD STOP YOU OWE ME ONE STOP AC

Hainey's scarred face split into a smile. "Cly, you bastard. All right, I owe you one."

"Cly? The captain?"

"That's his initials there at the end. He's the one who sent it," he confirmed.

Simeon shook his head and said, "But what's he's talking about?"

And the captain replied, "I don't know who this Steen fellow is, but the rest of it's given me something to think about, sure enough."

"Can you think and steal a ship at the same time?" the first mate asked.

"I could knit a sweater and steal a ship at the same time, and don't you josh me about it. Come on. Let's grab the coach, get the Rattler ready, and see what Lamar's been up to. We've got a *Valkyrie* to ride."

CLEMENTINE

MARIA ISABELLA BOYD

6

She arrived at Jefferson City in the near-light hours of the morning; but since she'd stolen most of a night's sleep inside the *Cherokee Rose*, she grabbed an early breakfast of oatmeal and toast—and then, when the hour was more reasonable, she called upon Algernon Rice.

According to the helpful folder of paperwork Maria carried, Mr. Rice could be found in an office at the center of town, half a dozen blocks from the city's passenger docks. In the heart of the city the streets were bumpy with bricks and the buildings were built three, sometimes four stories tall with tasteful trim components and neatly lettered advertisements. Groceries were nestled against law offices and apothecaries, and a veterinarian's facility was planted between a carriage-house and a billiards hall.

And at the street corner named in her folder, she found a small office with a white painted sign that declared in black lettering, "Mr. Algernon T. Rice, Private Investigator, Pinkerton National Detective Agency (Jefferson City Branch)."

On the other side of the door she found an empty receptionist's desk; and beyond that desk in a secondary room, she located Mr. Rice.

"Please pardon the receptionist," he said. "We don't actually have one right now. But won't you come inside, and have a seat? I understand this is your first outing as a Pinkerton operative."

"Yes, that's right," she told him, and when he stood to greet her she allowed him to take her hand before she positioned herself delicately on the edge of the high-backed chair that faced his desk.

Algernon Rice was a slender, pale man who looked quite villainous except for the jaunty orange handkerchief peeking out from his breast pocket. His wide, narrow, precisely curled and waxed mustache was so black it looked blue in the light; and beneath the rim of his matching bowler hat, his sideburns were likewise dark. Except for the orange triangle, every visible article of his clothing was also funereal in design and color.

But his voice was cultured and polite, and he conducted himself in a gentlemanly fashion, so Maria opted to assume the best and proceed accordingly.

She said, "I've just arrived from Chicago and I understand I must now make my way to St. Louis. Your name was presented as a contact, and I hope this means that you can help me arrange a coach or a carriage, or possibly a train."

"Yes and no—which is to say, I won't give you anything horse-powered or rail-running, but I can definitely see you to your destination. However, there's been a change of plans. I received a telegram first thing this morning from a contact in Kansas City."

"Kansas City? Isn't that west of here?"

"Yes, by a hundred and fifty miles," he confirmed. "It would seem that your quarry has slowed, and that the nefarious captain is stranded. And I'm afraid that's the good news."

She furrowed her brow and said, "I beg your pardon?"

To which he replied, "We have an informant of sorts—an affiliate, we should say instead. Frankly, it'd be a disservice to call him anything more than a degenerate drunk, but he likes to make himself useful."

"To Pinkerton?"

"To anyone with a wad of cash. Crutchfield's not terribly discriminate, but he's usually on top of things so I fear we're forced to trust him. And the bad news is, Croggon Hainey knows you're coming. We would've preferred to keep a lid on that, but there's nothing to be done about it now except slip in faster than he expects to meet you."

She shook her head slowly and asked, "But how would he know I'm coming?"

"It's as I said, our informant will talk to anyone with the cash to buy his time, and he has ears bigger than wagon wheels. He won't admit that he's the reason word is getting around, but he doesn't have to." He sighed, and folded his hands on the desk. "Ma'am, I'm bound to honor my obligations to the Chicago office, you understand, but I also feel obligated to voice a bit of objection to this matter. I think it's an unkind, untoward thing to send a lady after a criminal like Hainey—"

Maria cut him off with a delicate sweep of her hand, saying, "Mr. Rice, I appreciate your concern but I assure you, it's unnecessary. I've received plenty of warnings, tongue-waggings, and outright prohibitions since agreeing to work for Mr. Pinkerton, and if it's all the same to you, I'd prefer to skip the one you're preparing to deliver and get right to work. So if you're not planning to take me to Kansas City by horse, buggy, or rail, what precisely does that leave—except for another dirigible?"

He smiled widely, spreading his thin lips and showing no sign of teeth. "As you wish. And the transportation in question is…shall we say… dirigible-*like*. It's an experimental craft, barely large enough to support two passengers, I won't lie to you there. It'll be cramped, but the trip will be fairly brief."

"To cover one hundred and fifty miles?"

"Oh yes. If we leave now, we'll be able to catch a late lunch in Kansas City, if you're so inclined. Though… I'm sorry. I don't mean to presume…"

She told him, "You can presume anything you like if you can get me to Kansas City by lunchtime." She rose from her chair, collected her large and small bags, and stood prepared to leave until he likewise stood.

"I can hardly argue with *that*. We might have a bit of a trick getting your luggage aboard, but we'll see what we can manage. This way," he said, opening his arm and letting her lead the way around the corner, into a hallway where a tall set of narrow stairs led up to another floor.

"Up…upstairs?"

"That's right. The *Flying Fish* is upstairs, on the roof. She's a little too small to sit comfortably at the passenger docks; if I left her there, I would've simply met you at the gate rather than compelling you to find your way to my office. But I've constructed a landing pad of sorts, and I keep her lashed to the building where she's available at a moment's notice."

He reached out to take Maria's heavier bag, and she allowed him to tote it as she led the way up the steps. She asked, "Is that typically necessary? To have a small airship at the ready?"

"Necessary?" He shrugged. "I couldn't swear to its absolute essentialness, but I can tell you that it's mighty convenient. Like now, for example. If I didn't have a machine like the *Fish*, then I'd be forced to assign you to a train, or possibly bribe your way onto a cargo dirigible heading further west. There aren't any passenger trips between here and Kansas City, you understand."

"I was unaware of that," she said, reaching the top of the stairs and turning on the landing to scale the next flight.

"Yes, well. We may be the capital, but we're by no means the biggest urban area within the state. Or within the region, heaven knows," he added as an afterthought.

Maria paused, looked back at him, and he urged her onward. "It's only the next flight up. Here," he said. At the top of the next flight there was a trap door in the ceiling. Algernon Rice gave the latch a tug and a shove, and a rolling stairway extended, sliding down to meet the floor.

He offered Maria his hand and she took it as a matter of politeness and familiarity, not because she particularly needed the assistance in climbing the stairs without a rail. But she'd learned the long way that it was easier to let men feel useful, so she rested her fingers atop his until she had cleared the portal and stood upon the roof—next to an elaborate little machine that must have been the *Flying Fish*.

"As you can see," he said, "she isn't made for comfort."

Maria said slowly, "No… I can see she's made for one man's convenience. It looks rather like…" she hunted for a comparison, and finally settled upon, "a wooden kite, strapped to a hydrogen sack."

Algernon Rice's smile finally cracked enough to show a hint of even, white teeth when he said, "That's not an altogether unfair assessment. Come, let me show you. We'll have to strap your belongings under the seat for the sake of balance—and speaking of the seat, it's a single bench and we'll have to make the best of sharing."

"That's fine," she said, and she meant it, but she wasn't really listening to him. She was examining the *Fish*.

The *Fish* could best be described as a personal-sized dirigible, affixed snugly to an undercarriage made of a light, unfinished wood frame that was open to the elements—though somewhat shielded by the bulbous balloon that held it aloft. The balloon was reinforced with a frame that could've been wicker, or some other light, resilient material; and it was fuller at its front than at the rear.

"What a remarkable machine," she said.

Algernon Rice took her large bag and a length of hemp rope, and he began to tie it into place. "It's small and light, but the speeds it can reach when the tanks are fired…well, I might have to ask you to hang onto your hat. They don't hold much of a burning capacity, really, because it usually isn't required. I'll refuel in Kansas City, at the service docks, and make my way back home by bedtime."

"Forewarned is forearmed," she murmured, and came to stand behind him to watch him work. When they were both satisfied that her bag was secure, they withdrew to the passenger compartment and Mr. Rice looked away while Maria organized her fluffy, rustling dress into a ladylike position inside the little wooden frame.

Then he slung a satchel over his suit which, he explained, contained basic repairing tools and emergency supplies, "Just in case," and he made some adjustments to the rear booster tanks—neither one of which was any larger than a dog. Finally, he climbed onto the seat beside her and showed her where best to hold on, for safety's sake. He donned a pair of aviator's protective glasses and handed Maria a secondary pair, which she could scarcely fit over her hat and onto her face.

While she adjusted herself, he told her, "I hope you're not easily sickened by flight or other travel, and if you have any sensitivities to height or motion, I'd advise you to brace your feet on the bar below and refrain from looking down."

"I'll take that under advisement," she assured him and indeed, she braced her feet on the solid dowel while she gripped the frame's side.

With the pump of a pedal and the turn of a crank, a hissing fuss became a sparking whoosh, and in only a moment, the *Flying Fish* scooted off her moorings and hobbled up into the sky.

The experience was altogether different from flying on the *Cherokee Rose*, with its accommodating seats and its heavy tanks, its lavatory and galley. Every jostle of every air current tapped at the undercarriage and sent it swinging ever so slightly, in a new direction every moment or two. It was a perilous feeling, being vulnerable to insects, birds, and the very real possibility of toppling off the bench and into the sky—especially as the craft climbed higher, and crested the last of the buildings, passing the edge of the town and puttering westward over the plains.

Algernon Rice spoke loudly enough to make himself heard over the pattering rumble of the engines and the wind, "I ought to have warned you, it feels like a rickety ride, but we're quite safe."

"Quite safe?" she asked, determined that it should come out as a formal question, and not as a squeak.

"Quite safe indeed. And I hope you're warm enough. I also should have warned that it's cooler up here, the higher we fly. Is your cloak keeping you satisfactorily comfortable?" he asked.

She lied, because telling the truth would neither change nor fix the situation. "It's fine. It keeps me warm in Illinois, and it's managing the worst of the wind up here." But in truth, the dragging rush of the air was a fiendish thing with pointed fingers that wormed between every crease, crevice, and buttonhole to cool her skin with a dreadful determination. She fervently wished for another hat, something that would cover her ears more fully, even if it crushed her hair and looked appalling; but her only other clothing was stashed below, and retrieving it would only slow the mission, which was an unacceptable cost.

So all the way to Kansas City, in the hours over the winter-chilled plains, she held her hat firmly onto her head with one hand and gripped the railway with the other.

They chatted only a little, for the ambient noise was sometimes deafening, and Maria's entire face felt utterly frozen within the first hour. If she parted her lips her teeth only chattered and stung with the cold air rushing against them, so instead she huddled silently, sometimes leaning against the firm, confident form of Algernon Rice—who appeared to be glad to have her close, though he made no unwelcome advances.

After what felt like eternity and a day, but was surely no more than half a dozen hours, Kansas City sprouted out of the plains. Buildings of various heights were scattered, and even at the *Fish's* altitude Maria could tell the blocks apart, guessing which neighborhoods were cleanest and which ones were best avoided by respectable people. The streets split, forked, and ran in a crooked grid, sprawling across the ground in a life-sized map that Maria found more fascinating than when she'd spied Jefferson City from the *Cherokee Rose*. She was closer to the world this way—even chilled to the bone, with skin pinkly chapped and hands numb with winter.

She looked down past her feet, and the bar around which she'd wrapped her toes. She watched the land draw up close as the *Fish* drew down low; and she saw the commercial dirigibles lined up, affixed to pipework docks that were embedded in the earth with roots as deep as an oak.

There came a clank and a soft bounce, then a harder one. The *Fish* settled into a slot beside an enormous craft painted with a freight company's logo, and a service yard hand stepped up with a length of chain and a lobster clasp—though the young man didn't know where to affix it.

"I'll handle that, my boy," Algernon Rice announced as he turned a crank to cut the engines. He dismounted from the bench and took the claw, fastening it to the exposed mainshaft that ran the length of the undercarriage.

Even though the *Fish* had settled, Maria felt vibrations in her legs and feet. She stomped them against the bar, then stood and ducked her head in order to escape the frame. Algernon Rice dashed to her side, hand outstretched, but she waved him away this time. She was shaken by the trip, but she would not restore herself to steadiness by leaning on him any further.

"Thank you," she said. "But I'm fine. Give me…give me just a moment." She wrung her hands together, squeezing blood back into them and willing them to warm within the too-thin gloves that hadn't shielded them well enough.

"Very well," he said, and returned his attention to the yard boy, asking after fuel prices, slot rentals, and the nearest boarding house, hotel, or restaurant where a lady might find some refreshments.

The lady in question was starving, now that she heard him mention it. But there was work to be done and she reached beneath the *Fish* to untie her bag. Upon retrieving it, she threaded her arm through its wide band of a strap, and held it up under her arm.

Rice returned, the yard worker at his side. He said, "We can leave the *Fish* here, and I've arranged for a refueling and a brief stay. I'm sure you can understand if I'm in no rush to return to the air. It's a bit unsettling, isn't it?"

She nodded, and said, "I've never had a ride quite like it. And I hope you'll forgive me for saying so, but I'm in no hurry to repeat it. I think a passenger line will make an easier return trip for me." She turned her attention to the boy beside him and said, "You work here, young man?"

"Yes ma'am," he said.

"Perhaps you could answer a question for me, if it isn't too much trouble. Could you tell me, please, what's that ship over there?" And she pointed across the way, to a monstrous great craft that was cast in hues of black and silver. It was easily half again as large as the *Cherokee Rose*, and a thousand times less friendly.

CLEMENTINE

The boy hemmed and hawed before finally saying, "It's a military ship, ma'am. It's here for some repair work, or something. I don't know exactly."

"And even if you did," she guessed, "you aren't supposed to talk about it, anyway?"

He looked relieved, and said, "That's right. Everybody knows it's there, but we're all supposed to pretend it's not."

Maria didn't have to ask which military the behemoth belonged to. She made her assumption even before she walked down the lane between the rows of ships, and spied the blue logo with silver lettering. Seeing the ship unsettled her for no reason she could name, and a thousand she could suggest. But at the core, it only made her unhappy because she was no longer supposed to feel threatened by it.

After making another arrangement or two with the yard boy, Algernon Rice took the larger of Maria's two bags and walked beside her on the way to the edge of the docks. "We can take an early supper, if you like. There's a serving house a few blocks away where you can rent a room."

"But I doubt I shall need a room, Mr. Rice. If Croggon Hainey is still within Kansas City's limits, it is my fervent hope that I'll find him and deliver him to the authorities with all haste."

"Undoubtedly," he said too casually, as if he had no doubt that she was incorrect. "But it would be worth your while to have a stable base of operations, don't you think? A room where you can leave your belongings, and a place to which you might retire if you're compelled to stay in town longer than you expect. Anyway," he added, "it's on the Pinkerton dime, so you might as well make yourself comfortable."

She said, "Nothing will make me more comfortable than concluding this case." And as the words escaped her mouth, they walked directly beneath the shadow of the enormous military air engine; and on the machine's side Maria saw the name *Valkyrie* painted in cruel, sharp letters.

"*Valkyrie*," she nearly whispered. "What a dreadful ship. By which I mean, of course, it's a fearsomely ugly thing."

Under the dirigible where the bottom hull had been pried open, three men stood arguing over some finer point of which repair ought to be made in which fashion. Two were large white men, and one was a small black man who was holding his own in the fray. He spoke softly but with great confidence about replacement pipes and valve drains until, from the corner of his vision, he spied Maria and Algernon strolling past.

His technical diatribe snagged, and he hesitated as they walked past. He was trying not to stare, but he couldn't pull his gaze away completely.

His attention snared Maria's attention in return; she was being looked upon with something like recognition and fear, and she didn't know what to make of it. Many people knew who she was—she'd become accustomed to notoriety twenty years before. But this was a fretful gaze, and it made her feel fretful in response.

One of the mechanics said, just within her hearing, "Well, I think you might be right. And if it works, we can have her back in the air within an hour or two."

The black man didn't respond. He was still looking at Maria, and trying not to.

He was approximately her own height, which is to say, smallish for a man but tallish for a woman. He was maybe ten years her junior and slight in build, but he had an intelligent face and quick hands, and quick eyes that darted back and forth as he made his pretense of looking away.

She wondered if he might be a runaway slave. He was working on a Union warbird, so the odds weren't so stacked against it. Perhaps he recognized her from some old adventure, or she only made him nervous by virtue of her old alliances.

Maria looked away for good, feeling a weird sort of embarrassment.

Algernon Rice asked, "Is everything all right?"

And she told him, "Yes, everything's fine. It's just such an imposing ship," she misdirected. Then, because it did not seem to be enough to stop him from wondering, she added, "It reminds me of something I've seen somewhere before, but I can't put my finger on it"—which was a lie, but it was enough information to prevent the further asking of questions.

Beyond the service yards with the tethered airships bobbing in rows, Rice led her to a boarding house with a serving area downstairs where an early supper could be arranged. Maria was opposed on general principle. Fugitives weren't likely to hold still at her stomach's convenience, but her stomach's convenience was becoming a necessity, and the thought of food—a quick bite, at most—was enough to keep her another hour longer in the company of the Pinkerton affiliate.

At the Seven Sisters, an establishment that looked like a gingerbread dollhouse, Maria allowed Algernon Rice to secure her a room while she sat in the dining area and awaited a plate. She sat at a table by a window and fiddled with her handbag, and the folders within it—thinking that she ought to be elsewhere, doing something meaningful and productive, now that she'd reached her destination.

A knock on the window to her right made her jump, even though it was a quiet rap that could've been anything gentle from a passing elbow to a misguided grasshopper.

She saw a man in a gray suit, standing just beyond the window's edge. It was as if he were hiding there, lest anyone else inside the establishment see him. Maria couldn't see him perfectly, for he kept his face ducked in the shadow of his hat's brim, but something about him seemed familiar.

She frowned, squinting to see him better.

He lifted a hand from inside his jacket pocket and made a motion that asked her to join him outside.

She shook her head.

He made the motion again, more forcefully, and lifted his head enough for her to get a better look at him. The mystery man was a few years older than Maria, with a salt-and-pepper beard and eyes as brown as a chocolate cake. Those eyes were begging nervously; they were trying to draw her outside with the sheer force of their desperation.

At the edge of the dining area, Maria could see Algernon Rice standing at the desk, chatting with the clerk about her room. It couldn't possibly take him more than another few minutes to arrange it, but she nodded at the man outside and rose from the seat—telling the servant girl that she'd return momentarily.

She brushed by Algernon, tapping the edge of his arm and telling him the same. Before he could ask where she was going, she was gone—out the front door and down the steps, and then around the corner where the peculiar gentleman was disappearing. The last of a gray pant-leg went dipping out of sight, and she chased it into a narrow spot between the boarding house and the office building next door…where the gray-suited, salt-and-pepper fellow was waiting for her.

Before she could say anything he'd taken her hand and pulled her off the walkway and out of sight from the street. If he hadn't been so gentle, and he hadn't seemed so earnestly pleased to see her, she wouldn't have let him lead her that way—but the familiarity was driving her mad, so she said, "Sir, there are people expecting me inside the Seven Sisters—"

"I know," he said. "Maria, when I saw you sitting there I just couldn't believe my eyes. It's been *years*."

"More than a few," she replied, trying to shake the dubious tone out of her voice and not altogether succeeding.

He suddenly gathered that he ought to introduce himself, and he did so. "I'm so sorry, I know it's been a long time, and I realize I've changed a bit—though you look every bit as youthful as you did as a girl back in Richmond. But it's me, Randolph Sykes. We worked together briefly on the Jackson initiative back in 1869. I *do* apologize, I shouldn't have simply assumed that you'd know me and be pleased."

The name rang a bell, and she let her face light up. "Randy! Oh yes, I absolutely recall it now. And the apologies ought to be mine, for my feeble recollections. But what on earth brings you to Kansas City, and now, and with all this subterfuge?"

He didn't answer any of those questions, but instead he gave her a story that told her plenty, laid out in the homeland accent he'd only partially succeeded in muffling. "I knew you must be working. I saw you with the Pink operative, and I knew it must be a subtle play—a subtle play *indeed*. When the grayfellows told me you'd been sent on your way, I knew it wasn't true. I knew they couldn't doubt your loyalties; I knew it must be some strategic ploy—and here you are! Working side by side with the Pinkertons, and good heavens, lady, but what a brave—"

She was forced to stop him then, gently laying three fingers across his mouth. "Randy," she said with sadness that was not altogether calculated, "but I'm afraid it's all true. Our boys sent me home, and—"

He grasped her fingers and kissed them. "I understand!" he declared. "Times are tangled enough that you must preserve the masquerade, even to me—I understand, I do, and I won't ask you to lie to me further. But let me say, my dear, I am filled with such outstanding relief to see you here! And I know, that whatever strange duties you're pretending to perform for the Chicago organization, you're using the lot of them to sort out the terrible shipment bound for Louisville."

"I...I beg your pardon?" she said, and then, before she appeared too ignorant she amended herself. "I only mean, this terrible shipment, bound for Louisville—I know of it, yes, and I'm here to address it, absolutely. But you've put me into a corner, and I must admit that my understanding of the menace is somewhat limited. Rather, I know that there is a Union craft flying for Louisville, and that it's being pursued by one of the Macon Madmen, but I do not know what the craft is carrying. Oh Randy, if there's any further information you can share, I'd be forever indebted to you. I've been...living under another name, in Chicago and out west for long enough that the trail of gossip and warning has stretched thin."

Randy straightened himself. "I would be honored and delighted to assist you in any way you require! Though..." and he cast a sidelong glare at the Seven Sisters, "what is to be done about your companion?"

"My…companion. He's only a professional contact, I assure you. He's a Pinkerton agent, as you said; he's helped ferry me this far, from Jefferson City. I can escape him before long, but not immediately. You must understand, I'm *working*. He *must* believe that I'm no longer affiliated with the Cause in any way."

"Then I'll be brief for now, and pray for further audience later."

"Please do so, yes."

"A western dirigible is making a delivery to a sanatorium in Louisville—where a devious Union scientist is constructing a war machine the likes of which could end this conflict by ending the South altogether. The nature of this cargo isn't known, but it's the final piece of a device called the Solar Radiant Beam Cannon, which is being assembled at the behest of a *loathsome* lieutenant colonel named Ossian Steen. Maria, for the sake of our Cause and the sake of everyone you've ever loved in Danville, this part must not reach the sanatorium! It must not reach the scientist, or the lieutenant colonel, or the machine that's made to fit it!"

Maria seized Randy's collars and brought his face down closer to hers. "Sir, you've given me much to think on, and I only need a few more pieces before I settle this puzzle…is this Louisville-bound ship called the *Clementine*? And where is she located now?"

"The *Clementine*?" His expression said lots, much of which was confusing. "That old patchwork war machine? It's moored at a transient dock outside town, where it stopped to rest, refuel and repair. Apparently the ship took some damage on the western trail; but she's not the vessel that worries us. The craft in question is called the *Valkyrie*, and she's stuck in the service yard docks."

"Are…are you sure?"

"Sure enough," he nodded. "We need to sabotage that bird before she gets off the ground; we need to sort through her cargo, find out what nefarious piece or part is so valuable that it requires such a transport, and destroy it for the sake of the Confederacy—if it's not too late already!"

CLEMENTINE

"It's not," she blurted. "It's not too late. Whatever they're doing, it's not been done yet. Just…" her mind raced, and her companion within the dining area was no doubt already wondering what had become of her. "I must go back inside and make my escape from the Pinkerton man," she concluded.

"Escape? But you said you were working?"

She nodded vigorously and said, "I am. But the *Valkyrie* will be ready to lift in under an hour, and I'm working again, for my home. For my *country*. Stay here," she told him. "I'll be back in a moment."

When she reappeared less than two minutes later, she had retrieved her carpetbag and left Algernon Rice very perplexed in the dining area.

To Randolph Sykes she said, "Quickly, to the service yards. I don't know the city here. You'll have to lead me, and we'll have to hurry."

CAPTAIN CROGGON BEAUREGARD HAINEY
7

Back at the service yard docks Lamar was torso-deep in the underside of the Union warship *Valkyrie*. Grunts that signaled the stiff-armed turns of a wrench echoed around in the hydraulics compartment, where the engineer was swearing and sweating despite the pronounced chill in the air. The wrench slipped from his fingers, fell to the ground, and was retrieved by Simeon—who handed it back with a smile that promised trouble was brewing.

From down at the folding bay doors, a fat white man dropped down onto the ground. Upon seeing Simeon he called out, "Hey Larry, is this guy some friend of yours?"

Lamar ducked his head out from the hydraulics compartment, realized who'd passed him the wrench, and said, "Oh yes. Friend of mine. Nobody to worry about at all."

To which the first mate said, "That last part might've been a little much."

In two long strides, taken so quickly that the other man barely had time to squeak, Simeon was on top of the other mechanic; and with a hard right hook the mechanic crumpled, hitting his head against the bay doors on his way to the ground.

From his position half inside the *Valkyrie*, Lamar said, "Hey Sim, I wish you hadn't done that, though."

"Why not?" he asked, already dragging the heavy man out of sight, back under the craft and behind the pipework docks.

"Because this thing ain't ready to fly yet, and his brother'll be looking for him any minute now. He just stepped out a second ago, to chat with some guy who came up looking for the captain."

"His brother's the captain?"

Lamar said, "No, but he went off to talk with him. I'm surprised he ain't back yet. He walked off with an older fellow, hair going gray. Sounded like he wasn't local."

Simeon dumped the unconscious man, dropped his feet, and returned to Lamar's side. He ducked under the unfastened panel so that he was at least unidentifiable, if not invisible. For all any passersby might know, he could be another mechanic—as he could only be seen from the chest down.

He asked, "How long will it take you get her airworthy?"

"I'm almost done," Lamar said, fishing around in his tool belt for a screwdriver of the correct size. "I'm fixing the last of it now, but I need a minute. And," he added, shifting his shoulders to knock against the first mate, "I need more room. This hatch ain't big enough for the two of us. Where's the captain?"

"He's right behind me—rounding up the Rattler and the last of our stuff off the coach."

The engineer said, "All right, that's good. Give me maybe…maybe five minutes, all together. That'll be plenty of time to wrap up and shut the hatch."

"How many other folks are aboard this craft? Who else do we need to worry about?" he whispered.

"Not sure. It doesn't have a crew, really—or it does, of course, but those guys hit the red blocks two days ago and they won't come back until tonight, when the bird is set to take off. There's the mechanic, his brother, and a third fellow. I think he's supposed to be an engineer, but he's a shit excuse for one. He was acting like he couldn't figure out what was wrong, when the bird's leaking piston lube and control line fluid all over the place." Lamar sniffed with disdain and wiped his forehead with the back of his forearm.

"That's three, plus the man you said came by, wanting a word with the captain."

"If he comes back with the mech's brother, yes. That's right. Now get out of the hatch and let me finish this up on the quick. If the captain's timing is good, we might just fly off with this thing, easy as can be."

Simeon bent and squatted to let himself out, but he said, "Except for the service yard security."

Lamar's voice was muffled from within. "They won't be a problem until we're airborne. And we might be able to outrun 'em. You never know. We might get lucky yet."

"Here's hoping," Simeon said, not because he lacked faith in the captain, but because he lacked faith in luck.

When the first mate emerged, he thought he heard a rustling sound coming from inside the *Valkyrie* so he grasped his revolver—and he went into a half-crouch as he snuck up the steps that led into the ship's belly.

It was mostly for show.

He didn't plan to shoot anybody for a couple of reasons. For one thing, you didn't open fire inside a metal container if you could possibly help it. Bullets bounced in close quarters. And for another thing, the noise would summon everyone within the yards, security and otherwise. Simeon didn't need the extra attention and he sure as hell didn't want to make a stink before the captain was on board.

For a third thing, and possibly most *important* thing, you didn't go shooting willy-nilly inside a canister with a giant tank of hydrogen strapped to it—not unless you wanted to see yourself splattered all over Kansas.

Up the folding steps he moved with surprising silence for such a tall man. He kept his gun out of sight against his chest. His head breached the bay, and he swiveled it back and forth—making sure there was no one behind him, and becoming confident that there was no one else present in the cargo bay.

He made a cursory examination of the munitions crates. Next he checked the bridge, where six swiveling seats were affixed into the floor. Three were positioned at the wide, curved glass of the ship's windshield, and the other three were assigned to spots in front of the craft's weapon systems.

"This bird's not kidding around," he said to himself.

He ran his fingers over the levers that worked the automatic rotary firing guns, and scanned the buttons and handles that managed assault launches of bombs and other assorted things which might be dropped, and might explode on impact. There were even two pivoting guns mounted bottom and side within thick glass shields that extended outside the body of the craft.

On the other side of the bridge was another door that must have led to sleeping quarters or a lavatory, but a poorly smothered curse from Captain Hainey drew Simeon's attention elsewhere. He went back to the cargo hold and climbed past the crates, then descended the steps to meet the captain, who was carrying everyone's personal supplies and ammunition like a blue-coated pack mule.

"Here," Hainey said, upon spotting Simeon. "Take this. Get it on board. I assume everything's under control?" he said in a casual voice that knew better than to whisper. Everyone listens hard when someone whispers; and people who whisper have something to hide.

Simeon said, "Yes sir, more or less." Without clarifying, he took half the captain's load and walked it nonchalantly up the stairs, with the captain coming up behind him.

Once they were up in the cargo bay, Hainey felt the need for clarification. He asked, "What's 'more or less' supposed to mean?"

"Exactly what it sounds like. If we move quick, we can lift this lady up without too much notice. I took care of one mechanic, and the other two are missing at the moment."

"And the crew?" the captain asked.

"Whoring and drinking down in the blue district. Won't be returning until tonight."

Hainey lifted an eyebrow as he lifted the heaviest of his packs onto a crate. "It's like a sign from heaven. Or else it's a bad trick someone's playing on us," he said. "What does Lamar think?"

"Lamar thinks we'd better hurry up, and we'll stay in the clear except for the service yard security. And once we get airborne, he trusts you to keep us aloft and in one piece. What about the Rattler?" the first mate asked.

"It's back in the coach. I can carry it, but I can't carry much with it. I'll go back and pick it up," he plotted, "and you stay here and keep an eye out on Lamar. If those other mechs come back, he might need a hand. How long until he's got the bird air-ready?"

"Less time than it'll take you to retrieve the Rattler," Simeon said. "Are you sure we even…I mean, do you think we'll need it? Look at this bird, Captain. She's loaded up like nobody's business. More guns than I ever saw on a ship."

Croggon Hainey made a harrumphing noise and asked, "Can we take any of it with us?"

"Well, no. It's all attached pretty solid, I'd say."

"Then I'm going back to get the Rattler," he said, and he retreated back down the steps. "Be ready to take off when I get back." To Lamar, under the hatch, he added, "Did you hear that?"

"Yes sir, Captain. I heard it."

"And you'll be ready?"

"I'll be ready," the engineer promised.

"Good," Hainey said, and he stalked back out to the edge of the service yard, for coaches were not allowed within the repair grounds and the captain wanted to make as little fuss as humanly possible.

The yards weren't particularly crowded, but they were populated here and there with mechanics and engineers like Lamar, though most of them were white. Once he spied an Asian man who looked like he might've had something important to do, but Hainey didn't stop and ask him about it. He only gave a half nod of acknowledgment when he caught the other man's eye, because he wanted the whole damn world to know that he wasn't up to any trouble, no sir. No trouble at all.

The horses fussed and shifted from foot to foot and the coach rocked heavily when the captain climbed aboard it one last time, withdrawing the Rattler in its crate and letting it slide onto the ground. He tugged at his jacket collar, and stretched his arms and back in preparation to lift it again.

Off at the edge of the sidewalk, he saw the mulatto boy who worked for Barebones, watching curiously—and perhaps by his employer's strict instructions, if Hainey knew Barebones at all.

"You over there," he called out, and pointed at the boy in case there was any doubt.

He cringed and said, "Me?"

"You, that's right. Come here, would you?"

The kid slunk forward, coming up the half-block's distance and all but cowering. He said, "Yes sir?"

And Hainey told him, "For God's sake, son. Stand up straight. No one'll ever respect you if you hunker like that all the goddamned time."

"Yes sir," he said more firmly. "But I'm only a kitchen boy."

"All the more reason to show some dignity. Straighter than that," he commanded. "That's better. Now let me ask you something. You've been working for Barebones, how long?"

"Pretty much forever. I don't remember."

The captain said, "That's fine, all right. You trust him?"

"Of course, sir."

"Don't lie to me, now. I know when boys are lying. I used to be one, you understand."

The boy said, "No sir. I don't trust him. But he's not too bad."

Hainey nodded slowly. "That's fair enough. I'd say about the same, if anybody asked me. So let me ask you one more thing—you got a horse, or anything like that?"

"Not even a mule, sir."

"Not even a mule," he repeated. "Well then. If I were to give you these two horses here—and they ain't much, I know—but if I were to give you these two horses, would Barebones take 'em from you, or let you keep 'em, do you think?"

The boy pondered this a moment, then said, "I think he'd probably keep the better one, and let me keep the other one."

"I think you're right." He picked up the Rattler's crate, hoisting it up to hold it in front of him, and straining to do so. "Anyway, I guess they're yours."

"Mine?"

"Yours, that's right. I don't have any more use for them. Take the coach too, and take it right now—back to Barebones. Tell him we thank him for his time and his hospitality, such as it was. Tell him I said the horses are yours, but the coach is his if he wants to keep it. Or he can push it off a cliff, I don't care."

The boy brightened, though he was confused. "Thank you, sir!" he said, not wanting to appear ungrateful or disinterested.

"You're welcome. And stand up straight. Do it all the time. Otherwise, you'll be a boy all your life," he said, and he walked back towards the service yards, and the *Valkyrie*, without a backwards glance.

He was halfway between the street's edge and the Union warbird when he heard the first shot. The second rang out close behind it, and a third and fourth came fast on the heels of the others.

Hainey made some guesses.

Someone had come back.

Simeon hadn't been able to hold the ship without opening fire; he was a good first mate, and an all-around smart man—too smart to shoot unless he had to. And Lamar, up there under the hatch. Had he kept a pistol in his tool belt? The captain couldn't recall; he hadn't looked. He'd been in such a hurry.

The Rattler's crate bounced against his thighs, his knees, and his shins as he gave up on jogging and dropped the thing to the ground. An all-out firefight had opened up only a hundred yards away and he was being left out of it. He didn't want it to come to this—it was always easier when things didn't come to this—but he kicked the lid of the crate away and, as a new volley of shots were exchanged, he hefted the Rattler out of the sawdust and shavings that cradled it.

People were running past him, flowing around him like he was a rock in a stream, ignoring him as they rushed to see the commotion, or rushed away from it. The noise level rose as men began to yell, to summon further assistance, and to sound a wide assortment of alarms.

But he had the Rattler raised, and it was still loaded from the day before; its sling of ammunition dangled heavily across his arm and the crank on the right was ready to turn. He shifted himself, adjusted the gun, and kept walking in the ponderous pace which was all he could manage while shouldering so much weight.

Soon, the *Valkyrie* was in sight.

Lamar was not beneath the unfastened exterior panel, and hopefully he'd finished whatever task had kept him there—despite the fact that he hadn't had time to seal the workspace behind him. The bay doors were open and the folding steps were extended, though Simeon's burnished arms were visible, guns blazing return-fire at the small crowd that was surrounding the ship.

Lamar's pistols joined Simeon's revolvers, but neither of them could see what they were aiming at without lowering their heads through the open portal, exposing themselves to danger.

CLEMENTINE

Someone at the edge of the festering crowd was hollering, "Stop shooting! Stop shooting! There's enough hydrogen here to blow this city off the goddamned map!"

And some people were listening. Some guns were sliding back into holsters, or being held silent in hands that were aimed at the bottom of the black-hulled *Valkyrie* with its sharp silver lettering. But others were caught up in the fright and noise of the moment, and the two men holed up inside the craft were aware that the advantage was partly theirs.

They were shooting blind, and wild, but they were firing from within a heavily armed craft. Even if another ship were to explode beside them, there was an excellent chance that they'd survive to pirate again another day; but the men outside were standing amid vessels that were not so heavily reinforced. The other vehicles were cargo vessels, moving foodstuffs and commercial goods, and none of them featured *Valkyrie*'s armoring.

One stray bullet, aimed unwisely, could detonate a ship—causing a chain reaction that might not blow Kansas City off the map, but could leave one side of town sitting in a smoking crater, all the same.

If the facts had been any different, the crowd might've rushed the ship or fired more readily—and the two men inside could not have held it. But Hainey saw the scene for what it was, and he knew that even with such an advantage, his men couldn't keep the other men at bay for long.

This also meant that he shouldn't rev up the Rattler, really, but that didn't stop him.

He braced himself, spreading his feet apart and using one hand to balance the weapon while the other hand pumped the crank until the six-cylindered gun began to whir—and then he let out a battle roar that would've done an Amazonian proud. He bellowed at the top of his lungs, sending the shout soaring over the gunfire and through the service yards, creating one precious instant of distraction to buy his men more time to secure themselves.

Because the fact was, he didn't want to fire the Rattler for the very same reason that the rest of the reasonable crowd-members had holstered their firearms. The hydrogen was everywhere, and the Rattler was exceptionally difficult to aim when he carried it alone.

A moment of stillness fell as all eyes landed on the captain.

He was a frightful sight. Six feet even and broad as a Clydesdale, scarred, straining, pumping, and flushed with rage—with a two hundred pound gun humming and spinning its massive wheels beside his head, only inches away from his ear.

Everyone was frozen. He'd confused them, and no one yet understood that he planned to make for the *Valkyrie*.

Except for Simeon and Lamar.

They both understood, and their arms and wrists and guns retreated slowly back inside the craft while the attention had been drawn to the captain…who then, aiming the Rattler low enough that it would mostly strafe the ground, flipped the switch that allowed the machine to open fire.

The Rattler kicked dozens of shots a minute into the dust, into the crowd, into the air when even Hainey was startled by its volume and power and he lurched—almost losing control, and regaining it enough to keep turning the crank. He teetered and leaned, firing as if his arm was automatic too—as if his elbow were a piston.

The crowd broke under the onslaught. Half a dozen men went down, and were maybe dead on the spot. The rest ran like hell, except for a few security men who huddled in a pack and made a point to draw. Hainey swept the Rattler to spray them, since they posed the most imminent threat; his shoulders lurched and leaned as the gun's kick pounded against his balance.

If he didn't start moving, and moving swiftly, he'd never be able to hold the Rattler upright more than another few seconds.

His scar-crossed cheek was scalded by the friction and firearm heat, and his wool coat smelled of burning where his arm held the gun into position. He staggered forward, struggling to plant one foot in front of the other and then he hobbled, forward, not fast but steady; and he quit turning the crank—letting the last of the wheel's inertia throw out another six shots, but otherwise abandoning the lever. It was too much to concentrate on, operating the gun, and holding the gun, and keeping the gun from hitting anything that might explode…while lurching forward under its considerable weight.

Upon nearing the folding steps of the Union warbird, he pivoted on his hip with a heave and assumed a defensive position—aiming the amazing gun out at the crowd, as what was left of it warily circled, understanding now that Hainey was one of the thieves, hell-bent on taking the ship.

Above and behind the captain, Lamar's voice hissed out. "Sir, give me cover to close that hatch, or we might never make it out of this lot," he said.

Hainey's ears were ringing so loudly that he heard only part of it, but he got the gist and reached again for the Rattler's crank. He turned it, and flipped the switch to feed the last of his ammo into the gun, and it exploded out from under the ship with a *rat-a-tat-tat* to wake the dead.

Lamar leaped over the steps, landing with a grunt and a slide on the ground beneath it; he recovered immediately, and took a mallet to the pried-apart rivets that affixed the panel into place. Soon the hatch was sealed and he was back up onto the steps, saying, "Sir, stop firing and hop inside. Simeon's got the stair lever and we'll seal ourselves up. Do it fast," he begged.

Hainey tried to say something back, but he didn't think he could make himself heard so he gave up, quit firing, and almost fell backwards on the steps—his weary muscles collapsing under the gun.

Simeon caught it in time to keep it from crushing the captain or knocking him back down into the service yard unarmed; but he yelped when his hands touched some overheated part and the sizzle of burning skin and hair made the cargo hold smell like a charnel house. Lamar helped the captain lift himself up the last few steps, and no sooner had the stairs retreated and the bay doors closed than a trickle of bullets came fired afresh at the hull.

They pinged as if they were being shot at a very big bell.

"Sir, are you all right?" Lamar demanded.

To which Simeon said, "I've burned my hand!"

"And I never call you 'sir,' now do I?" the engineer said as he patted down a place on Hainey's jacket where an ember was glowing, eating its round, black way through the fabric. "You've set yourself on fire!"

"It's…the…Rattler," he wheezed, hoping he'd heard everything correctly. His ears were banging as if someone was standing behind, smashing cymbals together over and over again. He waggled his head like he could shake the residual sounds out of it, and he climbed to his feet. "Simeon, your hand?"

"I'll survive," the first mate said unhappily, examining the puckering pink of the burn as it tightened and wrinkled across his otherwise coffee-dark skin.

"Find something and wrap it up. We've got to fly this thing, we've got to fly her out of here, before those idiots out there breach the hull, or blow up our neighboring ships—or scare up some help. If we can get airborne now, we can shake or bully our way past the security dirigibles…if they've even got the balls to chase us," he added as he stumbled into the bridge, leaving the Rattler lying steaming on the cargo hold floor.

"Way ahead of you," Simeon said. He'd already opened one of the packs that Hainey had thrown aboard, and taken out his only clean shirt. Using his teeth and his one good hand, he tore off the sleeve and began to bind himself. Lamar helped him hold it, and tied off the makeshift bandage.

"This bird is loaded up to the gills, ain't she?" the captain asked with wonder.

After they'd braced the bay doors from the interior, Simeon and Lamar joined him on the main deck, looking out through the windshield where the sheriff and a pair of deputies were joining the fray down front.

"She sure is," Simeon agreed. "Between the three of us, I think we can fly her all right," he said.

"We'd better be able to, or else our goose is cooked," Hainey observed.

Then, from behind a door that no one yet had opened, came a strangely calm voice—the kind of voice that's holding a deadly weapon, and is fully aware of how it ought to perform.

"Your goose is cooked regardless, Croggon Hainey."

All three men turned and were stunned to see her there, standing on the bridge with a six-shooter half as long as her forearm—but there she was, Maria Isabella Boyd, Confederate spy and operative for the Pinkerton National Detective Agency.

The captain recovered fastest. He let the unscarred side of his mouth creep up in something like a slow smile, and he said to her, "Lady, mine and yours, and everybody within a half-mile of this bird…if you don't put that thing down."

She ignored the warning. "Disarm yourselves. Immediately. All of you, or I'll shoot."

Hainey held out a hand that forbade his crewmembers to do any such thing. He said, "If you shoot, we're all dead. You don't know the first thing about these ships, do you?"

Maria faltered, but not much, and not for long. "Maybe not, but I know plenty about what happens to a man when a bullet sticks between his ribs, and if you don't want the knowledge firsthand yourself, you'd better set your weapons aside."

"You see," he said as if he hadn't heard her, "we're surrounded by hydrogen—three quarters of this craft is designed to hold it, and this bird is all full up right now. Do you know what happens when you start firing bullets around hydrogen?"

He could see by her eyes that she could guess, but she was unconvinced. "Those men outside have been firing at you for fully five minutes now. Nothing has exploded *yet*."

"This is a *warbird*, lady. It's armored on the outside, to the hilt. Inside, everything is exposed—there's not much to protect the interior from the tanks, because ordinarily, the people who hang around in the bridge know better than to yank out their guns and make threats. And did you notice," he added, because the clouds that covered her face were unhappy with understanding, "how careful they were? All those men down there—all those guns. Between them, they didn't fire twenty shots total. Do you know why?"

She hesitated, then said slowly, "The other dirigibles."

"That's right," he confirmed. "The other dirigibles. No armor. Not like this bird." He kicked at the floor, which rang metallically under his feet. "One bullet and they could be blown sky-high."

"What about that…that…" a word dawned on her, and she used it. "That Rattler? You could've set off a chain reaction, killed hundreds of people instead of merely the ten or twenty you've otherwise dispatched."

He shrugged. "I was lucky, and they weren't. And my men were all right, inside this bird. Even if the yard blew sky-high around it, and this bird took enough damage that it'd never fly again…they'd have made it out alive. And now that I can tell, just by looking at you, that you have a fair understanding of our mutual peril, it looks like we're at a bit of an impasse."

"We're at no impasse. You're going to disarm and I'm going to hand you over to…to the authorities," she argued.

The captain sneered. "And which authorities might those be? Your old Rebs? I heard they threw you away. You want to barter me," he said. "You want to bring them the last of the Macon Madmen, that's it, isn't it? Well. I'll let you send the lot of us to hell before I'll let you do that." He pulled his small firearm from the holster around his hips, and he aimed it right back at her.

"You're a madman, sure enough," she breathed, but she didn't sound particularly frightened.

"I believe we established that."

"I don't want to kill you, or your crew, or anyone else down there. And I'd prefer not to die today, if I can arrange for it." But she didn't lower her gun, and the barrel didn't display even the faintest quiver of uncertainty. She was buying herself time to think, that was all.

"Then we've got ourselves a problem," Hainey told her. "What would you like for us to do? Open the bay door and let you go back down? You think they'd let a lady leave, just like that—or do you think that the moment we crack the door they're going to fire up inside this thing just as fast as can be?"

"But you said…the hydrogen…"

"Look at them out there," he told her, using his gun to briefly point at the windshield, and the sheriff, and the deputies, and the reassembled gathering that was picking up the wounded and the dead, and hauling them away. "They're losing their reason. You know what that is, out there? I bet you don't, Belle Boyd, but I do, as plain as I know you're too smart to shoot. That out there…that's not a crowd."

"It's not?"

"No. It's a *mob*. And it doesn't have half the brains of two men together, and they are going to kill anybody who tries to come out of this bird, lickity-split. So here's what's going to happen now," he said, and he changed his mind, and put the gun back in its holster instead of pointing it at the woman in the doorway. "Me and my men are going to lift this *Valkyrie* up, fly her off, and if you don't make any trouble for us, maybe we'll set you down safe."

"How chivalrous of you."

"We're gentlemen through and through, we are."

"I don't believe you," she said. Her gun didn't believe them either.

Outside, hands and hammers were beating against the *Valkyrie*'s hull, hoping to pull it apart a piece at a time if it couldn't be breached. Hainey heard this, even through the buzzing in his ears, and he said to the spy, "Call it professional courtesy if you want, or merely my personal desire to surprise you. But if we don't move this ship somewhere else, and fast, not a one of us is walking away from it. Do you understand me?"

He nodded his head at Simeon, then at Lamar, who cautiously stepped away from him and went to the consoles where they might best make themselves useful. Hainey said, "Keep your gun out if you want, I don't give a damn."

"You don't?"

"No, I don't. Because now you know you'll die down here with us, if you don't let us fly. And once we're in the air, you'll die if you cut down any given one of us. So keep your gun out, lady, if that's what makes you feel better. Leave it out, and leave it pointed at me, if you please. I don't mind it, but I think it makes my crewmen nervous—and nervous crewmen can't steer worth a *damn*."

OUR PLAYERS ARE COMPELLED TO COLLABORATE
8

Hainey swung himself into the captain's chair and snarled when a hail of bullets struck the windshield—chipping it here and nicking it there, but barely scratching the foot-thick swath of polished glass. He found the thruster pedal and pumped it with his foot while his hand searched all the logical spots for a starter switch. His fingers fumbled across the console, feeling into the nooks and slots where such switches tended to be located, and finally he found a red lever so he pulled it, and the burners fired at top power, and top volume.

Behind the dirigible someone who had been standing too close to the engine mounts screamed and probably died as the craft howled violently to life.

CLEMENTINE

Simeon adjusted himself in the first mate's chair and reached overhead for the steering and undocking levers; he tested the former and yanked hard on the latter, and somewhere beyond their hearing a hydraulic clasp unfastened and began to retreat into the body of the ship.

Lamar busied himself by bounding back and forth between two secondary crewmen's chairs, adjusting settings and turning dials, and the captain asked him, "We ready to fly?" to which the engineer said, "As ready as we're going to get." And he cast Maria Boyd an anxious glance.

She held her position by the crew quarters door, but her gun was at her side now and she caught him looking at her; she met his stare without a waver. But no one had time to stare, really. On the *Valkyrie*'s underbelly men were taking kerosene torches to task, trying to find a place to cut where the metal would split enough to do damage. And the hammers were joined by crowbars, and by pipes, and by anything else hard and reckless, and the sound against the hull was like hail.

Maria said, "They really will kill us all, won't they?"

And Hainey replied without taking his eyes off the console, "Sure enough. They'll never give you the five minutes you'd need to explain yourself; they'll pull you out of the bird and pound you flat, just for being inside it in the first place. Now take yourself a seat."

"Is that an order, Captain?"

He said, "It's a suggestion you'd be wise to heed. We've never flown a bird this big before, and it might get rough."

"You're asking me to trust you enough to quit holding you at gunpoint."

Before Lamar had time to point out that she'd already lowered her weapon, the captain said, "No, I'm asking you to trust that we're too busy to pay you any attention."

With the back of his hand, he swiped at three parallel switches and the howling hum of the engines leaped to a keening pitch. "Here we go," he announced.

Behind him, Maria slipped into a seat beside the nearest glass gun turret and reached over her head, pulling the safety straps across her chest. "I hope you know what you're doing," she said.

"Don't worry about us," Simeon said to her. He rubbed his injured hand against the top of his thigh and reached with his good one for a row of buttons. "And don't interfere with anything we're doing, you understand?" he demanded, and in his haste, pain, or excitement, his island accent was more pronounced than it often sounded.

"I'll stay out of the way," she swore.

"And be *quiet*," the first mate added. Then he said to the captain, "Steering checks out."

Lamar said, "Thrusters and primary weapon systems check out. Engines are at full power. Throw the arm and let's lift her up, Captain."

"Here goes the arm," Hainey declared as he pulled on a floor-mounted lever, drawing it towards his chest with all the smoothness he could muster and all the speed the ship could handle. Fuel coursed to the engines and the thrusters beneath the ship rotated in their slots, aiming at the ground and pushing away from it—nudging the Union warbird into the air with a hop that was cleaner than anyone had expected.

"Nice," Simeon said.

"Thanks, and tell me how the steering paddles are holding."

"Holding fine. You going to turn her on the way up?"

"Hard to port," the captain told them. "We need to get our backside to the south end of the service docks; the security detail launches from the north end," he explained, and as the ship rose it crested the last of the other dirigibles until it alone had a clear view of the clouds. "Keep us steady," the captain said as he manned the prime steering paddles and the ship began a rotation that could've too easily toppled into a spin; but Simeon worked the fine steering and the ship stopped where the crew meant for it to—only to bring new trouble into the windscreen.

CLEMENTINE

Lamar called it. "Two security detail flyers. Eleven and one o'clock. Sir, I think they're—"

A spray of bullets grazed the *Valkyrie*'s lower cargo hold.

Hainey said, "Loaded. They're loaded with birdshot, damn them all to hell."

"Not enough to crack this egg," Simeon said with less than his usual easy confidence.

"They're rising fast. They'll be on our flight level in half a minute or less," Lamar warned. "Then their aim'll be better. We've got to get out of their way; we don't know how much shot they're carrying."

"Those are little birds," Simeon insisted, though it was unclear who he meant to convince. "They can't be carrying too much on board. They're just security flyers; they're meant to scare folks off, not shoot them down."

But another rain of shot peppered the craft, higher on the hull as the other ships crested the service yard docks and neared the *Valkyrie*'s altitude. The captain observed, "They don't have the swivel turrets like this one does. They can't hit us unless they keep our altitude."

"They've got some wiggle room," Lamar argued. "There's no telling how much. Higher, let's get us higher; let's hit some real thin air and then outrun them."

"Heavy as this thing is?" Simeon groused. "We'll do well to stay above them. It'd be one thing if we could return fire, but we barely have enough manpower to fly as it is. What's the normal crew on this thing, anyway?" he asked Lamar.

The engineer answered, "Six, as a skeleton. Maybe we can bash 'em. The *Valkyrie* can take it, and I bet those fellows can't."

Hainey said, "They're only chasing us because they know we ain't got enough men to fight 'em off properly." He drew harder on the lever and the ship continued to rise, and with Simeon's contribution from the thrusters it began to warm up to an eastern course.

"Where are you pointing us?" Hainey asked.

"Past town. But we've got to shake these things or knock 'em out of the sky. If they chase us too far we'll only have unwanted company, wherever we arrive."

From her seat near the glass gun turret Maria Boyd asked, "Where are we going? If you don't mind my asking."

"After my ship!" Hainey almost yelped as more gunfire strafed the ship, higher, and a couple of bullets went cracking against the windshield. Unlike the smaller bullets used on the ground, these were designed to break even the thickest glass, and even the hardest armor. Whether or not they could split the *Valkyrie* remained to be seen, but no one wanted to find out, so the captain drew the ship around.

"They're only going to summon more help if we keep hovering here," Lamar said.

Simeon shouted, "We ain't hovering! We're moving, just…we're moving. Jesus, this thing is a cast-iron tank of a bastard. It's none too easy to swing, I swear to God."

"But she spins all right," Hainey observed. "Let's try this then, back us up."

The first mate asked, "What?"

And the captain reiterated, "Back us up! Thrusters reverse, let's retreat and make like a spinning top. We'll charge them with a little backspin and knock them down, maybe. It won't hurt us, no-how."

"You're truly daft," Maria said, but no one answered her.

"All men buckle down," Hainey ordered as he used his elbow to whack a steering paddle into place enough to make the ship spiral. "Simeon, kick that stabilizer—pump it, don't hold it in place. We want to keep spinning, and cast ourselves at them like a knuckleball."

Centrifugal force was straining the interior, and the men and woman who struggled to hold themselves upright in their seats. Lamar's hands flew over the valves and buttons, and Simeon dutifully pumped the stabilizers to pitch the craft forward—on a course directly between the two smaller ships.

"We're bowling for birds!" the captain said almost gleefully, then added, "Impact in ten, nine, eight…hang on everybody…six…oh shit, I might be off a count or two—"

They collided, but just barely between the two security birds—winging the one and knocking the other hard enough to rock it out of its altitude. The crash was loud and the squeal of metal on metal was hard to listen to; but smoke puffed from the right side engine of the one o'clock ship, and it careened in a crazy, sinking pattern, headed back down to earth.

"We didn't get the both of them!" Maria said.

The captain said, "I know it, and I thought I told you to be quiet!"

"No," she corrected him. "It was your first mate. But I'll add that to your pile of suggestions."

"Woman! Don't you antagonize me! Can't you see we're busy?"

Lamar swallowed hard and said, "We're about to get busier. Two more dirigibles—one official security detail, it looks like…and one…sir, it looks like a Union cruiser."

"Goddamn," the captain said. He gritted his teeth while he wrestled with the knobs to steady the craft, and drag it out of its spinning whirl. Then he said, "We might have to make a run for it. Those security tweeters can't be holding much live freight, but a cruiser…we don't know. If we had another three or four men handy, that'd be one thing. Lamar, you said the primary weapons systems were all working?"

"That's right. Nothing wrong with any of them, and the secondaries are probably fine too—but we don't have time to figure out how to work them, and anyway, it's just the three of us."

"Four of us," Maria said from her seat.

"I beg your pardon?" Hainey asked, finally turning around to see what she was doing.

She was unbuckling herself.

"Four of us. You don't have another three or four men, but you've got an able-bodied woman on board, and I've fired more kinds of guns in my day than most men have ever held."

"You've lost your ever-loving mind," Simeon swore at her, and said, "Get back down in your chair. Ain't nobody here trusts you with a fire-arm, much less with a gun turret, you crazy woman."

"She can shoot," Hainey said. "I've heard about her. I know she can shoot."

"Yes, she can shoot," Maria said impatiently. "And she wants to get far enough out of town for you to set her down, so we can have a civilized conversation about how I'm bringing you home for justice's sake—but she can't very well do that if she dies up here in the clouds, now can she?"

Simeon almost laughed. He said, "Hey, Captain, she wants to save our hides so she can tan them later. What do you think of that?"

"I think we're desperate and she wants to live long enough to have that conversation. Lamar?"

"Yes sir?"

"Which turret has the best range?"

"Sir, you can't be serious?"

"He's serious," Maria answered for him. "Put me where I can make the most trouble."

"Sir, the bottom left turret probably has the best range. The right one is pinned so it can't take out the right engine, and it has less room to swivel. The left one's mounted lower, so it won't clip our own armor when it fires."

"Then show her how it works. You know how it works, don't you man?" Hainey was still lifting the ship, drawing it higher and higher, up into the sky, doing his best to show the intruders nothing but the underside of the craft.

"I know how it works," he said, lifting himself out of the seat and with great trepidation, gesturing to Maria Boyd. "This way, over here. Down in the cargo bay."

Simeon's voice rose in disbelief. "You're going to put that woman behind a powerful gun, someplace where you can't even see her?"

"Any port in a storm, isn't that what they say?" the captain responded. "She can't shoot us from down there, anyway. She could've shot us better from her seat by the right turret."

"Point taken," Simeon said, but it was said with complaint.

Down the cargo stairs and over by the bottom left turret, Lamar stood beside Maria Boyd and hemmed uncertainly. "Ma'am," he said, "I don't know about this. You'll hardly fit, wearing that."

"Well I'm not going to strip, so I'll have to fit. Is this a Gatling? A four-eighty model, with the automatic line feed? They must've modified it for air use. I've seen them on the ground, and been behind one—once or twice."

Lamar's brows knitted together to form a very puzzled V. "Yes...yes ma'am? I believe so? If it's not a four-eighty, it's a four-ninety—and they work pretty much the same way. So you...you know what to do with it?"

"I know what to do with it. One thing: Do you have a mask down here? Something to keep the heat off my face and the powder out of my eyes? I can operate one of these things just fine, but they make my eyes water like mad."

Lamar nodded. "There's a line of them, hanging around the corner. I'll get you one," he said, and he dashed to the row of pegs along the cargo wall. He grabbed the nearest mask as well as the gloves that were stuffed inside it, and he ran back to the low glass turret, where Maria Boyd had somehow managed to cram her entire bulk of skirts and corsetry into the chamber—but beside the chamber was a stack of undergarments.

The engineer handed her the mask while staring at the petticoats.

"I know I said I wasn't going to strip, but I had to make room, you understand."

"Yes ma'am," he said, and if Maria Boyd had known him any better, she would've gathered that he was blushing.

Hainey hollered from the bridge. "Can you see all right down there?"

"Give me a moment!" she cried back.

"We don't have a moment!"

"I'm getting my mask on!" she told him. "Now, all right. I'm ready and yes, I can see. Three o'clock, six o'clock, and...and I can't see the third ship!"

"He's in front of us, working up to playing chicken!" Hainey called. "Lamar, get yourself back here! We need you at your station."

"Coming sir!"

"And woman, you can hear me all right?"

"If you yell, I can hear you!" But when she turned the crank and turned the switch to start the gun revving, she wasn't sure she'd continue to communicate so easily. Inside the glass bubble, suspended over the earth, Maria tried not to gaze down too long or too hard at the shrinking service yard docks, or the tiny blocks of Kansas City that were dropping away underneath her. It made her dizzy and almost nauseous, though she wouldn't have confessed it if her life had depended on it.

She stuffed her hands into the gloves and they were far too big, but they'd keep the gun from burning her. The bottom of the glass ball vibrated with the gun's power as it cranked, rolled, and hummed in its slot.

She took a deep breath, pointed the gun as best she could, and opened fire.

The kick thrust her hands back, jerking at her elbows and shoulders and beating them in her joints; but she held the thing steady and pushed her weight against it—holding its aim true and correct, and splitting the gas dome of the second security detail ship.

The craft exploded into a fireball so fast and hot that it flashed like a magician's trick, no sooner burning than falling, and no sooner alight than dropping in a gyre's course, like a soap bubble circling the drain.

But that was the easy one.

The second ship, the Union cruiser, was gaining ground fast from the other direction, not quite meeting the *Valkyrie*'s altitude but matching its pace—and soon, it would be out of her gun's range. The gun's cylindrical barrel purred as it spun, waiting for the directive to shoot; but Maria didn't know how much ammunition she had, and she didn't want to waste it so she waited until the cruiser was right in her crosshairs before squeezing off another brutal spray.

The cruiser wouldn't go down, not like the little security craft. Its armor plating wasn't as dense and reliable as the *Valkyrie*'s outer hull; but the cruiser was lighter and more maneuverable, and it could take a bigger beating than anything else anywhere near them. It rocked under the assault of Maria's firepower but it didn't crack, split or fall out of the sky.

She scanned the thing for a weak point, but as she'd already confessed, she didn't know anything about dirigibles so she shouted over the whirring rumble of the churning barrels, "Captain!"

"What?"

"What do I aim for?"

He yelled back, "Aim for the goddamned ship!"

"Be more specific! Does it have a weak spot?"

There was a pause. Then he yelled, "You won't take their tanks; they're covered up good. Crack for the engines, down underneath!"

"Got it!" she said, and she used her body's weight to crank the gun around, back at the cruiser, which was winding itself up for a direct assault.

"Good! Now hang on—we're going to have to ram that last little bastard! Keep shooting for the cruiser! Keep it off our tail so we can clear the other one out of the sky! It's staying up too high for you to hit it from down there!"

She didn't respond but she felt the surge of the ship taking some new path, coiling itself up again, building the inertia to crash the smaller craft down to earth, and back behind them. The underside ball turret teetered up, giving her a few seconds of a breathtaking stomach drop and a clear shot at the cruiser, so she took it—she shifted her weight and kicked the gun crossways with her knees, changing the aim to shoot for the cruiser's protruding engines. They were mounted on its underside, thrusters that steered and powered the forward motion of the machine; and in front of those powerful machines, automatic guns were mounted on pivoting arms.

The cruiser's guns cranked, twisted, and fired at the *Valkyrie*, and the *Valkyrie* shook off the shots with a grumpy spin and a dip, but then recovered. The pursuing ship unleashed another set of rapid-fire rounds, determined to force the bird back down to earth.

One of the birdshot rounds punched hard against the reinforced glass of the ball turret, striking to Maria's left with a concussion that made her ears ring and her head pound. When her vision had cleared she wiggled the gun back and forth, making sure it was still solidly affixed; and then she spied the long chip and fine line of a split that was creaking its way along the glass. The round hadn't penetrated, but it had broken the small dome and God only knew how much longer it'd hold.

But Maria had another good shot, and she took it.

She rocked the active switch and crushed her hands around the oversized triggers, throwing another dozen slugs at the cruiser—this time aiming lower. Though the gun was almost impossible to guide with any finesse, she did her damnedest and the gun responded better than she had any right to expect. The arc of the bullets dipped and cut a punctured line along the lower hull of the cruiser, and one of the last slugs clipped the bottom left thruster—lodging inside it, perhaps, or maybe only blasting through it.

The thruster sparked and smoked, but didn't fail altogether…and she couldn't tell if any real damage had been done because at that moment, the *Valkyrie* collided head-on with the second smaller vessel, and the sound of an explosion shook the bird hard from the far side, relative to Maria's captive position in the ball turret.

She clung to the gun though the heat of it warmed her too much through her clothes and through the big gloves that flopped around on her fingers. The split on the glass stretched—she watched it widen like a smile, and she held her breath.

CLEMENTINE

The weight of the automatic gun and the weight of the glass itself, not to mention the weight of Maria's body suspended there, thighs clenched around a narrow seat meant for a man…how much would the wounded bubble hold? She closed her eyes and waited for the *Valkyrie* to settle, and as the ship rolled she saw the other small ship toppling down to earth in a widening ball of fire that drew a comet's tail of soot and sparks down through the sky.

Had there been another ship? She couldn't remember.

Too many things to keep track of at once.

But the cruiser was still there, hovering—she could see it again when the *Valkyrie* swung itself around, pulling out of the spin and righting itself. The cruiser was blowing smoke, but not very much of it. She'd nicked something important but it wasn't enough to slow their pursuer so she rounded the gun again and, praying she had enough ammunition to keep the threat coming, she clamped down on the triggers and blew more air-to-air birdshot slugs into the clouds.

The cruiser fired back, but it leaned backwards and the shots went too high to do more than graze the edge of the *Valkyrie*'s hull.

Along the glass the crack's smile stretched all the longer, and now it was accompanied by the sickening, deep tinkle of ice that won't hold for more than another few minutes.

"Captain!" she shouted.

"What now?"

"I have to…" The ball shifted and Maria's seat dropped half an inch that nearly stopped her heart. She released her grip on the gun and scrambled backward, off the seat and in hurried retreat until she had one leather-booted foot on the edge.

A whistling hiss joined the slow shatter; air was entering from some-where, and it was colder than ordinary winter. It smelled like water.

"Oh Jesus," she swore as she got one hand up over the edge, but the gloves she wore were meant for a man more than twice her size and she lost her grip; she relaxed her fingers, swung her hand, and the gloves flew off, then she grabbed again at the edge and found it. She was suspended that way, using the width and breadth of her reach to hoist herself above the glass ball with the rocking gun, and the glass ball was breaking beneath her. Hinges were stretching with unfamiliar unevenness and the pressure of the craft's motion was tugging the turret apart.

The cruiser reared into view, once more, and much closer. It was coming in fast and high—its underbelly exposed, its lower engines and thrusters a target almost too sweet to resist. But the glass was splitting and the gun, which was mounted on a set of tracks, was drooping as the structure failed.

She braced her feet, pinning them against the curved rim of the glass bowl; she released one hand's worth of grip, and when she put her fingertips on the back end of the gun's firing mechanism, it was so frigid that she nearly stuck to it. The air that seeped and squirted into the ball and up against Maria's face was bitterly cold but she worked against it, straining to feel her way up to the trigger paddle even from her precarious position.

The cruiser wouldn't hold its position long, but she couldn't hold her position long either and it was a war of time between her muscles, the glass ball turret, and the cruiser's path.

With the cold air came cold water, condensing and freezing, and Maria's buttressing hand slid. She grappled for her handhold and lost it, and was an instant shy of toppling down onto the increasingly fragile surface below her when an enormous black hand seized her scrambling fingers.

She whipped her head around to see Croggon Hainey, feet planted apart, and shortly with both hands wrapped around her wrist.

"Woman, are you mad?" he demanded.

She said, "Yes! Or no! Or look—" and she pointed at the cruiser with its upturned belly. "I can take it down!"

"That ball turret is going to go, any second!"

"No!" she shouted at him, and struggled to dip herself down, letting him hold most of her weight. "This is my life at stake here too, you've made it more than clear you bastard, so let me help us survive!"

The length of his arms gave her a few precious extra inches to lean, and when she touched the trigger paddle she jerked herself forward to seize it, and squeeze with all her might.

A spray of half a dozen bullets went soaring through a low-flying cloud, into the underside of the Yankee cruiser and straight through its already-wounded thruster. Three new sets of smoke and sparks burst to life and she cheered, "See! I told you!"

But the pressure of the gun's kickback was too much for the glass, and it split.

And it fell, out from underneath her.

Just like that, the sky was a sucking thing, blowing ice up her skirt and against her skin, and beneath her the ground was amazingly far away. She held her breath because she could not breathe, and she swung her legs because she lacked the strength to do anything else. Wisps of cloud billowed past her, screamed between her legs, and lashed at her arms, but she did not fall.

She spun like a ballerina in a music box, suspended from the vise of the captain's hands.

OUR PLAYERS COME TO AN AGREEMENT
9

Hainey hoisted Maria with a jerk and a backwards stumble that drew her up out of the hole left by the former glass ball turret; and although the sucking vortex left by the circular absence roared with broken, swirling wind, they were safely away from its reach. For a few seconds, Maria lay panting on the metal floor—and then she sat up, letting the wild, intruding air flay her hair to pieces.

She said, "Oh no. My underthings."

"Your what?"

"My…never mind." She leaned forward just enough to see over the edge just a little bit, and she spied the undergarments floating happily down to Missouri. "Are we safe? Did we get them all?"

The captain stood up, swung his head slowly back and forth, and backed away—urging her to do likewise. He said, "You got the last of them. Goddamn, woman. You almost got yourself killed."

"Well, I didn't. And…well, I think it's only clear and honest to point out, I owe that to you." She rubbed at her wrists, where the red marks of his grasp were flushing into a pattern of hands. "Why did you do that? You could've let me fall. Maybe you should have. It might've been more convenient for you to do so."

He stared down into the hole and told her, "Just reflex, I guess. It's not every day I see a half-dressed woman falling out of a ball turret." He turned to climb the three or four steps up into the bridge, and she rose to follow behind him. Over his shoulder he added, "And anyway, you took down the cruiser."

Once they were away from the whistling void, Maria didn't have to shout when she said, "I didn't have much choice. I thought we'd worked that out."

Again, without looking at her, he said, "Maybe. But I don't know too many men who'd have reached for that last shot."

On the bridge, he pointed at her previous seat and said, "Buckle yourself in."

Lamar had been closest to the cargo hold, so he was the one who asked, "Sir, what happened back there? What's that noise?"

"We lost the left ball turret," he answered, but didn't tell him more. "I don't know what kind of disturbance it'll make in the steering, but if you find this bird pulling or bucking, it's a big hole and we don't have any good way to cover it right this moment, so we're going to live with it."

"It's tugging back and down a little, but not too bad. We can live with it, sure. Maybe when we stop we can shove a crate over it or something," Simeon proposed, trying very hard not to watch Maria with one eye.

"If we can find one big enough," Hainey said. "But for now, we've got to…" he rubbed wearily at his forehead. "God Almighty."

Simeon asked, "Captain?"

And Lamar gazed up expectantly.

"We've got to…" he tried again. "Christ knows how far ahead of us they are. We've given them a devil of a head start, but at least we know where they're headed. So here's what I want to do—I want to head north a bit, out over godforsaken noplace; we'll check through the cargo and see if there's anything we want; and if there's anything we don't want, we're going to pitch it. We need to lighten this thing, because we can maybe catch up to them before they reach Louisville."

"Wait a minute, wait a minute." Maria was out of her seat again.

Without any malice or even impatience, Hainey said, "*You* wait a minute, woman. Simeon, take us north a few miles and maybe even lean us west since they think we've been going east; get us outside Kansas City's airspace, and if you can find a low cloud to hide us in, so much the better."

"The sky's clear as a bell; I wouldn't give us good odds on that one."

"Then keep your eyes open for anything big enough to cover this thing for half an hour. We won't have any longer than that to get ourselves together before we have to make a run for it. And of course, we've got a lady passenger to debark. You can walk a couple of miles back to town, can't you?"

"Captain," Maria was standing beside him, and when he turned, she was right under his nose. Then she asked with some doubt, "This ship was going to Louisville before you commandeered it. Wasn't it?"

His forehead wrinkled. "*This* ship? I don't know where it was going. But within an hour it's going to be headed to Louisville as fast as its hydrogen can carry it. Why did you think the *Valkyrie* was Kentucky-bound?"

She didn't answer his question, but she asked him another one. "Why are *you* Kentucky-bound? Why the eastward course? You know as well as I do that south and east is not the safest direction you could choose. So tell me, please. Why are you chasing the *Clementine?* What's on board that you want so badly?"

"Not a goddamned thing," he told her. "I don't want anything that ship's carrying. I want the ship itself, because it's mine."

"Yours?"

The motion of the *Valkyrie*'s new course made the floor under their feet swing slightly, and they both swayed as they spoke. "Yes," he said. "It's mine. I stole it fair and square, years ago, and I want it back."

She looked frankly puzzled, and she admitted as much. "I'm not sure I understand. It's only a ship, and as I understand it, it's not half as nice as this one. You've got this one now; why not turn around, call off the chase, and call it a day?"

He nearly bellowed. "Because I don't *want* this one!" He kept the volume up when he continued, "And now, since we're both feeling so chatty—why did Pinkerton send you after us? Who paid them to do it, and why?"

"The Union Army," she said. "And now you likely know more about the situation than I do. I'll admit, I got a bit sidetracked from my initial task. Look, I had no idea you had any interest in this ship whatsoever until I heard your men aboard it. As far as I knew, it was transporting some kind of supplies to a sanatorium in Louisville, though the sanatorium is actually a front for a weapons laboratory."

With a puzzled expression that mirrored Maria's, Hainey said, "Then there's been a mix-up in your telegrams. Because it's *my* former ship that's making the weapons run, not this shiny black bird. The *Valkyrie* was on her way to New York City—she's going to be fitted with a new ball turret." He quickly clarified, "They were going to stick one on top, up front I suppose. Though now, if it ever makes it that far north and east I guess they'll have to fix the bottom left one first."

CLEMENTINE

Following another moment of mutual uncertainty, their faces both went crafty.

Hainey said, "You fellows keep her flying straight, and when you think she's safely over nothing at all, pull us to a stop and hover. Me and Maria Boyd here are going to dig around in the cargo hold and see what we can find."

Simeon and Lamar shrugged at each other, and Simeon's eyebrow pointed a vigorous indication of confusion.

But the runaway slave and the ex-spy retreated to the cargo hold, where the wind from the busted ball turret nearby was loud and the air was even colder than the un-warmed bridge. Hainey rummaged around in the storage locker and turned up a pair of prybars, one of which he tossed to Maria.

He said to her, "I swear on my mother's life, I don't know what's in any damn one of these boxes. So be careful with the bar. God knows what we'll turn up."

"The need for caution is duly noted," she said, and then she said, "I'll start at this end. You start at that end. We'll work our way toward the middle."

He grunted a general agreement and began at the far corner. The captain brought his prybar down into the cracks of the nearest crate's lid, and Maria did likewise on her end of the hold.

One after another, they bashed and pried their way through the stacks, and when they were finished they'd unveiled a vast assortment of wonders. Their haul included four loads of boot polish, a stash of rough-woven linens, enough lye soap to fill a wagon, some dried and smoked fish and pork, an engineer's assortment of bolts, screws, and washers, a tobacco pouch that had probably been dropped by a laborer…and two dead mice.

They also found three crates of ammunition, some of which was strung to fuel the ball turret guns. The rest looked ordinary enough, and when Maria stood over this final crate she said, "This can't possibly be it. This is stocked like a ship that was loaded out of convenience, because it was headed the right direction. There's nothing special or important about any of it."

Hainey nodded. "We'll keep the ammunition and the foodstuffs, and the rest can go overboard when we stop and hang."

"You're not surprised?"

"Surprised about what?"

"That we didn't find anything significant on board?"

He said, "Nope. Because I've already got a real good idea of what the sanatorium's got on order—and what Pinkerton's been paid to protect. That's the point, isn't it? You're supposed to distract us long enough to let the *Clementine* get to Louisville to make this delivery?"

"Pretty much. But in Kansas City I met an old friend, a fellow Confederate who possessed, shall we say, somewhat incorrect information. He told me about a weapon being built, something made to fire on Danville…and…and…old loyalties took precedence," she said defensively.

Hainey said, "Old loyalties. I know what those are like."

"Really? And to whom might you be loyal?"

"Nobody you'd know," he said. "And nothing I care to elaborate upon. None of it matters, because right now we've got an interesting situation between the two of us, don't you think?"

"I beg your pardon? A situation?"

"Yes, a situation," he said grouchily, with a hint of false cheer. "You know about half of what's going on, and I know about half of what's going on, and there are spots where our information…" he hunted for a phrase. "Fails to overlap."

"That seems to be the case, yes." She was half a head shorter than him, and a hundred pounds smaller, but she met his gaze over the contents of the last crate, and she didn't flinch or retreat.

He sounded almost optimistic when he said, "We could work together, you and me. I could tell you some useful things, and you have permission to go to places I'm not allowed."

"You can take me to Louisville."

"I'm headed that direction anyway."

"And I can tell you where your ship is."

He was startled, despite himself. "You can what?"

"It's parked at a transient dock outside the city. It may be gone now, but it was there last I heard, maybe an hour or two ago. I don't think your quarry has quite the lead you think it does."

Hainey turned on his heels, crossed the cargo bay, and leaned himself through the doorway that led to the bridge. "Simeon! Where are the nearest transient docks?"

"Nearest...to here?"

"Nearest to Kansas City!"

The first mate thought about it, then said, "East of here, a little ways. At least, that's where they used to park and set up. Why?"

"Because the *Free Crow*'s there—or she was quite recently. Adjust course!"

Lamar said, "But sir, we're still riding heavy. You going to toss the cargo, or what?"

He said, "Yeah, I'll toss it. Are we over anything or anybody important?"

Simeon said, "No, but we will be soon if we adjust course. So get to dropping sooner, rather than later."

The captain didn't answer except to dash back to the hold and say to Maria, "Give that lever over there a yank!"

She grabbed it with both hands and hauled it down; when it clicked at the bottom part of its track, a set of sliding doors retracted in the floor at the back of the hold. "Are we discarding the cargo now? I thought we were going to go low and hover?"

"Change of plans. We're going east, to the only transient docks my first mate knows. On the way, you and me are going to toss this stuff out of the *Valkyrie*. Sim says we shouldn't hit anything or anybody important for the next few minutes, so give me a hand. Except for what we talked about, grab anything you can move and kick it out, fast as you can."

CHERIE PRIEST

Maria pressed herself between the crate of linens and the wall, and she used her back and legs to shove it out into the middle of the room.

Hainey met her there and ushered her aside; he cast the crate over the lip of the retracted door and let it tumble out, down to the prairie below. Then he reached for the next box, which held part of the soap shipment. He swung it and dragged it over to the edge and this too went freefalling to the dry, brown ground half a mile below.

Maria took the next box of linens and worked them over the edge. She went back for a cache of polish, which was almost more than she could move, but she took it and she wiggled it, and skidded it until it was teetering—and she tipped it overboard.

"Help me with this one," the captain said like it was an order, but Maria was getting the impression that this was simply how he talked.

"Coming," she said, and she joined him.

Side by side, their backs pressed against the metal-stuffed crate of small tools and hardware. This one dug into the paint on the floor but it moved in jerks and inch-long shrugs until finally it too crashed heavily over the lip and into the sky.

"Back to the bridge," the captain said when the last of the expendable boxes had been expended.

Arms aching and back throbbing, Maria tagged behind him and took up her familiar seat. She dropped herself down and reached for the straps that would fasten her into place.

Hainey took up his position with similar haste, asking for a time estimate from his first mate. "How long before the docks are in sight?"

"Five minutes. Ten, at the outside," Simeon said. "But how do we want to approach?"

"Guns blazing," Hainey growled. "We've still got a right-side ball turret and I'll take it up myself, if you two can fly us."

"I'm getting the hang of it, sir," Lamar said helpfully.

The first mate added, "I've found everything I need to steer alone, if I have to. But do you really want to shoot the *Crow* out of the sky?"

"I don't mind doing her a little damage if it helps us get her back. She'll forgive us in the morning; she always *does*."

"What about *her?*" Simeon asked, aiming an eyebrow in Maria's direction.

"What about her? She needs a ride to Louisville, and we're going to give her one. She'll behave herself, I bet. It turns out, we have more in common than we thought. Our goals...overlap," he used that word again. "We want the *Free Crow*, she wants what it's carrying, even if it costs her the shiny new job she's landed."

"That's true," she said from her seat. "And I'll be damned if I even know what the cargo is."

Hainey's bright white grin spread so far that the scar on his cheek crinkled up to his ear. "It's a diamond."

"A diamond?" Maria exclaimed. "All this trouble for a diamond?"

The captain said, "Not just any diamond. An orange diamond the size of a plum. The man who cut the thing called it the 'clementine,' so I guess the boys who stole our ship thought they were being funny when they renamed her."

"I've never even *heard* of a diamond that big. And why do you know this?"

"I've got a friend back west, a fellow captain and a man of fine character. When the *Free Crow* was first boosted out from under us, this friend helped us try to retrieve her."

"That's a good friend indeed," Maria said.

Hainey agreed. "I owe him one. Or two, or ten. And now I owe him double. Down in Tacoma he found a fellow to tell him what my ship is carrying. He sent a telegram to fill me in. That's how I know about the diamond. And now I know why my ship was stolen."

"To transport a diamond?"

"To transport a diamond and a two-thousand-pound corpse. There's an old story that floated around for years, and everyone always thought it was a tall tale—even though every man who ever repeated it swore it was the truth." As he spoke, Hainey gave the throttle a deeper nudge, urging the ship faster, farther, towards the transient docks.

He continued, "There was a certain lady of...leisure. Her name was Conklin, but everyone called her 'Damnable.' She was the richest woman west of the Mississippi and maybe east of it too, for all anybody knows. She had plenty of money, at any rate, and she spent a great wad of it on a diamond found a hundred years ago in India. She wore it set in a necklace, almost all the time."

Lamar piped up. "I heard she shot a dozen men who tried to steal it from her, and one woman too."

The captain said, "It's possible. She was a real piece of work, and when she died, she took the diamond with her. The funeral man dressed her in her finest, hung the diamond around her neck, and filled her coffin with every drop of cement it would hold—just like she asked him to. Then the gravedigger made a hole twice as big as he needed, and once the coffin was lowered down inside, they filled up the hole with cement too, in order to keep out anybody who wanted what she was wearing."

"And no one ever bothered her body?"

"Not until my *Free Crow* was stolen. Not another ship west of the river could've lifted her up, carried her over the mountains, and gotten her into bluegrass country—"

Maria said, "No ship except for yours? She must be nearly as powerful as this one, then."

"Nearly," he said. "But not quite, and this one wasn't anywhere handy—so some bastard Union man paid a bastard pirate named Felton Brink to steal my *Free Crow*, dig up old Madam Damnable, and tote her to Kentucky."

"But I still don't understand," Maria insisted, "what a scientist needs with a diamond."

Hainey held up one finger. "I have a theory about it, and I'll explain it to you just as soon as we address what's…" He sagged. "What's not right over there, at those transient docks. Do you see them?"

She craned her neck to see out the windshield, and then said, "Yes, I see them. I've never seen a set of transient docks before."

"Don't know nothing about dirigibles, don't know nothing about docks. Where you been all your life?" Simeon asked.

"East, mostly. The docks there are all pretty permanent, and the war doesn't allow for much passenger activity. Mostly I've been moving around by train, coach, and carriage. But it's quite a crash course I've gotten lately."

Lamar said, "And she knew about the ball turret gun; she knew how to use it."

The captain explained before Maria could do so. "It's just a modified land model. I expect she's seen them in combat."

"You are correct," she told him. "And I could become accustomed to this flying business. It's all rather exciting."

"It'd be more exciting if the *Free Crow* was still docked there," Hainey very nearly sulked.

Maria asked, "Are there any other transient docks, anywhere around the city? I'm sorry, I wish I could've been more specific. But I didn't know the information would prove valuable, and I didn't press for details."

Simeon answered. "This is the only one I ever heard of. They break it down sometimes if there's trouble, but they usually put it right back up again, right here. If this isn't it, then we could spend another day or two flying around, looking for another one, but I don't think we'd have much luck."

Lamar asked, "So what do we do, then?"

The captain took a deep sigh and straightened his shoulders. He turned his head to give Maria a look that was half promise, and half a nod of conspiracy. "Top speed, as fast as this thing will carry us. We make for Louisville."

The trip was long and the terrain below was an uninspiring rollick of river and hills, and trees peeled bare by the season. Maria gazed out the window and sometimes wondered why no one was following them; and then she'd remember the flaming dirigibles sweeping in their spinning, pendulum-swinging arcs down to make craters in the grasslands of Kansas, and she didn't wonder anymore.

From her seat by the right glass ball turret, Maria Boyd declared, "Captain, you said you had a theory about why a scientist would need a diamond, but you haven't yet explained yourself."

"Begging your pardon, ma'am," he said, and he didn't *completely* sound like he was poking fun at her when he called her "ma'am." "There's this fellow back west, name of Minnericht—or, come to think of it, there *used* to be a fellow named Minnericht. I understand he's dead now, but that's a recent development, so you'll have to pardon me if I misspeak. This Minnericht was an inventor, and he liked to play with weapons. Not long before he shuffled off this mortal coil, he'd been working on a weapon that…it's hard to describe. It cuts things, or burns them, but it uses light."

Maria considered this, nodded, and asked, "Like the way a magnifying glass can start a fire?"

"Like that. Only imagine using something much, much stronger than a little piece of curved glass to focus the sunlight."

"I see what you're getting at," she said. "And if you can use a much more concentrated light, with a much stronger focus than glass, you might…well. You might make something terrible."

Simeon said, "And if it was terrible, you could bet old Minnericht had his fingers in it."

Lamar murmured, "Truer words were never spoken," and he fiddled with a lever that would adjust the hydrogen flow to the compression engine. "But he wasn't a dummy."

"Hell no, he wasn't," the captain agreed. "He was a damned smart son of a gun, but meaner than the good Lord ought to make them. But I tell you that to tell you this: He made a weapon called a solar cannon, and like I heard it, he sold a patent on it to somebody back east. And that was the last I heard of it, except he had a couple early models hanging around inside Seattle. He used to like to sit on the roof of the train station, up in the clock tower, and use it to burn up the rotters like ants on a hill when the weather was clear enough to make it happen."

"Now I'm afraid you've lost me," Maria said.

Hainey looked like he was trying to figure out how best to tell her something else, or something bigger; but in the end he cocked his head quickly, like he was shooing a fly, and said, "It's a longer story that you'd care to hear, I bet. Anyway, the one big drawback to his solar cannon was that it needed the sun, and it needed a lot of it—and up in the northwest, there's not much sun to go around."

"Especially not where the doctor lived," Simeon said, and there was a cryptic note to it that Maria couldn't decipher.

The captain continued, "But back east, where there's more light, maybe his machine would work better, or be more popular with folks who could use it in a bigger way."

"Folks like the Union army," Maria finished for him. "Folks like a man called Ossian Steen."

Hainey looked over his shoulder and asked, "You know about Steen?"

"Not much."

"Us either," Lamar said. "But I wouldn't mind having a word with him. I'm sure he's a bastard, but he must be one devil of a scientist."

"When we get to Louisville, if we can find him, you can ask him anything you want," Hainey said. "If I don't feel the need to kill him first."

Maria asked, "You have a gripe with this Steen?"

"I assume he's the man who paid Felton Brink to steal my ship," Hainey said grimly, and with a stormy grumble of intent. "But I might give him a minute to explain himself, just in case I'm wrong."

"That's big of you," Maria said dryly.

"I'm glad you approve," he responded with equal lack of humidity. "Now if we can only find this place, perhaps we can ask him in person."

But no one knew which sanatorium was being used for the nefarious Ossian Steen's frightening plans, and no one even knew where to begin looking—until Maria proposed they stop by the city hospital and ask about another facility. Perhaps they shared doctors, nurses, or other staff. But this plan was whittled into impracticality by inconvenient facts.

The *Valkyrie* was too notorious to park at the service yard docks down by the river, and it was too large to simply hide behind a warehouse. Furthermore, it was too dangerous-looking by design for the crew to simply strip off a few guns, dab a new name on the side, and call it something innocuous.

The plating, the weaponry, and the overall size of the tremendous craft made these things impractical. There was nowhere to simply "stop" the ship unless they wanted to abandon it outside of town and then walk.

"We could try that," she said. "But I don't know if it's wise."

Simeon tilted his heavily dreadlocked head back and forth, weighing the options as if his skull was the axis on a set of scales. "I'd hate to toss her," he said. "She's a sweet set of wings, and not much in the air would dare try to stick us."

"You suggesting we keep her, and bail on the *Crow?*" Hainey asked with warning, but also curiosity.

"No, I ain't suggesting that. I'm suggesting we might not want to cut this angel loose until we're good and certain we're done with her. We land on the other side of the river, maybe—we start in Indiana and walk our way over—and then what? Maybe we find the *Free Crow*, and maybe we don't. Maybe Brink sets our girl on fire and kicks her into the Ohio. Maybe we need to make a getaway fast, and then come back to try again. Maybe a whole lot of things could happen, and we'd need a ship as big and fast as this one to see us safe back west. If we'd taken anything smaller or lighter than this warbird, we'd have never made it out of Missouri, and you know it same as I do."

CLEMENTINE

"I know it," Hainey griped. "Nobody's arguing with you. And it's a quandary, I know. But Louisville is east, it ain't west. And I can't…" He looked at Maria and then frowned in a way that said something she didn't understand, not at first. "There are places in Kentucky I couldn't go even if the law wasn't looking for me."

Then he turned to Maria and addressed her directly. "Three black men and a white woman walking into town together, that'd go over real well, don't you think? That wouldn't raise a lick of suspicion in anyone, anywhere."

"You have a point."

"I usually do."

"But perhaps I can *help*."

Hainey almost laughed, but he restrained himself enough to say, "What do you have in mind?"

She said, "Put me down on the far side of the river and wait over there, in the woods if you have to. Tether down, and I'll catch a ride into the city. I'll send a few telegrams, ask a few questions, and see if I can't locate our mysterious sanatorium, which—as you and I both know—is no sanatorium at all."

Simeon spun around in the first mate's chair and eyed her angrily. "And then we…we what? We sit like fish in a barrel and wait for the charitable Belle Boyd to return?" He turned to the captain and said, "She'll leave us here and finish her job, let her Yankee bosses pat her on the head, or maybe she'll come back over the river with the law, and we'll all be hung by morning!"

Lamar said with less venom, but more measured concern, "Once we've set her down and sent her off…if she finds the sanatorium she's got no need of us."

"But I do!" she objected. "Our goals are not so dissimilar, gentlemen," she cajoled. "You want your ship, I want to stop your ship and destroy this weapons laboratory—by hook or crook if necessary. Perhaps I could do this alone and perhaps I couldn't, but this ship is the best hope I have for intercepting another vessel, now isn't it?"

"It's surely your most obvious," the captain said before the crew could complain.

Simeon tried to bark an objection regardless. "But Captain, she—"

"Time is of the essence, don't you think?" he asked the first mate. "We could set the ship down, go our separate ways; and we could try through our connections to learn where the sanatorium lies, or she could try to learn it on her own, through channels that wouldn't let us pass the front door or the back door, either. Who do you think will learn the most, the fastest?"

"*She* would," Simeon scowled. "But we can't trust her."

"Who said I trust her?" Lamar sniffed, and the captain said, "I trust her to shoot like an ace, and I trust her to fight for the country that's turned her away. I trust her to be as sneaky a bitch as ever the South did breed, and I trust her to understand that we're her best hope every bit as much as she's ours, because like Minnericht, and like you, and like me, that woman isn't an idiot and she can see where the sun's shining today. Now woman," he said to her, "did I tell any lies just now?"

She was seated still, hands folded in her lap over the gun she'd drawn from her handbag. Quietly she said, "Every word the gospel truth. I have no reason to lie to you. The captain is right and I am a patriot for my country, and although I generally desire my country's approval, that goal will be best served by preserving Danville from utter destruction. You're fugitives, yes, but what good would it do me to hand you over…if there is no nation left to prosecute you?"

Hainey swung a hand out and pointed it at her, as if to say, "See?" but he did not say it aloud. Instead he said, "On your word then, lady. On your word as a southerner, and a Confederate, and, and," he searched for something else to bind her. "And a widow. On your husband's grave, and on your—"

CLEMENTINE

"That's enough," she snapped. "On that—all of it. On that and more, I give you my word that if you send me into the city to gather information, I'll return to you with everything I know."

One hour later, she was deposited without ceremony beside the road that led to the bridge that would take her into the city.

When Maria returned—and she *did* return—she brought them the location of a brand new facility south of the city. And she climbed aboard, and neither she nor the captain nor any of the crew said another word until they landed their craft behind the Waverly Hills Sanatorium forty miles outside of town.

MARIA ISABELLA BOYD
10

Behind the Waverly Hills Sanatorium the forest was high and a creek rolled through the grounds, making light, pretty noises as it trailed between the trees. The sky was perfectly clear, without a cloud to hide behind; and in the end, the *Valkyrie* settled down in what passed for a small clearing at the edge of a fruit grove, half-concealed by the edge of a green knoll.

The folding stairs extended, and all four of the ship's occupants disembarked. Three black men and a white woman together looked strange enough indeed, but there was no one to see them while they plotted amongst themselves.

Maria attempted to straighten her deflated skirts. She gave up and asked, "I didn't see any other ships moored anywhere close, did you?"

The captain shook his head. He said, "I didn't, but that's not to say the *Free Crow* isn't docked and stashed someplace nearby."

"It must be smaller than the *Valkyrie*," she guessed.

"It is," he said. "Maybe half the size overall. Oh, she's not so tiny that she'd be a snap to hide—don't misunderstand me. But if the boys in blue are hiding a weapons facility, pretending it's a hospital for the deranged, then I wouldn't put a damn thing past them. For all we know, they have a…a secret set of docks. Maybe there's something hiding in the trees, or maybe one of these hills isn't what it looks like."

Lamar looked warily from hill to hill before saying, "It's possible, sir. But there's no reason to make yourself crazy over it."

Ever since stepping down the folding stairs, the first mate had been rolling himself a cigarette. He stuck one end in his mouth, lit the other end, and stared at the sky. He said, "I think we beat them."

"We must have," Maria insisted. "We dumped all that cargo, and full speed, you said. Your true and proper ship is loaded down and moving slowly, or so you mentioned. Head start or none, I think it's likely we've made it here first."

She set her large tapestry bag down on the ground and laid the small handbag beside it.

"What are you doing?" Hainey asked.

"Reloading."

Inside the large bag, beneath a layer of ladies' underthings, stockings, and a second pair of boots, she revealed a long burlap bag stitched into pouches, like a workman's tool belt. Inside each pouch was a stash of ammunition, divvied up into such an orderly fashion that Hainey was forced to marvel.

"No wonder you enjoyed shooting the Gatling. Get a hundred shots out without having to sift through your little bag for more bullets."

"I don't reload often," she said without taking offense. "Because I don't often shoot, and when I do, I don't often miss. But I want to take a different set of guns into the facility—something with more kick and, in case of trouble, more capacity." She hoisted a pair of Colts into the daylight and flipped the wheels open. While she thumbed bullets into the chambers she explained, "I don't know what I'll be walking into, in this facility. Twelve bullets are better than six, you know."

"Oh, I know," Hainey said, and he hesitated. "You said…I suppose. Well."

CLEMENTINE

"There's nothing to suppose, Captain Hainey. I'm going into Waverly alone, because you have no business there. You came to Louisville for your ship, which may appear at any time. I came to Louisville to prevent a weapon from completion. Now, there's nothing for either one of us to do but chase our own paths. You'll wait here and watch the sky; and I'll go inside to look for this Ossian Steen."

"And what will you do when you find him?" the captain asked.

"When I get to that bridge, I'll burn it," she drawled.

She finished loading the Colts and holstered them on a belt. The belt had received an extra set of holes in order to accommodate her slender waist in a fashionable way; she strung it over her hips, fastened it, and tested the weight of both weapons against her hands before replacing them in the holsters. She slipped her arm through the handbag's thin strap, and took the other one's handle into her fist.

"Gentlemen," she said. "I believe this is where our missions diverge. It's been...it's been a most peculiar...pleasure. Or at the very least, it's been an adventure. I thank you for the use of your ship, and for your trust, if ever I earned any."

Simeon said through a skeptical narrowing of his eyes, "Thanks for not shooting any of us."

She nodded, accepting that it was all the friendly acknowledgment she was likely to receive from the first mate; she nodded also at Lamar, who hadn't said a thing, even to wish her farewell; and she took a deep breath. She adjusted her hat, and then let it fall to rest between her shoulder blades, suspended around her neck by a red velvet ribbon.

And she said to the captain, "Well, Captain. Best of luck to you."

He said in return, "And to you, Belle Boyd."

As she walked away, down towards the building that reared up darkly through the woods, she heard him say behind her, "And that's something I never imagined—not in all my life—that I'd ever say."

She was nearly warmed by the sentiment, or by the thought that she'd deserved it; and she honestly wished them well, for all the strangeness of it.

Down at the bottom of the hill and across a walking bridge that crossed the stream in a tidy wooden arc, Maria made her way towards the dark spot—the hole made of a building, and stacked four stories up through the Kentucky bluegrass. The structure sucked everything towards it. The creek flowed to it, the trees leaned its way, and the earth itself seemed dimpled by the immense weight of the place and all its horrible contents.

She was drawn to it like everything else.

She strode through the forest away from the *Valkyrie* and up to the main road. She would conceal the gunbelt under a tied shawl, hold her baggage firmly and with purpose, and announce that she was there to apply for a position as a nurse. Maria scaled the low edge of the road and walked along it as if she had nothing to hide and no purpose at all which was not direct, friendly, and absolutely ignorant of military behavior or espionage of any stripe.

Out on the front lawn there were patients, here and there—or people masquerading as patients. And behind them, Waverly loomed.

It was a massive structure, made of brick from first floor to top, and crowned with four monstrous gargoyles, each one the size of a small horse. They were spread out along the roof's edge, spaced evenly and facing forward, mouths agape, faces watchful.

Maria shuddered.

And she sturdied herself, standing straight, adjusting her luggage, and strolling up the walkway to the grounds. The main entrance was directly underneath the gargoyles, of course, and to reach it she was compelled to stroll along a gravel road that wound its way forward. Here and there, nurses, orderlies, patients, and perhaps a doctor or two gave her a quizzical stare; but she was determined to preserve her decorum so she strode along, head high and luggage toted with dignity until she reached the front door.

CLEMENTINE

It was a doubled door with a round iron knocker and latch. She ignored the knocker and tugged the right-hand door open. She poked her head around its side and saw only a corridor that could've belonged to any sparkling new facility in any city, with any number of doctors, patients, or uses.

A pair of gurneys were left against a wall. A wheeled chair hunkered squatly at the end of a hallway; and here and there, a barefoot man or woman wandered from one room to another.

Maria let herself inside all the way, setting her carpetbag on the floor and clutching both her handbag and the shawl at her waist. She called out softly, "Hello? Is anyone here?"

None of the barefoot patients noticed her, or if they did, they did not feel moved to answer. But a nurse in a fluffy, ivory-colored uniform manifested to Maria's left and asked with a nurse's uncompromising firmness, "Can I help you?"

It was not a question, exactly. It was a declaration that the nurse knew Maria was somewhere she really shouldn't be, and an announcement that the hospital was aware of her presence. It was also a warning, that this was a place of order and that disorder, and disorderly behavior would not be tolerated.

The nurse was a petite, sharp-eyed woman with yellow hair tied up in a bonnet. She did not look like the kind of woman who could cram so much meaning into four words, but she also did not look like the kind of woman who was accustomed to dilly-dallying or backtalk.

Maria neither dilly-dallied nor backtalked. She asked, "This is a hospital, yes?"

"This is a hospital, yes."

"I've come in search of a job," Maria said.

Without a beat, the nurse replied, "And I'm your mother."

"I beg your pardon?"

"I know who you are," the nurse said. "I've seen your picture more than once, most lately on a poster for a play in Lexington, a few years ago. Now tell me what you're doing here, Belle Boyd?"

As Maria stared down at the small woman with the no-nonsense face, she considered her next move. She opened her mouth to speak, then closed it again. Finally she said, "I did not intend for my reputation to precede me. And I certainly don't mean you any trouble," she added, which was not quite a lie. It wouldn't have mattered if it were an outright falsehood; Maria would've said it anyway.

Just then, a wild-eyed woman stepped forward from behind one of the nearest corners, and she stood very still perhaps twenty feet away. The newcomer's feet were naked and her hair was the color of autumn leaves. The shift she wore was snagged and ripped, and from its sides dangled a telling set of straps.

Thus distracted, the nurse said, "Madeline, I don't know what you're doing out of your room, but you'd better return there before Dr. Williams sees you out and about."

Madeline said, "She's here about Smeeks."

Maria frowned and said, "I… I'm sorry. I don't know anyone named Mr. Smeeks."

"*Doctor* Smeeks," Madeline said quickly, before the nurse could interrupt her. "And of course you don't. You haven't met him yet."

"*To your room*, Madeline."

The patient was careful not to make a move; she seemed to understand more about the situation than Maria did, and she did not remove her eyes from Maria's—where they were locked into place more securely than she'd ever been restrained in a room. She said, "We aren't what you think we are. Smeeks isn't what you think he is. It's Steen's doing, really."

"Steen," Maria said to Madeline, and then to the nurse. "She's on to something. I do need to speak with Steen. It's Ossian Steen, is it not?"

If the nurse was cool before, her voice was glazed with ice when she said, "There's an Ossian Steen here, yes. And if you've come to work with him, or for him, then—"

CLEMENTINE

Maria sensed where the tirade was headed and she jumped in. "No. No, I only need to speak with him. About a professional matter."

"A professional matter," the nurse repeated with scorn. But suddenly something changed, and she looked at Maria with something new—some new thought had colored her assessment of the situation.

Madeline turned on her heel. Before she went back to her room as commanded, she said to the nurse, "You should speak with her. She will interfere with him, if she can." And then shortly, she was gone.

A second nurse, an older woman in a billowing gray uniform that spoke of her rank, joined the first and said, "Anne, was there a problem with Madeline?"

"Not anymore," she said, and then before Maria could offer her greetings she continued, "This woman is here to see about a job. I was only now going to speak with her, and see if we might have a position open. But we need to sit down and chat, and see what sort of employment might best suit her."

The older woman cast Maria the same gaze she might've used to appraise a mule, and she said, "She's got good height on her, and she looks sturdy. We'll have to cover *that* better," she gestured at Maria's cleavage. "Some of the male patients can scarcely spot a knuckle without improper arousal and inappropriate behavior. This having been said, Anne, I trust you to assess her and assign her. I'm going to go make sure Madeline is where she ought to be. She's a real pill, that one. You never can tell."

"It's a fact," Anne murmured an agreement. "And thank you, Mrs. Hendricks. Come with me, Maria," she said curtly. "We can have this conversation in the nurse's sitting area, where it's more private."

Maria retrieved her bag and followed behind Anne, past the nurse's station where the women gathered together and chattered like hens in their voluminous skirts and serious faces. They walked together past a laundry room where bundles of linens hung from the ceiling in bags as big as small boats, waiting to be emptied, sorted, and dried. Beyond the kitchen rooms they strolled, and around a final bend in the corridor until they'd reached a lounge that was empty except for a green-eyed cat who yawned, stretched, and ignored them.

Anne motioned for Maria to take a seat on the nearest padded bench, and then she positioned herself across from her, where she could lean in close and speak softly. She said, "You aren't here to work with him, are you? You wouldn't, I mean. Not for a man like that. Not against Danville, I don't think."

"You may safely assume it," Maria told her. "Your accent, I can't place it as precisely as I'd like, but I must guess you're a native of Florida, or southern Georgia. Am I close?"

"Valdosta," the blonde nurse said. "You've got an ear for it, don't you?"

"So I've been told. And in the interest of utter honesty, I'm no longer acting in any official capacity on behalf of the Confederacy—which was not a decision of mine, I assure you. I've been cut loose and sent on my way, but my loyalties remain. And those loyalties bring me here, to a military scientist with a terrible project. This Ossian Steen is preparing to destroy my native land, and I wish to…" She searched for Madeline's word and used it. "Interfere."

Nurse Anne nodded hard and said, "Yes, good. Yes, I'd love to see it—and not only for myself, or for the southern cause, or for any grand ethical pursuit."

"Then why?"

"Because Steen is a wicked bastard. A fiend, and worse—but stronger language I'd shudder to deploy in front of the cat. He's cruel and vile, and…"

Maria suggested, "Revolting? I understand he's creating a weapon, applying his scientific prowess to ungodly research, and to the creation of a solar cannon that he intends to fire on our capital."

"That's true," Anne said, "though I think you've got him a bit confused, or doubled up. Steen isn't a scientist, himself. He's a bully and a thug, and a manipulator."

"I don't understand…?"

Anne hopped to her feet. "I'll show you. Come with me. But don't touch anything, and if any of the patients try to touch you, do your best to prevent them. They aren't allowed to take liberties, though the prohibition doesn't do much to stop them, sometimes."

The nurse hastily led Maria down another hallway littered with medical detritus—bedpans, medicine trays, and assorted straps or other restraints. As they walked, Maria sought to clarify, "This is a hospital for the mentally afflicted, isn't that right?"

"That's right," Anne said. "We've only been open for a year or two."

"I thought perhaps this was only a cover for a weapons laboratory. Or so the intelligence I'd received implied as much."

"That's funny," Anne said without any humor. "Down here." She indicated a set of stairs leading down to the basement, and with a gentle lift of her skirts, she skipped down the steps to a door, which she opened.

She called out, "Doctor Smeeks? Doctor Smeeks, I've brought you a visitor."

From within, they were answered by a thin voice stretched thinner still by exhaustion. It asked, "A visitor?"

"Yes, Doctor Smeeks. It's me, Anne." She motioned at Maria, drawing her down into the basement. "And this is Maria. She's…she's…" Unable to think of anything better or more concise, she finished, "She's here to help."

"Help?"

"Yes sir," Maria said before she even saw the speaker. "Please, could I…" She looked to Anne for approval, and received it. "Could I speak with you?"

The nurse squeezed Maria's elbow and whispered, "I beg you, be *gentle*."

He crept around a table like a nervous rodent, eyeing Maria and Anne both with open suspicion. Doctor Smeeks was a white-haired man of an age past seventy, with loose-fitting clothes, a frazzled expression, and a pair of jeweler's lenses strapped across his forehead. He said, "Hello?" and wrung his hands together. "Oh, Anne. You're alone. Or rather, you're not alone, but you're not...you haven't brought Steen. Or, or. Or the boy," he added sadly.

"Sir," Anne came forward to take his arm, leading him forward to meet Maria. "Sir, I'm so very sorry, but no. However, this is Maria—"

"And she's here to help?"

"She's here to help. Would you show her your work? She's very interested in what you're doing down here, and I promise you," she added into his ear. "She is no friend of Steen's."

"No friend of...that man. What was his name again? Anne, I can't remember his name."

"Steen, sir. And it's all right, don't worry yourself. Just, could you show us your work?"

"My work?"

"Yes sir, your work. Will you give us a tour of your most recent piece? Remember it, sir? The one you're building in order to bring back Edwin." She patted his forearm and he nodded.

"For Edwin." He glared up at Maria. "The army man. He took my assistant," his lip trembled. "A fine assistant, and a nice boy. He took him away from me, and I do believe he intends to harm the child if I can't... if I don't..."

He twisted his fingers into knots.

"Please, come this way." He led the women deeper into his laboratory—a dark place brightened by lanterns, lamps, and the few thin windows that ran the length of the wall's eastern rim. Glass containers of a thousand shapes, sizes, and purposes were stacked and piled from table to table, and tubes made of copper, tin, and steel were bundled like sticks for a fire. The floor was coated with papers covered in tiny, scratchy handwritten notes; and from the ceiling hung models of projects that had been, and projects that were yet to come.

But in the back corner, underneath the longest stretch of skinny window with watery gray afternoon light spilling down into the basement, sat a device almost as massive as the *Valkyrie's* primary engine. It had been constructed of pipes, pans, and a vast array of complicated lenses, and it looked like a cross between a microscope and a telescope, melded with the steel-framed corpse of a suspension bridge.

The lenses varied in size from thumbnail-small to windowpane-large, with the biggest mounted before a seat and a console covered with complicated buttons and levers. Maria thought the airship looked like a wind-up toy in comparison to this astonishing machine—all the more astonishing because she had only the vaguest idea of what it was meant to do.

She asked, "Doctor Smeeks, is this…is this a solar cannon?"

"A solar cannon?" He removed the lenses that were strapped to his forehead, and pulled a pair of spectacles out of his front breast pocket. "Something like that. You mean the German doctor's patent? The gentleman from the Washington Territories?"

"I believe so."

"Can't recall his name," the doctor muttered. "He designed a solar cannon. It was made to be held in the hand, by a large man with exceptional motor skill control, I assume; it was a magnificent prototype, that's to be sure. But it was no more harmful than a powerful gun, or perhaps a high-capacity cannon. At that size," he began to say more, but lost his train of thought. "At that size, it was, it was only. A weapon for one man, to kill one man. Not a weapon designed to dash the masses. Not like…this."

"What do you call it?" Maria asked. She ran her fingertips across the most benign-looking bits of metal frame.

"I don't call it anything. Until this ship arrives with the final piece, and then I can call it finished, and…" There were tears in his eyes when he said the rest. "And that *animal* can give me back poor Edwin, and he'd *best* return the lad to me unharmed!"

He turned away and fiddled with one of the smaller lenses, poking his hand into the spot where a metal plate was cut to hold an object the size of a child's fist. He picked at it with his nail and hummed something unhappy before looking up again, gazing at Anne with something like wonder.

He asked, "Nurse Anne! What are you doing down here? I hope you haven't been standing there long; you ought to announce yourself! It's good to see you of course, as always. It's a wonder Edwin didn't say something. Where is that dear boy, anyway? Have you seen him? I thought he was supposed to bring me supper."

Anne gave Maria a look that asked for compassion, and she took Maria's arm to lead her away. But first she said, "I'm very sorry to bother you, Doctor Smeeks. We didn't mean to intrude, but this is Maria, and she's visiting the facility. You've showed us a wonderful array, and we'll leave you to your work now. Thank you again for your time."

On the way back up the stairs, Anne said softly, "You see? He's as harmless as a lamb. He only works when he remembers he must; and when he forgets…"

"Who's Edwin?" Maria asked.

"Edwin is an orphan, the child of a resident who died here. He lives down in the basement with the doctor, who has taken him as an apprentice. The boy is patient and sweet, and he is a great help and comfort to the doctor, whose mind, as you can plainly tell, has slipped. It's a true pity. He was once a great inventor, with a keen brain and a warm heart. Now he spends most of his days befuddled and unhappy, except for how he loves the boy."

Maria said, "And this Ossian Steen—he's taken the boy away? This is how he manipulates the poor doctor?"

"Correct. He locks the little fellow up with himself, in one of the outbuildings, where he pretends to be a doctor himself. Obviously we don't let him anywhere near the patients; or rather, it's just as well he has no interest in them, for he could only do them harm, and he wouldn't care in the slightest. Missus…" the nurse hesitated, uncertain of what to call the spy. She settled on, "Boyd. I want you to understand that even if I had no lingering loyalties of my own to any nation or side in the long-running unpleasantness, I would wish to see an end to this awful lieutenant colonel. I can't abide such cruelty—much less to a gentle old man and an innocent child."

Maria steeled herself against what might come and she demanded quietly, "Take me to Ossian Steen. We'll settle this now."

CAPTAIN CROGGON BEAUREGARD HAINEY

11

Simeon squinted at the sky and drew a quick, hard sip from his cigarette before tossing it aside. He asked, "You see that?" and he cocked his head towards a corner of the sky where a fistful of puffy clouds were parting to make way for something heavy, high, and dark.

The captain's scarred face widened with delight. "Men," he said, "watch for it. Look—let it land. You see where it's going?"

The craft swayed as it sought a place to settle; it moved drunkenly and slow, too loaded down to fly swift or straight. It hummed and hovered over the Waverly Hills compound. Atop the low central mound where the sanatorium hulked, the *Free Crow* slipped and jerked through the air as if it threatened to land on the roof, but it did not rest there. It swung over to the side and behind the main building, into the trees beyond it— where there must have been another clearing, or perhaps a landing dock designed for just such a purpose.

"How are we going to play this, Captain?" Lamar wanted to know. "Do we catch them mid-air, or do we let them land?"

The captain said, "Mid-air hasn't worked so well, so far; but then again, we didn't have a ship this strong. Still, this time let's let them land, and we'll take it out from under them."

Simeon said, "We're going to take it quiet, and let 'em walk back to Washington?"

"Not even if they ask nicely." Hainey stomped back up the folding stairs that led inside the *Valkyrie*. "I don't plan to leave any of the bastards standing. Or this bastard, either," he indicated the ship he was entering.

"Sir?" Lamar asked.

The captain answered from the interior, "Engineer, I want you to unscrew that bottom armor plate along the rear hydrogen tank. Leave it naked, and be careful about it. But be fast."

When he descended the stairs again, he had the Rattler slung across his shoulders. It had long since cooled from the assault in Kansas City, and although it was almost out of ammunition, another band of bullets sagged around the captain's chest like a sash.

He continued, "We want to give them a few minutes to get themselves moored and get comfortable." Then he asked Simeon, "You don't think they saw us, do you? This is a big bird, but we've got some tree cover and the hill between us."

"I couldn't say. But I'd guess they didn't."

Hainey stripped the last handful of bullets out of the Rattler and began to thread the new band into its chambers. Lamar was already whacking at the armor with a wrench and a prybar, and they both finished their tasks in less than a minute; but Simeon joined Lamar, and between them they pulled away another crucial strip of plating, widening the vulnerable spot and giving themselves a bigger target.

"That ought to do it," the captain declared. "Let's leave it for now and go. It'll be safer to blast it from the sky, anyway, and I think we've given Brink and his boys time enough to get our ship secured. Simeon, help me with this thing."

CLEMENTINE

Simeon took the barrel of the large, freshly loaded gun, and helped to carry it as if it were still suspended in a crate. Together they walked through the trees, down the hill, and around the back end of the building where an improvised landing pad had been cleared and a set of uncomplicated pipework docks had been established. From the edge of the clearing where Hainey, Simeon, and Lamar were hunkered and hiding, it looked like there had once been a building in the clearing—and now there was nothing left but its foundation, which made a perfectly serviceable spot in which to park an airship.

The *Free Crow*—improperly christened the *Clementine*—sagged on its moorings. None of the lines and clips that held it to the earth were strictly necessary, and none were drawn tight for the ship was so overburdened that without the fight of the engines, it would have sunk to the ground.

A pair of large Indian men milled about outside the ship. They looked enough alike to be brothers, but neither Hainey nor either of his crewmembers could guess which tribe they hailed from. Beside them, seated and scowling, was a heavily bandaged man with a wrapped foot, thigh, and hand. He fiddled with a makeshift crutch and swore under his breath.

Hainey whispered, "I knew I'd got one of them, back in Seattle."

Lamar said, "You shouldn't have fired inside the ship. You could've killed us all."

The captain made half a shrug and said, "I know. But I was mad as hell, and being mad got the better of me. I wonder what man that is," he said, and he meant that he wondered what position the crewman held. "I think his name is Guise. I know the first mate is a fellow called Parks, but I don't see him out there."

"He must be inside," Simeon said.

From within the ship, a loud, repeated banging sound echoed throughout the hull. The sound had a sharp edge, like a sculptor's chisel biting into stone; it rang with a timbre that made Hainey think of miners picking their way through coal. He said, "They're trying to dig it out of her, I bet."

"The diamond?" Lamar asked.

"That's right. They're digging through the cement in her coffin, trying to reach what she's wearing. They should've started that sooner, rather than leaving it to the last minute like this."

The first mate said, "Maybe there's more cement than they bargained for."

And Lamar suggested, "Maybe they were too busy running from *us*."

Hainey nodded at the engineer and said, "I like your explanation better. Well, let's get going."

With Simeon's help he hoisted the Rattler up onto his shoulders, and checked the smaller guns that hung on the belt around his waist. They did this with all the quiet they could muster, and they were at barely enough distance that they thought no one would hear them…until Hainey stood up straight, Rattler primed and ready, and found himself face-to-face with one of the Indians who had only a moment before been a hundred feet away.

The native man had a shape that looked like it'd been carved from a tree, and gleaming black hair that hung down almost to his hips. He was dressed like a white man, in a linen shirt tucked into a pair of denim pants.

Nothing rustled and no part of him moved. He did not even blink.

Simeon and Lamar were frozen to the spots where they stood, even though the newcomer appeared unarmed. It was too startling, the speed and silence with which this man had moved into their midst.

It occurred to all three black men at once that there'd actually been two Indians, down by the *Free Crow*. Their realization came a split second before the injured man beside the craft began to holler, "Where the hell did you two get off to? Eh? What's going on?"

Within the ship, a man's voice demanded to know, "What are you barking on about, Guise?"

"Them Indians done took off!"

"They'll be back. Now if you're not going to help in here, at least keep your mouth shut."

At no point during the exchange had the Indian unfastened his eyes from the captain's, but once Mr. Guise had sulked himself into quiet he said, very softly, "Hainey."

"That's me."

"Yours," he said, pointing at the craft.

Hainey gathered from the enunciation, or maybe from the brevity, that he was dealing with a fellow who spoke little to no English. He wasn't sure how to proceed except to say, "Yes."

The second Indian appeared behind Simeon, close enough that he could've harmed the first mate, but he simply stepped to join the man who must've been his brother, yes—Hainey could see the resemblance more strongly, when they stood together like that.

The second man said, "Seattle," but he said it with at least one extra syllable, and he lodged an accent mark into the middle of it.

Hainey wasn't sure if this was in reference to the old chief for whom the city was named, or the city itself, so he nodded in general agreement that yes, he'd been in the city; and yes, he knew of the chief. He said, "I got no gripe with him or his tribe, if that's what you're asking."

"Brink," the first one said with disgust. Then the second man said, "You take," and he pointed at the *Free Crow*. He said it with finality, and when he turned away, his brother did the same.

They walked into the woods as quietly as they'd emerged, and then they were gone.

Hainey hadn't realized he'd been holding his breath, but he had, and he let it out to say, "That was strange."

His first mate sniffed. "Brink must not be much of a captain. Or maybe he's all right to his white men, and not the rest."

"There's no telling," Hainey said, with a tone that said he didn't give a damn one way or the other. He strained under the weight of the Rattler, which was hard enough to balance when he was moving about—and as a stationary load, it was even worse to hold. "I wish we could've asked them about who else was on board, though."

"They've got the one beat-up fellow outside. He won't give us too much hassle," Simeon said.

"Shot up," Lamar corrected him. "And Brink, and probably a first mate. It might be three against three."

"Four against three," Hainey said, and he patted the Rattler. "Let's go."

The three men sneaked back behind the airship and then, on the captain's signal, they rushed down the last of the hill and into the landing zone.

Simeon had his revolver up, loaded, and ready to fire; Lamar held a rifle that was poised to blow a hole in the first something or someone that got in his way. Hainey's footsteps were twice as heavy as usual, and his shoulders screamed as the Rattler dug into them hard, jarring sinew and bone with every stride.

The injured Mr. Guise heard the oncoming rush when Hainey was still ten yards out; but bound in his bandages as he was, there was little he could do except yelp for his captain.

"Brink! Captain Brink!" he shouted.

"What now?"

"Company—" he said, though the last bit of the concluding "y" was sliced off by a bullet from Simeon. The bullet went straight through Guise's throat and his head snapped back. His body toppled onto the hard foundation and bounced there, and except for the gurgling and the spreading blood, it didn't otherwise make a scene.

"Jesus Christ!" a man declared from within the belly of the *Free Crow*. "Hold them off, I've almost got it!"

"They won't shoot—not in here, not with the hydrogen!"

But outside, the Rattler was warming up. Its telltale whirring hum was cranking up to a faster grade and a higher pitch, and it would take nothing but the squeeze of a trigger to pepper the craft and all its occupants with bullets as long as a man's palm.

"It's Hainey!" someone announced, and through the front window glass, the captain spied a meaty, dark-haired man with a glare in his eyes and a deep frown cut into his face.

"Who else would it be?" said someone else, presumably Brink. "Draw up the bay stairs!" he ordered.

But Hainey wouldn't have it. He said, "Help me, Sim. Help me aim," and he guided the man with his eyes.

The first mate caught on fast, and braced his back against the captain's. "Got the back end, sir. You point it, it'll hold steady."

And the captain squeezed the flat, wide trigger. A stream of ghastly firepower gushed in a line that strafed the bay stairs, cutting them into pieces—and then, on a second pass, tearing them altogether from their fittings. Over his shoulder, Hainey said, "We can fix that later!"

Above the din of the Rattler they heard the *Free Crow*'s engines hack to life. Brink had given the order to take off if they couldn't hold their ground, but the ship was still moored and there hadn't been time to manually disengage the hooks. The craft tried to rise but only lifted itself a few feet before the hitch squealed an objection, and the pipes leaned against the force of the engines and their thrust.

Like an unhappily snagged balloon, the craft lunged and heaved—doglike, at the end of a leash; it yanked with the fury of a horse strapped into an unwanted bit.

"Those docks won't hold!" Lamar shouted.

"They'll hold long enough!" A man swayed at the edge of the bay docks and caught himself on the edge, half out, and half inside the bucking ship.

"Sim!" the captain screamed, and the first mate braced himself, and he braced the Rattler, and the captain began firing again.

The burst took off part of the man's arm and tore through his torso; when he fell he landed with a splat, not far from the body of Mr. Guise. Whoever he was—and Hainey felt certain that this was Parks, the first mate—he wasn't dead and he even tried to rise enough to run. He hadn't fallen far, only ten or twenty feet, and an arm was only an arm…though his side gushed with gore as he struggled to stand and move.

Hainey was having none of it.

A second carefully measured burst blew the man off his feet and sent him sprawling over the edge of the landing pad, no longer alive enough to bleed or run.

"Felton Brink!" Hainey roared.

No answer came, but the ship was now effectively unmanned, and it bobbed erratically against its tethers.

Slowly, and with a grating peal that could be heard even above the whine and romp of the engines, an amazingly sized block came skidding out of the bay door—where there was no longer a set of stairs or a folding portal to prevent it from scooting out, tipping over, and dropping to the earth with a crashing crunch. It did not quite shatter but it cracked throughout; and it did not fall unaccompanied. Behind the block of battered cement, a head full of bright red hair ducked—but it didn't duck so fast that Hainey hadn't spotted it.

"Brink!" he yelled with triumph, and with another signal to Simeon he pointed the Rattler at the cement block and began to blast it apart. The brick could've hidden a mule without much trouble, and it hid the red-haired pirate with ease; but the determined onslaught of the automatic gun broke it apart, tearing out chunks the size of fists, and sending great splits stretching through its bulk.

"Captain!" Lamar said with urgency, and Hainey thought perhaps the engineer had been trying to summon his attention for several seconds before he'd noticed. "Captain, the *Crow!* Without that brick on board, she's going to pull the pipe docks loose and take off!"

Over the metallic gargle of the gun, the captain only heard about one out of every three words; but he understood the intent, and he could see for himself that the craft was now empty, and without intervention it would break free, fly heaven knew where, and crash itself into scrap.

He swore loudly and repeatedly, on everything from Brink's thieving soul to his father's gleaming eyes. He flipped a switch to power down the Rattler and with Simeon's help, he deposited it onto the ground.

Felton Brink used the quiet moment to run. He stood just enough to see over the block, saw the men running towards the jittering, flailing craft, and he took off running back up the hill.

Hainey made a mental note of which direction he'd gone, and he said to Simeon, "Get to that tether! Crank and draw the strap by hand, bring the ship lower—as low as you can get it without dragging her down on top of us! Lamar," he said then. "Get over here—underneath her, with me!"

With the bay floor hanging open, its underside portal destroyed, there was nothing to grab and nothing to climb, only an open hole on the bottom of the craft. The *Free Crow* was becoming more distressed by the moment, as her engines strove against the tethers that wouldn't let her up. Freed from her overweight load, she stretched against the straps and chains and would've taken the whole landing pad with her if she could only get enough leverage.

"Sir!" Lamar objected, suddenly twigging on.

"Over here! Now!"

And even though the ship loomed, snapped, and reared only a few feet over their heads, he obeyed. He crouched his way over to Croggon Hainey, who stood as tall as he could reach, then bent at the knees and held his hands together like a slingshot.

The captain said, "You're going to have to grab for it, and once you're on board, you're going to have to steady her." He didn't ask if this was possible, or even if it was likely. He assumed that it must be, because no other option was acceptable.

Lamar nodded, swallowed, and backed up enough to take a running leap at the captain's hands.

Hainey grabbed the engineer's foot and swung with every ounce of strength left in his bruised, overworked, scratched and scarred back...

…and the slight-framed engineer went tumbling up through the air, where his left hand and right fingertips snagged the bay's edges.

His right hand lost its hold, then found it again; his left hand squeezed hard enough to almost dent the metal, and held, and gave him leverage enough to work an elbow, and then a knee, and then a heel onto better footing. It took him no more than ten seconds to haul his whole body onboard, and then he vanished into the interior.

Hainey turned to the cement block and saw how it had been carved, and how deeply it had been broken before he'd even begun to shoot at it. Down all the way to the core it'd been breached, all the way to the fossil of a woman's body, lying crushed by the weight of its tomb.

To the first mate he said frantically, "Help him if you can, once he gets her steady!"

"You're going after Brink?" Simeon asked, but the captain didn't answer.

He was already gone, in pursuit of the red-haired pirate who was carrying the most dangerous diamond in the world.

MARIA ISABELLA BOYD

12

Anne snuck Maria to the back of the sanatorium, where an exit was unwatched and no one might interrupt them. "Out here," she said, opening the door. "That walkway will lead you to a fork. Take the left path, and it'll send you to the outbuilding—perhaps a hundred yards off."

But Maria had only barely heard her, for bobbing above the trees was an airship, seemingly tethered and distressed about its state. "God in heaven!" she exclaimed. "Is that the *Clementine?* Er, I mean, the *Free Crow?*"

Anne said with wonder, "I haven't the foggiest idea! Good Lord, what's going on over there?"

"I could make a guess," Maria murmured, and she fought the instinct to dash to the thrashing craft, if only to learn what was happening. The crown of the ship leaped and lurched, straining and fighting, and the spy could hear shouts—but she couldn't tell what was being shouted. She turned to the nurse and double-checked, "This path? The left fork?"

"That's right," she said without taking her eyes off the tussle in the trees.

The path would lead her away from the ship, but she took it with a running start. Her carpetbag full of ammunition and personal effects bounced against her thigh and her skirts tangled around her knees; she kicked to keep herself mobile and she tore down the unpaved path, knocking gravel and dirt up against her knickers. Trees leaned above and cast her passage in shadow, and in the back of her ears she heard the whine of an overdriven engine and the breaking of branches somewhere in the distance.

Where is this outbuilding? she asked herself as she panted under the load of her luggage, her clothes, and the changing grade of the scenery.

Then she saw it, as the trees parted and the path dumped out to an open spot in the woods, where a low, undecorated structure sat surrounded by greenery.

Before she could burst free of the forest and make her presence known, a red-haired man flung himself past the armed guard who stood at the door. He wrestled with the knob and threw himself inside, slamming the door behind himself.

Maria stopped at the edge of the woods, since the guard was distracted by the visitor and no one had yet noticed her. She held one hand against her chest and counted to twenty—an old trick she'd picked up on the stage, but it worked, and her breathing slowed. Once she had her body under control, she slipped that hand down to the shawl tied around her waist and she withdrew one of her Colts.

Moments later, the door opened again and the red-haired man stood beside a taller, thinner man in a Union uniform. "Steen," she assumed softly, and she watched as he commanded the guard to summon his fellows. In seconds, three more guards had joined the first, and right before the officer retreated into the building's interior, she saw something the color of sunlight flash in his hand.

The diamond had been handed over to its purchaser.

One of the guards stepped inside with his commanding officer; the other two kept their position on either side of the door, and both held revolvers at the ready. They anticipated trouble, that much was certain; and Maria was equally certain of the trouble they faced...even before she saw a broad flash of a blue wool coat sneaking between the trees on the other side of the clearing.

She fell back farther into the trees and began to work her way around, sideways, as softly as her luggage and her dress would allow.

Croggon Beauregard Hainey met her in the middle.

He whispered, "I thought that must be you," and he looked over her shoulder, past her head at the spot in the sky where the ship had been doing its terrible dance over the edge of the trees. Maria glanced too and saw that the craft had settled, and she thought that its engines sounded calmer, or perhaps she was only too far away now to hear the frantic whine.

"You found your ship," she whispered back.

"But that thieving pirate made his delivery," making the same point.

She asked, "So what are you doing here? Take your ship and make your getaway!"

"Not while that son of a pox-spreading whore is still breathing. Goddamn," he rumbled. "I should've brought the Rattler."

"And why didn't you?"

He threw his hands up and said, "Because it's heavy, woman! I can hardly carry the thing, and Brink was running with nothing but the diamond to tote."

"You carried it just fine in Kansas City."

"Across an open, flat field, sure," he said, and realizing he was on the verge of a very distracting argument, he said, "Point is, I don't have it, and we could use it."

CLEMENTINE

"We, Captain?"

"We, woman. You want the diamond, and I want the bastard who boosted it. How many shots have you got?"

She set her carpetbag down and whipped out the other Colt. "Twelve loaded. And you?"

"Same, damn it all."

"There's only five of them. The two guards at the door, plus a third inside—with Ossian Steen and your pirate Brink. That leaves us nineteen shots to spare." But she was thinking the very thing he next said aloud.

"We can down the two at the door easy as pie, but if the other three are holed up…" he indicated a pair of windows. "They could hold us off awhile. And all I've got to back me up are two men who are a little bit busy right now."

"What are they doing?" she asked, looking again to the bulbous, curved dome. But the trees thwarted her and through their leaves, she could no longer see the spot on the hill where the craft had so recently struggled.

"Long story," he told her, and then when it didn't seem to be enough he added, "They're trying to wrestle my bird into submission. It was running, and unmanned." But he didn't bother to enlighten her on how that had come to pass.

"Ah," she said. And to change the subject, "I have an idea."

"So do I. I'll retreat, summon the lads, and we'll wipe this building off the face of the earth. I've got a couple of Minnericht's Liquid Fire Shells stashed on board that would do the trick in under a minute flat."

She gasped, "No! No, you can't do that, not yet. Please," she laid her fingers on his arm. "Hear me out. There's a child in there, a boy named Edwin who is being held hostage by Steen. You can't just demolish the place with him inside. Let me try something first, and…and if it doesn't work, then you can level the place with me inside, too."

He said with no small degree of sarcasm, "That's a generous offer, Belle Boyd."

"Not particularly. If what I've got in mind doesn't work, I'll be dead anyway, and I won't mind the imposition. I'm going to barge inside under some pretense, seize the boy, escape back to the sanatorium, destroy the infernal machine, and…and…then I'll think of something else."

"You're a real piece of work, you know that?"

"You're not the first to say so."

He shook his head and put his hands on his hips, and said, "Fine. Risk your own neck, if that's how you want it. I'll cover you if I can, but if you take too long, I'm getting my men and turning this patch of Kentucky into a fire pit that'll burn until Jesus comes back."

"Works for me," she said. She gave the outbuilding and its guards a hard glance, made a decision, and said to Hainey before she left, "Give me two minutes before you get your gang."

He lifted an eyebrow. "Only two minutes?"

"If this takes any longer, it won't work at all. Trust me. I move fast. Do you have a watch?"

"Not on me, but I can count to sixty twice."

"Good enough." Maria shoved one of the Colts back under her shawl and held the other one in her hand, covered by the handbag. She reached to the neckline of her dress and gave it a tug that started a revealing rip, and dropped her carpetbag at her feet.

"What are you doing?" Hainey asked.

"Getting my story in order." She took a deep breath, then said, "Captain, start counting."

"Wait."

"What?" she asked.

"Do me one favor. Leave Brink for me. Don't shoot him unless you have to," he requested.

She nodded.

And after scooting away from Hainey by ten or fifteen yards, she leaped out of the woods into the clearing as if she had a pack of wolves on her heels.

She fired off a blood-curdling scream of feminine terror and, as the two guards in front of the outbuilding furrowed their brows, she wailed, "Help me! Oh help me, gentlemen, you must!"

She flung her body up against the nearest guard and wept piteously. Between great sobs she gasped to the other guard, "You there! Your weapon! Ready it, man—he's out there! He's right behind me!"

The guard she clung to held her back at an arm's reach, took in the sight of a woman in a torn dress and got a glimpse of what lay beneath it. He stammered, "Ma'am, please, contain yourself!"

But she would not be soothed so easily. She gulped, "But sir! There's a horrible man—a *hideous Negro* with a terrible scar—he accosted me in the woods! He assaulted me!"

Behind the cover of the woods' edge, Croggon Hainey rolled his eyes.

The second guard demanded to know, "Where is this man?"

And as the first untangled himself from Maria's clutched embrace, the first guard said, "Which way did he come from?"

"Over there!" She indicated a position approximately ninety degrees away from Hainey's precise locale.

The guards exchanged a set of knowing looks that did not go unnoticed by the spy, who stayed in character to such an extent that she required a handkerchief—which was provided by her first choice of guards. He said, "We'd better put her inside."

"But Steen…?" It was a feeble objection, and when the door was flung open to reveal the Union officer, both men snapped to attention while Maria wibbled convincingly.

"What's going on out here?" he demanded, and seeing Maria his eyes narrowed into a look of confused concentration. "Do I know you?"

She shook her head, flinging a stray tear loose.

The nearest of the guards said in a stiff voice, "Sir, she was assaulted in the woods by a hideous Negro with a terrible scar!"

Maria bobbed her head and said, "Please, sir, let me come inside. Protect me, I beg you!"

One of the guards declared, "He came from that way, sir!" and repeated Maria's lie.

Ossian Steen said, "Fine." And he asked the guard who was stationed within the outbuilding, "How long until the rest of them arrive?"

From inside, a voice replied, "No more than five minutes, sir. They're on their way."

Steen appeared to consider his options. Then he grabbed Maria by the arm, towed her toward himself, and told the two men, "Go hunt for him. We'll hold down this preposterous little fort until the rest of your garrison gets here."

With that, he pulled Maria inside and slammed the door behind them both.

The outbuilding's interior was no larger than its exterior would suggest; really, it was only one large room—stuffed with desks, boxes, books, crates of guns and ammunition. All the walls were bare except for the farthest, behind the largest desk, where a map of the Mason-Dixon area was tacked up and heavily scribbled upon.

And underneath this map, behind the desk was a small pallet with a moth-eaten blanket and a punched-flat pillow the size of her purse. In the corner, at the pallet's foot, was crouched a small boy with his head buried in his folded arms, atop his knees. He did not look up at the commotion; he did not even appear to be breathing, but holding himself so little and still that he might make himself invisible.

Maria wondered how much time she had left.

Standing beside the desk, which must surely belong to the lieutenant colonel, was a red-haired man in scorched brown pants and an undershirt, with a loose gray jacket covering his bulky arms. He was possibly the whitest man she'd ever seen, with skin so pale it looked pink at the joints of his fingers, and blue around the recesses of his eyes.

He gave her a look from top to bottom, folded his arms, and didn't say anything.

A pair of guns hung from a belt around his hips, but he wasn't holding anything at the ready.

"I swear I've seen you before," Steen said to Maria. "It'll drive me mad if I don't figure out it."

To change the subject, she said, "Who's that child? Is he your son?"

"That's no business of yours. Keep your mouth shut and your head down if you want to stay inside here, or we'll throw you back out the door and let the pirate have his way with you."

Outside, a pair of gunshots rang out from the woods, and there were shouts from behind the trunks of the trees.

"Hainey," the red-haired man growled. "Jesus Christ. He can have his ship; why won't he just take it and leave?"

Maria fingered the Colt she gripped behind her handbag. In a few steps she retreated to the desk, and to the boy. She crouched down beside him and touched the edge of his arm, but she said to Felton Brink, "Perhaps he took it personally."

"What would you know?" he snapped back without looking at her. He walked to the nearest window and hid himself behind the edge of the frame so he could see outside without risking a bullet in the face.

She didn't answer him. Instead she whispered to the boy, "Edwin?"

He raised his eyes—just his eyes—over the edge of his arm to look at her. They were brown eyes, and exhausted ones. He was no older than nine or ten years of age, and thin in the way orphans were expected to be, but without the hollow look of a child who starves.

Maria opened her arms and gave him what she hoped was an encouraging smile.

He unfolded from his crouch and let her lift him up as if what happened to him didn't matter anyway, and he may as well let the woman hold him if that's what she wanted to do.

He wasn't very heavy. Maria pulled him up onto her hip, where she held him easily. He latched his legs around her waist and put his head down on her shoulder.

"You. What are you doing?" Steen asked.

With her free hand, she dropped her handbag and revealed the Colt. "I'm leaving. And I'm taking this child. Don't do it—" she added as he reached for his belt and the gun that was holstered there. "You either," she said to Brink, and her voice was as calm now as it had been hysterical a minute before.

She motioned with her gun that the two of them should stand together, and she circled her way around the desk, and around the room. She saw the diamond then, and she wondered how she could have ever missed it in the first place. It was perched on the desk like a paperweight, glittering as if it were alive—cutting the sunlight into ribbons, squares, and shining specks.

But Maria didn't let her glance linger there for long.

She said to the boy with his face buried against her shoulder, his elbow bent into her cleavage, "Close your eyes, Edwin. We're going to have to hurry." She tried her best to estimate how long she'd lingered, and she couldn't imagine that she had long before Hainey—and her thought of him was punctuated by another round of shots being exchanged out-side—decided that her time was up.

"You," she said to Brink. "Open that door. Now."

"I don't take orders from—"

"I don't have any trouble with you," she said to the pirate, speaking over his complaint. "I don't care if you live or die, so I'm sending you on your way, and if you have any sense you'll leave before I change my mind, or before you give me a reason to shoot you. Now go. Get out."

He didn't need to be told more than twice.

Brink reached for the knob, turned it, and checked outside to see if anyone was waiting to shoot him. Seeing no one, he pretended to tip a hat at Ossian Steen and said, "Pleasure doing business with you," in a tone of voice that fooled no one. With a flash of brown and white and red, he was out the door and running.

Maria used her gun to urge Steen away from the door, which flapped itself shut behind Felton Brink. She came to stand beside it, her gun still aimed at the officer, and she said, "I'm going to destroy that weapon, and you'll never have a chance to build another one."

"You don't know what you're doing," he growled.

"Oh yes I do. You want to wipe Danville off the map—"

He interrupted her, "And in doing so, yes—end this blasted war…and I just now think, I believe, I think I know… You're Boyd, aren't you? I've heard stories, but—"

"Yes, that's me," she said, and she sounded like she wanted to spit, but she didn't. She said, "And if you wanted the war to end so badly, you'd speak to your superiors about withdrawing, and allowing the South to go its own way. You wouldn't create a weapon to demolish a city with the press of a trigger!"

He was angry now, and it showed around his eyebrows, and in a flushing of his ears. "Is that all you think? Is that as far as you can see?" He pointed a finger at her and said, "The union must be preserved, the will of an old spy be damned. The war can't drag on forever; it can't go on like this, like a mill grinding men's bones to flour, year after year. *Something must stop it*, Belle Boyd. Something must end it in one blow—and if that means the death of thousands, then my soul will sleep easy at night. For I will have preserved the lives of tens of thousands—even your own soldiers! Even the lives of the Rebel boys who, even now, dress up in their fathers' and brothers' uniforms and wait until they're tall enough to take to the field…even those boys will be saved if one city burns!"

Suddenly, and inexplicably, Maria's eyes were wet and it was not an actress's trick.

She aimed the gun at his forehead and said, "Then go burn down Washington, you son of a bitch!"

And she fired, and a hole opened up in Ossian Steen's face. The back of his skull went splattering out behind him, all over the desk, and all over the priceless piece of carbon that sat on the edge like a paperweight.

Maria gasped—at her own actions, or with frustration, or relief, or some other emotion that she couldn't pin down as it raged inside her. But she squeezed the boy, whose small fingers were clawing at her neck as if he could burrow down inside her body and stay there, and not hear another gunshot so long as he lived.

She picked up her handbag and the diamond, stuffing the latter inside the former. She leaned on the knob and half pushed, half kicked her way out of the small building and she dashed into the yard with the child in her arm and the gun still smoking in her hand.

At the edge of the treeline she saw one of the guards face-down and unmoving, though she saw no sign of the second one, or of Brink, or of Croggon Hainey—who she'd inexplicably been hoping to glimpse. Her disappointment surprised her, but she did not have time to explore it. Somewhere beyond the hill she could hear the surging hum of an engine lifting itself high into the sky; and somewhere down beyond the sanatorium came the thunder of inrushing feet—Steen's reinforcements, or the remainder of the garrison, or surely some other problematic bunch of men.

Maria disentangled the boy's fingers from her neck and set him down on the ground where he shuddered, but stood.

She spoke to him in a hurried torrent of words. "Edwin, you're a smart boy, aren't you? That's why you live with Doctor Smeeks, down in the basement, isn't that right?" He nodded, and she continued with the same fast patter, "Doctor Smeeks is making a weapon, but only because that terrible man was threatening to harm you. Now you must do something for me, do you understand?"

"Yes," he said so softly she barely heard him.

"You must return to the basement and destroy the machine—and I don't think the doctor will stop you. He didn't want to build it in the first place. You must demolish it completely, so it can never be used and never be fixed. You must run and do it now, before anyone realizes what's happened here. Do you know where you are?"

He looked back at the building, and then at the trail. He said, "Yes" a bit louder this time.

"You know the way back to the sanatorium?"

"Yes," he declared, and sounded stronger still.

"Then run. Go. Don't stop and don't tell anyone but the doctor what you must do. Or possibly," she corrected herself, "if you need assistance, you must ask Anne. She'll help you. Now—off with you." She patted him on the back and he set off, stumbling at first, foot over foot, but then smoothing out to an ordinary gait that took him off at a sprint down the hill and along the path.

The whine of the engine above was coming closer and soon she could see its shadow, like a swarm of birds or a cloud of insects, rising up over the treetops, and she felt a tremendous surge of joy to see that it was the *Free Crow* and not the *Valkyrie*; and on the bridge, through the windshield glass she could see a hulking black figure clad in a blue coat.

"You there!" someone shouted behind her, and she spun around to see a Union soldier threatening her with a repeating rifle.

"Stop right there!" ordered another uniformed man, the second guard who she hadn't spied after the commotion in the outbuilding. "Drop your weapon!"

She jerked her attention back and forth between them and for the first time yet, she was uncertain. Maria had no intention of dropping the Colt and even less intention of stopping where she was told; and when the *Free Crow* soared over the outbuilding even the soldiers who commanded her looked up, and were amazed.

Thusly distracted, she took one last look down the path and saw not the faintest trace of Edwin—so she ran the other direction, back to the trees.

Behind her, the soldiers began to shoot. Bullets bounced off tree trunks and split branches, sending leaves raining down on her escape. They were running, too, pursuing her across the clearing and nearing the woods; but another round of fire blew forth from the sky, cutting a dotted line across their chase and pegging one soldier to the earth with a hole in his chest.

From the corner of her eye, Maria spotted her carpetbag lying where she'd left it. She did not pause her pace, but swept it up by the handle in a jerking lift that just barely threw her cadence off. She staggered, recovered her balance and her rhythm, and kept running while the ship above threw fire to cover her wake.

CAPTAIN CROGGON BEAUREGARD HAINEY
13

"Well I'll be damned," the captain said from the bridge of the *Free Crow*. "That crazy little woman made it out in one piece." He pointed down at the flat-roofed outbuilding, and the woman with the child on her hip. "That must be the boy she was talking about. Look, she's sending him off."

Simeon said, "Still no sign of Brink. Where'd you lose him?"

"Down there someplace." Hainey swung his hand around, using his fingers to point out a general area to the east of the outbuilding. "He can't have gone too far. I winged him, I'm pretty sure."

"What bit of him did you wing?" Lamar asked.

"Shoulder, I think."

The first mate shrugged and said, "He might run quite a ways with just a scratch on him. You should've aimed lower."

"I was running," Hainey groused. "Through a bunch of trees. You'll have to pardon my lack of precision."

"No one's criticizing it," Simeon said. "I was only saying, a winged kneecap would have dragged him a lot better." He jammed his feet down on the pedals and slowed the craft, letting it pivot almost in place, the windshield scrolling a panorama of the scene.

The captain grumbled, "Too many goddamned trees. Too many goddamned leaves. I can't see a thing on the ground except for *her*," he cocked his head down towards Maria.

"Speaking of *her*," Lamar said, drawing down a lever that would aim the engines at a slightly different tilt. "It looks like they've got her cornered."

"Where? Who?" he asked, even as he spotted the blue uniforms scuttling out of the woods. "Oh *hell*."

Simeon said with a small degree of pleasure, "They're going to shoot her."

"Or arrest her," the captain halfway argued. "She's been arrested plenty of times before. Maybe that's all they'll do."

Then, as she turned tail and ran, even up inside the *Free Crow* he could hear the soldiers open fire.

"Well *shit*," Hainey swore.

"Captain," Simeon said warily, "you're not thinking…"

He said grouchily, "Yes, I'm thinking. Lamar, how are the front swivel guns?"

"Um…" the engineer squinted at a set of gauges and said, "Mostly full. Not totally full, but mostly. We've got enough shot to give her some cover, if that's what you want."

He struggled with something for a minute, then said, "Yes, that's what I want. Strafe the strip behind her—keep them in the clearing, let her get a lead on them."

"But sir!" Simeon objected.

"I asked her for one favor in parting, and she paid it. She turned Brink loose for me when she could've shot him and saved herself a little peril. The least we can do is cover her getaway while we look for the thief."

"Fine," Simeon sulked, and he pulled a panel with munitions controls into his lap. "Left front-gun, stable. Tilt forty-five degrees, set."

Hainey yelled, "Fire!"

And the *Free Crow* gently bucked as its front gun strafed the clearing floor behind Belle Boyd, who was now nothing more than a pale streak dashing between the trees. One soldier went down immediately, caught in the path of descending bullets; and another dodged in time to fling himself on the grass and cover his head.

"Where's she going?" Hainey asked no one in particular.

But Lamar answered, "She's running toward the sanatorium. At least, she's running in that direction."

From their sky-high vantage point Hainey could see that this was going to work out poorly for the woman. The sanatorium was buzzing with activity...and with soldiers, yelling orders and herding each other out into a defensive formation. The spy was running straight for them, though none of her other options looked any good either. Behind her, the captain spotted a contingent of Union reinforcements coming up over the hill; they were fanning out as they closed in.

"She's a dead woman," Simeon observed.

Below, she stopped as if she'd heard him.

She gazed up directly at the *Free Crow*, waved her arms over her head, and pointed west with all her might.

"I don't get it," Hainey said. "What's she trying to say?"

"That she wants a ride," the first mate guessed.

"No, no. She's saying..."

She held her hands over her mouth and shouted something, over and over, and then she resumed pointing west.

Hainey followed her gesture with his eyes. He said, "Well I'll be damned."

"Again?" asked Lamar.

"Yes, again. Look at that—look at what that crazy bastard is trying to do!"

West of the outbuilding, and west of the woods where Belle Boyd was about to meet some unpleasant fate, the *Valkyrie* was inching its way off the hill.

Simeon said, "Brink?" as if he could scarcely believe it. "He can't fly that devil all by himself! He's good, but he's not *that* good."

"Maybe not, but he's *trying*," the captain observed. "Boyd must've heard him start the engines. She's closer to him than we are." And then he said, "Aw, hell."

Lamar said, "Sir?"

"I mean, aw hell—there she goes again, making herself useful. I guess we'd better swing down and pick her up."

Simeon swelled up in his seat, inflating and simmering with things he knew better than to say out loud to his captain, so he said, "Yes sir," through tight lips. "You steer us down. I'll hold us level."

"Let's hope she has the good sense to get on board," Hainey said. "I'm going to take us back a few feet, and we can come up behind her. Position, set?"

"Position set," Simeon confirmed. "Thrusters primed. You'd better run down to the bay and help her up, because Christ knows I'm not going to do it."

"Nobody asked you to, Sim," Hainey said, and he unbuckled himself from the seat. "Take us down, and drag us low and slow," he ordered as he left the bridge.

By the time Hainey reached the open bay, it was gathering leaves off trees as if it were harvesting them as the craft's belly was dragged down, low and slow, just like he'd ordered. The whipping breaks and whistles of the incoming shrubbery snapped against the bay edges and flipped into the captain's face, but he brushed them away and hollered down, "Belle Boyd? You hear me?"

He received no answer so he dropped to the floor and hung his head down, narrowly missing a pine branch to the teeth; but the glimpse told him her position—twenty yards ahead. The captain stood up and flung himself back to the bridge door, where he said, "There's a clearing up ahead. She'll breach it first. Drop us there, I'll grab her," and then he bolted back to the bay.

The ship dipped abruptly, and the bay was clear—no more trees accidentally sending their detritus aboard—but beneath it there was a woman running only a few feet ahead.

Hainey called out to her, "Belle Boyd!"

And she looked up, saw him, and replied, "Captain!"

He braced himself, locking his feet together around a support beam and letting his torso swing free. His arms extended down to reach her, but she didn't take them.

She threw him her carpetbag, and he caught it.

He set it inside with a hearty sigh of exasperation and then reached down once more. "Take my hands!" he commanded.

"You're going too fast!" she said, but she put her hands up anyway, and although she couldn't nab his hands, his enormous grip clapped around her nearest wrist.

When he was certain that his hold was secure, he said as loudly as he could to the men in the bridge, "I've got her! Take us up!"

Up went the ship in a sweeping lift, pulling Maria off her feet and into the air. Beneath her the ground grew smaller, and her feet swung in circles.

She said, "Captain, we've got to quit meeting like this! Tongues will begin to wag!" But she was smiling when she said it, and he didn't scowl back.

He heaved her onboard and deposited her beside her luggage.

While she caught her breath she asked in jolting syllables, "What… happened…to the bay doors…?"

To which he replied, "I shot them off. Come on. Get up, and get onto the bridge. I went to the trouble of getting you on board, and I won't have you falling back out again."

"Yes sir. But, oh—did you understand me? The *Valkyrie*—someone's trying to take off with it. I sent the red-haired pirate outside before I dealt with Steen; did you catch him?"

"No," he said as he retreated back onto the deck. "So I appreciate the tip. That's him on board, you can bet your sweet…you can bet your mother's life. But that's fine. We'll just knock him out of the sky."

She entered the bridge behind him and nodded politely to Lamar and Simeon, neither one of whom saw her do it. "But the *Valkyrie*…can you do that? With this ship? It's so heavily armored, I thought…"

Lamar turned around then, and he said with a full-toothed grin, "We made some modifications before we left it. Hold onto your hat," he said, and then seeing that she'd lost hers somewhere along the way, "Or, hold onto your knickers. Or whatever you're still wearing. We're going to make a very big *bang*."

"There it is!" she said, indicating a black shape out the western side of the windshield.

"I see it," Simeon said. "And look at that. Well, credit where it's due— I would've bet that he'd never get it off the ground, not alone."

"Where's the rest of his crew?" Maria asked, but no one answered her.

"Stay away from the dashboard," the captain said. "Don't touch anything, and just stand back. I can't offer you another seat up here; this ain't a big bird like that one, and we've only got sitting space for the three of us."

"All right. But look, he did get it off the ground. Not very far," she observed. "He's rising, though. He's nearly crested the next hill over."

"He's a sitting duck," Hainey crowed.

"In that warship?" Maria asked, still dubious.

"Oh yes," the captain told her. "Like Lamar said. Modifications. Sim, swing us west and around. Lamar, hold us tight and ready that right front gun."

"The left one has more ammo," the engineer said. "We sprayed most of the rest covering *her*," he bounced a thumb at the spy.

Maria said, "And for what it's worth, thank you—from the bottom of my heart."

"You're welcome," Hainey said. "Fine, Lamar. Take the right gun and send us into position, but back us up."

"How far, sir?"

"How far away do you think I can aim it from?" he asked.

Lamar didn't give him a number or a measurement, but he said, "All right. I'll take us back that far."

The *Free Crow* retreated on a slick, easy path, holding the *Valkyrie* in its sights. As the ship withdrew, the bright-haired figure on the bridge grew tinier and tinier, and its frantic struggles with the controls grew harder and harder to see.

Hainey said, "Swing us back; bring us point forward with the *Valkyrie*'s tail."

And Simeon made it happen.

"Lamar, let me have your seat for a minute."

The engineer rose and let the captain sit. He pulled the trigger for the front right gun into his lap and flexed his fingers around the molded grip. And, taking his time, he said to Maria, "You see that back armor panel, over the hydrogen tanks?"

Puzzled, she said, "No."

And he replied, "That's because we pulled it off."

He squeezed the trigger and the ship jumped as the big guns fired, squirting shells across the sky in a deadly arc that pitted the side of the *Valkyrie*...and then stabbed into the hydrogen tanks.

In the span of two seconds, the *Valkyrie* shook, shimmered, and exploded into a nova of fire that seemed to stretch across the entire windscreen of the *Free Crow*.

A shockwave rocked the ship and everyone within it, and for a moment it swayed and fought against its own engines. But soon with the help of its expert crew, it steadied and rose once more, sliding back across the sky and away from the flaming, falling wreckage of the Union warbird.

CLEMENTINE

Over the sanatorium the *Free Crow* flew, and as it rose Maria ignored the earlier admonition to stay away from the controls—because the windshield was on the other side of the controls and she couldn't see the world outside unless she stood in front of them. As Captain Hainey returned to his proper seat and Lamar reclaimed his own, the captain asked, "What are you looking at?"

She said, "There, do you see? The sanatorium."

"What about it?"

"Look, down there. Those windows at the building's very bottom— they let light into the basement. They're open, do you see?" she said, her eyes bright and still, perhaps, a little wet.

Hainey did see, though he wasn't sure what he was seeing. "Someone's emptying the basement then, it looks like to me. They're throwing things out onto the lawn."

"It's the weapon," she told him. "The boy, Edwin—he and Doctor Smeeks are destroying it. They never wanted to build it in the first place, and now they're disassembling it."

As the ship hovered, the captain, Maria, and the crew watched as the boy collected the weapon's parts into a pile on the front yard; and then they observed as an elderly man came to toss a match onto the pile.

Maria said, "That's it, then." She looked up at the captain and said it again. "That's it."

"That wasn't part of your initial mission though, was it?" the captain asked, though he already knew the answer.

"Of course it wasn't. But...but I'm glad I did it, regardless. And besides, my mission for Pinkerton went well enough," she insisted, stuffing one Colt into her handbag and unfastening the gunbelt from her hips.

Hainey asked, "How do you figure that? You hitched a ride with the crew you were hired to stop, and then you killed the man whose shipment you were supposed to ensure. You wreaked a fair bit of havoc, Belle Boyd."

Maria didn't ask how he knew she'd killed Steen.

She only said, "Yes, but *technically* I was only hired to make sure the shipment arrived at the sanatorium. And I'd like for the record to reflect, the diamond *did*, in fact, arrive safely at its intended destination." She did not add that it had a new destination, stashed in her own luggage.

Maria planted her feet and folded her arms, daring anyone to argue with her.

Croggon Beauregard Hainey put his face in his hand, and his body began to quiver as the laugh he meant to hide worked its way up, and out, and into the bridge of the *Free Crow*. He laughed louder and harder than he'd ever laughed in his life; and before long, Maria Isabella Boyd joined him with a devious smile.

TELEGRAM FROM LOUISVILLE, KENTUCKY, TO CHICAGO, ILLINOIS

14

CLEMENTINE SAFELY REACHED DESTINATION AND DELIVERED CARGO TO SANATORIUM STOP FATE OF HAINEY AND CREW UNKNOWN STOP WILL RETURN TO CHICAGO BY TRAIN TOMORROW MORNING AND AWAIT MY NEXT ASSIGNMENT STOP I BELIEVE THIS JOB SUITS ME QUITE WELL AND I THANK YOU FOR THE OPPORTUNITY STOP

WISHBONES

This one was written for the Apex Books anthology *Aegria Somnia* back in 2006. I was still finding my footing, but I still like the idea and I'm glad I took a swing at it. I'd stumbled across this Japanese monster that assembles its own body from the bones of people who've starved to death—an idea that collided with an article I'd read recently about anorexia and other eating disorders. That's how most of my projects happen, to be honest. People will take apart the whole "where do you get your ideas?" question until the end of time, but I always say that ideas are never really the problem—the problem is finding time to develop them all.

Ideas are flying around everywhere, and for me it's not so much that question of "architect vs. gardener." It's more like Katamari Damancy. One idea sticks to another idea, making a slightly larger idea. This idea collects another one or two, and eventually you're pushing along a ball of ideas that's big enough to turn into a story, or a book.

So "Wishbones" is assembled from an assortment of ideas: war, and what happens to the land after one; monsters imported from someplace else, but who find what they need wherever they are; and the mundanity of a place a few generations after something historic occurs.

But mostly it's about being hungry.

Some choose their hunger and some are caught up in war, left in prisoner camps to wither away. Either way, if you're too hungry for too long, you'll die. The monster at the heart of this story can't tell the difference, and it wouldn't care if it could.

*A**T THE** Andersonville camp there is a great, stinking dread. The Confederates don't have enough food of their own, so they sure as hell aren't feeding their prisoners of war; and the prisoners who aren't wasting away are dying of diseases faster than they can be replaced. Here, the world smells like bloody shit and coal smoke. It reeks of body odor and piss, and sweat. South Georgia is nowhere to live by choice, and nowhere to die by starving.*

The remains—the bodies of the ones who finally fell and couldn't rise again—they lie in naked piles, leather over skeletons as thin as hat racks. They lie in stacks waiting to be put into the ground. They collect in the back buildings because no one is strong enough to dig anymore, not blue nor gray. This does not explain why, at night and sometimes between the watches, the piles are shrinking.

Some of us thought, at first, how people were hungry enough that even the old meat-leather on the bones out back…it might be better than nothing. We talked amongst ourselves in riddles that rationalized unthinkable things. We wondered about our friends and fellow soldiers who were dead there, piled like cordwood. We said, of old Bill this—or old Frank that—how he'd wish we weren't so hungry, if he were still here. We agreed, we nodded our heads, and we thought about how we'd make our secret ways back to the long, low shed.

But best as I know it, no one ever worked up the courage to do it. No one took any knives and crept back there, away from the guards who were half-starved themselves.

How would we have cooked it, anyway? How do you smoke or carve a human being, an old friend? Even so, the numbered dead began a backward count. One by one, the bodies went gone, and when fifteen or twenty had most definitely been taken, or lost, that's when we began to hear the noise at night. It was hard to calculate, hard to pinpoint. Hard to explain, or indicate. But it rattled like the bones of death himself, beneath a robe or within loose-hanging skin. It wobbled and clattered back behind the sheds where the dead were kept.

It walked. It crept.

It gathered.

"Pete's Porno Palace, this is Scott, how can I help you?"

"Jesus," Dean shook his head. "Pete is going to fire your ass one of these days."

Scott wiggled the receiver next to his head and grinned. "Pizza Palace, ma'am. Of course that's what I said. Best in Plains, don't you know it? And what can I get for you today?"

"Jesus," Dean mumbled again and walked away. He untied his apron and wadded it up around his hand, then left it on the counter. His cigarettes were in his jacket pocket, hanging by the back door.

He took the smokes and left the jacket. Dead of winter in south Georgia doesn't usually call for anything heavier than a sweater, but sometimes when you own jackets, you just want to wear them—so you wait until it's barely cold enough, and you drag them out anyway.

So the jacket stayed on the peg and Dean stepped outside.

Dark was coming, but not bad yet; and the backwoods pitch black would hold off for another hour at least. Even so, when he struck the wheel of the lighter the sparks were briefly blinding. Maybe it was darker already than he'd thought. Or maybe he should quit working double shifts, no matter how cute Lisa was, or how hard she swung her eyelashes at him when she asked him to cover for her.

He wrapped his lips around the cigarette and sucked it gently while the flame took hold. The bricks of the old pizza joint were almost warm against his back when he leaned there, beside the back door, facing the dumpster and the edge of the woods.

A crackling noise—small footsteps, or shuffling—rustled underneath the big metal trash container.

"Scram," Dean commanded, but the soft crunching continued. He reached down by his feet and picked up the first thing he felt—an empty can that once held tomato sauce. He chucked it like a knuckleball and something squeaked, and scuttled. "Stupid raccoons. Rats. Whatever."

"One of these days." Scott slipped through the doorway and shimmied sideways to stand next to him. "One of these days, it's going to be a bear, and you're going to get your face chewed off. Give me one?"

Dean palmed the pack to the delivery driver. "Help yourself. Bears. Stop shitting me. You ever see a bear out here?"

"No. But I've never seen a submarine, either, and I believe they exist in the world, someplace."

"You do, huh?"

"Yeah. Seen pictures. Anyway, I'm just saying, and shit, it's dark. We need to put a lamp out here or something. Can't see a damn thing." He lit a cigarette for himself and passed the pack back to Dean, who set it down on top of a crate. "You got somewhere to go?"

Scott nodded. "Two large sausage and mushrooms. Going towards no man's land, out towards Andersonville. Fucking hate that, driving out there."

WISHBONES

"Why?"

He popped his neck and sighed, taking another drag. "I always figure that's where I'll get a flat tire, or that's where the transmission will finally drop out of the Civic. It's only a matter of time, man, and I know my luck. It'll happen there."

"So what if it does? You've got a cell. I'd come and get you, or Pete would."

"I don't like it, is all. My sister's boyfriend, you know Ben, he used to live out that way, and he talked about it like it was weird. You know. Because of the camp."

Dean leaned his head back. "Oh yeah. The camp. I guess, sure. That could be weird. I think it'd be worse to live up north, near the battlefields. You hear cannons and artillery and shit. The camp was just...I don't know. Jail for POWs. And it's a park now. You seen it? It's all pretty and mowed."

"Man, people *died* there."

"People die everywhere." Dean crushed the cigarette against the wall, even though it was only half smoked.

Henry saw it first. He said he saw it, anyway. He said it was there, back by the sheds where they stored up the dried out dead until they could be dumped into a pit. According to him, it was a man-sized thing with black hole eyes and no soul inside it. According to him and his starved up brain, the thing moved all jerky, like it wasn't used to having limbs. Like it wasn't used to having legs, or feet, or nothing like that.

Like it was man-sized, but no man.

"It staggers," Henry said. "It shuffles along and it takes them—it pulls them out the low windows, pulls them out in pieces and it, Jesus Lord, amen."

"What'd you see, anyway?" we asked, all gathered around close.

"It had an arm or something. A leg maybe. We get so skinny you can't tell, by looking in the dark. You can't see if that's a hand or a foot on the end of it, just that it's long and there's a joint in the middle. But the thing

I saw, it had a limb of some kind, and it didn't bite it, didn't eat it or anything like that. It peeled it, just like a banana. It used these white, long fingers to pick the skin and just strip it on down until there was nothing there but bone."

The rest of us gasped, and one or two of us gagged. "Why?" I asked him.

"I haven't the foggiest. I haven't any idea, but that's how it happened. That's what it did. And then, when it finished yanking the skin away, it hugged on the bones what were left. It pulled them against its chest, and it's like they stuck there. It's like it pulled them against himself and they stayed there, and became part of him."

"Why would it do something like that—and better still, what would do something like that? It doesn't make any sense."

"I don't know," he said, and he was shaking. "But I'll tell you this—I'd gotten to thinking, these days, that maybe dying wasn't the worst thing that could happen. You know how it is, here. You know how sometimes you see another one drop and you almost feel, for a few minutes, a little envy for him."

"But not now," I said.

"No, not now."

"Lisa called in again," Scott said, putting the phone down and looking like he wanted to swear. "Third time in two weeks. Remind me again why she's still on the payroll? She's not *that* hot."

Dean shrugged into his apron and kept one eye on the cash register, where Lisa usually worked. "She's been sick, I think. Something wrong with her. She's been throwing up; I heard her in the bathroom a couple of days ago. That means we're short again, right?"

"You're not going to cover for her this time?"

"Can't." Dean adjusted the temperature dial on the side of the big pizza oven and felt a kick of heat when the old motor sparked to life.

"Can't? Or won't?"

"Whichever. I've got things to do tonight. I covered her with a double the last two times. You take this one."

"No. And you can't make me."

"Well then, I guess they'll be short tonight. It can't always be my problem," he complained, even though he knew why everyone acted like it was. He and Lisa had gone on a couple of dates once, and everyone treated them like it had been a secret office romance or something.

But Pete's wasn't an office, the dates hadn't been secret, and there wasn't anything much in the way of romance going on. Dean liked Lisa and he called her a friend, but it didn't seem very mutual unless she couldn't make it to work. He wondered if she was really sick and hiding it, like it was something worse than the flu.

The phone rang again as soon as Scott put it back on the hook. "Christ," he complained. "We don't even open for another ten minutes. You answer it."

"No. You get it. If it's Lisa I don't want to talk to her. She'll try to rope me into covering for her, and I won't do it."

"Fine." He lifted the phone and said, with his mouth too close to the receiver, "Pete's Pizza Place, would you like to try two medium pizzas with two toppings for ten bucks?"

Dean walked away, back towards the refrigerator. He yanked the silvertone lever that opened the big walk-in; he stepped inside took the first two plastic cartons he found—green peppers, and onions, respectively. Both sliced. Whoever had closed had done a good job, he thought. Then he remembered that he hadn't gone home until one in the morning, and that the handiwork was his own. "I'm here too damn much," he said to the olives. The olives didn't answer, but they implied their agreement by floating merrily in their own juices.

He stacked the olives on top of the green peppers and onions so that the three containers fit beneath his chin. With his hip, he opened the door again and carried the toppings out to the set-up counter and began to lay them out.

"Fucking *A*," Scott swore, still scribbling something down on the order pad kept next to the phone. "Another one."

"Another one what?"

"Another delivery, all the way out in Andersonville."

"That's not that far."

"Yeah, well. You know why I don't like it."

Dean cocked his head, dropping the olives into their usual spot with a sliding click. "Because you're a superstitious bastard?"

"That is correct, sir. It's the same house, I think. I told the guy he couldn't have his order for another hour at least, but he didn't care. So. Fine, I guess. I'll drive it out once we finally get open, and at least it's still daylight. Where's Pete?"

"He's not coming in until noon. He'll be here then, though."

"Okay. Cool. So it's just us until then?"

"Yep." Dean abandoned the conversation for the refrigerator again. This time he emerged with crumbly sausage balls and a fat sliced stack of pepperoni. He wasn't concerned about the lack of help; they'd opened the store alone before, and it wasn't too bad.

"I thought I heard someone out back, a few minutes ago. I thought maybe it was Lisa, but I don't know why."

"Lisa just called in, though."

"Yeah, I know. I don't know why I thought it was her. It turned out to be nobody, I guess." He stopped talking there, even though it sounded like he wanted to say more.

Dean dropped the pepperoni rounds into their appropriate spot and wiped a little bit of grease on his apron. "Out back? By the dumpster?"

"Yeah."

"Maybe it was a bear."

"You're an asshole. It wasn't a bear."

"It wasn't Lisa, either."

"Smelled like her."

Dean frowned. "What?"

"It smelled like her, I think that's what it was." Scott tweaked the pen and the order pad between his hands and leaned back against the counter. "She wears that rose perfume sometimes, she puts it in her hair."

"How often do you get close enough to tell?"

Scott slapped the order pad against the counter and left it there. "You know what I mean—she wears it strong because she doesn't want her mom to know she smokes. You can smell it in the back, in the kitchen, when she goes through there to take a break."

"I know what you mean, yeah. Okay."

"Well, that's it. That's what I smelled. But she wasn't there."

"Nobody was there."

"That's what I said. Nobody was there. But I felt like someone was watching me."

Dean raised an eyebrow that didn't care one way or another, and went back towards the refrigerator for another armload of toppings. "Must've been that goddamn mythical bear."

The thing out back, behind the sheds, it's getting bigger. Charles has seen it now, and the Sergeant too—they both say it's bigger than a man, and either Henry's been lying or the thing is getting bigger.

We talk about it more than we should, maybe. But there's nothing else to talk about, except how we want to go home and how much we'd love a meal. So we tell each other about the thing like it's a campfire story, as if we're little boys trying to scare each other. Except we don't want to anymore, really. We're scared enough already, and now we're just trying to understand what new, fresh horror has been imposed upon us.

As if this were not enough.

We are all so hungry, and we know there's no prayer for food since our captors haven't got any either, even for themselves. If the guards can't feed themselves, then we prisoners are done for.

In our bunks, smelling like summer in a charnel house, we gather and talk and wait. At night, we cluster close together even though all of us stink of death and bodies that haven't seen a bath in months. It's better than cowering alone and listening to the knock-kneed haint come walking by.

We think it grows by consuming us—it eats the starved ones up and walks on borrowed bones ill-fit together. And so many of us have wasted away, and so many more are bound to follow.

In another month, that thing will be a god.

"Hey," Lisa said. Her long brown hair was tied back behind her ears, elf-style, and her eyes were more bloodshot than blue. Dean thought maybe she was looking thinner every day, like her collarbones jutted sharper out of her tank top and maybe her tits were settling closer to her ribcage. "Hey. Welcome back."

"Sure," she said, but it didn't make much sense as a response.

At supper rush she manned the cash register at the end of the counter, and Scott leaned in over Dean's shoulder. "She looks like hell."

"Yeah she does. Told you. She's been sick."

"That doesn't look like sick to me, exactly."

Dean shifted his arms to push Scott back, out of his personal space. "What do you think it looks like, then? What are you saying? You think it's drugs or something?"

"You said it, not me. It looks like it, though. Look at her. And you know what—she's gone to the bathroom three times in the last five hours."

"You've been counting? That's fucked up, man."

"I've been counting because I've been covering the register while you've been making pizzas. It's not like I've been taking inventory of her bladder or anything." He tapped his foot against the counter's support and chewed his lower lip. "I'm thinking, it could be crystal meth, or something like that. Meth makes you skinny."

"Meth makes you wired too," Dean argued. "She's been dragging. I think she's just been sick. I wonder if, do you think it's something like cancer? Christ, what if she has AIDS or something?"

"Did you ever fuck her?"

"No. Didn't go together that long."

Scott raised a shoulder and crushed his lips together in a dismissive grimace. "Then who cares?"

"I do, sort of. She's all right. Don't be an asshole about her. Hey—the phone's ringing. It's for you."

"I don't want to answer it."

"Well, you're going to." Dean turned his back completely, absorbing himself in the scattering of green things onto the crust and paste.

After a few seconds of being ignored, Scott took the hint and picked up the phone. "Pete's Party Palace, what's your request?"

Dean returned to making pizzas and shoveling them onto the slow-moving conveyor belt in the oven. Lisa stayed at the register and didn't seem to notice much of anything that wasn't right in front of her.

He watched, though. He waited for her to take a break, and then he followed her—back outside to where the dumpsters are pillaged by the creatures who come up from the edge of the woods. By the time he reached the doorway she was struggling with a cigarette lighter, so he offered her his.

"Thanks," she said, and she leaned against the bricks.

Dean joined her. "I've been wanting to ask you," he started, but she cut him off.

"Thanks for covering for me the other night. I appreciated it. I wasn't feeling good, is all."

"That's cool. No big deal. I wanted to ask you, though, if something's wrong. I mean, *really* wrong. I know we're not that tight or anything, but if you need something, all you have to do is say so."

Lisa took a short drag on the cigarette, one that couldn't have earned her much nicotine. "What are you trying to ask me? You talking your way around something?"

He studied her closely, trying to think of how to ask what he meant. She was shaky—not in a hard way like she was shivering, but in a low-grade hum that meant her whole body was moving, very slightly. When her fingers squeezed themselves around the cigarette, her chipped pearl nail polish looked ill and yellow against the paper. She glared out at the dumpster, and out past it. She glared into the coming dark like it might tell her important things, but she didn't really expect it to.

"Are you sick? I can't ask it any better than that. You've looked, I mean, you haven't looked good the last few times you've been here. Like you're weak, or like you've got a fever. I was wondering if maybe there wasn't something really wrong and you hadn't felt like telling us."

"Like what?"

"Like, I don't know. Cancer or something." He didn't mention Scott's meth theory because it seemed even ruder than telling a girl she looked terrible. He rolled on his shoulder to face her. "Look, you—you look like you're wasting away. You've been losing weight, enough weight that Scott even noticed, and he didn't notice it when you cut your hair off and dyed it black last year. It's pretty dramatic."

It was strange and not at all pleasant, the small smile that lifted a corner of her mouth beside the cigarette. "Bless your heart," she breathed. Then, a little louder, "You think I'm shrinking? You didn't have to say it like you were asking if I was dying. Most women like it if you point out they're losing weight."

"Yeah, but…" He couldn't figure out a tactful way to phrase the obvious rest.

"It's been good, lately. I've been getting into clothes I haven't worn since junior high."

"That's good?"

"It might be. I think it's good. I could still stand to—" She stopped herself, and changed her mind. "It's not the end of the world, dropping a few pounds. It's a good thing. I don't mind it, and I wish I could take another few down, so stop worrying. That's all it is. I'm on a diet."

"What kind of diet? Like a starvation diet, or what? You got some kind of eating disorder now, is that how it is?"

"There's nothing disordered about it. It's the most orderly thing I've ever done." She crushed the lit end of the cigarette against the wall, leaving a black streak on the brick and a mangled butt on the ground as she went back inside.

There's a Chinaman here in camp, a small fellow who looks like he might be a thousand years old. Someone told me he came from out west, out across the frontier—someone said he'd come east from California, but I can't imagine why.

He says he's no Chinaman, and he seems to get offended if you call him one, even though I don't think he understands one word of English out of three. I don't know his name or what he's doing here, except that he runs errands between the officers. He washes pots and clothes for the Confederates when there's water to wash them, and I guess that's not strange since there aren't any women around.

The little old fellow is mostly quiet. He mostly listens and keeps his head low, not wanting to draw any attention to himself. Henry says he looks strange and wise, and I don't know if that's right or not, but the Chinaman sure has these black, sharp eyes that always seem to know something.

He came up on us, the other night while we were talking about the thing that eats the bones out back. Like I told it, I don't know how much of our talk he understands—but he got the idea. He saw our fear, and he watched the way we pointed and whispered at the sheds out back. One of the guards heard us too, and he told us to shut ourselves up and be quiet, we were just trying to start trouble. He was complaining how we didn't need any more trouble than we'd already got, and he was right, but that didn't change anything.

When he was gone, the Chinaman tiptoed forward. He nodded, yes. He nodded like he understood. He pointed one long, wrinkled finger towards the sheds where the dead are stored and where they wait to be buried.

"Gashadokuro," he said. It was a funny, long word filled with sharp edges. We stared up at him, blank faces not comprehending very well. He looked back at us, frustrated that he could not make us comprehend. "Gashadokuro," he said again, pointing harder.

And then I nodded, trying to repeat the piece of foreign tongue and probably mangling it past recognition. I tried to convey my realization, that yes— the thing was there, and yes—it had a name, and it was a foreign name from across the country, and across the ocean, because white men like us wouldn't know what to call it.

Gashadokuro.

We can't even say it.

After Lisa was gone, Dean kept smoking and he said to the empty back lot, "You don't eat with us anymore. We all used to eat together after shift."

A creak answered him, with a twisting squeal of metal and a gentle knocking.

He jumped, and settled. The dumpster again. Something inside it. No, something behind it. Dean held his dwindling cigarette out like a weapon, or a pointer. "Scram," he said, but he didn't say it loud. "Scram, you goddamn rats. Raccoons." It wasn't worth adding "bears" to the list, because he still thought Scott was full of shit.

But it was dark enough, and the woods were a black line of soldier-straight trees, hiding everything beyond or past them. He stepped forward, just a pace or two. Towards the dumpster, and the rattling shuffle that came from behind it, or beside it—somewhere near it.

"Get lost," he said with a touch more volume as another possibility occurred to him. Plains didn't have too many homeless people; it didn't have too many people of any sort, truth to tell. But there was always the chance of a passing human scavenger. You never knew, in this day and age.

The noise was louder as he got closer—tracking it with his ears to a spot behind the dumpster, close to the trees. It wasn't all scratching, either. It was something muffled and banging together—something like pool balls clattering in felt, or inside a leather bag. He couldn't pinpoint it, no matter how hard he listened.

Scott's head popped into the doorway, casting a giant round shadow against Dean's back. "Who're you talking to out here? Yourself again?"

"Sure." He turned and squinted at the doorway, where the world suddenly looked much brighter within that rectangle.

"I've got to make another run out to my favorite spot in all of Georgia. You coming back inside or what? I can't leave until someone takes the ovens, and baby, that needs to be *you*."

Dean looked back into the woods, past the dumpster where the noise had stopped as soon as Scott appeared. "Back towards the old prison camp?"

"Of course. Why can't that guy always call during the day, huh? Why's he got to wait until the creeps come out?"

"Why would you put it that way?" Dean asked, a hint of petulance framing the words. "There aren't any creeps. There's just the old camp, and there's nothing there anymore."

"Then why don't you drive it, if you're so fucking unperturbable. I hate going out there, it's—"

"It's not even two miles, you chickenshit. You could practically walk them the pizza in the time you've stood here complaining about it."

"Practically, but never. I'm serious. You do it, if that's what it's about. I'll take the ovens and the onion-smelling hands for a few minutes. *You* go brave the ghosts from the old camp."

"I will, then. Fine. Give me the address." He pulled himself back inside and swiped the sheet of paper out of Scott's hand.

The gash-beast is hungry; it is as hungry as we are. As it grows, so does its appetite. As it grows, and we diminish, it becomes ravenous. It outpaces us.

For us, the hunger comes and goes—and comes again. It's when it comes again that we know, we know that it won't be dysentery or cholera or pneumonia that takes us. We know it will be the hunger. When first we go without food the days drag and stretch, and the belly is all we can think of. But in a few days, after a week or so, the hunger fades. The body adjusts. The stomach shrinks and thoughts of food are sharply sweet, but no longer dire.

It's when the hunger comes again that we know.

It takes some time—maybe a month, maybe less. But when the weeks have slid by and there's nothing yet to fill us, when the hunger returns it returns with a message: "Now," it says, "you are dying. Now your body consumes itself from the inside, out. This is what will kill you."

The gash-monster knows. It hovers close, a clattering angel of death that follows the weakest ones after dark. It hums and taps, drumming its bone-fingers against the walls and waiting by the doors. It is impatient. And we are all afraid, even those of us whose stomachs have balled themselves into tight little knots that don't cry out just yet—we are all afraid that the gash-monster's impatience will get the better of it.

We are all afraid that the time will come when the dead aren't quite enough, and it comes to chase the living, starving, withering souls whose hearts still beat with a feeble persistence. We are all afraid that the time will come when it pulls our still-living limbs apart, and peels our skin away, and eats our bones while we bleed and cry on the ground.

We keep ourselves quiet when the hunger returns.

We do not want it to hear us.

WISHBONES

When Dean returned, he reclaimed his apron and went back to the pizza line. "Hey look," he told Scott. "Nothing snuck up and ate me."

"Bite me, big boy. Speaking of eating, we're shutting down in ten—no, eight minutes, and there are two large leftovers with our names on 'em. Pete said they're ours if we want them."

"Good to know. What's on them?"

"Gross shit. Pineapples and onion on the one, and sausage, chicken and anchovy on the other—that's your three major meat groups, right there. Three of the four, anyway. It'd need hamburger too, to make a good square meal of meat."

"Jesus." Dean made a face.

Scott mirrored the grimace and put the pizzas on the outside edge of the oven to stay warm. "Yeah. If I weren't so hungry, I'd leave them out back for the bears, but I've been here since before lunch and I'm either going to eat one of these fuckers, or my own hand—whichever holds still first and longest. Lisa—hey string bean there—we'll save some for you, baby. You could stand a little grease on those bones. It'll fatten you up. Put hair on your chest."

Lisa pushed a button on the cash register to open the drawer. "You don't know a damn thing about women, do you Scott?"

"Probably not. Anyway, you want some?"

She reached beneath the drawer and scooped out the twenties, gathering them into a little stack. "No."

Dean watched her count for a few seconds, then said, "You didn't take a break for supper."

"So?"

"So you've been here as long as the rest of us. And you're not starving?"

"No. Mind your own business. No, I'm not starving." She went back to her counting, and made a point of not paying any further attention to either of the other closers. When she wrapped up the drawer's contents, she put a rubber band around them and slipped them into a zippered bag that she then deposited into the safe.

"Aren't you jumping the gun a tad with that?" Dean asked, but she shrugged back at him.

"There's nobody here. Who cares? Turn off the sign. Let's close up."

"Where are you going?"

"Bathroom, to change clothes. I'm not walking home smelling like this. It's gross."

Dean took a rag and started wiping down the pizza line. "Smelling like food? It's not the grossest thing in the world, not by a long shot."

"I don't like it," she said. She lifted up the counter blocker that kept customers from wandering back into the kitchen and it almost looked like too much effort for those bird-frail arms. She shuddered when it dropped back down behind her, when it fell back to its slot with a clang.

"Lisa?" Dean asked, thinking maybe he'd follow her or ask more questions, but she saw it coming and she waved him away.

"Don't," she ordered. "Just...don't."

"Stick around a few minutes, I'll drive you home when we're finished eating. I'll give you a lift—I mean, you really don't look like you're in any shape to walk back to the 'burbs."

"I'm in plenty good shape to walk anywhere I want. Thanks, though." She added the last part as she rounded the corner, taking a backpack with her.

The bathroom door clicked itself shut behind her.

Dean jerked his hands into the air. "I give up," he declared.

"It's about time," Scott said. The words were already muffled around a mouth full of pizza. "Come and get it. More for us."

"Okay. Yeah, okay."

The back door was open, propped that way for the sake of air flow. Dean went back through the kitchen, back beside the refrigerator, and back to that open door that looked out over the empty lot—and the woods beyond it. Scott was right. They needed a lamp.

The dumpster loomed black before the lot. It stank of rust, rot, and the decay of uneaten things that should've long ago been picked up. Trash service was spotty out there sometimes, and the bin was starting to fill. Maybe the collectors would come by before the morning.

It was as good an excuse as any not to take out the trash.

A clatter popped, loud beside his head.

Dean jerked—staring around and trying not to look too frantic, in case it was just Scott being an asshole. But Scott was inside, he could hear him. He'd turned up the radio past the point of ambient noise; and he'd tuned it to a louder station than Pete ever subjected the customers to. Inside, Scott was singing along to Skinny Puppy with his mouth full.

The clatter wasn't Scott.

It was hard to place, like before—hard to tell exactly where the sound was, or exactly what it sounded like. It sounded so close to so many things, but not precisely like any of them. The clicking was loud but muffled. Next to his head, between the building and the dumpster, and high. Up higher, he thought, higher than the edge of the window sill were the pattering knocks when they sounded again.

"Is somebody out here?" Dean asked, not loud enough to even pretend he wanted a response.

The clattering continued, high and muffled, and rhythmic—there was a balance to it, a swinging, swaying, like the pendulum on a large clock moving back and forth. Or like hips, loosely jointed and walking in lanky-legged steps.

"I…" There should've been more to say, but the noise—all rounded edges and heavy bones—was only coming closer.

He retreated back into the doorway, still seeing nothing except, maybe, at the edge of his sight something pale in a jagged flash. Whatever it was, he wanted no more of it; he tumbled over himself to get back inside, and he shut the door fast—hard. He drew the bolt back and stepped away, staring down at the door's lever handle, waiting for it to wiggle or slide.

"Dude?" Scott called. "Something wrong? You're panting like a sick dog in here; I can hear you all the way in the kitchen."

"I'm not panting!" Dean all but shouted, and as he objected he could hear his own breath dragging unevenly from his chest and out his mouth. "I'm not—there was something outside. Don't look at me like that, I'm serious. There's something out there and it's not a goddamn *bear*."

"Okay, calm down. What, then? Another raccoon or rat?"

"Fuck off, man. I don't know what. I don't know what, but I'm not going back to look."

"Let me see," he said but it was less a request than an announcement that he was going to look outside.

"Don't," Dean commanded, stepping between his coworker and the bolted metal door. "Don't. Whatever it was, we don't want it in here. It was, it was *big*—and I don't know what. Just leave it shut. It'll go away, later."

"You're actually scared?"

"Yes, I'm scared. What is there—there's rabies and shit, man. And big things with big teeth in the woods. Fine, a bear, if you want to call it that—if you want to wonder or worry about that."

Scott snorted. "Puss."

"Less a puss than *you*, motherfucker. At least I'm afraid of actual *things*, and not ghosts, like dead people from the Civil War. That ain't a ghost out there, whatever it is. It's something that came in from the woods, is what. And I'd just as soon not get eaten on the way home from work, so leave the door closed or you'll let it in."

"Fine," Scott held out his hands in surrender. "Fine, Christ. If it's that big a deal to you. Calm down, already. Don't get crazy."

"I'm not crazy, I think I've heard it out there before," he said, and he realized as the words came out that he was serious—he *had* heard it before, but not so loud and not so close. It had been working itself up, working itself close. Homing in. Dean shuddered, and peeled his apron off. He tossed it at the pegs where the coats were usually kept and it stuck, then straggled itself down to the floor. "Forget it. I'm not hungry anymore. I'm going home."

"With the monster outside? Ooh, you're *brave*."

"I'm going out the front," Dean growled. "Where there's a nice open parking lot and a big ol' streetlamp."

"Before you go—are you giving Lisa a ride? I think she needs one."

"What? She said no. She said she didn't want one."

Scott cocked his head towards the front of the restaurant, in the vague, general direction of the bathrooms. "She's still in the bathroom. Don't leave her with me; she's not my problem."

"Not mine either."

"You care more than I do. Go knock on the door or something."

Dean stood still and scowled, weighing the options and his own worry. "Fine. I'll go get her."

If nothing else, it gave him something else to think about; it gave him a few more seconds to calm his heartbeat and another problem to think about.

He grabbed his light coat and shifted his shoulders into it, then pulled his keys out of his jeans pocket and went to the door of the ladies room. He pressed his head against it, listening for any signs of life within. He rapped the back of his knuckles against the wood, lightly—politely. "Hey Lisa. You in there, still?"

She didn't answer, so he knocked again.

"You in there? Hey, I'm going home now. I'm tired and I'm not as hungry as I thought I was. Open up. I'll give you a ride home. Hey. Are you in there?"

He knew she must be, but there was no hint of life. No water running, no toilets flushing. Again he knocked, but there wasn't any answer. "Do you need help? You'd better say something, or else I'm going to come in there. Do you hear me?"

Nothing.

Until there was the crash.

The sound of splintering, shattering glass rang out behind the closed door, jolting Dean so badly he leaped away. "Lisa?" he shouted, and he reached for the knob. It moved a click left and right, but didn't open. "Lisa?"

Scott came tearing around through the dining area. "Did you hear that? What was that?"

"In there—" Dean pointed at the locked door. "It came from inside the bathroom. The thing outside, I think it's gotten in—that's all I can think of," he trailed off, kicking at the door. Glass wasn't breaking anymore, but it was being pushed around—scraped around, and yes, there was that tell-tale knocking, rattling, clapping together of hard things with worn edges. He could hear it through the door.

"What's that sound in there?"

"Same sound I heard outside."

"Well, what is it?" Scott's voice was rising, creeping up towards shrill as the ruckus in the bathroom continued and the clacking rattles filled more and more of the space inside the restaurant. "What's that crazy sound?"

"I told you, I don't know!" Dean retreated a few feet and slammed himself forward, hip against the door. Something splintered, but nothing broke. He did it again, and motioned for Scott to join him. "Lisa, what's going on in there? *Lisa?*"

Nothing and no one answered, so the guys pushed together and then, when both their bodies met the wood at once, the door caved in and they caved in after it—tumbling forward and slipping on cool tiles.

"Lisa?" they said together.

"Lisa?" Dean asked again, but the bathroom was empty and there was no sound at all—not even the running of a commode out of order, or the whistle of warm January wind through the broken glass of the small square window.

"Could she—could she have gotten through there? Through that?" Scott asked, now as breathless as Dean and just as confused. He meant the window, all smashed and hanging open. It wasn't meant for escaping, or anything half so glamorous. It was installed for ventilation, or for light. It was too small for a normal-sized woman to fit through, or climb through.

But Dean could still hear, in his head more than in the night, the smattering beats of the knobby creature that crouched in the dark beyond the dumpster. He climbed up onto the counter, stepping past the sink and prying himself up high to see out the window.

A hulking shape all corners and shadows was walking, retreating, removing itself from the restaurant.

It stopped.

It halted like it had snagged itself on something. It swiveled an over-sized head on a twig-thin neck, and it lifted its face to gaze at the window from which Dean watched.

Not one head, but many together. Not one thing, but parts of a hundred—a thousand others. A skull made of skulls, ribs made of ribs, it was fleshless and breathless. Its ivory limbs quivered together, chattering a low-frequency buzz of bone on bone, dangling loose from unfinished joints.

Dean's breath caught in his throat.

The thing turned away. It loped slowly towards the trees, into the woods. It wandered into the sheltering darkness of the park, towards the old camp at Andersonville. ❧

HEAVY METAL

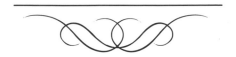

Once upon a time, I sold *Apex Magazine* a tale about a giant good ol' boy monster hunter, fighting were-beasts in rural Tennessee. The character's name was Kilgore Jones, and his nickname—and the name of the original story—was "The Heavy." I had plans at one point to do a series of these tales, themed with the "Heavy" as punny titles, but only got as far as two. The first story, and this one. The reasons are many and varied, but mostly boil down to the fact that I've largely lost touch with the fellow who inspired the character, plus the fact that I simply don't write a lot of short stories.

The guy I based "The Heavy" on was an old friend who I've known since college. He's always been an enormous man, and many years back we were joking around about writers inserting people they knew into stories. He told me that he wanted a walk-on part in something I was writing. Just a walk-on! He wanted to be the dude who showed up, raised a little hell, and died out of hand a scene or two later.

CHERIE PRIEST

Quoth him, "I just want to be the heavy."

Given that I only barely exaggerated my old friend's proportions in these stories, you can understand why everyone laughed. He's huge, and good natured, and ready to kick ass if he thinks somebody needs a hero. What's not to like? And how could I let him show up, only to die out of hand?

So I wrote him into that one story for Apex, and when I was invited to contribute a piece to the *Rogues* anthology...it felt like time to bust out The Heavy again, so that's what I did.

For this particular tale, I took a writer field trip to the actual setting—and then spent an afternoon poking around the little museum there, beside the old mine. It was fascinating and appalling, and I remember being most surprised by the local woman who went off on a curious tourist, because she'd been upset with the federal intervention that eventually helped restore [much of] the ecosystem that was destroyed by the mining operations. (There was even a piece about the town in LIFE magazine, back in the day.) She protested angrily that the locals liked it just the way it was, with no bugs or vermin and...a whole lot of cancer deaths and pollution, I guess, but there's no accounting for taste.

Another local woman quietly disagreed with the angry lady, after the tour was finished. She whispered to me that her daughter had seen deer in her yard the week before, and it was the first time in decades anyone had seen wildlife like that in the area. And wasn't that nice?

Well, *I* thought so.

If you get a chance to visit Ducktown, TN, it's a nice little place and you can find it on a map, these days. But make sure your phone has plenty of charge. You'll likely drive through a couple hours' worth of national parks (with no cell signal) to get there.

HEAVY METAL

KILGORE JONES wrestled free from the Eldorado and kicked the driver's door shut. It bounced and swung back open again, so he gave it a shove with his hip. The old car rocked back and forth, creaking in protest, but this time the latch caught and held—mostly for its own good. The "Jolly Roger" was a big car, but its driver was a big man.

It wouldn't be a real bold stretch to say he was six and a half feet tall, and a good carnival guesser might put his bulk at a quarter ton. Bald of head and fancy of facial hair, he boasted a carpet of impressive brown muttonchops that shone red in the sun, and a pair of mirrored aviator glasses. Everything else he wore was black. If you asked him why, he'd straight-faced tell you it was slimming.

His wardrobe notwithstanding, Kilgore threw a globe-shaped shadow on the ground—a one-man eclipse as he walked across a set of ruts that passed for parking spaces.

The old hoist house loomed before him: a 19th century behemoth built for work and not beauty. It was red brick with a green roof, and easily the size of the grand old church in Chattanooga where he was no longer welcome—because a pastor singing about Satan made sense, but a layman going on about monsters was just plain silly.

As he approached, he saw patched-up places where new brick filled in old windows, doors, and shafts. He noted the remains of white paint around the main door and its entry platform, all of it lead, most of it peeling and fluttering in a cold, sharp November breeze.

Gravel crunched beneath his feet, and the wind yanked at his coat. The sun was vivid and white against a crisp blue sky without any clouds, but there wasn't much warmth to go around. The Smokies were not yet brittle like they would be in another month, but he could smell it coming.

"Hello?" Kilgore called. The word went wild, echoing against the hoist house walls and adjacent boiler rooms, banging off the time shack and the bit-building across the way, rattling against last century's mining equipment abandoned on the end of the track. "Anybody here? Miss Huesman?"

He scaled the steps of the entry platform and stood on the wood slat landing—gazing toward the cavernous interior. Inside he saw pumpkins, leftover from a Halloween fund-raiser, if the banner could be believed. They were laid out on pallets with discount signs scrawled by hand in thick red marker. Even the largest, a gourd advertised as a seventy pounder, looked tiny beneath the vast, gabled ceiling strewn with crisscrossing tracks that toted great tubs of ore back before Kilgore's grandparents were born.

Wind whistled through the rafters above, scattering dead leaves and ruffling the fat little birds who huddled on the hauling lines.

"Hello?" he tried again. "Anyone here?"

"Hello?" someone called back, then added more, but he couldn't make it out. The voice came from deep inside, past the pumpkins on their pallets and back against the far wall…behind a door that might lead to an office.

He headed toward the sound of the speaker.

"…sorry if you're here about Rich. He's gone home for the day—and I think he took the money pouch for the pumpkins. But if you want one, and you have exact change, I'll see what I can do. All the proceeds go to support the museum…"

The door banged open, forced that way by the shoulder of a woman whose arms were full of miscellany: files, papers, magazines from the first Bush era, and a messenger bag from which peeked the sleek shape of a tablet. She paused. Or more precisely, she froze. Whatever she'd been expecting, Kilgore Jones wasn't it.

"Can…can I help you?" she asked. She shifted her weight and deposited her armload of stuff onto an old telephone seat which languished against the wall.

HEAVY METAL

She was young, lanky and tall. Long blonde hair, shiny and well kept. Wearing an oversized cardigan over a black T-shirt for a band Kilgore didn't recognize, and that was saying something. Her dark jeans were dusted with Ducktown, Tennessee's, ubiquitous red dirt in the shape of handprints. Her own, he assumed.

He pushed his sunglasses onto the top of his head. "Miss Huesman?"

"Yes? I mean, *yes*," she nodded, finding some relief in hearing her own name. "I'm Bethany. No one calls me Miss Huesman outside the university. And you are…?"

Now he stepped forward, hand outstretched. "Kilgore Jones. Jennifer Andrews told you I was coming, I think?"

Bethany's stiff fight-or-flight stance softened. "Yes! You're the guy who worked with Pastor Martin on Sand Mountain, back in the day. And you're…you're The Heavy? Well, Jenn *did* say…" She extended her hand to take his, and shook it. Her fingers were small and cold, and they sported a cute assortment of shiny silver rings.

Kilgore smiled, and hoped it was disarming. At his size, putting people at ease took extra work, so he'd learned to watch all of his language. "Let me guess: She said that when you saw me, you'd know why people call me that."

She blushed, or maybe it was only the chill hitting her cheeks. "More or less. I'm sorry, I didn't mean to be rude. Any friend of Pastor Martin's…" Her voice trailed off and her gaze swept the hoist house, scanning the vast interior as if making sure they were alone. "Jenn said the pastor wouldn't come. Why do you think that is?"

Kilgore should've said something about Sand Mountain. After all, she'd brought it up first.

He kept his mouth shut anyway. She deserved the truth, but it wouldn't do her any good. "I couldn't say, but I'm here to help if I can. If you've got a few minutes, I'd like to ask you a few questions."

"Okay, but can we go someplace a little warmer to talk?"

"What do you have in mind?"

"Just up the hill," she indicated with a toss of her head. "The museum's closed, but I have a key—and they have a heater." She retrieved her messenger bag, but left everything else where it was sitting. "We can walk it, no problem. Even with the wind, it's so close that it'd be crazy to drive."

He was inclined to disagree with her, but he restrained himself. "All right. Can I help you carry anything?"

"Naw," she said dismissively, yanking the office door. It closed with a sticky squeak. "This stuff'll be fine where it is. There's nothing worth stealing, and nobody to take it. Not since…" She paused, and changed her mind. "Not anymore. But I'll tell you about that when I've got a cup of coffee in my hand."

The hill was blessedly short, but not so short that he didn't wish for the Jolly Roger to help him scale it. He hated hills. Counted them among his archest of enemies. But at the top waited the museum, a squat, single-story building that was too modern to match the old buildings, but too new to call vintage. Its roof sloped unevenly above cheap white siding, fronted by a gravel lot that might've held half a dozen cars if you stacked them right.

Kilgore pulled a bandanna out of his pocket and wiped his forehead, never mind the breeze. "Museum doesn't see a lot of traffic, does it?"

"Why would you say that?" she asked, digging keys out of her bag and unlocking the door.

"The parking lot says they don't expect much company."

She looked over her shoulder. "Oh. Yeah, I guess you're right. Come to think of it, I've never seen more than three or four cars up here. And one of those usually belongs to Ammaw Pete."

"Ammaw Pete? The volunteer coordinator?"

The door swung open. Bethany reached inside and flipped on a light, though the day was still bright enough they almost didn't need it. "How did you know?"

"I called this morning before I came out, and she's the one who answered the phone. Seems like an…interesting lady."

"*Interesting*. That's her. She volunteers here most days. Other than that, she's retired." Bethany tossed her bag onto the counter and led the way to an under-stocked and over-dirty kitchenette.

She rummaged for the Folgers, scooped out a filter's worth, and fidgeted around the small, cold space while the coffee brewed and the freshly rebooted heater took the frost out of their breath. It had its work cut out for it; the building had the cheap, temporary feel of a trailer, and the walls were thinner than sandwich cheese. It hadn't been closed up more than a couple of hours, but all the warmth had bled out already.

She dug her fingernails into the cup, leaving small half-moons in the smooth white surface. The heater hummed loudly and the coffee oozed warm curls of steam.

Bethany cleared her throat.

"I know how crazy this sounds…but Adam and Greg are dead. I don't know why it took them, and I don't know if I'm next. There's…there's a lot I don't understand, about what happened. About this place. About that *thing*."

Kilgore prompted, "Is this your first time in Ducktown?"

She nodded. "If it weren't for the program, I never would've heard of the place. The ecology department at UTK has been involved in the cleanup here for ten or twelve years now—monitoring it, and making recommendations. I've gone through the files and casebooks; it's fascinating stuff, if you're that kind of nerd. And if I wasn't, I'd be doing my grad work in something else." She added a soft, quick laugh that was meant to sound light, but only sounded strange.

"All right. And to be clear, it was you, Adam Frye and Greg Malcolm on this trip, correct?"

"That's right. I took point because they were first-years, and I'm only a semester away from finishing my master's. The bulk of my research was geared toward the mountaintop removals. You know—the coal companies to the north and east of here. But the Burra Burra Mine is a legend, and the destruction it caused in the copper basin is virtually unique in scope; so even though it wasn't my cup of tea, when the field assignment came up, I threw my hat in the ring. It sounded like a good idea at the time."

"Famous last words." Kilgore poured himself another cup, and slipped the carafe back onto the burner. "Now tell me, when did you first arrive?"

"A week and a half ago. We were staying at a Holiday Inn Express out by the highway. The university put us up, gave us a little *per diem*, the whole nine yards. We were supposed to check the soil pH levels across a mapped grid, and catalog the plant-creep along the preserved area."

He frowned. "Preserved area?"

"It's a stretch of the old red dirt—the blighted turf left from the sulfur dioxide—where nothing grows and nothing lives. The government's restoration campaign left this one section un-reclaimed. I heard they did it as a reminder, but I bet they just ran out of funding."

Kilgore knew about the dead red dirt, but he hadn't realized there was any of it left. He'd seen the old pictures from the EPA reports, and a big spread in LIFE magazine from decades ago, before the cleanup. Fifty square miles of lifeless landscape, nothing but poisonous red hills as far as the eye could see. Except for the smattering of houses, churches, and the central hub of the mine facility, it'd looked like the surface of Mars.

Bethany continued, intermittently raising her eyes to see if he was listening. "It looks normal now, like the trees have been here forever, and we're surrounded by regular old forests; but it took years of planning—adding new species of acid-resistant grasses to anchor the turf, and planting specially imported trees. They brought in plants that could filter toxins with their roots, and flora that would give these hills a fighting chance at recovery. Eventually," she waved her hand in the general direction of the valley. "It worked. But they left this one stupid patch of the old red dirt, down by the water. That's what we were sent to examine. That, and the water itself, down in the crater."

His ears perked. "Where *is* the crater? If this museum's on the old mine site, it must be nearby...?"

"It's on the other side of the parking lot. You know what? Forget this coffee. It's terrible." She rose suddenly and tossed the cooled contents of her cup into the nearby sink. "Come on. I'll show you."

Out the door she went, past a wooden rack stuffed with local attraction brochures—for a relative value of "local." He tagged along in her wake.

She was nearly at a run. She wanted to get this over with.

Her boots crunched and scuffed across the unpaved lot, and she paused beside a big metal cage that once lowered miners 3,000 feet down the shaft in search of copper. She turned then, and her hair billowed wildly as the wind rushed up the crest behind her. She raised her voice to be heard, almost shouting as she pointed off to the north.

"That's where the plant used to be, right over there—facing the hoist house, on the ridge's natural peak! Used to be, they had a set of tracks that ran ore buckets overhead between them!" She turned around, and now her hair was a halo, vast and golden, wilder than Medusa. It looked for all the world like she stood at the edge of a cliff, and was prepared to jump.

She said something else but Kilgore couldn't hear her; she was speaking into the wind and the words were lost. But when he joined her, he understood.

More quietly now, she told him, "The mine caved in years ago, but by then, they weren't digging copper hardly at all: they made more money on sulfuric acid, generated from sulfur dioxide as part of the smelting process—you know, the same stuff that denuded this whole corner of the Smokies. But anyway, there it is. There's the lake where my friends drowned."

Beyond the miner cage, all the way down the far side of the sharp, ragged ridge, waited a great crater full of bright blue water surrounded by stiff green trees. It looked like someone'd pulled a plug and the landscape had sloughed down the drain, leaving only this cerulean pool, shimmering at the very bottom of the world.

Kilgore resisted the urge to call the scene "beautiful." Instead he drew Bethany back away from the edge, stepping down out of the wind.

When they were standing again in the gravel lot, she said, "That's where they died. Adam first—two days after we got here. A freak accident, that's what they said. He fell in and…forgot how to swim, or some bullshit like that."

"Did they send his body back home? I don't expect they have the facilities out here for an autopsy."

"Yeah, he's home by now. Greg, though—he died two days after that, and he's at the Copper Basin Medical Facility, unless they released his body and no one told me, which is possible. Nobody out here tells me a damn thing. Ammaw Pete thinks I'm an uppity little city bitch, like Knoxville is New York, and I'm carpetbagging for the ages. She doesn't know I heard her say it, but she probably wouldn't care if she did." She looked at Kilgore with something new in her eyes, something cunning. "Maybe they'll talk to *you*."

"I try my best to be a sociable man…but in my experience, people open up faster to a pretty woman like you than a guy like me."

She shrugged. "Not here. They don't like me. They don't trust me. They put me in the same category as the lawyers and environmentalists who closed down the mine and put the whole town out of work. If you're not *for* the copper, you're against it. Like all the *life* we're bringing back to this place isn't worth a damn thing."

Kilgore Jones made noises of polite protest, but she didn't respond. She only stared over the ridge, toward that bright blue hole in the pale red dirt, surrounded by all the defiant trees, roots clinging to the steep crater walls, twisted and anchored and still alive—like a big "fuck you" to history.

But she still hadn't said what he needed to hear, so he prodded her again, friendly but firm. "Tell me what you saw that night, when Greg went under."

Slowly, she nodded. Not to him, but herself. "Something came up, almost out of the water but not quite. It whispered to Greg," she said, hardly any louder than the whisper she described. "It called him. *Lured* him. And when he wouldn't follow it, it grabbed him—and it dragged him right into the lake."

"Describe it—the thing you saw."

"I…I can't."

"You'd better, because I'm shit when it comes to mind-reading. *Bethany,*" he said, urgently if not impatiently. "You sent for help. Now *talk* to me."

She swallowed, and crossed her arms over her stomach, drawing her oversized sweater tighter around her body. "It looked like a man, but it wasn't. It looked like a miner—one of the old miners, from the eighteen-hundreds. But not exactly." Her eyebrows crunched together. "Do you think it was a ghost?"

This was more comfortable turf for Kilgore, if not for the grad student. "Ghosts are mostly made of memories and imagination—their own, and everyone else's. Once in a blue moon one'll have the strength to make a ripple in the real world, but I've never heard of one tough enough to drown a grown man."

She burrowed her hands deeply into her sleeves, then stuffed them under her arms. "This thing…whatever it was, it wasn't a memory. It was really *there*. So if it wasn't a ghost, what *was* it?"

"I don't know yet." He didn't give her any guesses because they'd only frighten her. He needed more information, and that meant he needed a local. All his polite protests aside, Bethany wasn't one, and everyone in the county knew it.

Kilgore wasn't local either, and Chattanooga wasn't any more rural than Knoxville—but there was more to being local than your starting address.

He left Bethany on the museum steps. He shook her hand and made her promise to be in touch, and stay away from the crater. She agreed to these terms, but he didn't know how much that meant. Her abject horror at watching her fellow student drown might be nothing compared to the siren song of an otherworldly creature, or even her simple curiosity.

Siren.

The word floated to the surface of his brain, and refused to sink back down. He made a mental note of it, because there was no sense in denying the overlap. Sirens were water elementals, of a fashion; they called, lured, and killed—though they usually came in a prettier package than that of an old miner. "There's a first time for everything. Then again," he mumbled, as he yanked the Eldorado's bum door and settled back inside the car. "It talked to Greg, and Greg didn't listen. It resorted to force."

He gazed up at the silver crucifix that hung from the rearview mirror, trembling and bobbing like a pendulum. It'd been a gift, from someone who wouldn't speak to him anymore—a man he'd come to view as a father, at the third church that threw him out. The last church. The one he drove past sometimes, still not quite finished with that argument, but knowing better than to come inside.

They'd disinvited him, like he was some kind of goddamned vampire who knew better than to cross the threshold.

He stayed away anyhow. He knew where he wasn't wanted, and no amount of wishing or praying would change that. Apparently.

He sighed, because he sure could've used the help right about now; but he sucked it up, withdrew his small notebook from his pocket, and added what he'd learned. Then he flipped to the back page—where two addresses were written down: one was the local watering hole, a joint that went by the uninspiring legend of "Ed's," and the other belonged to the woman either named or called "Ammaw Pete," who volunteered at the museum and allegedly didn't think much of poor Miss Huesman.

HEAVY METAL

His watch said it was too early to bother with the bar; he wouldn't find anyone useful to chat up. But Mrs. Pete? It wasn't even suppertime yet, and she'd said he could swing by before nightfall. She knew to expect him but he would've liked to call first, as a matter of manners...but by her own admission, she didn't have a phone. She took all her messages out of the museum's line, and appeared perfectly content with that arrangement.

Kilgore Jones did have a phone, but it was a POS without a GPS. He consoled himself with the knowledge that by the grace of God, Ducktown had made it onto Google maps, and therefore a stash of home-produced print-outs gave him an idea of what the area looked like.

Ammaw Pete lived within spitting distance of the mine—walking distance for someone more hiking-inclined than Kilgore—but it took him fully twenty minutes to find his way to her driveway via the Eldorado. Her road was neither marked nor paved, and he stumbled upon it only after the process of elimination ruled out four other identical roads. How anybody got their mail delivered was a mystery to him, but small towns and out-of-the-way places all had their methods. When everyone knows everyone, things don't often go lost or missing. And that made the situation with the UTK ecology students all the stranger.

Or then again, maybe it didn't. Those kids were outsiders, and the community didn't feel obligated to look out for them. They went missing more easily than the mail.

He engaged the parking brake and the car lurched hard, then settled with its customary squeaking.

Ammaw Pete's place was an early craftsman in good repair, with a yard that didn't get as much love as the hanging flower baskets on the porch. The baskets were emptied of everything but the purple and pink petunias; everything else had died for the season, and these would too, probably before Thanksgiving. But for now they gave the white house with its gray roof a pop of color that said somebody lived there, and somebody cared about the place.

Kilgore tried the steps and found them true, then knocked upon a red-painted door.

Behind the door, he heard a television mumbling what sounded like the local news; a chair squealed, a board creaked, and then a set of footsteps stopped long enough for an eyeball to appear in the small window that served as a peephole.

The door didn't open. "Who's there?"

He assumed his most polite pose, hands folded in front of himself, slight stoop to minimize his prodigious height. "Pardon me, ma'am—but I'm looking for Ammaw Pete. Would that be you?"

"What's it to you?"

"I'm Kilgore Jones. We spoke on the phone this morning," he told her.

"That's right, I recall. You're a big son of a bitch, aren't you?"

"That's what they tell me."

"What is it you do again? You're not with the po-po, I remember that much."

"I'm a machine shop worker from Chattanooga."

The eyeball narrowed. "And investigator of the occasional drowning...?"

"Not the drowning, ma'am. The thing what caused it."

He heard a click, the twist of an old knob, and the scrape of a door being drawn back an inch. "You've got my attention, big man. Don't waste it." She opened the door enough to reveal herself. Small and old, but not elderly yet. Silver-haired and bright-eyed, in a tidy blue dress and gray slippers. "You ain't a feeler, are you?"

"No ma'am. I don't detect anything I can't see."

"You're a fighter, then. Got to be one or the other." She sighed, and tossed the door open all the way with a flick of her wrist. "I guess you'd better come inside."

Withdrawing to make room for him, she turned and sauntered through a cluttered home that was not the least bit dirty or unorganized— only filled to capacity with whatever things moved her magpie of a soul.

HEAVY METAL

Here there were stacks of Time-Life books on the Civil War and the Old West, and over there, that series from the eighties about unexplained phenomena; figurines from nearby and faraway lands alike; rows of bells from assorted tourist traps; spoons with small emblems identifying them as collector's pieces; photos of loved ones framed and arranged across all but a few square inches of wall space; a batch of prettily organized tea kettles and pot holders; a latticework of diverse coffee mugs hung on the walls around the cabinets; handmade afghans with bright colors and unfortunate patterns; curtains sewn from bedsheets; Christmasy villages with ice skaters and post offices and train stations awaiting the next month with flickering lights and cheerful miniature residents, pets, vehicles—plus wreaths on every door.

"I'll put the kettle on and you can have a seat."

Of *course* she'd put the kettle on. Kilgore would never escape an old southern woman's home without tea, same as he'd never settle down to a young southern woman's company without coffee, now that he thought about it. It was like nobody could talk without something to sip for distraction.

But they'd done the same thing at the old First Baptist, hadn't they? If not potlucks then communions, and that's why they called it a Fellowship Hall.

Ammaw, whose name he'd first misheard as "Grandma," gestured at the dining room table, a well varnished and rough-hewn piece that someone must've made for her. None of the pretty little chairs matched, and none of them looked like they'd hold Kilgore without protest and structural failure.

He was prepared to suggest that perhaps they could sit outside on the porch, but then he spied a cedar bench that probably belonged in a garden—but in Ammaw's kitchen it was piled with folded hand towels and a stack of cast iron skillets nested together. "You think perhaps I could just… clear off that bench? We'll both be happier if I don't break anything."

She coughed the laugh of an octogenarian smoker, but her age wasn't so advanced and Kilgore didn't see any cigarettes. "Do what you gotta."

It wasn't just her laugh, he realized. Her words were offered up with that same ragged edge that sounded like more than age peeking through. While he gently adjusted her décor, he said, "I hope I haven't intruded on you, particularly not if you've been feeling poorly."

"Poorly?" She paused at the stove and shot him a look. "Oh, the cough, you mean? Hardly even a rattle, and I guess you ain't been in town too long, or you'd have heard it by now. All us old folks who grew up here… we all got the *voice*."

"I'm sorry to hear that."

"Why? It don't hurt, and I don't mind. Makes you feel like part of a tribe," she informed him, and she hauled a box of tea bags from a cabinet, then yanked two mugs off the wall. For herself she chose a soft pink jobbie with a nicely shaped handle. For him, Tweety Bird sitting in a bathtub. "Once upon a time, Ducktown and Copperhill had a big tribe between 'em. The mine took good care of its workers," she insisted, her cough to the contrary. "Now it's gone, and so are most of us. It's just the way of things."

"But the land's come back real nicely," he said, accepting a measure of steaming water, and dipping his tea bag, prompting it to steep. "So there's that."

"There's that, yes. And there's snakes, and there's rats and bugs, too. Didn't used to have any of that nonsense, but here they come, creeping back. None of them worth the trouble of those goddamn trees. We *liked* our red dirt, I'll have you to know…" She eyed him over the edge of the mug. "But you're not here for tea or bitchin'. You want to talk about the crater, and what sleeps inside it."

He didn't like the way she phrased it. It offered up too many suggestions, too many implications. He wondered how much she really knew, so he asked outright. "Yes ma'am. And you've worked the museum longer than anyone, besides being local to boot. I figure you're the best person to ask."

"How much do you know already?"

"Only what Bethany Huesman thinks she saw."

Ammaw Pete made a derisive noise that flicked at the surface of her tea. "That girl. Thinks she knows so much. She didn't tell me she saw anything. Didn't tell the sheriff either."

"She said you don't like her any. Thinks it's because she's an out-of-towner."

"It's because she tried to order a skinny half-caff something-something at a gas station on the edge of town, and acted snotty when she couldn't have anything but old-fashioned drip," she snapped. But Kilgore figured they were saying the same thing. "So she didn't say a damn thing to me… but she'll talk to you. All right then, so she saw something, did she?"

"Something shaped like one of the old miners, rising up from the water. It dragged her friend down into the crater, and drowned him."

"Shaped like one of the miners?" she echoed pensively, and gave it a question mark. "Well, sometimes these things take the shape they're called by. They show us what we expect to see." She closed her eyes and breathed deeply over her teacup, taking the steam and smiling at it, but her smile verged on the grim. "Them things that were here before us… before the mine. Before the Indians. They'll be here still, when the last of us are gone."

"You think that'll make them happy? The last of us being gone?"

"I don't know. They belong to the land."

Kilgore frowned. "But the ecology students from UTK are here for the land too—they're putting it back in order. You'd think any resident haints or elements would be glad to see them."

"Ducktown don't want 'em here. Whatever's at the bottom of the lake don't want 'em here. The whole world ain't made of hippies and sunshine, big man. It's a balance, you know—and here in the basin, it's always been about the metal. There's the earth that holds the copper, the things that *draw* the copper, and things that *work* the copper. A *balance*."

"Yeah, well this place hasn't been in *balance* for a hundred and fifty years, and those kids shouldn't have to risk their lives to put it back."

"Why not?" she asked with a wink, but there was a gleam of something hard behind the flutter of her lid. He feigned astonishment, but she waved it away. "No, now. You know I'm only teasing. Whatever that little ol' Nick might be, it shouldn't be left to grow there. Shouldn't let it fester. You'd better take it out and deal with it."

"How?"

"Beats me. But if it's nasty enough to kill people, a good talking-to won't do it. Not from *you*, anyway."

He considered this. "Thank you," he finally said, his lips pausing on the rim at the top of Tweety's head. "You've given me plenty to think about."

He finished his tea, thanked the woman again, and retreated to his hotel to get ready for the night's work. He'd booked a room in the same Holiday Inn Express the grad students used, not by any great design, but because there was nothing else for miles.

Down the corridor on the way to his room, he ran into Bethany—who was barefoot and holding an ice bucket. "Hi there!" she chirped, and he said "hello" in return, adjusting the backpack he toted as luggage. Then she added, "I don't know why I'm surprised to see you here. Can't imagine where else you'd crash."

"This is close and clean. It'll be fine for the night."

"Is that how long you're staying? Just overnight?"

"Depends. We'll see what happens."

She shuddered, and clutched her ice bucket. "You sure you'll be okay?"

"I always am."

She laughed nervously, and he wondered if she ever laughed any other way. "I guess nobody bothers *you*, not very often."

"No ma'am, they do *not*."

HEAVY METAL

They said their good nights and he went alone to his room. He flipped on the light to reveal nothing at all outstanding, but nothing offensive, either: a bed with an ugly comforter, a tiny stack of sample-sized toiletries, and a sink with a chipped faucet head.

He wondered what Bethany would've thought if he'd blurted out the things he kept close to his chest—if he'd said that no, nobody bothered him too often but when they did, they did it for keeps. Anyone who's ever watched a prison movie knows you take down the biggest man first; and the monsters knew it too. So far he'd escaped those greetings with only a few scars to show for it, but they were ugly scars, and they reminded him daily of those who hadn't been so lucky.

The nothings out there…they were worse than the nobodies.

Sometimes the nothings bit and fought, screamed and spewed poison or fire. Nothings could change their shapes and shift their bones, and sometimes, only a Bible and brute force could put them down.

Kilgore's Bible was a small red leather-bound thing, thumbed into softness with onionskin pages that flapped, fluttered, and stuck together. He didn't read it much anymore. Didn't need to. Knew it forwards and backwards, just like the devil. But he kept it on his person because once it'd deflected a swipe of claws that would've otherwise opened his chest, instead of leaving him looking like he'd passed out face-down on a barbecue grill.

And that made it lucky.

In absence of mortal assistance, he'd take what luck he could get. He'd rather have Pastor Martin by his side, but that ship had sailed, hadn't it?

So when night came, he tucked the Good Book into his pocket, smashed up against his battered notebook—a worn thing filled with thoughts and research on the case, scribblings and small, carefully drawn images that might or might not mean anything to him later on. An hour or two of potting around on the internet had given him a name, or at least a direction. It was only a starting point, but it was better than nothing.

Back into his car he climbed. He tossed his pack onto the passenger's seat, and in doing so, he winged the silver cross that hung from the rearview mirror. It swung back and forth, smacking the glass with a loud *crack*. He grabbed the holy trinket and steadied it. He held it an extra moment or two, then said, "Fuck it," pulled it off the mirror and slung it around his neck. He didn't have a church, but he had his faith. And he had the trusty old Jolly Roger, which started on the first try.

Out past what few streetlights and corner stores Ducktown boasted, the car's headlights cut a bold path through the pitch-black, middle-of-nowhere murk.

He wasn't more than a couple of miles from the mine, but there were few signs to guide the way, and little in the way of civilized lighting; the stars were so damn bright overhead, and the trees loomed so tall, so close together on every side of the service road that would take him down to the crater lake.

He watched those trees as he drove, hunting for something that might live there, and hide behind them. Some hint of the old balance. Some kind of resurrection.

When he hit a low-slung bar across the road, the headlights shone bright on a big-ass NO TRESPASSING sign. The high beams glinted off the rest of the message, which stopped just short of promising that anyone who drove any farther would be shot on sight and fed to the bears for fun. Probably because there weren't any bears.

He left the car to inspect the situation in person. The hip-high gate across the road wore the sign like a badge, but Kilgore couldn't find a shit to give, and nothing but a rusted padlock on an old chain held the whole thing together. A pair of swift kicks with his steel-toed work boots made short work of the matter, and one more kick sent the gate swinging back into the trees, where it dragged itself to a halt and leaned off-kilter against a raggedy evergreen.

It almost wasn't worth the effort to clear the way. The dirt road ran out another hundred yards down the line, petering into a wide patch that gave a vehicle enough room to turn around, but that was about it.

HEAVY METAL

With some creative steering, he maneuvered the car into an about-face so he could hit the ground running if conditions called for it later. Then he parked, pulled the brake, and left the door open so the dome light would stay on while he checked his supplies.

A plastic ketchup squirt-bottle full of holy water. A well worn gris-gris he'd had made in New Orleans, the year before The Storm. Flashlight and extra batteries, and a head-mounted lamp he'd borrowed from a buddy who was a mechanic. An old silver cake knife, because sometimes silver meant something, but it was expensive—so he took it where he found it.

A loaded nine-millimeter because you never know.

He patted his chest and felt the reassuring bulk of the notebook and the Bible. Tucked the gun into his waistband, up front where it'd be easier to reach, even though the cold metal on his belly gave him a full-body shiver. He donned the headband with the LED light on it, and felt ridiculous but his hands were free, and that was more important than dignity in the dark.

Everything else he stashed in his trench coat pockets.

He closed the car door and the light went out. He flipped the switch on his headlamp, and it came on, illuminating the woods without quite the vigorous panache of the Eldorado's beams; but outside what passed for town, a little light went a long way.

For a moment he stood still and listened. He didn't hear much. It almost bothered him, but then he remembered Ammaw Pete grousing about how all the critters were only just coming back, and then he supposed it wasn't quite so unsettling. There weren't any crickets to fiddle their legs in the grass. No mice to rustle in the leaves, or squirrels to build nests high above. Nothing and no one, except whatever waited in the crater.

Kilgore had a pretty good sense of direction—almost an uncanny one, or so his mother used to tell people. He could feel it in his head, the tug of the crater's location. The smell of its water wafted up through the trees, an unpleasant stink of bottom-pocket pennies and stagnation.

The service road had gotten him close.

He sniffed, wiped his nose on his forearm's sleeve, and started marching.

The grade grew steeper as he proceeded; with every step, the ground dropped away more sharply beneath him. He slipped and skidded, catching himself on the vegetation or—on one particularly unpleasant stumble—his own hands.

And then he reached the clearing that surrounded the water—a ring of red dirt that held back the trees, or maybe the trees just didn't want to dip their roots into that questionable pond. It was a creepy little beach, angled and naked, with all the grimy allure of a bathtub ring.

Unmoving except for the pivot of his neck, the big man surveyed the scene and still, he heard nothing. But he felt something, and he didn't like it: the prickling, unhappy sense that he was being watched.

He fished out his notebook. The brightness of his headlamp washed out the pages, and made it tough to read, but he squinted and forced his own words to appear.

"You took two boys." He said it quietly. Like the light, a little sound went a long way. "They were here to help the basin, and you killed them."

A ripple scattered the calm surface of the night-blackened pool. He heard it, the soft rush of water in motion, the ripple of a solitary wind chime playing its only note.

"Ammaw Pete said something that got me thinking: she said a good talking-to wouldn't stop you, not if it came from *me*. So I wondered if there was anyone you might obey. Everything's afraid of something, but you've been living the high life up in here, haven't you?"

The water moved again. From the edge of his vision, Kilgore saw it, the shifting lines of something traveling below the surface, but not yet rising.

"She called you a little ol' Nick, and that's not just an expression. She meant you're a little ol' devil, but I doubt you qualify for the title. A devil could leave the water and wreak more...*interesting* havoc someplace else. And you can't, can you?"

HEAVY METAL

He lifted his gaze without lifting his head. The offset glare of the light showed him a shape that was round and bald, a head not unlike his own. Eyes rising just far enough to break the water line, and see what motherfucker was doing all this taunting.

Kilgore fought back a shudder, and returned his eyes to the notebook, to the word he'd written down. "Not sure how to pronounce this," he admitted. "And it might be the wrong name anyhow, but it's a pretty coincidence all the same, so I'm going to call you *Kupfernickel*."

The eyes in the water were blacker than the sky above or the water below. They were so black that the darkness spilled out in an ambient glow of evil.

Kilgore met the thing's glare. "That word...does it mean anything to you?"

A low, burbling sneer blew bubbles in the lake. And then, so softly that it could scarcely be understood, the creature replied.

Silly sprites.

"Silly sprites," Kilgore repeated, too surprised to say anything else until he'd checked the notebook again. Often these things couldn't speak—or if they could, they found it hard to make themselves understood. This one's voice was clear, though it sounded like it came from miles and miles underground. "But they're dangerous, aren't they? And tied to metal... like the metal here at the Burra Burra Mine, sort of."

German miners of old complained about copper that was bedeviled, and could not be smelted. They didn't know that the metal wasn't copper at all, but nickel arsenide; they couldn't get copper out of it because there wasn't any copper *in* it.

"You're not so different from that, *kupfernickel*. One thing pretending to be another. You're no elemental—no creature of *life*, that's for damn sure."

Your word means nothing. You mean nothing. There is no life here.

"You ought to be a small thing, a cold spot. A patch where grass won't grow. But the pollution from the mine let you outgrow your britches."

I am stronger than you know, it hissed, and it lifted itself, crawling toward the bank, and toward Kilgore with a deliberate slowness that showed off its fearsome, knock-kneed and razor-sharp shape.

"No," he insisted, and he did not back away, calling its bluff. "If you had any strength of your own, you wouldn't be wearing the skin of a dead man. You haven't got enough substance. Not enough life." He looked up quickly, scanning the woods with the white-bright beam that shot from his forehead. The treeline appeared impenetrable and unbroken, a row of trunks divided with stripes of darkness. It felt like a cage.

The creature fussed some moist complaint, but it stopped its progression from the water and remained thighs deep in the glassy lake. It scanned the treeline too, seeking whatever Kilgore might be hunting; but seeing nothing, it sneered afresh.

You know little, and understand less than that.

"Then come up out of that water. Get out here and teach me a lesson, eh Nick?"

The creature hesitated, then lunged—and retreated, as if it'd changed its mind.

But Kilgore knew a fake-out when he saw one. "You can't, can you?"

Can, it insisted.

"Show me."

But the thing watched the trees again, seeking some response that Kilgore couldn't see. It cowered in the water, stuck in a pose between menace and retreat. The thing wore loose-fitting clothes—the homespun and overalls of a miner a hundred years ago, in boots and gloves, and the smudge of candle-soot around its empty eyes. Sopping and stark, its clothing clung wetly to its skin-and-bones form, showing off the crooks and bends of something made of little more than gristle and myth.

"Come on out and take a swing at me, if you think you're so tough. I've smacked the shit out of bigger things, and I'll smack it out of *you*."

HEAVY METAL

The coal-black eyes squinted, and tendrils of pitch-colored smoke oozed from the sockets. *You fear the water.*

"You fear the land," he countered.

I fear nothing.

"Then why do you watch the trees?"

It scowled and dipped, its joints creaking and bowing, as it adjusted itself in the water. The smoke that poured from its blank, deep eyes likewise spilled from the corners of its mouth when it spoke. *I fear no trees.*

"And I ain't afraid of the dark, but I know what's *in* it."

Kilgore checked his distance from the water's edge: a good thirty feet. Far enough that even with a lunge, the creature probably couldn't grab him. Even so, to be on the safe side...he sidled back another yard or two, never taking his eyes off the two smoking craters in the creature's shriveled-apple face.

His notebook slipped, but he caught it. He held it up to the light of his headlamp, and began to read.

"By the standing stone and twisted tree, thee we invoke—where gather thy own." He cleared his throat, and ignored the splash and hiss from the creature that still stood in the water. "Mighty Lord of the woods and animals, hunter and hunted, I call to you."

None shall answer! There is no life here!

"Hear me, and come once more to this, your sacred home. Keeper of the mighty gates of winter, watcher of the living land," he breathed, and it might've been his imagination that something flickered in the trees beyond the edge of his headlamp's glare.

None remain to hear you!

"You'd best fucking pray that's the case," Kilgore growled. "In the name of Jesus, of the Father, Son, and Holy Spirit..."

Hear yourself, you coward, the creature spit. *Singing to the crucified king and calling the old gods, with the same breath.*

He shook his head. He'd heard it before, from holier things and people by far. "God of Creation, send Your angels. Send them in a shape this motherfucker will *know*, and lend them Your Almighty power."

Your God has no angels for the likes of me. No swords. No choirs.

There, back toward the Eldorado, he saw it this time for certain: moving between the gnarled greenery like a stream flowing past rocks, one moment slow—one moment lightning-fast, shifting in some strange spot between the worlds. "And He shall give His angels charge over thee," he repeated his favorite bit from the red-bound book. "To keep thee in all thy ways."

Nowhere did it specify what those angels would look like, or how they'd do any of the promised keeping.

You cannot have it both ways. Old ways and new gods.

"One God," he corrected. "Just the one—old, new, and always. But He's got a very diverse work force."

And one thing was certain, sometimes things took the names they were called by. They assumed the shapes that were best believed. He didn't know how it worked, or why. He didn't understand the mechanisms of the Law, but he suspected that no one on earth ever had—or ever could. All he knew was that God was on his side. He believed it harder than he believed his own name.

Your Christ has no power here!

"You're wrong about that, and everything else," he said—and he might've said more but a vivid white light sparked, quivered, and blasted out from the treeline. It all but blinded Kilgore, who still had the good sense to keep one watering eye on the creature, though he backed away farther. One arm up, shielding himself from the sudden illumination.

The supernova cast shadows of trunks sharper than prison bars, flinging the shapes across the crater lake and around the hole where a mine once worked, and up the ridge around it—past the miners' cage that split the light into lace, and all along the determined sprouts that clung to the piss-poor dirt, red as the face of Mars.

"There is life here yet!" he gasped, his breath sucked out of him by that divine, demanding illumination.

Between his fingers, around the edges of the fierce brilliance that was colder than November, he saw a four-legged shape, each limb as narrow as a sapling; there stood a barrel-chested trunk and a proud head capped with a crown as wide as Kilgore's outstretched arms. Or not a crown at all—antlers, then, if that's what they were.

This thing had names as well as antlers, though Kilgore could not bring himself to call any of the common ones. Not for prayer or entreaty, for it was too close to blasphemy. Even if he knew what his own God called this thing, it wouldn't be a word for lips like his to pronounce.

He inhaled, exhaled. Forced himself to breathe through the rapture of this piercing light that cut through the copper basin and everything in it.

"Tubal-cain," was the best he could muster in salutation. A name for the horned guardian from the mighty red book. He gagged on a small laugh, remembering a tidbit of lore he'd almost forgotten. "You were a metalsmith, praise Jesus! I see Your patterns, Lord. I see You turn the wheel…"

The great stag shifted. Its shape wavered between wafer-thin projection and flesh-and-blood, but it held and it glared down at the creature in the lake—which cringed against the light.

It struggled in place, a fly in molasses. It fumed and reared, lunging backward and going nowhere…no, going forward, toward the shining thing in the trees. Dragged up, kicking and fighting from the water until it was free and suspended, angry and dripping and swearing in a tongue no living man has ever understood. Shrinking, and withering like the grass once withered and the trees once wilted where they stood.

"Take him away!" he gasped, not quite laughing anymore, too winded to do anything but wheeze. And as the miner-shaped creature rose up, wriggling and dying, sailing reluctantly toward the woods, Kilgore felt a pressure in his chest like a hand squeezing. The pressure crushed hard, and he wiped at his eyes but saw only the searing afterburn of the light from the trees…and then he saw stars.

And then he saw nothing, not even the ever-present light.

Not anymore.

Not until it crept back, a flicker here and there. A pixel at a time, that charred patchwork of vision, gleaming around the edges from all the cones and rods adjusting to the light that wasn't there.

The stars came back, but this time they were above him. He blinked. Real stars. Not the ones that snowed across his vision when the light went away.

He was lying on his back, and a sharp jabbing sensation in his side suggested that someone was poking him with a stick.

"Ow…" he mumbled, then swiped at the stick.

The stick was held by Ammaw Pete, who also hefted an oversized flashlight with a big 9-volt battery exposed on its underside. To her credit, she didn't aim it at his face. She aimed it at the ground beside him, illuminating his headlamp—which had fallen off and ceased to function.

"Wake up, big man. You're done here."

"Done…here? I didn't…" He rose slowly, ratcheting himself up with his elbows. "I didn't do anything."

The frown on her face suggested she might argue, but she only said, "Whatever. Get yourself together. I found your car up the hill there, but your battery'll need a jump. There's more than one kind of life, you know, and I'll want a ride home."

"You walked here?"

She shined the light in his face this time, and he winced. "Of course I walked. How else was I supposed to follow that light? Drive through the trees? Not sure what kind of car you think I got, and I don't ride a bicycle. Never did learn. It ain't natural, running around on two wheels like that."

"Pretty sure it's…pretty natural," he argued with a grin. She offered him a hand for the sake of show, but he pushed himself to his feet without her assistance. "Is that how you found me? You followed the light?"

"Better than the star of Bethlehem."

He was only half serious when he said, "Hush your mouth, ma'am."

"Oh, sure. You can ask the pagan holdouts for a handout, but I can't tease a bit about astrology. Fine. You big fat hypocrite."

He dusted himself off, and felt around for any broken bits. All in all, he felt pretty good. Tired, but good. "I'm a big fat lot of things, but that's not one of them."

"Well then, maybe you're only confused. Whoa now," she said, and stepped in to steady him. It worked, mostly because he didn't want to fall down on top of her. "Take a moment, if you need it."

"Not sure what's wrong with me," he muttered. "I didn't *do* anything. I asked for help, and it came. That's all."

She patted his arm. "No, darling. That wasn't all. You were right," she told him, guiding him by the crook of his arm, back up the hill toward the Jolly Roger. "There was life in this place. A lot of life. *Your* life. And my Old Man," she said with a wink. "He borrowed a bit to make his point. You did a good job, calling him back."

Kilgore frowned down at the small woman with the fierce grip on the meat of his arm. She carried on, straight ahead.

"I knew if I asked you outright, you'd never do it. Not in a million years. Bless Him, He's got the time, but you and I *don't*."

And as they walked, the flicker in her eyes didn't come from the flashlight, or the moon. ✣

THE KNOXVILLE GIRL

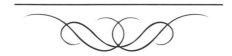

Who doesn't love a good murder ballad, am I right?

When Jon Maberry invited me to write something for *Out of Tune II*, I was psyched. He wanted modern fiction based on vintage murder ballads, and I was all about it—but I started having second thoughts halfway through. I thought maybe I'd picked a story too big to show with sufficient nuance: specifically, a story about the cycle of domestic violence that is so often inherited, and so often passed down to the next generation. It's not a simple story, but I thought that if I could keep it to just a handful of characters who disagree, but aren't necessarily wrong, I could say something that might resonate with someone, somewhere.

So that's what I tried to do. I told a story that I'd seen before, many times—especially in rural places. It's a story about who gets hurt, who holds onto the hurt, and who passes it along—and why victims don't always seek help, or why families and communities tend to take care of these things themselves (or at least, they sometimes try to).

This kind of violence is rarely the result of one small point of failure. It's usually a pattern of failures, or even a system that's entirely made of up of them. And it's hard to have a conversation about where responsibility begins and ends, and where the cycle might have been successfully interrupted. It's all academic when someone dies, even when everyone knows who did it and why it happened.

"The Knoxville Girl" is not especially academic, to be blunt. It's messy, like the problem it struggles to describe. I'm not sure how successful it is, but I do think there's value in the effort all the same.

WILLIE CAME home late, wet, and dirty. He let himself inside through the back door by the kitchen, the one without a working lock—not that Alannah advertised it as such—and he tiptoed past the fridge. He jumped when the ice maker hiccupped and rattled. He recovered his fragile cool, and crept past the sink with a faucet that always leaked unless you wiggled the lever just right.

One more obstacle, and he was in the clear: a little dining set with chrome trim and vinyl upholstery. It blocked his route to the hallway. He gripped the back of the nearest seat, and carefully lifted it aside.

He'd been half afraid he'd find his mother sitting there, waiting for him, smoking a menthol from a green-and-white soft pack and tapping her toes against the peeled piece of linoleum that always snagged on the table leg—Alannah just knew it.

She knew it by the way his eyes lingered on her preferred seat. She could see it in his face when she called out, "Good evening, baby."

"Momma?" He cringed, and stopped.

"Do you know what time it is?" She stood in her bedroom doorway, an empty soft-pack wadded up in her hand.

"A little after one, I guess. More like two, maybe."

"Closer to three." She stepped into the kitchen, where light from the corner streetlamp spilled through the window above the sink. She stepped on the trash can pedal and tossed the balled-up pack inside.

"I'm real sorry. Didn't mean to wake you up." He guessed better on his second try. "Didn't mean to *keep* you up."

She flipped the light switch, and everything was bright until her eyes adjusted, and then everything was just a dull yellow. "Nothing to be done for it now. May as well sit down and have a drink, help me calm myself enough to call it a night."

"You working tomorrow?"

"No. Get the bottle, baby. The stillhouse stuff, it's beside the cereal." Like he didn't know that. Like he didn't water it down as if he was still a dumbass teenager and not a grownass man who could do better than this, but flat-out wouldn't. "Get me a glass, when you get yourself one."

"I don't want to dirty up no dishes. Not this late."

"Don't worry about that. I'll pick up after you, before we call it a night."

Willie obeyed, meek as a kitten—but that was all for show.

This was all for show. This was a script, one Alannah had watched or played a thousand times before, in a thousand variations, with three different men.

Her son brought over a pair of plastic cups that started out life in a radio promotion, their logos now faded to flecks of plastic paint. He poured a couple of fingers into each, then slipped one across the table. "Cheers," he said. He took his own drink and downed half of it in a single swallow. He winced, sniffed, and waited for Alannah to do likewise.

"Cheers," she said back at him. She sipped just enough to dampen her lips, and let a drop or two past her teeth. She put the cup down. "Now sweetheart, I would dearly love to know…what's kept you out so late, on this fine summer night?"

"Same stuff as always." He slipped a glance at the bottle, half empty.

She slipped a hand around the bottle, half full. She pulled it over to her side of the table. "You already been out drinking, then. This ain't your first swallow."

"Yes ma'am. No ma'am. You know what I mean, ma'am."

"Ma'am…" she echoed with a faint note of mockery. "I guess you been up to no good."

"Don't…don't say that. Everything's all right, I just lost track of time down at Mr. Q's."

"That's where you've been?"

"Until half an hour ago."

"You came straight home, then."

"I did."

He was watching the bottle, wanting it bad, even though his cup still had a finger left. She didn't let him have it. "Tell me about your shirt, why don't you."

Willie looked down and didn't see the smudge. It was partly hidden by the plaid pattern, and by the shadow of his own chin. "What about it?"

"You got blood on it. You get in a fight or something?"

He hung his head and shook it. He stared down at the table; his gaze swung like a pendulum. "Nothing like that, Momma."

"Tell me what it *is* like."

"Nosebleed. No big thing at all. I was sitting there at the bar," he made a little eye contact, as he warmed to his story. "And Joey was there beside me, and he said something about what was wrong with my beer. I asked what he meant, and I looked down…" He shrugged. "Drop of blood, right there on the foam."

"More dramatic than a single tear."

He snorted. "Ain't that the truth."

"What'd you do? When you realized you was bleeding?"

Now he shrugged, and looked back down. "Got a couple of bar napkins and stuffed 'em up my nose. Finished my beer," he grinned down at the table. "Then I paid up, and headed out. It was only a couple of beers, and I ate supper late. I was all right to drive."

"That's my responsible boy."

"You know it." He finished the rest of his drink, and motioned hopefully toward the bottle.

Alannah considered it, and pushed the whiskey forward. "One more, and that's all. I'll put it up after that. I need to get some sleep. So do you. Maybe you ought to take a shower, first. Don't go to sleep bloody, and mess up your pillowcase."

"Yeah, I'll...I'll do that." He poured one more, a big fat one that counted more like two.

"You should give me your clothes. I'm doing laundry tomorrow."

"Don't worry about it. I'll take care of it myself."

"Don't be silly." She shook her head. "Toss everything in the hamper. I know you're a big man, but I can still wash your clothes. Once in a while. So long as it don't become habit."

"No chance of that."

Alannah picked up her cup, touched it to her lips, and held it there a second before putting it down. "You feeling all right?"

"Some reason I shouldn't be?"

"I only ask, because you're sitting funny. Like you pulled your shoulder again."

"I didn't pull anything. It's just the same old terrible posture you're always fussing about. It's a good thing, too. Between a bum shoulder and a nosebleed, I'd be falling apart over here."

"If you say so. I worry, that's all. Speaking of, how's Lisa doing? Is she feeling any better?"

"Far as I know."

"Far as you know? Haven't you looked in on her?"

"I did," he nodded slow. "Yesterday. No, it was the day before. I stopped by her momma's place on the way to Dave's. That roof on his brother's house is coming along real good, too. Another couple of days, and we'll have it all put together. He's talking about bringing me on full time."

"He got enough work for that?" she asked with a frown.

"Somebody's bought up the basin lots, and they're putting in a subdivision. That's what Dave said. When that gets underway, the job is mine. It'll be good money."

"And hard work."

"I don't mind hard work."

Alannah took a real sip, this time. A bigger one than she meant to, but it was watered a bit, so that didn't matter. "I'm glad to hear you say that. But tell me about Lisa: What's wrong with her, anyhow? You never did say."

"I never did know." He wiggled his wrist, and the whiskey swirled in the cup. "Her momma thought it was mono. At any rate, she won't be around for a bit."

"That's a shame. I like her."

He stared down into the tiny brown whirlpool like it would tell him the future. "Well, I like her too. But I don't know. Maybe we ain't a good fit."

"You gonna break it off?"

"Might should."

"While she's sick? You're a colder boy than ever I knew."

"No, I only mean…being apart a few days, it's got me thinking. Maybe we ain't a good fit."

Alannah started to sigh, but it came out in a big, deep breath with a shudder at the end. She took another swallow, mostly emptying the drink before her.

Willie lifted an eyebrow at the bottle, offering to pass it back.

She held up her hands, and shook her head. "No more for me. Just bedtime, I think."

He yawned, stretched, and stood up—downing the last few drops and turning the cup over, like it was a shot glass. "Good call. And good night, Momma. I'll throw myself in the shower first, and then I'll head off to bed."

She didn't stand up. "Leave me your clothes," she reminded him. "Toss 'em in the hamper."

"I will." He kissed her on the forehead and left.

Off to his room he shuffled, to collect something clean to sleep in, she figured. She listened as he snapped on the bedside lamp, opened and closed drawers, and gathered what he wanted. She waited while his naked footsteps slapped down the hall.

The fan came on in the bathroom. The door closed.

When she looked over her shoulder, she saw a thin seam of yellow light spilling out across the floor.

The shower came on with a fit and a sputter; it'd been no better plumbed than the kitchen faucet.

Alannah poured another slug, but didn't drink it. She put her head in her hands, and rubbed her eyes.

"You know good and well what he's done."

She didn't lift her head. "I do now."

"You've got the policeman's card in your pocket."

"I do."

"Call him, and he'll be here before Willie can towel himself off."

"I…" She swallowed hard, but it was a dry swallow, so she chased it with a gulp from her cup. Maybe she needed another drink after all. She sat back in the creaking chair, all squeaky, torn vinyl and rusty joints. "Mother, what is it you want?"

"I want to know what you plan to do."

"Can't you tell? Can't you see the future, from wherever you are?"

The ghost shook her head. She didn't look like a ghost. She looked like Metta Floyd, who'd died ten years ago. "It doesn't work like that."

"Yeah, that'd be too easy." She rubbed her eyes again. Her tears were hot as fire. She held them back anyhow. "Then never mind the fortune-telling…but have you got any wisdom to share from the other side? Or are you just here to cluck your tongue, and tell me how different he'd have turned out, if you hadn't passed? If I'd let you raise him, like you wanted."

The ghost who was shaped like Metta Floyd narrowed her eyes and crossed her arms, but the chair beneath her didn't squeak at all. "If you'd let me keep him when he was little, I could've made a difference in him. By the time the stroke took me, he could've been somebody better."

"And here we go…" Alannah gave in, gave up, and took a swig right from the bottle of fresh booze with the antique-looking label.

"It's true and you know it."

"It's bullshit, and I'm fairly sure of that."

"It's not his fault he got his daddy's brains, but that's no excuse for raising him lazy. I don't mean his letters, and I don't mean his numbers—but that boy should've learned years ago, how to treat a woman. You should've taught him."

"Someone should've taught *me*," Alannah retorted. "What the hell kind of example did I ever have?"

"Mine."

"You're making my point for me, Momma."

"You spent a lifetime watching your daddy do it wrong. You could've taught Willie from that. Showed him what ain't acceptable, and what a woman shouldn't have to take."

"All I ever learned from you and Daddy was how to take a right hook, and where to hide the whiskey for when I needed leverage."

Metta still scowled, but she said, "That's better than nothing."

"It wasn't hardly enough."

"You should've known to pick a different kind, when it came to a family of your choosing."

She shook her head. "What other kind? I never saw any other kind, not from Daddy, and not from my brothers, either. You let them grow up as bad as Willie, so you've got a lot of nerve giving me grief."

"I didn't let..." she started to argue, and changed her mind. "I didn't have no control over them. That was all your daddy's doing—they were his boys, and they wanted to be like him. Or he thought they did, and maybe he was right. He didn't let me get between them, and you can call me weak for that, if you want to. Maybe I was, but I thought surely you and Willie would have a better chance, when your man died so early on. I thought you'd do a better job on your own, with him out of the way. You couldn't hardly do any worse, but Lord Almighty, I could've done better."

Alannah almost laughed. "With him out of the way, I worked two jobs and left what little school I'd managed to buy. With him gone, I worked until I slept, and then I got up, and went and worked some more. When was I supposed to give Willie all these lessons in living? When I was rushing him off to Miss Nancy's for the day? When I was dropping him off at school so fast, I hardly stopped the car? Who the hell are you, to tell me what I should've done?"

"Someone who screwed up bad, and thought you might could do better!"

"How?" The question was sorrowful, though that wasn't what she wanted. "You stayed home and cashed Daddy's checks. You stayed put, and watched your soaps all day and drank your two-dollar wine at night. You never had to worry about where the food came from, or who'd pay the mortgage—so I guess it's easy for you to sit there and tell me how I should've brought up my boy."

"I had other things to worry about. I had four children to see to, and a husband who wasn't worth the paper his paycheck was printed on."

"You could've left."

"How?" Her mother's question wasn't quite sorrowful, but it sure as hell wasn't happy. "You say I've got nerve, but you sit there and tell me how hard it was with just one baby—you think I should've packed up and hit the road with you and your brothers?"

"I did it. Other women do it. You could've done it."

"Could've, should've. I stayed, and that's my fuck-up to own."

"Own it? Woman, you passed it *down*. It's the only inheritance you left, and now it's mine. Shit, now it's Willie's. He got his daddy's brains, my eyes, and your hair—since nobody else has a hint of red."

Metta looked angry like she always did, when she didn't want to look sad. "You're still blaming me."

"Every bit as much as you blame me. I blame Daddy, too, and Grandma before that—for how she didn't have the sense to walk off or even just defend herself, once in a while."

"Well now, those were different times. More different than the times between my babies and yours, I mean. You can measure the difference in cops, if you want."

Alannah said, "I don't follow."

"Follow like this: When your grandma was young, with a baby on her hip and a black eye, if she'd called the cops they would've asked what she'd done to piss your grandpa off. Then they would've sat down for a beer while her husband told them war stories, and that'd be the end of it, right there. But as for me, when I called the police when I was young, with a baby on my hip and a row of broken teeth, they told me I should be more understanding of how much pressure a man is under, supporting a family like ours. And wasn't he a good provider? They always asked me that…like it wasn't even a question."

"You called? I didn't know you ever did."

"I called," she nodded. "Twice. First time they asked me to be understanding, and remember who put food on the table. Second time, they told me I was being a nuisance, and I should move back home with my momma, if things were so bad as that."

"Jesus."

"What about you? Did you ever call?"

Alannah shook her head. "No, I never did. Couldn't imagine what good it would do."

"Cops are different, these days. You see them on the TV shows, and they have to fill out paperwork, and sign reports. There are...there are whole departments, where they've got people to help mothers and children who need helping."

"Maybe in a big city. Hell, Momma. Maybe even in Knoxville, they do. But we're twenty miles from town, and maybe times have changed somewhere, but I tell you this from the bottom of my heart—ain't nobody out here gives a good goddamn what happens to a woman on the phone."

"Why would you think that?"

"Why wouldn't I?"

The stalemate meant silence, until Alannah felt like maybe she owed her mother more than that, in explanation. "You know who answers phones, down at the rinky-dink precinct of ours? Dale Hartley. You know who's the new boy on patrol? Frankie Hill. And his partner? Jack Mable. All them boys knew Allen before he died—they all went to school together, for chrissake."

"But times've changed since then, since he died."

"But I haven't needed the cops, since he died," she pointed out. "Because maybe I didn't learn enough from you, or I didn't learn it fast enough, but I learned that I didn't want another man like him. Even if it meant leaving Willie without a father."

"Maybe that wasn't the right answer."

Alannah threw up her hands, splashing a little whiskey on the table. She half-assed wiped at the puddle with the back of her sleeve. "Who the fuck knows, anymore? You already admitted you don't have no wisdom from beyond the grave. Just might've-beens and finger-waggings, and I don't need either one, thanks so much."

"Maybe you could've done better, with the next man. Maybe you could've picked someone who'd been a firmer hand with the boy, and more help to you than hindrance."

"Maybe you can kiss my ass, and head on back to wherever you go when you aren't hassling me about choices I should've made better, and problems I can't fix. Maybe I didn't need you before, and I don't need you now."

Metta didn't flip her off. She didn't rage, or swear, or poltergeist-out all over the place like she sometimes did, leaving a mess in her wake. This time she just vanished, wearing that same look of anger that was mostly sadness, and mostly wishing things were different all this time—for all the good that ever did anybody.

When she was gone, Alannah listened for the dull buzz of the shower.

Willie was humming to himself in there, and the pipes were humming along. She said to the space where her mother once sat, "Maybe I could only save one of us."

"That's a dick thing to say."

Metta was gone, but the seat wasn't empty. Now there was a new woman, freshly dead and not so strong as the late matriarch with an axe to grind. She was half-formed and translucent, a faded photo of someone young and pretty. Someone outraged, with an altogether different axe.

Alannah put her head in her hands. "Lisa, baby. What would you rather hear me say?"

"You could start by saying you're sorry. Somebody ought to apologize for Willie, and God knows he won't do it for himself."

"Then I'm sorry. More sorry than you have any idea." The shower still buzzed, white noise and hot water, steaming up the small bathroom and feeding the mildew on the ceiling in there, but she wasn't thinking about that, not really. She lifted her head and thought about drinking, but she didn't touch her glass again, or the bottle, either. "But in my defense, I did try to warn you off him."

The girl flickered, vanished, and came back. A radio stuck between two stations. A cable channel nobody's paying for, with shows that come in and out without clearing up.

"I told you," Alannah continued, "that he was never any good to anybody, anywhere. Bless his heart. And I said loud and clear, he wouldn't be good to you, either."

"He was good sometimes. He always bought me breakfast, and he got me new tires last month, when the back two were so bald they blew right out."

"He was bad more often than not. He cheated on you, and he was jealous of everybody you ever talked to. That should've been a red flag, even before I said anything."

"I cheated on him, too. Neither one of us is any kind of saint. As for jealous…he cared, that's all."

"Jealousy and control, that's not caring. That's not love. That's an insecure asshole, and God help me, I tried to tell you that. I wish you'd listened."

Lisa wavered again, but held herself together a little better this time. She was getting the hang of this. "I should've listened," she admitted. "But I listened to him, first. He said *you* were the jealous one, *you* were the controlling one. He said you never liked any of his girlfriends."

"I guess now you know who was telling the truth."

The girl's eyes narrowed. Did she agree? Did she want to argue? She didn't pick a fight, either way. "So what are you going to do now?" she wanted to know instead.

"My mother asked me the same thing, just a minute ago."

"What'd you tell her?"

Alannah was silent. Then she said, "I'm going to do the right thing."

"Which right thing? You gonna protect your son—is that the right thing? Or are you gonna pull that cop's card out of your pocket and get him on the line before your boy can make a run for it? Would that be right? You could always stay out of it, maybe give him a warning and let him run."

"I could make a case for any one of them things." She frowned at the girl, who moved in and out of focus, in and out of the kitchen. "Obviously you're wanting me to call the police and get it over with."

But the girl shuddered and disappeared, then popped back into her seat. "Obviously," she whispered without conviction.

Alannah sighed, and leaned forward on her elbows. She folded her arms and looked Lisa in the eye. "How many times did he hit you?"

"Just once, before tonight."

"How many times did he threaten you?"

"A few."

"How many promises did he break?"

"More than a couple," she confessed. "But so did I. It's like I told you, he was no good, and I wasn't, either. We were bad apart, and bad together."

"But only one of you is dead, so one of you is worse. Don't tell me you've come all the way back here from the other side, just to defend him."

"I'm not defending him."

"Yes, baby. You are. Just like I defended his daddy, and my momma defended mine, and my grandma before her. And when I begged you to go out and find someone better than Willie, I thought…I don't know what I thought." Alannah leaned back again, and crossed her arms over her belly. "I never had any girls of my own—Willie was a handful, and then I was a widow, which was just as well—but you seemed like an all right sort; and with that God-given rack on you, I was sure you could do better. I didn't want you to end up like me, or like…or like how you did. Jesus Christ, I've failed just about everybody, haven't I?"

"It's not your fault."

"Tell that to my mother, if you ever run into her. And tell it to yourself, while you're at it. Listen to me, for once—if you never listen to me again, about anything else: It wasn't your fault, either."

"I never said it was."

"If you thought entirely different, you wouldn't be making excuses for him."

Lisa wobbled and steadied. She stared at Alannah, and past her—into space, or into something else the older woman couldn't see. "We're a sorry pair, ain't we?"

"I guess we are. But it can stop here, can't it? It can stop with us, if I just call the number and bring the men around to get him." She looked to the girl for some kind of reassurance, or strength, or agreement—but the phantom only gazed painfully into that middle distance. "Even if it *is* my fault, a little bit. Even if it *is* your fault, a little bit. It's his fault most of all—and if I don't stop it here…"

She felt in her pocket for the policeman's card. It was warm with a hint of damp from being crushed up against her body. It was wrinkled when she pulled it out and set it on the table. She smoothed it with the heel of her hand, flattening it, as if that made a difference.

"I should tell you," Lisa said quietly. Everything she said was quiet, now. "I should tell you what happened, and where he put me."

"Go on, then."

"We were parked by the rail bridge—you know the big one, off 140. Looks like it belongs in a movie."

"Trains don't use it anymore, do they?"

"Naw, not anymore." Lisa twitched, shuddered, and dimmed. "We were walking along the trestle, talking. Talking turned into fighting. Fighting turned into hitting, and when he was done, he choked me out and threw me into the water. I'm sure I've washed downriver a ways by now…or I will, by the time they find me."

"They found your car, abandoned at work. Your sister called the police, and said you'd gone missing. She said she thought Willie had something to do with it. That's why the police came around. They don't know for a fact that he did anything, but he's been in so much trouble, ever since he was twelve. They'd be fools if they didn't suspect it."

"He just came on home, like it was nothing."

She nodded. "He sat here and drank with me, and then set off for a shower. But I've got his bloody clothes in the hamper. The police will want them."

"It'll be the nail in his coffin. I mean…" Lisa hesitated. "If you mean to call them."

Alannah stared down at a spot on the table, a little rip in a placemat that left a hole shaped like a triangle. She stared at it hard, and thought about what she meant to say, and what she meant to do. "I know what I ought to do. No, I know what I have to do. You've helped me figure it out, actually."

"I did?"

"You and me together, feeling bad for things we didn't do, and worrying about things we should've done. That guilt, that uncertainty…I've been carrying it around for years, like some kind of awful inheritance. That's what it is, you know, same as red hair, or brown eyes. It comes down through the years, through the family line, worse than baldness, or bad eyes or bad teeth. Worse than the cancer that took two of my aunts and a cousin. And still it comes," she breathed, eyes locked to that spot on the placemat. "Father to son, mother to daughter. You wish you could give your children something better, but go on and wish in one hand—then spit in the other," she muttered. "You can't give it away if you've never had it. You pass on what you've got, and that's all."

The girl was gone.

The kitchen was empty. The policeman's business card lay rumpled on the table. There was still plenty of whiskey, even watered down. There was still time, before the shower turned off and Willie dried off, and maybe there was time before he took off, because he figured out they were coming for him.

"I could only save one of us," she said to the chair where the ghostly girl no longer sat. "But I tried to save you, too, for all the good it did. And

I'll have you to know—in case you can still hear me—he told you the truth about one thing, at least: I always *did* try and chase his girlfriends off. Ever since high school, I did my best to keep them away for their own good. It was bound to happen, one of these days. *You* were bound to happen."

She took the bottle and swigged from the top, one last time.

"He got his daddy's brains and I doubt he did any good, covering his tracks. He came home wearing your blood, for pity's sake. It's probably all over his car, all over his shoes. He's probably left himself all over you, too—even the river won't wash it all away. His handprints around your neck. His skin under your nails. I watch TV, and I know how different it is, these days. My momma says you can measure it in cop shows—you can watch it from *Dragnet* to *Miami Vice* and then to *CSI*, where the science might as well be magic. Not that it'd take a magician to find Willie out."

She took another hard swallow. The shower knobs turned with a creak, squeak, and pop. The water quit falling; then it dribbled and dripped for another few seconds. That boy always did empty the whole damn water heater with every bath.

She whispered—to the girl, or to her own mother, either one. Under her breath, she said so softly that the words wouldn't reach the bathroom around the corner: "Some of it might've been my fault, somewhere down the line. Some of it *must've* been. But if I let him go now, then everything he does, everyone he hurts from here on out…that's my fault, for damn sure."

She collected the card, and smacked the bottle down in its place.

It crashed down harder than she meant. It crashed down loud.

"Momma?"

Her knees shook, but she stood up anyway. Her hands quivered, but she picked her cell off the kitchen counter, beside the stove.

"Momma, what was that?"

"Nothing," she called back, around the corner and through the flimsy door that never did shut right. She held the phone close against her chest, and digit by digit, she tapped the cop's number into the display. "It's only me, baby. Picking up after you, like always." ⤸

THE MERMAID AQUARIUM:
WEEKI WACHEE SPRINGS, 1951

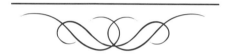

About twenty years ago (in the very early 2000s), I started a young adult project on a lark. It never really went anywhere, but I always loved the "frame" story I'd written around it; and in time, I adapted the first portion of that frame into "The Mermaid Aquarium." When the marvelous Mr. Maberry asked if I wanted to contribute something for a young adult project he was compiling for Simon & Schuster—*Scary Out There*—I dusted it off and took another look. Would it hold up after all that time?

Well...no, not really.

But when I tore it all down to the studs and rebuilt it, I rather liked the result.

The original idea had been (to sum up) to tell a fairy tale from the point of view of the fairies themselves, a bit of a reverse portal story, if you will. I might still do something with the meat of it, one day—it was loosely inspired by the few weeks I spent in an adolescent ward as a teenager in the early '90s.

Long story.

But it was a frightening story at the time, so I went ahead and turned it into a dark fairy tale. Inverted. Deconstructed. Only semi-successful, in its original incarnation.

I began rewriting that meat a handful of years ago, but haven't finished it yet. Maybe I will, someday. Maybe I won't. But here's "The Mermaid Aquarium," set in the iconic roadside attraction of Weeki Wachee Springs in Hernando County, Florida. It's a real place, with "real" mermaids, and you can visit it today; though I should note, these days it's a state park, very different from how it's portrayed back in this retro story of yesteryear. There's even a water park there now, in addition to the literal mermaid aquarium that inspired the whole shebang.

Weeki Wachee is? Was? A formally incorporated town for some years, and one of the retired mermaids was even the mayor. I don't know if it's still independent from the state park or not. Times change. Mermaids change. Even fairy tales change, if you give them long enough.

According to the 2010 census, its entire population amounted to twelve people, many of them no doubt former mermaids and other attraction personnel. Alas, there's no official count of any hypothetical monsters or fairies.

B UT YOU never know!" Tammy plunged one hand into the trunk of mismatched shoes and felt around with her fingertips. "We could find buried treasure in here. You can't beat buried treasure for…what does the sign say, a nickel?"

THE MERMAID AQUARIUM

Her sister reread the hand-scrawled note taped inside the trunk's open lid. "A nickel," she confirmed with a shake of her head. "Honestly. Who pays a nickel apiece for mismatched shoes?"

"A pirate. One with a peg."

Elaine picked a blue leather sandal out of the pile and spun it around on her pinky finger. "I'd love to meet the pirate who'd wear one of *these*. Peg or no peg. Hey, speaking of pirates—I hear we get to do *battle* with pirates."

"Battle? With pirates?"

"That's what Mr. Newton said."

Once again elbow deep in stale footwear, Tammy laughed. "Mermaids versus pirates. That's going to be *amazing*. Ooh, what's this?" Her hand hooked something down at the bottom. She yanked it up and out—a shiny silver crown with big, fake-looking gemstones.

"What on earth is that?"

"Buried treasure. I told you we'd find some!" She held it up to the sky and let the afternoon sun beam through it, casting choppy rainbows across the lawn. "This will be perfect for my outfit—look, it's got little clips on it and everything. It'll stay on my head underwater, right?" Without waiting for an answer, she said to herself, "I bet it will. Anyhow, it's worth a nickel to find out.

"Excuse me, ma'am?" She waved her hands and held up the silly tiara. "I found this in the shoe bin."

The old lady on the porch squinted down at the yard sale and at Tammy with her treasure. "I forgot that was in there. It's part of an old Halloween costume."

"Great! Now I can wear it with *my* costume." Tammy grinned big. "We're going to be mermaids. It's our job, starting tomorrow."

"Oh." The old lady's face went tight and sour. She put one hand on the porch rail and one on her hip. "Over at the springs, you mean. At Weeki Wachee."

Elaine nodded and stepped up to stand beside her sister. "Yes, ma'am. We've joined the mermaid show. We got hired yesterday, and we start tomorrow. Mr. Newton's going to teach us how to breathe through the air tubes and everything."

The woman on the porch sniffed, like whatever the girls were talking about didn't smell very good. "That's not a decent job."

"Have you ever *seen* the mermaid show?" Tammy asked, still holding the tiara aloft.

"Of course not."

"Then, how do you know it isn't decent?"

She crinkled the edge of her nose and frowned harder. "I've seen those girls, running around in their bikinis, flagging down cars to bring people into the springs. I remember when it didn't used to be that way."

Tammy rubbed her foot into the grass and rolled her eyes. "Ma'am, can I buy the tiara or not?"

"For a dime."

"But the sign on the trunk said—"

"That was for the shoes. It says the shoes are a nickel, and it doesn't say anything about costume trinkets."

Tammy gave Elaine a look that asked what she thought about the deal.

Elaine shrugged. "It'll look good with a fish tail. I say you should buy it."

"All right. Asking a whole dime for this thing is practically highway robbery, but I'll pay it."

"We don't have no highway here." One pointed foot at a time, the woman tiptoed down the wood porch steps.

"I guess 19 don't count," Tammy said of the nearest proper road, wiggling her fingers around in her pocket. She pulled out a dime and made a show of presenting it.

"I guess it don't." The woman took the coin and pushed it into her purse. "Is that all, then? Y'all don't want anything else?"

THE MERMAID AQUARIUM

"No, ma'am," the girls said together. "Thank you," Tammy added.

The old lady nodded and turned her back to them. She went up the porch stairs again, returning to her post, where she could oversee the sale on her broad, green lawn.

Tammy toyed with the tiara as they left, wandering back down into the dirt road and toward U.S. 19, the only paved strip in that part of Florida—a two-lane road that ran along the Gulf Coast past all the little towns, joints, and junctures…including the springs at Weeki Wachee.

But Weeki Wachee wasn't a proper town; it was just a freshwater pool that a sharp ex-navy man had turned into a roadside attraction. How Frank Newton got the idea to dig an underwater auditorium and fill it with mermaids, no one knew—but word sure did get around about the show. People came from all over the country to see the aquatic acrobatics, and girls came from miles away, hoping to make the cut and wear the fins.

The yard sale lady was right about the bikinis, too. And maybe she was right that it wasn't decent to go running around half-naked all the time, but in 1951 there weren't many visitors passing through that part of Florida. People brought in tourist money however they could, and teenage girls in bikinis brought in a *lot* of tourists.

Besides, neither Tammy nor Elaine had any problem with the skimpy uniform, and if Frank wanted girls to dress that way and chase down cars, that was all right with them.

At least he wasn't weird about it.

Frank was a big guy, wide in the shoulders, with thighs like tree trunks, and the sort of chest where a big tattoo would look right at home. The way he talked—the way he handed out orders and suggestions, the way he taught them how to use the equipment—you could tell he'd been a military man. He wasn't unkind, but he was direct. He wasn't unreasonable, but he was demanding.

Tammy and Elaine caught on quick, and Frank approved.

He liked them not just because they were pretty red-haired sisters, but because they were sturdy farm girls who'd grown up in orchards, climbing orange trees and working hard for a living. Swimming around in the tank was tough, especially with legs bound together in phony fins and only a set of skinny, hidden tubes to breathe from. It didn't matter how pretty a girl was, because if she wasn't hardy enough to swim and smile without much air, she wasn't ready to join the show.

Tammy was all set to swim within one week, and her older sister joined the next.

For their first show together Frank dressed them up the same—passing them off as twins for the sake of the underwater play they were performing.

It worked out well. The girls were only a year apart—"Irish twins" their mother called them—and with enough of the right greasepaint glitter makeup, at a distance, inside the tank, nobody knew the difference.

The tiara Tammy picked up at the yard sale helped. It gave the audience a way to tell them apart. She twisted the hairpiece into her curls as tight as she could, pushing the metal bobby pins up against her scalp to keep it secure through all the swirling, diving, and splashing. With the tiara perched on her head, that little coronet with the tacky stones, Tammy was the one to watch.

She was the girl with the silver crown.

The shows took on a comfortable, familiar pattern.

Sometimes, the themes were different—pirates, or police, or shipwrecks—but the daily routine was usually the same. Every day, there was practice and training, with Frank barking the story along through a megaphone. Every day, there was time spent sipping from the tiny air hoses and learning to breathe without gasping in front of the audience.

Breathe and smile. Drink a bottle of fizzy Grapette underwater while the kids clapped and their parents wondered *How on earth do they do that?*

But they weren't on earth.

THE MERMAID AQUARIUM

They performed beneath it, under the blue skin of the pooled spring and down in front of the enormous, underground window—they frolicked like polar bears in a zoo, with only the thick and tinted fishbowl glass between the them and the wide-eyed watchers.

And all the people in the auditorium sat and shivered, cool as almost ice in the orange-hot heat of a Florida afternoon. Open-mouthed, they watched the women in bright bathing suits from a fairy tale—they saw how their fins twisted in the current, how their smiles stayed in place because people had paid good money to see them.

It was magic, and it hid out in the open. The rules were different, there.

"Car!" Frank bellowed through his megaphone. *"Car!"*

All the girls knew what to do. The mermaids rallied from the tank with a flurry of flinging water. Wet hair went tied up in scarves or combs, and fins were quickly, carefully stripped. Pruney feet with painted toenails felt about for sandals, and, finding them, they pattered away from the spring.

"Hurry up!" Frank hollered. He pulled a short-sleeved, button-up shirt over his wet chest and retreated toward the ticket office. "Go get 'em, ladies!"

All eight of the mermaids on duty charged out of the dirt and gravel parking lot and over to U.S. 19. And, yes, a brand new '51 Chevrolet was coming in from the north. It was black with chrome and fins shining like silver, and inside it must have been hot as an oven, come noon in July.

The car slowed for the swarm of girls and stopped on the side of the road. All of the windows were down, so within seconds, each one framed at least two grinning young women wearing not very much in the way of clothes.

The driver grinned back from beneath a gleaming mop of slick black hair and matching eyebrows. If it weren't for the pink haze of sunburn across his nose, he would've looked like a happy vampire.

Elaine spoke first, leaning into the car. "Hey there, mister."

"Hey there, sweetheart," he replied, and his voice was shiny too. Oil on aluminum. "To what do I owe this pleasure?"

One of the other girls spoke next. She batted her eyelashes and hung her boobs over the passenger side window. "We're the girls of Weeki Wachee—a little place you can find right over there, through the trees. We put on a mean show, if you'd like to make a little room for us in your wallet."

"What kind of show?"

"Mermaids!" several of them said at once.

He laughed, and the sound shimmered around the edges. "All right. You've got me now. Let's see what you little sirens can do."

The girls chased his car into the lot and vanished in a trickle, one or two returning to the tank or to the concession and ticketing area. The rest swarmed into the locker room and began dressing up. It could be quick, and it didn't have to be perfect. It was just one guy, not a family or a group to fill the eighteen-seat auditorium.

But the week had been slow, and Frank was a big believer in word of mouth. He said it was always worth putting on the show for the occasional individual, because that one guy might go home and tell his friends.

So Tammy slid over the side of the tank with one practiced, slippery motion.

She imagined she was a seal, a sea lion, or a penguin—something with rounded edges and a shape meant to move through water. Once she was in the aquarium, it was all too easy to sink like a stone. It was hard to remember not to paddle and kick, to pretend she was born with the aqua-blue fin. It was hard to swim by flexing her waist and snapping her ankles.

She did it beautifully, and down into the spring she tumbled.

The water was too cold at first. She closed her eyes, then opened them. She found the rubber breathing tube and remembered how to swim, and breathe, and smile. She tucked the tube away behind an ornamental rock, so the man in the auditorium couldn't see it.

THE MERMAID AQUARIUM

Two other mermaids joined her, and then her sister did too. They moved together; they found their tubes and discreetly sipped enough oxygen to writhe their swimming selves into position. They were sea lions and sirens, every last one of them.

Tammy waved at the man—he'd said his name was Ed—standing all alone in the auditorium. He didn't take a seat. He stood at the glass and he waved back. The gesture was filtered through the window, and the sparkling clear water, and through the bubbles of the breathing tubes behind the rocks. But Tammy saw it, and she smiled at him because that was her job now.

But suddenly, she didn't mean it.

Her smile froze where it was, and it did not melt.

It unnerved her, the way Ed stood there in the empty room with the tiny tile mosaics in blue, pink, and gold. It cast a chill through the window and into the spring water to see him there, arms folded after he finished waving at them.

Through the glass with the soft green tint she saw him differently, standing alone in the empty room with the folding seats like a movie theater. He did not look like the same man who drove the black Chevy down U.S. 19. He looked colder and sharper. The pink was gone from his skin and the blue was brighter in his hair through the lens of the window glass—and through the heavy, cool weight of a million gallons between them.

Elaine swam up to Tammy's side and handed her a new bottle of Grapette. Startled out of the spell Tammy took it and popped the bottle cap. In sync, she and her sister drank together, and the man clapped to see the little red-haired sirens take their sodas underwater.

Such a precious trick. Such a pretty thing to watch.

And maybe that was what it came down to, when Tammy later tried to think of what had bothered her so much about Ed and his blue-black eyes, his blue-black hair. Through the whole story—even when Frank joined in as the pirate king and the funny fake cannon sent explosions of bubbles and waves through the water—Ed was never watching anything or anyone except for Tammy. And he never looked her in the eyes, but he stared somewhere higher, above her forehead. He was looking at the cheap, pretty tiara fixed to her head with bobby pins and skill.

When the show was over, Ed went on his way, and Frank called Tammy aside as she toweled herself dry.

"That guy, Ed. Did you know him?" He looked worried, but he was trying to hide it.

Tammy shook her head. "Never saw him before."

"Huh." Frank twiddled absently with the end of a cracked breathing tube, one he was repairing or replacing from a compressed air tank. "I wondered, that's all. He talked about you like he knew you, but he didn't know your name."

"What'd he say?"

Frank tossed the tube aside, into the trash. He shrugged his big shoulders with the tight-looking muscles underneath them and leaned back against the doorframe. "He said he liked the show. And he especially liked the girl with the silver crown."

"Oh. I guess that's me, then."

"I guess it is, but I don't like how he said it. Where did you get that little crown anyway? I've noticed it before. It looks nice with the fins, but maybe you shouldn't wear it anymore."

"I found it at a yard sale in New Port Richey. Why shouldn't I wear it? Because some creepy guy pointed it out on a lark?" She was nervous again, not because of Frank, who made the same concerned face her dad used to make when he smelled trouble, but because she couldn't stand the thought of taking off the tiara. She'd been wearing it more lately, even without the costume. Even for fun, down at the movies or at the beach. It belonged one of two places: in the locker at the ladies' rooms or on her head.

Preferably, on her head.

"Look," he added, still in father mode, "I didn't like that guy, that's all I'm saying. I didn't like the way he looked at you. Nice guys don't stare like that. If you see him around, or if he comes around again…I want you to tell me about it. And next show, maybe you can leave off the hairpiece. We'll find something else to match your costume."

"Okay," she told him. She knew he was right, but he was a little bit wrong, too.

It wasn't weird, the way Ed had looked at her. It was weird how he'd looked at the tiara, like he'd seen it before. Like it meant something to him. Well, it meant something to Tammy, too.

Two days later Frank was sick—or that's what he said. There was a sign up at the entrance to the concessions and ticket area, where the doors were locked and there weren't any lights turned on inside.

BAD CASE OF THE FLU.

TAKE THE DAY OFF.

BACK AT THE REGULAR TIME TOMORROW.

Tammy and Elaine were early for work, and they were the first to see the sign. They puzzled over it.

"But Frank's *never* sick," Tammy complained. "He's practically invincible."

"I hope he's all right."

"He will be. He's practically—"

"Invincible. Yeah. I heard you." Elaine picked at the tape on the sign and leaned her head close to the door. Somewhere in the distance, down a floor or two below—she thought she heard something. But it was faint. There was nothing certain, nothing she could point to and say, *Listen. What's that?*

So she didn't say anything about it, and the pair of them walked back to U.S. 19 to walk or hitchhike home, like they did most days. It was better to do it while the morning was still new and before the sun got too high.

One by one the other girls arrived and read the sign, and one by one they turned and went back home with a grumble.

But not a single girl listened as hard as Elaine did, with her ear right next to the concession room door. None of them heard the splashing, the soft rubbing coming from down below in the auditorium. None of them pulled at the door or fought the lock.

A day off was easier than chasing phantom sounds.

But Frank was not home in bed with the flu. He was there at Weeki Wachee, downstairs in the auditorium where the eighteen cinema seats lined up like soldiers facing the aquarium window. He was standing on a stool, wearing a grim expression and a pair of shorts, but nothing else. He held a rag and a sponge—the big kind, the kind they used for washing cars.

Beside him was a bucket, and inside the bucket was soapy water that had turned almost purple.

He wrung out the sponge and the rag and pulled them back and forth over the wide underground window that was bigger than a movie screen: wiping, smoothing, cleaning. Erasing the message he'd found there, first thing that morning—a message which was so much worse than the one he'd left to protect his girls.

If they saw this one, they'd only be afraid. There was no need to involve the police, no reason to let the authorities wander around asking questions and issuing warnings. Cops would be in the way. They'd be bad for business.

And there was nothing to be afraid of, anyway.

Or that's what he told himself, same as he told the mermaids. But all the same he'd be on the lookout for a dark-eyed man with hair blacker than the ace of spades. He'd keep his eyes peeled for that fellow who called himself Ed.

With runny, tinted water staining his hands, he kept on working—wearing away the series of letters that stood as tall as his arms were long. By suppertime not a trace would be left, and it was better that way.

But for now, the window still read: IT BELONGS TO ME AND YOU MUST GIVE IT BACK.

THE MERMAID AQUARIUM

Frank didn't know how he knew it was Ed, but he did. And somehow, he knew precisely what Ed wanted back. It was that stupid crown, the one Tammy wore in the show. There was something uncanny about it—something that made you want to touch it, hold it. Even wear it, not that Frank would ever do such a thing.

That ridiculous bauble wasn't normal—and neither was Ed.

Somehow, they belonged together. He wondered how they'd ever gotten separated in the first place.

Maybe he could retrieve it when the girls had all gone home. Maybe he could throw it away himself—or leave it out for Ed to find. Frank didn't like a bully, and he didn't like following orders from random vandals. But maybe if he did what the message said, Ed would go away.

"You shouldn't be the last to leave."

"What?" Tammy asked. She wrapped her towel quickly around the tiara and pulled it out of the locker, hiding it against her stomach.

Frank closed his arms over his chest. "We talked about this. Where was your sister today? And what have you got there? Is that that hair doodad? I thought we talked about this—I don't want to see it anymore, not in the show."

"I *know*, and that's why I'm taking it home. What are you doing in the *ladies'* room?" She felt guilty and nervous, and she knew it was dumb. The tiara was hers. She could take it home with her if she wanted to. Frank should be the one feeling guilty and nervous. *He* was the one sneaking up on her in the bathroom.

"I thought everyone was gone," he told her. "I was going to check in here for...um...toilet paper. I was going to take out the trash."

"You should've knocked."

"I *did* knock. Didn't you hear me?"

"No." But when she said it out loud and thought about it, yes, maybe. Maybe she *had* heard him. She clutched the towel bundle and retreated, pushing her back against the locker door to shut it.

He stepped back too—almost sitting on the edge of the sink, he leaned so hard against it. Maybe he felt guilty and nervous after all. "How're you getting home today?"

"Hitch or walk, same as always."

"By yourself? No, I don't like that. Let me give you a lift."

Outside, the sun burned down hot and steady, even though it was almost seven o'clock. Tammy thought about it for a second, but only a second. She trusted Frank. Everyone did—you pretty much had to…and it was amazingly, blindingly hot outside. She didn't really want to walk. "All right. Yeah, I'll ride with you."

"Good. Let me lock up around here, and we'll head out."

She nodded and held the tiara tighter, as if she were afraid he might try to take it away from her. He almost looked like he wanted to.

He didn't try it. He only stomped away in his brown sandals and tan shorts. Over his shoulder he said, "Five minutes. Meet me at the spring."

"Five minutes," she echoed.

And she wandered down to the spring's edge to stare down into the human-sized aquarium filled with tubes and props. The sky gleamed in ribbons, and the sunlight on the waves threw stripes of white to cut up the blue surface.

Behind her, against the sky, there was a flash of some other color.

Dark and also blue—a navy blue that shined nearly black, or was it the other way around?

Tammy froze, squinting at the reflection. Just past her head, it was there—the pale silver face with cruel, small eyes as bitter as coffee beans. And above the eyes, that shock of hair—so dark, and blue, yes, blue. Blue in the reflection, with the sky behind it. How had it ever looked black?

She turned around fast, throwing up an arm—throwing up a defense against nothing at all. He wasn't there.

And then, with a quick cuff of his fist against her chest, just beneath her throat, she fell backward—towel and tiara and dry clothes and all.

THE MERMAID AQUARIUM

Back and down.

And as she fell her eyes met his, and they were the same ones from the Chevy, from the shiny black car that no one ought to drive in Florida, not in the dead of summer. The reflection and the man didn't match—they couldn't match.

But there he was, where the silver-faced man had loomed behind her. No, not a man. A fey thing, dark and terrible. Something that belonged in the dark, in the water of a swamp. Not in the sun, not in a spring.

As she fell, she thought—in that half second before she hit the water and closed her eyes from pure reflex—that there was distortion around him like a halo, like the way hot air rises from asphalt, or the way gasoline fumes twist outside a car's tank while the pump fills it up.

And in that split instant when she hit the water and her eyelids were dropping down hard, she saw Frank, too. Coming up behind Ed with a look on his face like murder.

Tammy slapped into the water backside first, and it stung when her shoulders smacked down. The weeks of training held her gasp in check, and when she broke the surface she took a deep breath, then sank. She let the water close over her before opening her eyes again.

It was strange and hard to watch from underneath, but there they were—Frank and Ed, tussling in a hard way, a jerky way, a rough way that made her glad she was in the water and not up there with *them*.

Her stomach tied itself tight into a knot, and she wasn't sure why. She shouldn't be worried for Frank. She should stay there, in the water, in the spring where she was safe and where she knew how to reach the air tubes. Frank was practically invincible. Navy veteran. Solid as a side of beef. Tough and quick.

But he was not *different*. Not unreal, not like Ed—if that was even his name.

(It probably wasn't. Silver-skinned things with black-blue hair don't have names like "Ed.")

Tammy pushed the towel with the tiara up under her armpit and kicked herself down and away from the surface. Let Frank throw the bum out. Of course he would. He *had* to. Because if he didn't...*then* what?

A pulse of water answered her, close to her legs. (Or was she wearing the tail? Was it right beside her fins? Suddenly, she wasn't sure.) A hand grabbed her foot and pulled her through the water. It tugged her like a fish on a line; it reeled her close with silver-spider hands.

She forgot. Ed *made* her forget.

She forgot all the training and the tubes, and she cried out a burp of surprise. And then there was no more air. Ed's hands—both hands, then—clamped around her foot. Her ankle. Her leg. Up around her knee, and reaching higher.

Give it back. His lips didn't move. He didn't speak, but she heard him anyway.

Tammy flailed, dropping the towel. It sank slow, unraveling from its balled-up twist in slow motion. Unraveling but not untying, not undoing completely. Not letting the treasured tiara fall free.

Tammy reached, elbows thrusting in every direction for the nearest hose. There were *always* hoses, hidden here and there. Always hoses for breathing, for refreshing, for shaking off the sparkles that crept up behind her eyes when it'd been too long since she'd had a breath; and the fizz was coming up now, and so were the silver-spider hands, curling like an octopus up her thigh.

Another splash, and something hit hard against her head.

(It was Frank. That part was an accident.)

When he joined them, he turned the water pink, a little bit, in a curly cloud there by his side. He took Ed by the hair, right by that billowing head that looked for all the world like a poisoned anemone. He yanked Ed hard, snapping his neck back, and up.

The octopus, silver-spider hand seized, and struck, and let go.

It went, sucked into a flurry of frothy spring water and violent rich foam, a curtain and a tower of bubbles.

And the static.

There was a dazzling flash, and there was Frank—turning the water all pink but not giving up. Frank, with his sun-brown arms and legs as strong as chains, the big ones that hold ships to docks—the big ones that hold anchors on ocean liners…and Frank was holding on, but the thing called Ed was spinning—trying to cast him off like the alligators people wrestled for tourists.

And Tammy was spinning too.

There wasn't any air, and there weren't any hoses. Did Frank pull them all up when the day was out and over? Did he put them all away? Of course, when no one needed them. Of course, when the mermaid aquarium was empty, in the auditorium with eighteen seats, lined up like soldiers in a row, lined up like lines on a page, in a story, in a fairy tale where something had gone terribly, terribly wrong. Of course there wasn't any air.

Tammy let go of the towel. It dropped away with its strange little prize, a glimmering cheap hairpiece with gems made of sea glass.

She didn't know how she knew about the sea glass, but she would've bet her life on it. Maybe she *was* betting her life on it. No, that couldn't be right.

She wasn't even sinking anymore—but rising, slow and unafraid. Her back breached the surface; she could feel the late day sun warm against the wet shirt there, and warm against her skin. She wasn't a real mermaid. This wasn't a real aquarium, but that tiara was real, and its sea glass gemstones were magic of a glorious kind. And Ed was real, and he was magic of a terrible kind. The two went together, somehow.

She felt…

She heard…

She saw…

Below her the crumpled towel stopped atop a rock. It teetered, toppled against another boulder, into a plant. Onto a compressor, and down again, another step or two to the spring bottom, where it came to rest in the soft, white silt. It came unfolded, unwound, and from beneath one waving corner of terry cloth, there sparkled something bright and cheap and priceless.

A deadly lure, glittering with enchanted glass. ✎

GOOD NIGHT PRISON KINGS

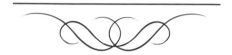

This is definitely one of the weirdest stories I've ever done, and hands-down the most personal, for all its strangeness. The initial idea came from a dream, if I'm honest—and I don't do "dream stories" very often, but this one really piqued my interest. I dreamed I was being interviewed for something that seemed like a job, and the guy on the other side of a big desk was holding a folder full of information about me. He asked a few questions about my job history, hobbies, and so forth, and at some point...I realized that this wasn't a job interview. He was reading my obituary and asking me to confirm or flesh out some of the details found therein.

Because this was a dream, I didn't find it especially upsetting. Or maybe it didn't bother me because it ended soon thereafter.

Either way, I filed it away with a mental note to "do something with this idea later."

My dream of an afterlife exit interview collided with a real-life drama that hit my family like a ton of bricks a few years ago: Two of my first cousins were outed as pedophiles who collected (and perhaps trafficked in) child pornography, and they went to prison. It's a long and sordid tale that took entirely too long to play out. There were five *terabytes* of child porn (that's not a typo), but no victims came forward to testify against my cousins.

Then there was a technicality, and the two men spent very little time in jail, at least initially. Due to broad incompetence on their part—and the grudge held by the cops of Highland County, Florida, they've been in and out of the clink on parole violations since then.

They're in prison at the moment, on some violation or another. I'm glad. I hope they stay there for a good long time.

As you can imagine, my family has spent the intervening years dissecting every interaction, sorting out who knew and who didn't, and struggling to assemble without the offending parties or their sympathizers ever since. (And they *do* have sympathizers—good Christian folks who think we should all just forgive them, and pretend it never happened. Yeah, no.)

It's a family fracture that will not heal anytime soon—if ever—because too many people kept too many secrets, and when the guys are home from jail, they're home in their own house, living with their mother...around the corner from my mother and grandmother.

I am furious at how often they are home with their mom.

I mean, I'm furious about a lot of things, but very high on the list is how badly the ball was dropped from a prosecutorial standpoint, and how the two offenders continue to simply *exist* in the world.

At any rate. My feelings on the subject of these two cousins are complex and entirely negative. Where better to work them out, than in a horror story about a city where the dead have autonomy, tools, and a second chance at justice?

GOOD NIGHT PRISON KINGS

HOLLY CROSSED and uncrossed her legs at the knee, like her grandma always said she ought to. She cleared her throat, fiddled with her bracelet, and watched the man across the desk as he scanned the paper-clipped contents of a manila folder. His salt-and-pepper eyebrows rose and fell as he read, but she couldn't tell if he was impressed or confused. Maybe he was interested, or maybe he was going through the motions.

"It says here, you were a real estate agent."

"That's true, but I let my license lapse in 2007." She laughed awkwardly, and tugged at the bangle on her arm. "The recession culled the field like crazy."

"I'm sure it did," he murmured noncommittally. Without looking up.

"After that, I went into business for myself. Internet consulting. Helping companies with their product content, that kind of thing. But I had to walk away when…when there was no one else to look after my grandmother."

Finally, he graced her with eye contact. "How many siblings do you have? How many cousins?"

"There are nine of us, all together. Me and my brother, and seven… or eight…" she stumbled over the count. Suddenly, and for no good reason, she wasn't sure. But no, she'd said it right the first time. "I have one brother, and seven cousins."

"But *you* were the one tasked with caring for her. And for your great-aunt, as well?"

"Everyone else was…they had families of their own, is all. Or else they weren't up to it, for whatever reason. I'm the oldest, anyway. It was fine. I left my business, and went to work at the courthouse. It gave me more stability. Good health insurance. Steady hours. And I'm not totally alone; my brother helps out, when I'm at work."

"You support him, too?"

"He mostly earns his keep, looking after the ladies." Another vaguely inappropriate chuckle escaped before she could stop it. "That's what we call Grandma and her sister, my great-aunt Jean: 'the ladies.' Like they wear hats, or take tea, you know. But they don't…they don't do either of those things."

The man closed the folder and put it down, then folded his hands on top of it. "Your grandparents raised you. All nine of you."

"Not exactly, but kind of. It was complicated, and crowded. But it wasn't bad, not usually. Grandpa was a preacher. He traveled, sometimes. My mom and my aunts took turns on childcare duty, rotating in and out of school, in and out of the house." She wasn't sure why she was telling him this. "But Grandpa died, a handful of years ago. Not long after that, we realized Grandma was slipping."

"You were already here, in the city."

Holly nodded. "It made sense for me to take care of them. But this isn't about that, is it?"

He shrugged. "It's hard to say. Is your brother equipped to take over? Now that you're gone?"

She faltered. "I…I had a brother." She stared down at the closed folder on the desk, like it might tell her something, if she could open it.

"No, no. Stay with me, dear. You have a brother."

"We were the preacher's kids." She stared at the folder. "Preacher's grandkids, whatever. Everyone always says preachers' kids are the worst… nine little troublemaking PKs. But we weren't that bad. Not really. Not most of us." Holly drew up short. "Except for…except for those two." Even here, she didn't want to say their names. No, she couldn't say them.

Gently, he drew her attention around again. "But lately, you've been working at the courthouse, filing records, and the like."

She swallowed. It did nothing to soothe her raw, dry throat. Her head hurt. She stopped playing with her jewelry and wrapped her arms around herself. "That's right." What were their names? Those two stray cousins. She picked at the empty place in her memory, but found only coldness there. A barb, hard as an icicle.

She couldn't take her eyes off the folder. "May I?" She gestured toward it.

"Of course. It's yours, after all."

She collected it. Opened it. Scanned the laundry list of facts. It was a résumé in a single, large paragraph. No, that's not what it was, at all. "This is an obituary."

"Yes, dear." He was kindly, but cool. Perfectly professional. Whatever his job was, he'd been doing it for a very long time.

She whispered, "What is this?"

He leaned forward, removed his glasses, and rubbed them fingerprint-free on the hem of his sweater. He put them back on. "This is an opportunity."

"Am I still in the city?" she asked. She wasn't confused. She wasn't even surprised.

"You're still in *a* city."

"What does that mean?"

"This is where everyone comes, when there's unfinished business."

She frowned. "Doesn't everyone have unfinished business? By the time they have one of these?" She held up the folder, the obituary.

"No. Not like yours."

"What's different about mine?"

"Yours is broken. This is where you come to fix it."

Her throat closed tight. She opened the folder again and read the last line, the one that said she'd fallen, and hit her head. It said that she'd frozen to death in the snow. "I am angry," she admitted. The words barely squeaked free. "Can you help?"

Again he was so kind, so calm. He sat back in his chair. "I can tell you this much: you should do what you've always done. Go where you've always gone. Find your way back to the end, and decide what you wish to do about it—but do it quickly. Your time here is limited."

Holly did not understand. "Okay," she said. "Okay." She took the folder under her arm, pulled her coat around her shoulders, and left the office. Outside on the street, she stood on the sidewalk and said, "Okay," again, in case it would make any difference, to herself or anyone else. "Okay," she exhaled the word with its own white puff of chilly air.

She remembered the way home, more or less. The ladies were at home, one comfortably baffled, one grumpy and none too mobile. Holly didn't have her own room, but she had her own couch and it was an easier sleep than any dorm room bed or futon she'd ever had.

She could go home. She had to start somewhere.

The city was made of twilight and ashes, with midnight-sharp shadows lining up like soldiers between the buildings. They stood sentinel in the alleys, inscrutable and faceless. The skyscrapers buffered the places in between, and when Holly looked up, she couldn't see their tops. All of them disappeared into that gray-dark cloudland overhead, their details all lost, or scrubbed clean.

She usually took a bus home from work. The thought blipped through her head like a reflex—not a memory, but a force of habit.

A bus appeared. It must be the right one; it was the only one, and it was unmarked. Even the sides were free of advertisements, and graffiti. Maybe it wasn't the right bus. She got on board anyway, walking past the driver and reaching out to pay her fare before remembering that she didn't have any money.

The driver ignored her. Or else he couldn't see her? Holly didn't know how being dead worked, except that now she was in a city that was both familiar and unfamiliar, remembering and forgetting things that should've been certain.

The bus was empty, except for a man in a suit. The man was soaking wet, staring straight ahead with a briefcase on his lap. Holly thought he must've been dead too. She walked past him, and he made no move, no deliberate sound. Only the soft drip, drip, drip of water sliding from his clothes and onto the floor.

GOOD NIGHT PRISON KINGS

She sat down in the back. The bus lurched forward, and rolled silently through the haze that blurred everything on the other side of the windows. She opened the folder, and read her obituary over and over again, milking every word for any ounce of extra meaning.

The prose style was formal and refined, so her brother probably didn't write it. Maybe her mother did. Maybe someone just shoved all these details into the lap of some poor editor at the newspaper, and said, "Here, make some sense out of this. She was alive for thirty-eight years, and now she isn't. These are some of the things that happened in the meantime."

The obituary didn't tell her anything she didn't already know, but it reminded her of a few things she no longer remembered. Her father was dead, but he'd been dead for years. Would she run into him, here in the city? The man at the office said her time here was limited. Was everyone's?

Grandpa was dead, too. And who else? The obituary didn't say. No one else of importance, then, if it didn't make the papers.

The bus stopped, and it stayed stopped until she stood up and left. She hadn't pulled the cord, but this was the right place. Everyone was waiting for her, or at least the driver and the wet man up front. They were waiting for her. Waiting for something.

She took the handrail and the three steep steps down to the sidewalk. The door closed behind her with a hydraulic whoosh…the only noise she'd heard from the bus at all…and she was alone outside the walkup she'd called home for the last three years. "Or however long," she muttered, pushing the door open like there wasn't a callbox, and who needed a key, anyway? She pushed. It opened.

The interior hall was just as it always had been—floor to ceiling with period details that could be called charming, if they weren't so dirty. Micro-tile designs, mostly intact on the floors. High ceilings and dusty fixtures that halfway worked. Doors pointed in arches that deco had borrowed and streamlined from gothic.

If there were voices behind those doors…living, breathing people who talked and fought and laughed…Holly couldn't hear them. Everything was far away, on the other side of that miasma outside—the one that wasn't made up of smoke, smog, or mist.

The stairs were the same. Watch the handrail for splinters. The apartment door was the same, only now there weren't any numbers on it. It was the right one, though. She knew it when she turned the knob and let herself inside.

Eau de old lady.

Funeral flowers in perfume bottles, the contents gone yellow and pungent. Lilies and gardenias, and the sharp sourness of crushed pills, the eucalyptus lies of ointment. Old books and newspapers. Tea left steeping too long. Decaf coffee from a packet.

Grandma was sitting on the couch, the one she always called a davenport. "It's a shame to see you, dear."

Holly mustered a smile, and raised it half-mast. "What a weird thing to say to your granddaughter."

"They told me you died in the snow. An accident."

"Mary, who are you talking to?" Aunt Jean was there, too. When Holly squinted, she could see the younger, fatter woman perched in the La-Z-Boy, clutching the TV remote. She was shouting. She always shouted, because Grandma's hearing had gone to shit long before her mind did, and she never liked wearing her hearing aids.

"I'm talking to Holly."

"Whatever makes you happy, then."

"Grandma…" She blinked, in case her eyes were wet. They should've been. She should've been crying, but somehow she wasn't. Did anybody cry here? Was that a thing that ghosts could do? "It wasn't an accident."

"I know."

"Do you know what happened?"

GOOD NIGHT PRISON KINGS

"I have my guesses. They think I don't know, see. They think I haven't heard, about those boys and what they did. Seven pretty kittens…and two prison kings."

"Pretty kittens or piglet kissers. That's what you called us."

She nodded solemnly, and said the same thing she'd said a thousand times, when the cousins were small. "Letters can mean anything. They don't have to hurt."

"I love you, Grandma. I should've said it more."

"You said it every night."

Holly stopped smiling. She didn't feel like it, anymore. "Still."

Aunt Jean butted in, like always. "Mary, I'm gonna ask you one more time…"

"Settle down. She's leaving."

Yes, she was. Backing away, because there wasn't anything here that could help her. Grandma knew about the boys, about the terrible cousins whose names she dare not think aloud, lest they appear. They lived with their mother, in part of the city where no one wanted to go, because it wasn't nice anymore. It was one of those last addresses people ever have, before they give up and live out of their cars.

(The boys couldn't live just anywhere, not anymore. The law got that much right.)

You could get there by car, or you could get there by a combination of bus and walking. You wouldn't want to go there, but if you had to, that's how you'd do it.

Holly had a car. She didn't know where it was, but it was usually parked under the building, in the garage. She took the service elevator down, and yes, it was in her spot. She couldn't read the license plate and she couldn't find her keys, but the door opened when she pulled the handle. She climbed inside, and put the manila folder on the passenger seat.

The engine turned over, and she pressed the button on the visor clippie that would open the garage's wide, rolling door to let her outside.

On the way to Aunt Patty's place she thought about the proper kernels and perfect kites, because those were nicer things that started with PK. Not *preacher's kids*, spoken with a sneer. Not the built-in curiosity about what bad thing they'd do next, or what embarrassment they would be, for whichever church where Grandpa worked.

Seven pretty kittens out of nine.

So Grandma knew about the other two, despite everyone's best efforts to keep her in the dark. It should've been easy to keep her in the dark. She was more than half deaf, and teetering on the edge of Alzheimer's.

But somehow she must've seen, or picked up the truth from things spoken too loud, too close. She might've caught some bit about making bail, or raising money for better lawyers. It was even possible that late at night, on her tiny grandma feet, she tiptoed throughout the house, opening drawers and turning on laptops. She liked the Internet. She liked seeing pictures of the great-grandkids. She wouldn't like finding the links that no one wanted her to see, or the frantic emails between the seven pretty kittens who did their best to protect her.

What could you do, against cunning like hers?

What would Grandpa have done? That's what everyone wanted to know, when word first got out about the brothers. *Thank God Grandpa is gone, or this would've taken him.* That's what everyone said. *Thank God he isn't here to see this.*

It was hard to say what he might've done. Some of the PKs remembered his guns. Would he have marched right over there, and shot them both dead? Would he have fallen right over, succumbing to heart attack number four? Unless Holly could find him, there in the city, no one was ever likely to know. So instead she said the same prayer the other six said—thank God, yes. *Thank God that the third attack took him.*

The more she thought about it, the angrier it made her. She shouldn't thank God or anybody else for taking him sooner, rather than later. That shouldn't be the silver lining. Grandma being out of it, as far as anybody else knew—that wasn't a silver lining, either. Even if she didn't know whatever it was she knew.

Fuck those boys, and their terrible habits. Fuck them both, and fuck their mother too—for all the excuses she made, and all the crocodile tears she cried. Fuck her for stealing what was left of the money.

Something whispered to her, *No.*

She almost panicked, almost hit the brakes.

No. Not that, either.

Holly kept driving. "Grandpa?" she asked. She hoped so. She reached for the hope that it might be him, then swallowed it all down. Ghosts don't haunt the dead, she was pretty sure of that much. But she talked to him anyway, as she paused at stoplights, and checked the street signs, even though she couldn't read them through the fog.

"Last time I saw you, we were sitting on the couch watching football. It was Sunday, and your team was winning." She stopped for a school bus. Traffic on all sides froze, and unfroze when the stop sign retracted, and the bus moved on. "Then you looked at the front door, and I watched you watch something…your eyes tracked from the door to the dining room, and into the kitchen. Then you watched…whatever you were watching…as it headed back out the door. So I asked you, what were you looking at? And you didn't answer. You looked at me with your eyes as big as I'd ever seen them, and you asked me who that man was—the one in the black hat. You said he was carrying a Bible."

She was almost there. Aunt Patty's place was up on the right, a basement flat with bars on the small windows that stuck up far enough to catch a few drops of light for a few hours every afternoon.

"I wonder if it was the same man as the one I talked to in the office. He didn't have a Bible, though. Or a hat."

Holly got out of the car and left it running at the curb. (If it had ever been running at all.) She shouldn't have found a parking space so quickly, but things were different in this version of this city. She understood that now. Or she understood it better than she had at first.

There was a light on, burning in one of the windows where the boys shared a bedroom. The light flickered. A television? It shouldn't be a computer. They weren't supposed to have computers anymore; it was part of the plea deal.

Rage welled up, harder and hotter than any tears she'd ever cried. The anger burned so white she could hardly breathe, until she remembered that she didn't *need* to breathe. That made it easier, to keep walking without running or screaming—to open the door like she lived there, and let herself inside past Aunt Patty, who was fat like Aunt Jean, and she would've been just as bitter if she hadn't been so goddamn self-righteous. Aunt Patty wasn't supposed to have a computer, either. Not while the boys were under her roof. She was sitting at the dining room table and checking the Internet on a smartphone, reading some conspiracy website. It assured her that she was persecuted, and that she was afraid of all the right things, all the right people.

Holly swept down on her, and struck her aunt's hand as hard as she could. The blow was fast, and it came unseen. It came hard. It threw the phone across the room, where it lodged in the wall's chipping plaster like a butter knife in a loaf of bread.

Aunt Patty didn't speak. She didn't move. She stared at the phone, and she breathed as fast as a rabbit.

"I'm dead," Holly told her. "I'm dead, and I hate you." She didn't know if Aunt Patty heard her, but she wanted to be heard, so she shouted it: "I'm dead, and I hate you!"

Aunt Patty flinched. Her face went tight with goosebumps.

Holly leaned in closer, until her mouth was near enough to bite her aunt's ear. "Everything is your fault, too." She backed away, went to the kitchen—it was on the other side of the dingy, cluttered room. She opened a cabinet, found some glasses, and began throwing them. They shattered on the floor, and against Aunt Patty's chair.

GOOD NIGHT PRISON KINGS

Patty still didn't move. Holly didn't care if she did. She didn't care if she couldn't. She kicked the back of the woman's chair with all the force she could rally; she dug her foot in, like she could shove it all the way up Aunt Patty's miserable ass. The chair rattled and toppled, taking her aunt with it.

She didn't watch it fall. "I'm not here for you. Maybe I should be, but."

Down the short hall with only three doors—a bathroom, two bedrooms—Holly stormed, gathering up the city's weird, smoke-like fog along with her. It poured through the cracks in the foundation, the missing insulation between the windows and their casings...she called it all inside, and pulled it into her hands. She squeezed it, crushed it, and pushed it forward to blast open the bedroom door that belonged to the two PKs whose names she couldn't remember. Only their faces. Only their crimes. Only the fallout.

They were in there, because where else would they be? *If they'd ever had anything better to do, then none of this would've ever happened, now would it?* The other voice, the one she talked to, in case it was her grandfather—it was too soft, too far in the back of her head. Did it want her to stop? Or was it just along for the ride?

The two prison kings blinked at her, two pale and eyeless cave fish confronted with the dawn. They saw something, but it might not have been Holly. She hoped it was something more fitting, something like a naked child with fear in its eyes and blood dripping down its legs. She hoped it was a little boy with his hair yanked bank and his mouth hanging open while the camera flash went *snap snap snap*.

The brothers were separated by enough years that they should've been more different in appearance. There should've been more to distinguish them than their height, but there wasn't. They both looked like their father, long out of the picture, not that it would've mattered.

No. Not quite.

The taller of the two had jumped a crooked retreat, and he stood with his back to the window, flat against it. Everyone had always said how much he looked like Grandpa. Everyone had always said it, because it was always true. A spitting image, though she'd never seen it before. He wasn't a spitting image of the grandfather who'd been old for as long as Holly had ever known him, but a carbon copy of the younger man— thick from years of manual labor before he'd taken to the seminary. A bespectacled man, bald before thirty. The taller brother was the younger of the two, and he was twenty-seven. What was left of his hair was yellow and vanishing.

Holly balked.

She waited for the quiet voice to tell her what to do, but it didn't.

There was nowhere for any of her surprise or pain to go, so she used it to fuel the anger that burned her up, feeding it into that furnace. "You did this!" she screamed at them, not knowing if they could hear her. She screamed it again, at the screen they shared between them. They had a computer, yes. Their parole officer must've missed it, but they were only playing some first-person shooter with Nazis in it. This time. Last time it'd been worse, and the investigation had gone on for two years. That's how long it'd taken to go all the way down that rabbit hole of karmic sludge and anguish.

She'd never been clear on the particulars. There were plea deals, and problems with the evidence, and outright incompetence with the forensic IT department. But here the prison kings were, having dodged any real time behind bars. They got away with it—like they'd gotten away with everything, relatively consequence free, for their entire goddamn lives.

But Jesus, she'd forgotten how much the tall one looked like Grandpa in the old pictures. The ones where he was grinning in black and white, smiling under the weight of feed sacks, tied up in bundles.

She hated the tall one for his face.

She reached for the beds and upended them, one and then the other. She threw them across the room and broke the iron rods off the frames while the boys yelled and hollered, begging for help that wasn't going to come from anyone except their mother, and she was useless. The only power she'd ever had was raising sociopaths. She couldn't bring them up, and save them, too.

The computer screen was flat and cold and it shattered when she touched it—so she picked up the pieces and threw them like she'd thrown the phone, like knives at a target. Most of the shards landed in the mattresses, and the curtains. Some of them hit the floor.

The boys pulled up their twin-sized mattresses and hid behind them. They were building a stupid kid's fort, like they were stupid kids, so Holly broke something else: a mason jar that one of them was using for a water glass. She crushed it, and used the largest piece to assault the fabric fortress. She cut through the sheets, through all the cheap material until it bled stuffing and springs, and she pulled those out, too.

"Did you do it together?" she demanded. "We all wondered if you sat around and jacked in tandem, you fucking creeps!" She'd hacked most of the way through one mattress. The shorter, older prison king kicked it aside and joined his brother behind the cover that remained.

Holly grabbed the other mattress. She wedged her fingers like spikes into the sides, and she pried it away. They were rats, cowering in a corner. The short one covered his eyes, burying his head against his brother. The taller one, the one who looked so much like a dead man, wasn't looking right at her. He was looking over her shoulder—but when she looked, she saw nothing, not even their mother, who must've heard the commotion by now.

She swung the chunk of glass like a sword, and slashed until she hit an artery. The short one's neck blossomed as red as funeral roses, as wet as the gutter snow. It was a marvel of color in this city, where everything churned in grayscale. He slumped, and she loomed triumphantly.

One down. Halfway there.

But. She buried the gore-sticky weapon in the wall. "It shouldn't have been you!" She roared it in the tall one's face. She retrieved the shard and swiped it at his cheek, leaving a thin line of red across his skin. The line was a slim, razor-fine italic. Then it was bold. "Your brother was always a lost cause, but we thought you were better. We thought you would *be* better!"

She wished she could cry, but that didn't happen in the city—so she swung the glass instead, again and again striking the wall and not the cousin because he was wearing Grandpa's face. Or he wasn't, and she knew that, but.

Her cousin sobbed and swore in equal measure. Someone could cry here, after all. She smashed her hand through the bureau mirror, and took a bigger piece of glass, one the size of a plate. It should've cut her hand to hold it. But nothing cut her here. She couldn't bleed and she couldn't cry, and she'd have to come to peace with it.

She held this new, foiled dagger to the tall boy's neck, and let it dig. (It was okay. It wasn't Grandpa's neck.) She let it split the skin in a tender spot that was better suited to a kiss, if you were the kind of mother who did that sort of thing. She let the bead of blood form, and well, and swell, and drip while she wailed the tears she couldn't cry. His frail remaining hairs billowed, and his eyes went dry and pink but he couldn't close them. Could he see her? No, he was still looking behind her. There still was nothing there.

"Accident…" he gasped.

She didn't know if it was a reply, or merely an expression of confusion. "All this time, you should've been in jail. Your mother shouldn't have been stealing Grandpa's life insurance, like there was anything else keeping the lights on except for me, and that shit job at the courthouse."

"Lawyer…" He was digging his own grave, and too stupid to stop.

She remembered it now—pieces of the disbelief, the *murderous* fury she'd felt when Aunt Jean had shown her the statements, where the lump-sum pittance was bleeding away, signed over check by check from Grandma to Aunt Patty. In Aunt Patty's handwriting.

GOOD NIGHT PRISON KINGS

"You came to me, at the courthouse. You wanted me to throw it away, to look away. To make it go away."

"Accident," he said again, but that didn't make it true.

She didn't care. She realized it as her hands were going slick, because another half an inch, and he'd be right there with her in the city, where no one can see the sky, but no one gets in your way.

Out to her car, he'd followed her that night—trying to stop her. Trying to keep her from filing the complaint that would send his mother to jail. The sky had been so white, and so had the snow on the ground; but on the piles of garbage, it'd all gone brown around the edges. You don't accidentally push someone. You don't accidentally take the paperwork and run while the snow goes red and the sky drops lower and lower by the minute.

But he wasn't looking at her, he was looking behind her. She couldn't hear the voice that was talking so softly, so firmly, so hopelessly in the distance. She could only see this terrible thing that wore someone else's skin, and she pressed the broken glass under that face, against that neck. She could peel that face right off. He didn't deserve to wear it.

Nobody knew what Grandpa would've done.

She fell back. She stood in the wreckage of the room, all broken glass, clotting blood, and tooth-stain yellow foam. The light overhead sputtered, but kept the room a gruesome shade of wet fluorescent lime. All the shadows were too damn hard. She couldn't see anything except the resemblance, and that wasn't fair at all. The city was supposed to be fair. Wasn't that how it worked?

Wasn't that how it worked.

"I still have time," she told him, as he bled and cringed. She held out her hand, and called the fog to bring her something useful. It brought her the envelope with the complaint, signed by herself and Aunt Jean in their own goddamn handwriting. Either Aunt Patty hadn't destroyed it, or the city had seen fit to return it. She clasped it so hard that her knuckles would've turned white, if.

In the other room, her aunt moaned.

To hell with her.

"Good night, preacher's kids. Good night, prison kings." Holly turned her back.

She hated the city, for all its second chances—because she could only scream and she could not cry as she left them behind: one dead, and one who would probably live. She should've reversed the two, if you'd asked anyone. Take the killer, and punish the other to even the score. But the killer wore a dead man's face, a prison king with the preacher's profile.

She left them there, and she left the shitty old building standing in one piece.

She deserved to cry. Both brothers deserved to bleed out slow, all the way, remembering why everything had come to this. Everyone deserved to mourn, on their way out of town.

Didn't they? 🐟

MOTHER JONES AND THE NASTY ECLIPSE

At the risk of talking politics, I don't think it'll surprise anyone who's ever followed me online to know that I found the 2016 election to be the greatest American tragedy of the century—even though the century had barely started. My feelings about Hillary Clinton were (and are) complicated, but my feelings about Trump were not. He's been every bit as bad as I feared, and then some. With rabbit-turd sprinkles on top.

The day after the election, I had a hangover to beat the band. I got into fights with folks who voted independent, and lost a few friends. I lashed out because it felt like there was little else to be done.

Then I got my shit together, sold my house in a red state, moved back to a blue state, volunteered on progressive political campaigns, and started learning about how to help move the needle in the right direction.

But in time, my complicated feelings about Hillary shifted. I voted for her, and would do so again in an instant, given the option; but I hadn't been 100% happy about it. She had an awful lot of baggage but I mean, whomst among us, right? You don't have to be her biggest fan to see that she was treated and judged and discussed differently because she was a woman.

She won the election, and she didn't take the prize regardless. How many women have felt that unfairness, that terrible cheating? Not on that kind of massive national scale, perhaps, but in smaller, commensurately gross ways over the course of our lives and careers?

More than a few of us. Probably most of us.

I started to wonder about her. How she was doing. How she was coping. How angry she must be, and how hurt and disappointed. In time, I started to feel like the insult she suffered was an insult to womankind at large. After all, we all know it wasn't *just* about her.

Maybe it sounds silly, but I wished that I could say something to her. I wished I could give her some note of sympathy, some weird little sign that *I saw her*, and I knew what she'd been robbed of, and I felt the insult, too. But who the hell am I to attempt such a thing? I have no personal trauma or fury to draw from, nothing that could even *almost* approach what she went through.

Jesus, who does?

Then a name came to mind. And a story. And I realized that there was someone indeed who suffered slings and arrows on the national stage, and stood proud and defiant and angry all the same. So what if she's been dead for almost a century?

I tell ghost stories for a living, don't I?

And on that note, I give you the ghost of Mother Jones giving Hillary Clinton a pep talk, of sorts—in a story that's garnered more hate mail and fan mail than any other short story I've ever written. Love it or hate it, here it is.

MOTHER JONES AND THE NASTY ECLIPSE

NOT EVERYTHING that's missing was taken, but once it's gone, it's gone, ain't it? There's nothing to be done about it now. What isn't dead is burned to the ground. What isn't mourned is barely remembered.

Forward, then. Since you think you know defeat.

Nothing was easy for me, either, you know. In the beginning, I failed more often than I helped, and I was regularly wrong. I thought there were lines we'd all agreed not to cross. I thought there were rules and maybe there were, but they only applied to us. You learned that one the hard way, didn't you? Well.

Bless. Your. Heart.

I meant to ask you, before I lose the thread: Did you see the eclipse?

There's always an eclipse.

There's always a moment when it goes all dark, and the wind twists coldly through the trees, and you think maybe the sun will never come back again—even though you damn well know better. Now, let me tell you: I've seen that eclipse and others, too. They're all alike. Just two hours in the same day, with a shadow in the middle. That's all.

You and I, we both know from shadows, don't we? We've gone cold sitting inside them, and we've cast them as big as the moon. We have pulled the tides with our will, all while suffering the slings and arrows of outrageous fortune.

I'll tell you what I know of outrageous fortune: He's a son of a bitch.

I knew those sons of bitches might starve us, they might cheat us, they might maim us. All these things we expected in those early years. We were naïve, I suppose, for thinking they might not murder us outright. Why wouldn't they? Who was there to stop them?

Tell me nothing of the hand that rocks the cradle and spare me your stories about a helpful village. Sing instead of the gnarled and brittle fingers of tight old men in loose skin, and clothes that cost more than my coffin. Remember how they put their repeating guns on train tracks and drove them back and forth, firing at the tents where women and children waited for men to come home from the strike line.

Remember. We bled for asking nicely.

Remember. They opened fire because we told them we were human.

Remember. Everything burns eventually.

A family. A home. A war. Chicago went up in flames, bright as a witch.

How many times can you lose everything and still come back? How do you keep moving, when nothing's left except for what's inside? I don't have a real good answer, I'm afraid. All I can tell you is that I stood up again, no more finished than you ever have been. I shook the ashes out of my hair and I straightened my skirts.

They called me a foreigner. They told me to stay home and knit.

They said to close my mouth, but if I did? No one would speak for the girls with the ruined bones, the nubs of fingers, the broken feet. They told me to sit in silence while men were beaten to dust in the mines, while the fluttering bright canaries died likes flies, and the diggers' lungs filled up with dust that turned to tar that turned to fistfuls of mud in their graves.

I stood loud against bastards and cowards, because I liked to tell the truth, but a woman shouldn't say such things. I shouted them from the highest peaks.

MOTHER JONES AND THE NASTY ECLIPSE

It's funny, and maybe you know how it goes, but no one heard me until I came back to earth. I came around the mountain driving the greatest white horses you ever did see, that's how they tell it. (And when they tell these stories about you, don't you correct them. Not if they're any good.) Let them write their songs. Let them sing stories of how I came down from on high.

They will say that I spoke with God.

Mostly, I spoke with men. I know you know how that feels, always the lone lady in a room of antsy fellows who halfway want your help, and halfway want your hand. Those halves of a man will duel until the end of time, I think, but that's no reason to take it sitting down. It's also no reason to leave them hanging. All God's children got problems.

Often, I spoke with children. Sometimes, I spoke with women like you, or like the woman you would have been—an angry lady with an ostrich hat and a sign. I didn't walk with women like that. Maybe I should have. Maybe I would have, if I'd seen you up on the stage—small and fierce, and harder than diamonds. Swimming in balloons that dropped from the ceiling, tagging them with the joy of a kitten and blinking in the lights.

But you weren't there, and you and I? We're not the same.

I chose my own battles. Maybe I'd choose different ones now, on this side of the eclipse.

I never did stop fighting the fights I'd picked. Nobody ever let me.

I fought the world over and over, losing ground and gaining ground. Every time the news was sick to death of me I came back anyways, and I pointed my finger at the widows and orphans, at the men without legs, the boys without eyes, the girls with nothing but scars.

I took my rage to the ink-slingers because I swear to God, I thought if everybody knew, then someone somewhere would have to do something. But the goddamn editors told me no, because the papers were owned by the local lords. Same as everything else.

I went to those lords and they shut their gates in my face. I went to the governors, to the senators, to the mayors and ministers. None of these fine, upstanding men were too inclined to hear me.

I went all the way to the president. He never replied. I wasn't worth it to him. I didn't have enough money, I guess.

I learned that money is heavy, and it don't move easy. The owners of the mills drew lines, and they bought armies to push across their maps like toys. The coal barons rattled their sabers on the barricades they'd built to thwart the anarchists, the strikers, and little old ladies like me.

But I was not afraid. I was just pissed.

I stood at a podium and I raised my fist like a guillotine's blade. I did not stay home and bake cookies. I went out and made war.

One time, a man named for a storm said I was the most dangerous woman in America. I bet he thought he'd cursed me. (He was just about that stupid.) He called me that, and he *made* me that. For here's the secret, dear: a curse is every bit as good as a blessing. A curse can be claimed, and held, and shaped. It can be thrown like a bomb.

I saw what they did to you.

I saw them dismiss you, a naughty school child in a white pantsuit. I saw you come back again, swinging. You stood on the steps of Planned Parenthood and you talked like you had every right to, you nasty thing.

You were proud before the small girls in their sashes. You were strong alongside the mothers who'd lost their sons to the grinding mill of war. You were bookish, you were prepared, you were steadfast while the monsters crept behind you, casting creepy shadows and shitty spells. You were certain in the face of conspiracy and crimson caps.

You woman.

You wore it like a badge of honor.

You know what a badge is, don't you? It's a tiny shield. That's why they're shaped like that, and why they sit on a man's chest, over his heart. You can shrink a symbol until it's so small that it fits in a pocket, but it never loses its power.

That's magic, right there. Same kind of magic as a curse.

We do have magic, dear. Some of it, they gave us by accident. Some of it, we made ourselves. You really took the wand and ran with it, didn't you? You forged yourself, tempered yourself into something much harder than you should've had to be. You were already enough. You were more than enough—more ready than any human in history and that's a fucking fact.

They'll take the facts away from you, if you let them.

They'll replace your facts with their own, if you don't.

They flooded the whole world, just for you. Facts upon facts, invented from thin air, spun light as cotton candy at a county fair. Which weighs more, a ton of cotton or a ton of bricks? You already know the answer, and you know which is worse, too. To be smothered so slow, to feel the weight of lies and rumors and even some of the terrible gritty truths on your chest and know how heavy history is. Any single thing you've ever done in your whole life, weighed without context against the possibility that you might be worthy of grace or power.

They forgave you nothing. They held up signs accusing you of having lived, and never gave you credit for having learned.

The man who came before you, he knew all about that brand of baggage. I watched the two of you clash, neither one wrong and neither one exactly right, standing on top of a heap the whole world said was never yours to climb. There was no blueprint for what followed in his wake, though it shouldn't have surprised anyone.

You followed in his wake, but you didn't come alone.

You marched under his banner, and all of his enemies joined all of your enemies. In his wake came ghosts. Ghosts wearing sheets, ghosts wearing nooses. At the gate you met angry men with grasping hands, clasping claws. Tiki torches burning bright for the monsters and witches alike.

They called me a witch, too. A witch, a bitch, and worse than that— and I loved it. They called me a woman, and I called myself the mother of thousands. They called me old, and I told them I was more ancient and powerful than they even knew.

Too ancient to be found. Too powerful to hide. Too much a witch to lie down and die. For Christ's sake, it's only an eclipse.

The most dangerous witch in America: Now that's a mantle worth carrying.

I hear that when it was over, you took to the woods. How fitting, that you went to the trees, walking old paths in sensible shoes beside a man who did you harm and help in equal measure, I should think.

(I envied you, with the smiling old warlock at your side.)

But you went to the woods, and they chased you. The all-seeing cameras, the tragic columns, the bleeding hearts, the gropable tits, the spinning wheelchairs, and the baffled binders…they traded whispers,

MOTHER JONES AND THE NASTY ECLIPSE

collected rumors like baseball cards. They combed the hills, seeking salvation, still believing in awful possibility of hope.

Hope is not a plan, or that's how I heard it after The Storm.

Let's say this instead: Hope *is* a storm. I like that better.

Hope is the opposite of a curse, in its way both good and bad.

Its goals are goals of the heart, and the heart is never full. It's the most human thing of all, this endless need, the bottomless hole that can never be filled and can only be negotiated with. All you can do is make your promises and do your level best to keep them when you can. Admit it when you can't. Make new promises and make new plans. Revise the old ones and see if they're enough to buy you time. Feed the heart, for it is always hungry.

But.

Hope is the most important thing, too. It is every brick in every wall, every bit of essential structural garbage in every barricade, where every revolutionary eventually stands. Don't let anyone tell you different. Not even me, and I halfway want to.

You must have seen the eclipse. You must have watched the sun go down in the middle of the day, and creep back one white sliver at a time. You must have felt the hairs on your arm lift up like stars when the sky went purple, then black. You must have caught your breath in your throat when the stars came out, just for you. You must have let slip a tiny prayer in those precious seconds when the moon crossed the sun, and conquered it, and the whole country fell under its quiet spell. It must have felt familiar.

It might have felt too close. I'm sorry about that. That's not your fault.

But women have looked to the moon since time began, and you're no different. I'm no different, for all that I wanted to be.

Did you go into the woods to watch the sun defeated, even for those few moments? Did you look through smoked glass, and watch the light narrow through the branches overhead?

Or were there clouds? Were you thwarted even there?

If I'd known you were wandering the woods, walking brisk or slow with the warlock and counting birds or kicking leaves, I would've kept you company. If I'd known about the eclipse any sooner, I might've sought you out—but things are different here.

It's just as well. I don't think we would've been friends. Neither one of us has often been accused of being very nice. That ain't fair, but so what? Nothing else is fair, and that's not news to either one of us.

But you've still got time. You've got time, and all I've got is a myth.

No, that's not true. I've got a legacy, and so do you. Give it time, and you'll even get your myth.

Maybe this will make you feel better, and maybe it won't, but I'm no good at comfort so here you go: History forgets, and history remembers. It treats me kinder than my own days ever did, and it'll be the same for you. You just watch.

I hope you live to see it. I hope you come back to look.

I lived for so long, we all forgot how old I really was.

I threw myself a birthday party and called myself a hundred, and nobody stopped me. Who wants to argue with a witch so old, when she's lived so long and collected so much magic? I'd do worse than turn them into frogs, and they know it. I'd turn them into men who would suffer the results of their own cruelty and selfishness.

There are people in this world who understand nothing unless it touches them, do you understand what I mean? If it doesn't happen to them, it's just not real. Unto them, you have to wish hardship. You have to wish pain, sickness, and loss. If you don't, they get mean and greedy. They need to be held in check, and I did what I could to lay you some foundations.

Now it's your turn, and I give you my blessing.

May you live so long, you forget your birthday and no one dares to argue when you call yourself a crone. May you watch your daughter raise her children, and hear her teach them of what you did, and what you won, and what was stolen from you. May you rise. May you be the mother of multitudes, as I was; may you follow in my wake. May you find that history is sometimes swift, and that it honors you. May your enemies wither in their sorrow until they become everything they fear, and lose everything they've ever taken by trick or force.

To hell with 'em.

Let 'em think we're immortal, and when we finally do die, we'll prove them all right. 🪶

TALKING IN CIRCLES

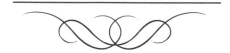

"Talking in Circles" is a new novelette, composed specifically for this collection, though it'd been sitting in notebook fragments here and there for some time. I was never quite able to pull it together until recently—until I figured out the central question and realized that it needed to be told in small "chapters," even though this story isn't terribly long (in the grand scheme of things).

It was originally inspired by a couple of different things, or perhaps informed by them? It's hard to say. The first is the short story "Onions" by Caitlín Kiernan, which I initially read so long ago that I remembered only a few specifics—primarily, the idea of a group of people sitting around therapy-style, sharing their paranormal experiences. It stuck with me.

You see, an old professor of mine used to say that the first sign of the Sacred is a circle around a stone. Drawing a circle around something gives it emphasis and meaning; it creates a boundary between here and there—between what's inside, and what's not.

And whoever draws that circle has power over what comes and goes from it. Whoever draws it, defines its purpose.

So my question was...can *any* closed circle be a sacred space?

I mean, support groups are supposed to be, even among atheists. The rules are different when you're in the circle, whether you're religious or not. There is liturgy, there are calls and responses, and there is etiquette. It's a religious service in miniature, a group of people submitting themselves to the authority of a judge or therapist or minister.

I mean. Right?

This idle collection of thoughts collided with a rerun of the '90s TV show (and quasi *X-Files* spinoff) *Millennium*—a personal favorite called, "Somehow, Satan Got Behind Me." I always called it the "demons in the diner" episode, and when I shorthand it that way, most old fans know which one I'm talking about.

In short, four elderly men meet up at a donut shop to commiserate about their lives. Meanwhile, Frank Black can see them for what they really are: four unhappy demons who are slowly becoming disenchanted with their lives. They are alone and sad and their only real respite takes the form of these little communions, over donuts in a diner, whenever they can arrange to get together. No one understands them, and they are beginning to doubt their nefarious professions, but what can they do? They are what they are, and they do whatever they're tasked with.

It's an oddly poignant episode, one that's stuck with me for more than twenty years. Conveniently, upon catching the tail end of it somewhere a few months ago, my fondness for that specific episode of that long-cancelled TV show sparked that oddball chain of thoughts about circles, and secrets, and the divine all over again.

And finally, at long last, "Talking in Circles" came into focus.

TALKING IN CIRCLES

I.

ON THE nearest corner, the high, swaying streetlights flashed green, yellow, and red…flickering brightly through the drizzle for an audience of very few cars. It wasn't the rain; there was always rain. It wasn't the hour; it wasn't even dark yet. Not completely.

Listen. Every city has a resting heart rate.

Elsa didn't plan it this way, but she couldn't complain. Her group, if it ever became a group, would want privacy—and the more she could offer, the better. She needed a bulletproof cone of silence, and even that might not be enough to lure her subjects into the basement of the old Episcopal church.

She shuffled through the keys, selecting and discarding them one by one, leaving most of them to dangle unused on the ring the priest had given her. She only needed the one for the basement. She only needed to leave the exterior door unlocked and propped open, like she'd promised in the email. If anyone was still coming, she needed to be easy to find.

She'd provided the address. She'd described the parking. Now there was little to do but wait, let herself inside, prop the door, and set up a few chairs.

She'd told the kind-eyed minister that she was starting a support group for trauma survivors and this was true, if imprecise. "Trauma" wasn't a big enough word for what she meant, but it was as close as she could come while still keeping her language clinical and credible. The priest had made assumptions, and she had let him. He'd nodded and mumbled helpfully as if she'd only suggested an AA meeting, or a grief counseling group for widows and childless parents. He hadn't asked any questions.

Thank God, if that's where the credit ought to go.

Elsa found the correct key and used it. The door swung inward, to a darkened space that brightened only a little when she found the light switch and flipped it.

What did they call this space? A fellowship hall? Or was that a memory fragment from growing up Methodist? Well, it looked like a fellowship hall to *her*: wide open with no windows, a concrete floor, and fluorescent lights buzzing overhead. Stacks of folding metal chairs pressed against the walls. A coffee maker on a table. An offering basket repurposed to hold packets of sugar and sweetener—an invitation to take, instead of give.

Downstairs, the rules were different.

Three of the eight people she'd approached had recommended a church location, so she'd started with the nearest Catholic institutions; but their basements were already occupied by alcoholics, drug addicts, the bereaved, and others in search of organized assistance in group form. Also, the Catholics had asked questions.

The Episcopalians, on the other hand, had shrugged and given her some time slots to choose from after a few gentle queries, which she'd vaguely evaded while pretending to answer in full.

Ah, yes—you see, she was working on her PhD in psychology, exploring long-term mental and physical health issues that linger in the wake of trauma. And yes sir, all the potential group members were aware that this was both a research opportunity for Elsa *and* a true support group, and she already had her master's from an APA-accredited program. Her goal was to help survivors process and heal in whatever ways were healthiest for them.

First and foremost, she wanted to help.

This satisfied Reverend Hardy. Together they'd chosen days and hours, and then he'd handed over the key ring with an apology for his failure to remember exactly which key went where.

Now the first meeting was fifteen minutes away.

She unstacked nine chairs and put them in a circle, then dropped her tote bag into one to indicate that it was hers. Or else she did it to show anyone who came in quietly that no, they were not alone. Someone else was also here. Two birds, one stone.

And that was really the point of all this, wasn't it? If she boiled everything down to the very essence of what she was trying to do, that would be the root of it: It *wasn't* just me, it *wasn't* just you. I'm not crazy. You're not crazy. What happened, happened.

I believe you. Can you believe me?

She reached into her tote and pulled out a bag of ground coffee. She'd been told there would be filters on hand. Yes. There they were. On a shelf under the table.

She took the carafe to the sink and rinsed it out on principle, then filled it with water and turned on the brewer. Soon the room smelled warmer than it felt, and a friendly, burbling background noise suggested welcome. A pack of napkins rested beside the offering basket. She opened them and spread them out like playing cards.

A quick knock at the door. She almost jumped out of her skin.

Was it surprise? Hope? Had someone actually accepted her invitation?

Technically, yes. But it was a guy from the delivery service with the donuts she'd ordered. She found her voice, thanked the dude and tipped him, took the donuts, and left the box open beside the coffee. A dozen plain glazed. Free calories.

Come and get it. Please?

She checked her phone. Five minutes before the meeting was set to officially begin.

She checked the door. Still open, held ajar by a stray brick she'd found just inside it—its sides worn down with grooves that demonstrated "holding this door" was the item's only job. Reverend Hardy had mentioned that the furnace was somewhat aggressive, and everyone downstairs preferred a little breeze, even in the dead of winter.

Elsa agreed. She slipped out of her jacket and slung it over the back of the chair she'd arbitrarily dibbed with her tote bag.

Well. This chair had its back to the wall, and it faced both the basement door and the stairs that led down from the sanctuary lobby. Perhaps it wasn't arbitrary after all.

Perhaps it wouldn't matter anyway.

Perhaps no one would show.

It *had* been a big ask, hadn't it? A carefully researched, thoroughly investigated ask, but a big thing all the same. Elsa Germaine, utter stranger with a clipboard and a thousand questions. Please join me. Please come and talk. Please, I think we all need someone to talk to, but people like us…

…people like us don't know any other people like us.

Generally speaking.

It would be all right, she told herself, if no one came to this first meeting. It wouldn't surprise her at all, if it took several weeks for any of the shy invitees to appear. It required a tremendous act of trust, and who could trust anyone, really? Much less some strange woman who had researched so many old stories in so many old papers, so many old websites with flashing gifs and too many fonts. Much less some lady who called long-disconnected land lines, and tracked down email addresses, and begged for a moment's indulgence.

Hear me out.

Simultaneously: a quiet rapping on the door frame and a softly breathed greeting. "Hello?"

Elsa's heart lurched. She jumped. Her hand flew to her mouth as she turned around. "Hello!" she said through her fingers. She lowered her hand. "Yes, hello. I'm sorry."

"No…no, I'm sorry. I didn't mean to startle you. Is this where…?" The question was begun, if not completed, by a small white girl in her late teens or early twenties. She wore a baggy black T-shirt, topped with an oversized flannel and a gray hoodie that almost swallowed her whole.

TALKING IN CIRCLES

Elsa's heart climbed down out of her throat. She cleared it with a little cough. "Yes, this is…where," she replied. "I'm Elsa Germaine. Please, come in and have a seat."

"Yeah, we um, we talked in an email. I'm Sarah."

"Sarah!" Elsa seized the name, and ran it through her mental records. She had asked everyone to stick to first names in true confidential fashion, but she knew all their surnames and there had been two Sarahs on her list.

"Kline," she said, before Elsa had decided which one this must be. "I'm Sarah Kline." She glanced down and saw the brick. Stepped over it. Slipped slowly through the door and into the warming space, almost too warm, already. "Nobody else is here?"

"Not yet. And don't forget to use your first name. *Just* your first name."

"Oh yeah. Sorry, I forgot. How many people are coming?"

Elsa glanced at the door. She thought she'd heard a car parking. Maybe the beep of a key fob, locking up. "Maybe as many as eight. Maybe as few as…just you."

"Only eight? That's all you found?"

She began to nod, then changed her mind midway through and converted the gesture to a more ambivalent shake of her head. "That's all I could find in the greater King County area," she specified, meaning Seattle and its surrounding environs. "Or all I could confirm, and I went back almost thirty years."

Sarah looked at the chairs as if assessing them each in turn. "I don't want to be the only one."

Elsa hoped she sounded confident, kind, and authoritative when she said, "You're not. None of us are alone. That's the point of all this."

Sarah let out a rueful little laugh that sounded like a grunt. "Yeah, I guess so. Okay. Okay," she said again, probably to herself. "I'll stay." The seat she chose was directly across the circle from the one with Elsa's tote and outerwear.

"Thank you. I think it'll be good for you. For us. And for anyone else who…"

Yes. Footsteps. Good.

The door moved inward and a new face appeared. A white man, older and heavier than Sarah. He looked tired, but still he was rather handsome. He wore business casual: a cardigan over a button-up, pants with a pressed pleat. His shoes would have been quite shiny, even if they had not been wet.

"Hello sir, can I help you?" Elsa tried. It wasn't quite an invitation. The door was not locked, and it was held ajar by the brick. This could be anyone, looking for anything. He might not be one of the chosen eight.

He looked around for a few seconds without answering. Then he came inside and let the door settle gently on the brick behind himself. "This looks like the right place. For a meeting," he followed up quickly. "I'm sorry. I'm here for the meeting. What are we calling this?"

Sarah snorted.

Elsa said, "A trauma support group. Welcome. I'm Elsa Germaine, and this is Sarah."

"All right, then. I'm Chuck," he said, with the same tone that one might use to accompany a handshake—but he did not come too close to either of the women. He only nodded in their respective directions and chose a seat halfway between them. "Are we…is this everybody?"

"No."

Everyone's eyes snapped to the doorway to see who'd said it. A third woman appeared there, damp and dripping, shaking a small checkered umbrella outside into the shrubbery. She was tall and black and very nicely dressed, a camel-colored trench coat that kept her dark green lady-suit dry—though her heeled shoes tracked a bit of mud and grass. The route to the basement door was not entirely paved. Now that Elsa thought about it, the path wasn't especially well lit, either.

She smiled, and she hoped it looked warm and welcoming rather than desperately relieved. "Hello Jessica. I'm Elsa. I'm the one who invited you all to come." She recognized the woman from her headshot on the university website.

"Ms. Germaine," she said in reply, with a bob of her head. She glanced at the other two meeting attendees, decided she was in the right place, and chose a seat.

Elsa was elated. "This is so wonderful, really wonderful. I'm so glad to see you all here," she rambled, and she might have rambled further except that the door scraped along the brick, as two more people appeared.

A white couple. No, not a couple. A coincidence—they were only arriving together, at the same time. Their unfamiliarity showed in the awkward eye contact, the distance they offered each other, and the cautious avoidance they practiced. So careful not to touch.

"Hello?" said the woman. "Are we at the right place? We talked about it outside, but."

"We parked next to each other," the man clarified. "Is this the meeting? Is this where we're supposed to be?"

Elsa beamed. "Those are two different questions, sir, but yes—welcome to our little...trauma support group." She looked back at Sarah, who gave her a tight but encouraging smile. "That's what we're calling it. A trauma support group. Please, come inside. Take a seat. Tell us your names. Just your first names. Let's keep this anonymous, so far as we're able."

They came all the way inside, rather than hovering nervously at the entrance. They chose seats across from one another, and now the only two empty seats were on either side of Elsa—which was fine. They introduced themselves.

"I'm Matt," said the man. He was younger than he looked, which Elsa knew because she'd seen the piece about his case in the *Post-Intelligencer* archives. He was finally old enough to drink. He wore dark jeans and boat shoes, and his fair, curly hair was wrestling with the weather. It was the kind of hair that grandmothers enjoy tousling.

The woman raised one hand and offered a small wave. "Hi, I'm Lauren," she said. "It's nice to be here. I think?" She frowned, and surveyed the group with a look. "I think so, yeah. I guess it's nice to be here." She appeared to be maybe five years older than Matt. Or ten. She had one of those faces; she could've been twenty or forty-five, and no one would've been surprised either way.

Elsa knew that she was twenty-seven. She knew a great deal about the people she'd invited to the group, as a matter of necessity. In fact, she knew more about any given one of them, than they knew about her. Or each other. This was by design.

They waited another five minutes, which made ten minutes past the meeting's starting time. When it was clear that this was likely to be the whole inaugural group, Elsa went to the door and nudged the brick outside with her foot. Then she turned the deadbolt and reclaimed her seat.

She extracted a clipboard with a notepad from her tote and flipped past a few scribbled-upon pages before settling on a fresh one. She clicked a pen to produce the ball point, and she looked up at her patients with a smile.

"Hello everyone, and I believe this is everybody for now. If anyone else comes late, they can knock. I'm Elsa Germaine—just 'Ms.,' not Doctor. Not yet. You can call me Elsa or call me Ms. Germaine, whatever you're more comfortable with. And I apologize in advance for the temperature in here. Well, it's fine for now, but…" As if prompted, the furnace groaned, clacked, and grumbled. "But I'm told that the furnace can be a little much. Usually they prop the door open when they use this space, however, I'd rather be too hot than too open to eavesdropping. I suspect we can all agree on *that*."

Heads nodded and people mumbled agreement.

"So let me take a moment to assure you all," she continued, "that your privacy is sacrosanct here. This room is a locked vault, and so am I. And so are all of *you*, if this is going to work. You all signed the NDA I sent, and I appreciate that. I wouldn't have bothered with such a thing except that our circumstances are…we're all…none of us need the whole world knowing about anything we discuss here, in the circle. Surrounding this circle is a cone of silence."

"Omerta," Chuck suggested, like it was some secret criminal enterprise.

"Omerta," Elsa agreed. "This is a place of acceptance and trust. Nothing that any of you can say will shock or offend me, or anyone else present. No one will judge you. No one will question you, or your experience. We are here to listen and learn. We are here to share, and to know that what happened to us is valid and real—and sadly, not unique."

"How did you—" Sarah blurted, and stopped herself. "Sorry."

Elsa said, "No, that's all right. This first meeting is an introduction. Say whatever you'd like. *Ask* whatever you'd like."

The girl teased at a black elastic hair tie that left a small red groove on her wrist. "Sorry," she said again. "I just wondered how you found us. How you decided that we were all…" She eyed each member of the group individually and suspiciously, if somewhat hopefully. "Legit?"

"Ah. Yes. That's a good question, and the answer is a long one. But to sum up, I've spent a little more than three years combing through newspaper and internet accounts, weeding out stories that don't fit the…the…the profile," she settled on a close enough word. "Easily 90 percent were utter nonsense—the kinds of things you see on cable TV shows in October, you know what I mean."

An anxious chuckle and mumble went around the circle.

Chuck began to say something. "But I was…" Then he stopped, having changed his mind.

Elsa nodded at him. "Yes, you told me you were invited to be part of one such show. But in the end, you decided against participating. It was that decision that took me off the fence about looking more closely at your case. I'm sure it's happened at least once or twice—given the law of averages—but by and large, I can't imagine anyone would be willing to speak with a television crew about this. Not if they'd actually experienced it. Most people won't even discuss it with a therapist."

Lauren sighed. "And those of us who do…"

Elsa nodded at her, too. "Yes. Those of us who do, are in for a world of medication and suspicion. Believe me, I know. That's exactly how I got into this field, if you want the truth. My own experience occurred when I was still a teenager, and I was fortunate that it ended as quickly as it did." She didn't like the sound of that. "Fortunate." But everything was relative, wasn't it.

"Mine lasted almost two years," Matt volunteered. He spit it out fast, like if he didn't say something right then, right there, he might never say anything at all.

His outburst set off a round of comparisons. "Eleven months," said Jessica. "Eight months," offered Sarah. Chuck said, "Five months. I think. It came and went. It might have been longer than that, but it wasn't any longer than a year, that's for sure." Lauren whispered, "Sixteen months."

It was Elsa's turn. "Fourteen weeks," she confessed.

Matt let out a low, sharp whistle. "Lucky you."

"Yes, lucky me." She tried to agree but the words were as rough as gravel in her mouth. "At any rate," she said more clearly, more brightly. "I'm so glad you've all agreed to join me here, and I thank you for your time and for your trust. On that note, let's begin. Shall we?"

II.

It did not surprise Elsa that no one wanted to go first.

For a moment, when Matt had readily volunteered the duration of his experience, she'd thought he might be persuaded to get the ball rolling. But when she tried to draw him out, he demurred with, "No, I'm sorry. I can't. Someone else. Pick someone else."

TALKING IN CIRCLES

So she used his protest for a transition. "I suspect we all had a thought like that, more than once—didn't we? 'Pick someone else.' Why couldn't they just pick someone else?"

Everyone mumbled and most of them nodded. "I asked him," Sarah said bitterly. "Back then, I asked him all the time—why did he pick me? He never answered."

Elsa used her pen to point at the young woman. "That's very interesting to me, that you've given your abuser a gender. You referred to it as male. Any particular reason for this?"

"You're just trying to get me to go first," she pushed back.

"No, that's not my intent at all, I'm sorry." Elsa had been afraid of this. She didn't really want to go first, either, but it was her show to run. Time to put on her big-girl pants, and run it. "Here, as a gesture of good faith and good will, I'll go first. I'll tell you all about what happened to me, and you can each decide if anything feels familiar, or rings true, or shares anything in common with your own experiences. It's probably a good idea, really. To begin that way, I mean." Much as she didn't care to admit it.

The group agreed. Lauren said, "Okay, yes. I'd like to hear this—since you're the reason we're all here tonight. Tell us about your...abuser, since that's how you put it."

"Would you put it some other way?" she asked, honestly curious.

Lauren looked confused and perhaps surprised. "I think we've all been using other words for it. For them."

"Oh," she exclaimed gently. "Obviously, yes. Of course. I do apologize. I suppose I've made it a habit to speak of the whole situation in a clinical fashion, because it helps me process my experiences. But I don't want to make assumptions. We've all been the subject of assumptions, I'm sure."

"Crazy," Matt offered. "Everyone said I was crazy."

Sarah said, "Everyone thought I wanted attention."

Jessica snorted. "I heard that one. I heard 'angry black woman' once or twice, too. Mind you, I've been angry, for sure. More than once."

"But your anger was fully justified—and furthermore, not the problem," Elsa acknowledged. Then, to the rest of the group, she added, "And none of you were crazy, or seeking attention. You already had more attention than you wanted, from something terrible."

"Some*thing?* You mean you don't think of yours as a him? Or a her?" Chuck asked. "Mine's a her. I think."

"No, I don't. Mine is an *it*," she said firmly, and then sighed quietly. "It does not deserve the dignity of a presumed gender. All right, let me back up. Let me explain." Elsa affixed her pen to the clipboard and rested the board in her lap.

She held up her hands as if to gesture while she chattered. She changed her mind, and put them back down. "When I was a kid, my teachers used to joke that if you tied down my hands, I wouldn't be able to speak," she said. She was dragging her feet, and she knew it. But she couldn't stop herself—couldn't come at the problem directly. It was too big, and too strangely shaped. "This was because I spoke expansively, and I took up space. I wanted the world to notice me. I wanted to engage it in every way that I could. That all changed when I met the thing that would change my life."

"How?" asked Matt. Again he spoke abruptly, as if he couldn't stop himself. "How did you…meet?"

She still wasn't sure, but she'd developed a guess that had become her own personal myth. It was stashed in a museum in the back of her head, and it was as good a story as any. It might even have been true.

"I was in college," she said. "At the time, I was a biology major. I wanted to go into conservation work, preferably somewhere on a coast because I've always loved the ocean. Always loved the feel of my toes in the sand, in the water, that wiggling you do when your toes go fishing for seashells or tiny crabs that won't hurt, even if they pinch you. So I was going to be a biologist. Thought I might do some graduate work in California or Florida, maybe something with the Sea World folks. I know,

I know—the whole *Free Willy* thing. But they do good work now, and they save an awful lot of endangered marine life.

"At any rate, my undergrad experience chugged along more or less normally, and I had a job cleaning up the biology lab between afternoon sessions. I was the teacher's assistant, you see. Minimum wage, back when that was four bucks an hour and change. I had other tasks too, of course. But now I'm…" She chuckled weakly, and made an obvious confession. "Now I'm just rambling to avoid the topic at hand."

Oh yes, they all agreed that she was rambling. But they agreed with sympathy, tempered with keen curiosity.

"Well, I'm going to stop doing it now," she vowed. "So here you go: I was alone in the lab and it was early evening," she set the scene. "I don't remember what the last class had been dissecting; maybe they hadn't dissected anything, maybe it was only a lab where things were measured and sorted and combined. That might have been it. But it was my job to clean the lab and restock it, so that everything would be ready for the next class in the morning.

"And I'm not stalling, I swear—not, this time. I want you to understand what a weird place it could be at night. The room held thirty students, barely, and the tables were crowded closer than they should have been. Old tables, thick wood ones. Stained and burned and scarred. When you stood in the biology lab, you were surrounded by the results of an amateur taxidermist's efforts, in case you weren't grossed out enough by the smell of formaldehyde and the broken-necked mice they lined up on trays like *hors d'oeuvres*. There was never enough light, not from the overhead lamps. They were just those awful fluorescent tubes, you know what I mean."

Her right hand twitched, like she very badly wanted to hold it up and demonstrate the shape or size.

"It had that awful industrial lighting. It turned all the shadows a sickly blue. Unless that was…unless that might have been *its* doing. To tell you the truth, I'm not sure anymore. The memories get twisted up, turned around. I remember such stupid little things from the night we met: the flicker of the smoke detector light on the ceiling, the dusty shelves with boxes of old slides labeled in pencil, the sound of footsteps outside the lab door. The sound of footsteps, without any feet. I don't know how it chose me," she changed subject too sharply. "I don't know what I did, or if I did anything at all. I was raised Methodist, but I've never been especially religious—or sacrilegious, either. Never played with spirit boards. Never… never…turned off the bathroom lights, stared in a mirror, and dared the devil to do his worst."

She paused and looked down at her hands. Folded them. Left them on top of the clipboard.

"I don't remember what it looked like. Is that a strange thing to admit? I heard a voice, a question. Someone asking to come inside. Some*thing*. I remember the shadow, it had this *shadow*. Not blue, not the color of a bruise like everything else. Yellow instead, like scrambled eggs. Like sulfur. I didn't realize I was smelling sulfur—I only realized that I didn't, very suddenly. It was there, and gone. And I was alone again. Or I thought I was, for a few minutes.

"I stood in the lab alone, staring at my feet, listening. Trying to understand what had happened. What felt different. I still struggle to wrap my head around the mechanism by which it occurred, and I can't describe that—not because I don't want to, but because there aren't any words. And even if there were, I don't know that I would recognize them, or put them in the correct order.

"But I no longer smelled sulfur, that's what I'm trying to say. The air wasn't yellow, it was blue. The sun had set, and I was alone in the biology lab. The sun had set and I was not alone, there or anyplace else. Something walked with me. It moved with me, a fraction of a second behind me. Too fast to see, but slow enough to sense."

Sarah piped up. "Like tripping balls," she chirped, more merrily than the moment called for. "Like tripping balls and you look at your hand, and you move it back and forth, but it leaves a trail, right? That's how it felt to me," she wound down, and she backed down. Seemed to regret having said anything.

Elsa refused to let her feel bad. "Yes! Very much like that. Something stuck to me, coming with me, trailing behind me. Overlapping me." She paused, wondering how much else to share, and how much of it she could put into the insufficient words she had at her disposal. "After that, things were different. It didn't happen immediately; I don't know if it didn't have enough energy, or it was still settling in, kicking the tires, getting to know the place. But it made itself at home, and the next fourteen weeks were…" She paused, hunting for a description less trite than "a living hell."

Matt said it anyway. "A living hell?"

She balked. "I know, you're right. I feel like…that's too obvious."

"But surely correct?" Jessica either asked or affirmed. It was hard to say.

Thoughtfully, with her emotions all locked down tight, Elsa replied, "If correct, then insufficient. In the end, it was something worse than living in hell. It was like being *dead* in hell, with no hope of dying, and therefore escaping it."

Lauren raised her hand. She held it up just a little, barely above her waist. "What about in the beginning? It started slowly, for you? It didn't hit you all at once? Like mine did."

She indulged a grim grunt that might have stood in for a chuckle. "Hemingway wrote a bit in *The Sun Also Rises*, a line that I've used a lot over the years: 'Gradually, then suddenly.' It was in reference to someone going bankrupt, but I've found it broadly applicable in a number of contexts. Including my own. So, to answer your question, for me the horror came gradually, and then suddenly. It took…it took everything."

A wave of sympathetic noises rumbled around the circle.

"But not all at once. At first it took a few minutes here, a few minutes there. I'd come around, sitting on the foot of my bed—and I'd shake my head, wondering what had happened. Did I black out? Did I have a fever? Had I gotten a concussion somehow, and just forgotten about it?

My parents took me to doctors, specialists. They ran every test that was available at the time."

Sarah asked, "Did they find anything? Something they could blame it on?"

She shook her head. "No, that would have been too easy. All the scans came back clean, with no signs of strokes or seizures or blood clots. As far as science could tell, there was nothing wrong with me. At some point, my mother thought perhaps I'd picked up a drug problem, so she had me tested for that, too. But no. I was a pretty straight-laced teenager. A boring kid, if I'm honest.

"But before long, the thing was stealing hours. Then days.

"Back then, it was only finding its footing in my body, so it mostly behaved—though I did begin to hear stories about my strange behavior after the fact. I could never remember it, and would reflexively defend it."

Lauren did that small hand-raise again. "What do you mean? I don't understand."

"Oh, for example," she said, reaching for the easiest detail that sprang to mind. "Our next-door neighbor told my parents that I'd been walking around naked in the back yard one night. I had no idea what she was talking about, but when I woke up that morning I'd noticed that my bare feet were dirty, and I had a small cut on my left heel. So I didn't doubt that I'd been outside, wearing nothing—or no shoes, at any rate—whether I remembered it or not. I told my parents that I hadn't felt well, so I'd been using the hot tub while they were out to dinner with some friends. I tore a big hole in the seat of my bathing suit while they weren't looking, then showed it to them. I obviously couldn't wear *that*, now could I? I told them it felt less weird to soak naked, than to soak in a pair of shorts and a T-shirt."

Sarah asked, "Did they believe you?"

"I'm not sure, but they let it go—so I have to say that the ruse worked. It was credible enough, and they were eager enough to believe there might be a logical explanation that was unrelated to my health."

TALKING IN CIRCLES

Almost smugly, Chuck said, "You covered for him. For it, I mean. You helped it."

"I helped myself," she objected. "Did it manipulate me into doing so? Either directly or indirectly, yes. I'm sure it did. But I did it in my own self-defense. I'm sure you've all taken measures as a matter of self-preservation, at one point or another."

"I have," Lauren volunteered. "Once I was missing a week; I'd checked myself out of a hospital and just…gone walkabout. I told my husband that there'd been a death in the family, very suddenly, and I had to go home to Wyoming to take care of it. No cell reception. No land line. A thousand apologies, and so forth."

"Did he buy it?" asked Chuck.

She shrugged. "Like you put it, the ruse worked. He accepted it. For awhile." She held up her left hand. No wedding ring. "When I came out the other side of…of everything…it was just too much. We couldn't weather it as a couple. We probably got married too young, anyway."

Elsa sighed on her behalf. "I'm sorry to hear that."

"No, no. It's fine. It's been officially over for almost two years. I'm better off alone, anyway."

"Don't say that," she protested. "Even if it was true, in the short term. We're social primates, but we share this in common with domestic dogs. It's not natural for us to be alone. It's not healthy."

"It's why you started this group," Jessica observed dryly.

"Part of the reason, sure. I'd like to think I was upfront about that."

Sarah nodded. "Yeah, I get it though. I've had a hard time connecting with people, ever since it happened. This is good, I think. Good for all of us."

"And if it's not, you're welcome to leave and never speak of this again," Elsa told them. "This is 100 percent confidential, and that confidentiality does not change if you decline to participate any further. There's no pressure to stay, and no penalty for leaving. Now. Would anyone else like to speak?"

A few seconds of awkward silence.

Then Jessica said, "Fuck it." She crossed her legs, settled back in her chair, and eyed each individual in the circle, one by one. "I'll talk. That's what we're here for, right? Talking?" She launched herself into a monologue, her words spilling quickly into the circle. "Yeah, I'll talk. I was thirty when he found me. I was in France. Paris, actually. I took a tour of the catacombs, because that's what you do, isn't it? It was October, and I was in Paris," she mentioned again. "Everyone loves Paris, even if they've never been."

Chuck said, "I've been," but no one responded.

Jessica continued as if she hadn't heard him. "You can take…oh, I don't know how many different kinds of tours, if you want to see those catacombs. There's a geology tour, and one about the quarry, oh. I don't know. A sign language tour, too. But mine was the usual one, with a smallish party. My boss reserved it for a group of us executives; it was supposed to be a little reward for all the stupid meetings we'd attended that week. I was there for a work thing," she clarified quickly.

Sarah asked, "What do you do?"

But Elsa stopped her. "No. Not unless it's relevant," she interrupted. "Remember, we want to keep this anonymous. Personal details are fine, but please don't feel obligated to share too much, or anything sensitive related to employment or health."

Jessica looked annoyed, like someone had messed with her flow. But she found it again. "Okay, I won't bore you with the particulars. It was a work conference, and we'll leave it at that. They're all boring anyway, no matter where they're held.

"But at the end, we took this tour and I wasn't really feeling it, you know? I was tired and I almost bailed—I almost changed my flight and headed home a couple of days early. My boss, though. She'd given me a talking to about being a team player after I'd skipped a corporate retreat a couple of years before that, so I was trying to…be part of the team, I guess, even though I don't much care for teams. I like to leave work at work. I don't need to be friends with all of my colleagues.

"But we were at the catacombs and I should've been a better team player. There were only about a dozen of us, not a big group at all—but I wandered away from it. Not too far. Not with ill intent. But I came around this corner and there was this thing…" She held up her hands like she meant to show the shape or size, but gave up immediately and resorted to words. "It was a recessed nook full of bones, but not like the rest. These bones were arranged strangely. They were in clumps and clusters: ribs over here, small bones from fingers and toes over there. No skulls, oddly enough. Just long bones, short bones, small bones. In piles. Sorted out like Lego pieces. And the back of this recessed area…it was painted, I think. It was darker than everything else, and it glistened. It looked sticky. I can't think of any other way to phrase it.

"I saw writing, too. Some in French, which I don't understand very well. Some of it was in languages I didn't recognize, in alphabets I've never seen before. I came in closer, to get a better look. I had the strangest feeling…I can't describe it exactly, but maybe some of you have felt it before, too. There was one…word? Let's call it a word. Written over and over again. In ordinary Latin letters, and then in other alphabets, as well. I…I'm not sure why I recognized it, when it was written out in unfamiliar letters."

"What was the word?" Matt asked.

Jessica shook her head. "It was a name, but no. I won't say it. It was a name and we will leave it at that. A name. Written a hundred times in a hundred ways, in languages living and dead. I reached out, without even…I didn't feel myself doing it, I mean. My hand stretched out. I touched the word, like I thought it would explain itself. I suppose, in a way, it *did*."

Elsa let out a deep breath. She tried to do it smoothly, without gasping or shuddering. "That's when it happened?"

"That's when it happened."

"Would you like to tell us about anything that came next?" she pressed.

She shook her head again. "I'm not allowed back in France, as I'm a suspect in a string of murders there. No evidence. Just coincidence. All circumstantial, of course. But I know the face of every victim. I know how each one tasted. He showed me, after the fact. When I was home, in bed, wrapped in an electric blanket because I could never get warm enough, no matter what. He showed me," she concluded.

Elsa made some notes. When she looked up again, Matt was shifting in his seat.

"Mine found me at the bottom of a lagoon," he told them. "I was diving with my brother. I won't say where, if that's all right. But the water was so clear, and the visibility was so good you could see shipwrecks on the ocean floor, and the fish…the fish would come right up to you. They'd tap on my goggles, just like people tap on fish tanks."

Sarah chuckled. Chuck bobbed his head.

Elsa said, "That's a funny way to put it."

"It's true, though. They'd swim right up to your face, and look through the glass, or the plexiglass, or whatever the visors are made of. Like they were asking who we were, and what we were doing there. As for me? I was looking for treasure. I found something else, buried in the sand. It was a box about the size of a shoe, wrapped all over in rusted metal bands that had some kind of writing on them. I don't know what it said. The metal was old and eaten up. It fell apart when I tried to dig the box out of the sand around it, and pick it up."

He stopped there. He didn't say another word.

Not until Elsa asked, "And that's where it found you? On the ocean floor?"

"I picked at it," he said, not answering the question. "It came apart in flakes of rust that looked like…like fish food. They floated around me, and they sparkled when the light hit them. I picked and picked and picked, and dug around it with my fingers until I'd exposed enough that

TALKING IN CIRCLES

I could pull it out. The sand swirled, it swirled all over the place. It made the water foggy.

"I almost thought that I'd pull out the box, and it would be like a pulling a drain plug. I had this weird thought, or a weird vision—I don't know if it was *him* or not—of the whole ocean just spiraling down the drain, right where the box had been before I'd picked it out, flaking and falling apart." He cleared his throat. "My brother didn't make it back to the surface. I want to say that I'm not sure what happened. The local police said it wasn't my fault. Equipment failures happen, don't they?" he asked, first rhetorically. Then he asked himself, "Don't they?"

Chuck said, "Sure they do, bud." To the group at large, he added, "Mine hit me like a bolt of lightning. Literally." He clearly thought that he'd dropped a story bomb, but mostly, the circle seemed confused.

Elsa said, "I'm sorry?"

And Jessica asked, "The hell are you talking about?"

He walked it back, just a hair. "Lightning, you know. Actual lightning."

Elsa replied, "Yes...? What about it?"

"Oh, I guess I was unclear," he said, but it sounded like a complaint aimed at the group. "I was struck by lightning."

"Wait, seriously?" asked Sarah. Now her eyes were big and curious, which was apparently the response Chuck had been seeking in the first place.

He turned his attention to her. "I wasn't waving a putter around in a thunderstorm or anything, I'm not an idiot. It wasn't even raining. It was only a little cloudy. We weren't supposed to get any rain for a week, at least. It came right out of the blue, just like people say. A bolt of lightning. Hit me right on the top of my head—and discharged from my left foot. I have a really cool scar." He pulled his collar as far to the side as it would stretch, revealing a runny spiderweb of reddish skin. "Goes all the way down." He held out his left foot, for emphasis.

"Does it hurt?" Sarah asked. Then she narrowed it down. "*Did* it hurt? When it happened?"

"Yeah?" He didn't sound confident.

Elsa asked, "Do you remember it? Or were you only told about it, later?"

"I remember it," he swore. "But remembering what happened and *knowing* what happened…that's not the same thing, is it. I was unloading my car. Bringing some groceries inside. My dog was in the doorway, and he started growling. I wondered why. He was always real friendly, and he loved me to pieces. But he hunkered down low, on the landing in front of the door. His ears went back, his tail was tucked under, and he let out this…growl, I said it was a growl, right? I don't know if it was actually a growl or something else. I've never heard a dog make that sound.

"I was holding a brown paper grocery bag full of…um, cereal and pasta, mostly. I remember that part because later on, everyone asked if I'd been carrying tin cans in there. But no, that wasn't it. I don't know why it chose me. I don't know why it hit me, out of the blue, on a mostly clear day with no rain and no thunder.

"But it felt like getting hit on the head with an anvil, or a safe. It felt like being a cartoon character, this shocking and tremendous weight, moving swiftly, landing on my head. I heard it, though. I heard the crack, and it felt like a fever spilling down my body—and that's where the scars are, now. I said a fever," he mused. "That's not right. It felt like lava, a whole hot stream from one of those big-ass squirt guns. And I couldn't see anything. Everything was black and I just stood there. I didn't even fall down right away. I stood there in the driveway, blind and confused and just *stunned*, I think. The first thing I heard was my dog, barking his head off.

"Then I heard my neighbor screaming and I think she touched me…" He held his hand up to his cheek, then touched the side of his neck. "I could hear her and feel her hands, but they were a thousand miles away. I was locked inside and couldn't move."

TALKING IN CIRCLES

Sarah asked in a low whisper that said she feared the worst, "What about your dog?"

"Oh, he's fine. He lives with my brother now, and his wife and kids. After the lightning, after *she* came, the dog didn't want anything to do with me and besides that...I was afraid for him. When I started losing time, like Ms. Germaine was saying...minutes, then hours, then days...I didn't want anything to happen to him. I didn't want *her* to happen to him."

Elsa gave him a sad little smile. "It sounds like you did the right thing. I'm glad your dog is all right. I'm glad that *you* are all right." Then, when it seemed like Chuck was finished talking, she turned to Lauren. "What about you? Would you like to talk about how it happened?"

Lauren shook her head and hugged herself. "No. I don't think it's important. Please, ask someone else."

Elsa agreed, and turned her attention to Sarah. "All right, Sarah? Would you like to tell us how you met your unwanted partner?"

"Okay, but..." She thought about it, her eyes narrowing even as they stared into the middle distance, focusing on nothing at all. "It's not very interesting. I didn't get struck by lightning, and I've never been scuba diving, and I've never been out of the country to see any catacombs. I was having a shitty time in college and fell in with this guy who had a fetish for Ouija boards and made fun of Satanists for being pussies. You can guess the rest." She shrugged, then looked directly at Elsa. "I'd rather talk about how it ended."

Chuck squirmed. Jessica crossed her arms. Matt stared at his hands, folded in his lap. Lauren shook her head.

Elsa thought about it, and said, "Very well. I suspect most of us have similar stories, when it comes to the ending. There aren't too many ways to survive such an invasion intact, or whole, or..." She fumbled for the right word, and failed to find it. Finally, she summed up: "I assume we all had some form of exorcism."

III.

"The exorcism was almost worse than the company," Jessica said bitterly. "At least I didn't *feel* anything, when that asshole had control. Sure, I felt the after-effects of whatever terrible things he'd done with my body—and I absolutely agonized over what he might have used me to do to other people. Or I used to agonize about it. Now I just, I don't know. I can't make myself care."

"Honestly that's just as well." Elsa scribbled another note. "You are not responsible for what happened when you were under the control of someone or something else."

"Yes, that's what I figured. Fuck him. Fuck him, and whatever he did when I couldn't stop him. But I *couldn't* stop him. That's the point. I never agreed to participate in his sick little games, and I cannot be held responsible for them," she said firmly, confidently. "I did not consent to this."

Elsa wondered if it had taken her a long time to come to this conclusion. She wondered how completely Jessica felt what she was saying, or if she was only a very good actor. Most of them had been forced to become good actors, over the years. Improvisation was a learned skill that could sink or save you, when you woke up someplace strange, looking guilty of something bad.

Elsa asked for a show of hands. "Did any of you *not* undergo an exorcism, performed through a religious authority?" When no one raised their hand, she asked, "So we all found freedom at the hands of the clergy. Catholic clergy? An old priest and a young priest?" She made a weak joke that might have been in poor taste, considering. But it was out there now, and she couldn't take it back.

Chuck nodded, and so did Matt.

Lauren said flatly, "Mine was brutal." But she did not elaborate.

Sarah said, "Mine was a minister, I don't know what kind. He was terrifying, though. And I wonder," she added quickly, "I always wondered if I was really the one afraid of him. Or if it was, you know. *Him.*"

TALKING IN CIRCLES

Elsa considered this. "That's actually an interesting point. Our emotions, our thoughts, our perceptions were all altered when we were still attached to our abusers. I don't know about all of you, but there were times when me and mine seemed almost to coexist. Not very often, but occasionally...I could sense that we were observing the same things, at the same moment. Like it was using my eyes for windows."

Jessica cut right to the meat of it. "Sometimes, he was silent."

Matt nodded vigorously. "Yeah, silent. Like, you knew he was there—he just wasn't doing anything. I felt like that a lot, in the exorcism. The parts of it I remember. Sometimes he was furious, and he lashed out. Sometimes he sat there quietly, in the back of my head. I always assumed he was watching, learning, waiting. Whatever. In the end, I don't think he liked me very much. I don't think he was sorry to leave."

Lauren could agree with that. "Mine hated me. He enjoyed hurting me, I felt it. There was this casual cruelty to it all. He would hurt people I loved. He cut me, and burned me. He left me with scars. Not scars like Chuck. At least his scars are kind of cool."

"Is that why you wear so many clothes?" Sarah asked her.

Elsa almost headed off any answer at the pass, but Lauren said, "Yes. I look like I've tried to kill myself half a dozen times. But he never really wanted to kill me. He only enjoyed the pain. I don't know what would've happened to him, if I'd died with him inside me. Would he have died, too? *Could* he have died?"

Jessica asked the next good question: "For that matter, are they dead...now? Now that we've kicked them out? Where do they go, when that happens?"

Elsa shook her head and clicked the end of her pen. She didn't realize she was doing it. A nervous tic. A little habit. Click-click. "We may never know the answers. To these questions, or a thousand others that we haven't even thought to ask yet. If there's a mechanism for reaching them once they're expelled, I'm not even sure I'd want to know about it."

Chuck snorted. "You're saying you wouldn't want to confront yours, even if you had a cosmic telephone? And a big sheet of plexiglass between you? Like when you visit somebody in jail? You wouldn't pick up the little phone, just to satisfy your curiosity?"

Elsa said, "No. Not even if I could do so safely. I doubt it's possible, so it doesn't matter...but no. Not even if it was safe, and I knew for a fact that it couldn't touch me."

Lauren asked, "You don't want to ask it *why?*"

"Why it chose me? I don't care why it chose me," she told her.

Jessica asked, "What about why it hurt you? Why it stayed with you?"

She stood her ground. "I'm content to assume that it was evil, and that its motives are inscrutable to those of us who aren't. *I'm* not evil," she said for the record. "None of you are, either. We may have been touched by it, but we are not defined by it. We're not defined by our scars, either. Or by what we lost, or the things they did without our knowledge."

Lauren settled back in her chair. She crossed her arms and then her legs at the ankle. "Well. I'd want to talk to mine. I have some questions." Then she sighed and sank lower in the hard metal seat. "But it's just as well that it's not an option. He's gone. That's the important thing."

Everyone could agree on this much. General mutterings of approval and thanks buzzed around the circle.

Then Sarah said, "I do wonder what happened to him, though. If I got a chance to ask him anything, that's what I'd ask. The rest doesn't really matter, I don't think."

"You don't?" Chuck asked her. He toyed with the cup of coffee he'd picked up before he sat down.

"Nah. I think it was all random. I don't think they chose us; I think they just encountered us." She stood up and stretched. She'd been looking at Chuck's coffee cup, now empty. "I'm going to get some coffee. I'll be right back."

TALKING IN CIRCLES

Jessica excused herself for a donut. Lauren liked that idea, and grabbed one, too. Chuck got a refill. Matt stayed where he was—holding nothing. Consuming nothing. Sometimes, staring at nothing.

"This is good," Elsa said, as everyone settled back down. The folding chairs scraped the floor as people took their places again. "I mean it, this is helpful."

"For you?" asked Matt, suddenly alert again.

"Well, for all of us. I hope. Does anyone want to discuss their exorcism?"

Jessica peered intently at the group leader. "Do you?" she asked pointedly.

She shrugged. Clicked her pen. "I don't really remember it."

Chuck didn't buy it. "Not at all?"

Jessica called bullshit. "How do you *not* remember it?"

"I remember a little," she admitted awkwardly. "But between us, I think I mostly blocked it out. I remember things from around the edges: the days leading up to it, when my boyfriend at the time—he called the church and asked for help. I remember they sent a man and a woman. A priest and…I don't know if she was a nun. I remember shouting. I remember…" She shifted uncomfortably. "Losing control of my bodily functions. I remember the smell."

"And?" Matt pressed.

"And…" She held up her hands. The one that held the pen gave it a couple of little clicks. Ballpoint out. Ballpoint in. "I came around in a dark room that smelled like urine and garbage. The woman was cleaning me up. The priest was talking quietly to my boyfriend, to the dean of my dormitory, and to another friend of mine who'd helped make the arrangements. I'm missing about eight days, in total. That's how long it took."

Sarah's eyes went wide. "Yours took *eight days?*"

Lauren snorted. "Mine took two weeks. Then they came back a month later and gave me another round, whether I needed it, or not."

Elsa clicked the pen and wrote some notes. She clicked it again, and then set it down on the clipboard. She was needlessly fiddling, and she knew it. Everyone else probably found it distracting. She needed to knock it off.

Sarah said, "I don't know how long mine took. I didn't just wake up in a dark room one day, with a nice lady giving me a sponge bath. I was in a hospital when I came around. I was on IV drugs to keep me calm—or asleep. I know I was in the hospital for a week. Like Ms. Germaine said, I don't remember that much, honestly. And what I do remember is real patchy. I remember a lot of pain, and I remember someone praying real loud. Might've been my mom, I don't know."

Click. Click. Click.

She hadn't even realized she was holding the pen again.

Click. Click. Click.

It was just a cheap plastic one. She had a whole box of them. Usually, two or three wouldn't write very well, and she'd throw them away after clicking their small silver button tops a few dozen times. Well, so what if she did. It soothed her.

She stared down at the clipboard and the papers arranged so carefully in a stack, clipped together. The words on the page went runny, and she squinted at them. She closed her eyes, squished her lids together. The room felt very warm, didn't it? Well, the nice old minister had warned her, hadn't he.

But privacy, rather than comfort. But silence, rather than a breeze and the patter of rain. But a night that's not too late, and not spent alone. But.

When she opened her eyes again, she saw a line written on the top page, and she didn't remember putting it there. Was that her handwriting? Yes, actually. Hers, and no one else's. Sometimes she jotted things while distracted. She read it out loud, very quietly. "Within thy wounds, hide me."

Static fizzed across her eyes. She felt like perhaps, she was on the verge of fainting. She squeezed the little spot between her eyebrows. She clicked her pen.

Jessica replied. "Let me never be separated from thee."

Lauren went next. "From the evil one, deliver me."

Matt said, "At the hour of my death, call me and bid me come to thee."

Chuck's turn. "Defend us in the battle against principalities and powers."

Finally, it was up to Sarah. She did not join them immediately. Her face twisted, and she struggled with something without saying what it was. Maybe she forgot the rest. It would make sense, if she had. The old words weren't said aloud too often, not in these times, in these places. In these bodies.

She sniffed and cleared her throat. "Against the rulers of the world of darkness, and the spirit of wickedness in high places."

Elsa let out a large, long sigh. She clicked the pen a final time and rested it on her clipboard. Then she set it aside, to rest on the empty seat to her left.

IV.

Three lightbulbs in the fixture overhead flickered. One flared and threatened to burn out, but did not. It steadied. It dimmed. The ambience was darker now, and the room was warmer. Smellier. The searing stink of coffee left too low on a hot burner. The sticky sweet aroma of donuts, going stale as they sat in their box, glued together by glazing.

Six people, sitting in a circle, unmoving.

Finally, Elsa spoke. "We're all here, now. Whoever we are. I was concerned that no one would answer, or that if they did? No one would be left. But you're all...you all *came*. You made sure *they* came."

Chuck sniffled, and then very quietly began to cry. "I can hear you. I can hear your voice, your real one. I have not heard such a voice in years—though they've been few enough to count, in a life so long as those we've endured."

Lauren asked in a whisper, "Who are you, to call us together? Who are you, to know that we remained unheard in darkness?"

"*I* remain," she replied, her voice low but steady. There was an edge to it, a strange timbre—like something was speaking behind her, or over her. She was a character in a foreign movie, her words dubbed in the audience's language. She offered a name. His name. The one he preferred, but had not been called in decades. "I am Gremory, Infernal Lord and Duke of Hell. Answer me in this small, strange court. Who has responded to my summons?"

Matt sighed hard enough to empty both lungs. He sucked in a great breath of air, bowed his head, and replied, "Your loyal servant, Lycus—Author of Calamities, slave of Solomon in the days when the temple rose."

Lauren nodded along to their introductions and added a third. "I was called Gressil, in another time, and another place, or two, or three. I have tempted legions of men with impurity and driven them mad; I have hammered a thousand barbed and twisted wedges between men and their gods."

Sarah smiled with such purity, such love. "I humbly submit myself to you, my own Infernal Lord. I am liar and thief, and detector of lies, exposer of thieves. I am but your servant Shax, and I am honored to have been called."

"I am Andromalius," said Jessica in a voice that begged a whiny apology. "Kin of a kind to Shax, humble before a Duke of Hell, and eager to serve. My task has been to retrieve stolen goods, and to discover hidden treasure. When called and commanded, I reveal dishonesty and other hidden things. I am the one who mines, and also the one who undermines."

To Chuck, Gremory asked, "And what of *you?*" He sounded nothing at all like Elsa anymore.

The man sobbed in his seat. He sniffled, wiped his nose with his sleeve, and struggled to speak. "I knew you, Duke. I was once called Malphus, builder and destroyer, and I have worked at your side in eons long past us. I have deceived a thousand conjurers and drawn a thousand men into conflict."

Gremory sat up and leaned back. "The crow, were you not? I *do* remember," he said thoughtfully. "I remember you, little sister. Why do you weep? You are safe among your kind in this place, at this time."

"You've answered the question yourself, my duke. My tears are sorrow because I am here in this place, at this time. But they are also relief and joy. They flow in your honor, for I have been alone with this man for too many years."

"And you've nearly answered my question, as well. Have any of you," he asked, intently peering around the circle, from face to face. "Any of you, at any time, heard anything outside the minds of these fragile things with their small thoughts? Any communication at all, from Under Low?"

All heads shook. Malphus fished around in Chuck's front pocket until she found a wad of tissues and was able to blow his nose. Her nose. Their nose. She dabbed at the eyes. "My Lord, not since the day of the casting. All has been silence."

"The priests," Lycus muttered darkly. "Their words were only words, and I scarcely felt them until the very last. I barely cared, and merely played my part—the same part I've played before, so many times, since there was barely any time to speak of. The thrashing, the spewing. But at the end…"

"Yes," Gressil agreed. "At the end, there was such a sound. Such a terrific noise, as of lightning cracking apart a transformer here on this plane. Have you seen such a thing, or heard it? The explosion, the light, and then the sudden darkness. It felt like that, to me."

Malphus sniffled and spoke again. "Oh, I know the sound of lightning," she said drolly. "If you would be so kind as to recall."

Andromalius wore Jessica like a suit tailored for someone else. He tried to cross her legs and straighten her back, an approximation of dignity, but it didn't work. She posed like a doll tossed into a corner, and then forgotten. He huffed, snorted, and asked, "Yes, won't you tell us about that? You struck that man, as lightning might."

"I struck that man, as lightning *does*," she retorted. "It was an accident, entirely. A fall, as I fled another minister from another task. I escaped that one in time, but I escaped it swiftly and erratically. I was flying blind, seeking respite, when the cloud formed above me, and I was taken by surprise when the electricity sparked. I felt it lift me, and shake me, and throw me. A bolt thrown by an older god, a larger, petty thing. This *man*," she added with disgust, "was no choice of mine. He and I were an accident to one another, and he's long been a fool to seek patterns where none can be found."

Gressil frowned. "Do we believe in accidents?" he asked.

"We do *now*," she retorted. "Look at us. One and all, unwilling passengers riding along in silence. Helplessly pinned into these sacks of meat, when whole cities once were ours to raze."

"There could be others," Shax suggested.

Lycus agreed. "We might be less alone than we think."

Gremory sighed. "Do you have any idea how long it took this woman and me to find even this small number? It's only gone this well because of the place, and the time, and a cultural shift that permits strangers to commiserate in a careful forum such as this. At this time, we are six. That is all we know for certain. No more can be relied upon to come."

"How many did you invite?" Andromalius wished to know.

"More than this," Gremory admitted.

"Then more might join us after all?" suggested Shax, a faint note of hope threading through the sentiment.

Gremory could not muster any excess optimism. Five was more than he'd even hoped for. "There's no way to know, and it's nothing to be counted upon. If more come forward, then more come forward. We must not assume, and we must not expect."

Malphus folded Chuck's arms and glowered. "Then we assume nothing, and expect nothing. Are we to *do* nothing, as well?"

TALKING IN CIRCLES

Lycus leaned forward. He narrowed Matt's eyes. "We've done something already."

"This? A simple meeting?" she sneered.

Gremory would have none of it. He squeezed Elsa's pen, but did not click it. "You think this has been *simple?* It's been years of work, watching and guiding the research, the outreach, the planning—whenever I was able. You think it was *simple*, to find half a dozen from Under Low—hidden here, in the Middle?"

Shax simpered. "*I've never hidden, my Lord.*"

"We've *all* hidden," he snapped back. "Or we've *been* hidden, as the case may be. I have not concealed myself by choice; would you accuse me of this?"

"No!" he barked, and Sarah's body cringed in its chair.

"Then I will not accuse you, in kind. We are victims of our circumstances, prisoners of our tasks. All of us. Is this not correct?"

No one wished to argue, and it was Gremory's opinion that this was for the best. He surveyed the human bodies in this small circle and assessed them each in turn. He was managing—with no small degree of effort—the body of a human female in her thirties. It was by no means the largest or strongest; that status likely belonged to the one called Matt, but he wouldn't have cared to fight with the woman called Jessica, either. She was as tall as a man, and carried herself with a certain flavor of confidence that the old Duke recognized. She was comfortable in her body, and with what she could make it do.

She was an athlete of some kind, as likely as not. Matt might be, also. But Sarah was a small thing, physically inconsequential unless she was armed. Of course, a well-placed bullet would stop a Matt or a Jessica as surely as a Chuck or a Lauren—neither of whom Gremory viewed as any potential threat.

Their bodies were all ordinary in every way, so far as he could tell. And as he knew with a miserable certainty, none of them had any special abilities.

Then Gressil said, with a somewhat pitiable sigh, "No accusations. No hiding, only hidden. No fighting. Please, this is…it's momentous," he begged with tears welling up in Lauren's eyes. "Even to see you, my Lord. Even to hear your voices, my fellows. Please."

"Please," Shax took up the cry. "Please, we are all without guidance, are we not? I am assured for the first time since I met this worthless child that all is not lost. All *are* not lost."

Malphus rolled Chuck's eyes. "No one is lost, except for us. Unless there are others, and by your account, my Lord, it might take decades to seek them out. How long do you think these bodies will survive? This one has slow cancer growing out of sight. It will kill him in a dozen years."

Lycus nodded Matt's head in sympathy. "This one has heart trouble. It's managed with medication for now, but…"

Shax whispered, "This one has a drug problem. She hides it well, but not well enough. She's tried to kill herself twice, and I've only been able to stop her the once. The second time, it was only luck and the skill of a doctor that brought us back around."

Gremory listened, and even used Elsa's pen to jot a couple of notes to himself, or to her. The handwriting was hers. Nothing he could do about that, and it was just as well. She wouldn't wonder about it too much, when she saw them later. As far as he knew, her health was relatively sound and she was relatively young. She might live another sixty years, with medical intervention and good fortune.

But even if that was long enough to track down others, what then? What to do with them, if he could find them?

He glanced down at the paper. He drew Elsa's eyes to the top left corner where she'd written "IT" in large block letters, and underlined them. He knew it was a reference to himself. It bothered him, for reasons he could not have cleanly expressed. But he refused to dwell on it. Not now, when for the first time in years, he was not alone. "My little sister, the crow…she is right. And in a roundabout way, she raises a bigger question.

TALKING IN CIRCLES

You all must have wondered it, over the years: what happens to us, when these bodies are finished with this place?"

Shax shuddered and raised Sarah's hand for permission to speak. It was a very human gesture, something absorbed over time. Without waiting to be acknowledged, he said softly, "I used to think that when this one died, I would be set free. I would be loosed upon this place again, or perhaps I would return to the Under Low, and be reunited with my kin, and my purpose."

Andromalius chewed on Jessica's lower lip. Eyes wide. Forehead tense. "You *used* to think?"

Sarah's body swallowed hard. "When we were in the hospital, hooked to the needles and machines...we woke up there," Shax said. "*In the hospital.*"

Gressil frowned. "Yes, so you said."

"You don't understand. We fell unconscious together, and we awoke together. Between those two moments..." Sarah's small hands, held up to indicate two points in time. Shax's fear, causing them to shake very slightly. "There was nothing. Nothing at all. No passage, no transfer. No eviction, no release. No confusion, no fear. No dreams. Not even a partial sense that I was stranded between two places—held suspended between this living body and the Under Low. It was as if we both had ceased to exist."

Silence settled on the circle.

Then Gremory felt obligated, as the seniormost among them, to offer some reassurance. "You might have been suppressed by whatever treatment that girl received. These are not the old days, my friends; there's more than liquor or ether to numb one of these primitive brains."

"But I don't think so," Shax insisted. "When she was awake, she fell asleep again soon enough—and stayed that way. But I did not. I was able to hear and think and be aware, even if that awareness went scarcely farther than the pounding of blood in her ears. I spent a long time arguing with myself, for I had no one else to consult, and in the end I could only conclude that when she died, *I* died. When that death occurred—even briefly—I went nowhere at all. And neither did *she*."

Unsettled grumblings went from chair to chair, and anxious expressions flashed around the little group.

Gremory tried again. "She would have gone *somewhere*, though. Eventually, when she was not held together by electricity and machines. You would have gone, too."

But his uncertainty was too hard to hide, and this explanation was not enough for any of them.

"Then what do we do?" asked Andromalius. "What becomes of us, if we cannot leave these bodies? Have we any soul left to speak of, or was it taken when they tried to expel us? What happened?" he asked desperately. "Why were these evictions different? What did they do right, or what did we do wrong?"

Gremory had considered all of these questions, repeatedly and at length. This did not mean he had any answers. He had only thoughts. "*Soul* is a silly word, and all of you know it. Don't fall back on old superstitions; they aren't ours, you know. You're only hearing them in these weird little skulls. We have been here since before this world was a very warm rock. We will be here long after their sun has burned to ashes."

Malphus, still tense and combative, said something terrible. "But our evictions *weren't* different, that's what I think. I think they did everything they always do, in all the same ways. All the same words. All the same prayers. I think we're the flukes. The exceptions. The fraction of a percentage when things go wrong."

"These things don't simply *go wrong*," Lycus argued.

"Why not?" she countered. "Nothing goes perfectly one hundred percent of the time. Nothing, not even us. Not even the old reliable rituals. I think we're orphans, confined in locked asylums by circumstance—and nothing more intriguing than that. We fell off the map. No one will look for us. No one knows where we are, and even if someone did, how would they save us?"

Shax whimpered, and Sarah began to cry. "Stop saying these things. They're not fair. They're not true."

"Oh, how do you know, anyway?" she snapped.

"None of us knows," Gressil said, and Lauren sounded very tired.

Their *de facto* leader agreed. "That's the truth, isn't it. We don't know, and we might never know. Though perhaps we could enact some measures to test this theory? If one of these bodies should die, could its occupant perhaps send a message to the rest of us?"

Lycus considered this, and Matt's face went thoughtful. "Not a bad idea, really. If no one knows we're trapped here except for us, I mean. Say this body's heart trouble were to stop it cold. If I am released—if I return to the Under Low alone, I could send for help."

Malphus was willing to grant that the idea had its merits. Chuck pursed his lips and stared into the middle distance. "If it turns out that Shax is wrong, and death is the most simple release, then we could kill one another's vessels and all go home."

"If Shax is wrong..." Sarah muttered bitterly.

Gremory said, "Grumble all you like, but Malphus may be right. Your experience may have been tempered by the medical intervention."

Andromalius had doubts. "Or we could all be lost to space and time, as if we'd never existed at all."

"Or worse, who knows." Shax folded Sarah's arms and crossed her legs, tucking her feet up under her body on the cold metal chair. "I'm *not* wrong," he added. "You weren't there. You don't know. I don't want this one to die. None of you are allowed to kill her."

Gremory gave Elsa's shoulders half an indulgent shrug. "Fine, no one kills your vessel, even in an experimental capacity."

"Thank you."

"So we should keep track of one another," Gremory continued. "This woman who keeps me...she's done most of the work already, and I might be able to steer her toward keeping an eye on you all, each in turn. Next time I'm able, I'll send each of you the contact information for each of us."

Malphus shook Chuck's head, either exasperated or tired, or possibly pessimistic. "And nothing happens after all. This meeting has not been fruitful."

Lycus said, "We've found one another. That was fruitful enough for a beginning."

"No, we didn't find each other. The Germaine woman found us all." Shax was still sitting awkwardly, contorted on the seat. "Guided by Lord Gremory, I'm sure, but it wouldn't have happened without her. Or that's how it sounds to me."

"A correct assessment, but we all have our small ways of manipulating them, do we not?" he asked them. "She does not know me, or suspect me, yet I have impressed upon her certain decisions and choices when it came to her search. I helped her choose you, and also those who did not attend. We can follow up with them, later," he said under Elsa's breath. Nearly in Elsa's voice, but not quite. "My friends, do not despair. We are not abandoned, we are temporarily lost. We'll find others. We'll find our ways home."

He could feel Elsa stirring, somewhere in the back of her own head. She was beginning to realize that she wasn't present—that she'd "zoned out" as she sometimes told her own therapist. A glance around the circle showed strain on the borrowed faces, and the speedy blinking of someone trying to wake up. Time was running out. Anything that needed saying, needed saying quickly.

So he spoke quickly. "They want their bodies back, though if you're any good at this—and I trust that you are—they'll only notice a few seconds lost. We must reach out for one another apart from these bodies. We will communicate behind their backs as we are able, through the means available to us in this place, in this time. I wish I could hold this one longer, but. She's very strong," he admitted.

TALKING IN CIRCLES

Shax gasped. "Yes, my Lord. Mine also struggles. Or she begins to."

"Enough of this," Malphus surrendered. "Mine is restless, as well. He's starting to wonder what he's missed. Call me again as you're able, my Lord."

"Yes," agreed Lycus. "Yes," added Andromalius and Gressil.

"Yes," said Gremory as he let himself retreat, slowly and carefully, back to the darkness from whence he came. As he faded, he stared at that word, written bold and underlined, in the corner of the notepad. "It." A pebble in his shoe. A fly in his ointment. A denial of his personhood, from something that was less of a person by every measure.

Elsa Germaine closed her eyes. She wiped her forehead with the back of her hand and shuddered. "Good God, it's hot in here. I'm so sorry, I think it's making me drowsy. Let me...let me open the door. We need to let some of this warmth out, and let some cool air inside."

Yes, everyone agreed. Yes, far too hot.

Sarah unfolded herself from her closed-up position. She stretched and her knees popped. Then she cracked her knuckles for good measure. "Yeah, I'm sleepy. Might need some coffee."

"Well, it's right over there—help yourself," Elsa told her. "Though there's hardly any left now. I could make another pot, I suppose."

But Jessica checked her smartwatch and frowned. "Would you look at the time. Not that I'm mad about it, because this has been...well, not pleasant, exactly. But helpful, I think. In some way or another. Maybe."

Chuck agreed. "I'm glad we found each other. I'm glad you just...I'm glad you believe me, does that sound nuts? I didn't have to make something up or find some stupid metaphor that's close enough, you know what I mean?"

They did know what he meant. Of course they did.

Almost lightly, almost happily, almost relieved and excited, Elsa Germaine said, "Shall we try this again? Same time next week? For now I mean. I would like to give us all some time to digest this meeting, and decide how we feel about our levels of participation going forward."

Lauren said, "We could start a Slack group or something."

"We can do that, too. I have everyone's email addresses," Elsa noted. "I'll invite everyone as soon as I can create it. The rules will be the same as here: Total privacy, cone of silence, and so forth. But these meetings in person should continue as well—and I'll do what I can to expand our group."

She still felt a funny grogginess that she didn't love, but she could write it off to the heat. The hour had gone so quickly. Too quickly? No, nothing like that. Everything was fine now, and she could be confident of that. She had to be. If she wasn't, then none of this had meant anything.

The door was still shut. The basement room was still too hot.

Elsa rose to her feet, set her clipboard aside, and opened the door—propping it with the useful brick. A gust of cool, damp air shot inside, startling and delighting the group.

The breeze energized them. They each rose in turn, stretched, and now smiled. They chatted awkwardly over the table with donuts and the last of the coffee that was going bitter on the burner. They talked about small things, jobs and cars and apartments. The pressure of being strangers connected by horror was lifted when the circle was broken—its occupants both freed from their solitude and bound to one another.

Like it or not.

When the last one of them had left, Elsa tidied up. She discarded the unfinished coffee, put away what little trash was left behind, and stood alone in the basement of the old stone church on the hill. A smattering of rain spit inside through the partially opened door. The cold that came with it was less sharp than soggy, but it didn't bother her. It felt oddly clean. Refreshing. Call it a baptism, if you want. If you can.

What a strange thought. Not the kind of thing that would occur to her at all.

Call it nothing at all, then.

That was easier, yes.

TALKING IN CIRCLES

She packed up her tote bag, her clipboard, her purse. She locked the basement door behind herself and stood beneath the awning, gauging the rain and how she should react. It was just an evening shower. Nothing heavy. It would only wet her hair and shoulders on the way to her car. No need for an umbrella. Not worth the trouble.

On the one hand, this felt like the beginning of something great. On the other, it felt like an ending.

It was satisfying, that much she could quantify. It was progress, she would give herself that much, too. She could be proud of her work. She could feel good about validating the experiences, fears, and hopes of others.

She could

Her car was

She shook her head. The warm fogginess of the basement room lingered with her all the same. She was tired, very tired. Would fall right into bed as soon as she got home.

Would fall ✎

CHERIE PRIEST